The Wedding Proposal

The Wedding Proposal

Sue Moorcroft

Published 2014 by Choc Lit Limited
Penrose House, Crawley Drive, Camberley, Surrey GU15 2AB, UK
www.choc-lit.com

A CIP catalogue record for this book is available
from the British Library

ISBN 978-1-78189-171-1

Printed and bound by CPI Group (UK) Ltd, Croydon, CR0 4YY

For anyone who was ever young.
And made a mistake.

Acknowledgements

Writing a book might seem a solitary affair but I rely on lots of people for help and advice.

I'd like to thank Lynda Stacey for sharing her diving expertise (and cooking me a lovely lasagne). Rowena Quinan for helping me with the IT content and reading and correcting the relevant parts of the book. Mark Lacey for the crimes and police procedure – it's a bit scary how many of my books he advises on. Oliver Winbolt for inviting me to the Southampton Boat Show and showing me around the twin of the *Shady Lady* so that I could get the details right. Robin and Vicky for information about marinas. Julie Miseldine for her experiences of working with children and where to access current safeguarding and protection guides. Janet Gover for information on UK citizens wishing to live and work in the US.

When I was a child I lived in Malta and from our sitting room window could see Ta' Xbiex Marina, where the *Shady Lady* and *Seadancer* have been moored for the duration of this book. To conduct additional research on a couple of my regular visits to the island was an absolute pleasure but my knowledge of the language is sadly lacking. My thanks to Tom Restall for the Maltese translation (and dinner at the Ta' Xbiex Water Polo Club).

Gratitude also goes to my lovely beta readers: Lynda Stacey and Julie Miseldine for reading the manuscript for errors and omissions. Mark West and Dominic White for their invaluable manly observations, reflections on human nature, comedic sarcasm, mickey taking, occasional outrage and analytical spotting of holes in my plot. Your feedback is a highlight of the writing process.

As always, massive thanks to the Choc Lit Team.

Never complain, never explain,
Never volunteer.
And never own up.

Prologue

To: Simon.Rose
From: Elle.Jamieson
Subject: (Nearly) All at sea

Hi Simon,
Nearly ready! The tenants have moved into the house, the car's sold and I'm in a Travelodge near the airport, ready to fly tomorrow. It's cost a fortune in baggage charges but I've got enough for the summer and left the rest of my stuff – especially the business suits – in the attic.

I can't believe I'm going to live in a marina in Malta. Wooooooo! You're so lovely to let me stay for free. (But I'm worried I'll do something stupid and break your boat. ☺) I'm so excited! But also mega nervous. This whole adventure is so not me.

Elle xxx

To: Elle.Jamieson
From: Simon.Rose
Subject: Free on board

Of course it's you because you're the one doing it. You'll love it. Malta's fantastic and the centre where you're volunteering is lucky to have you and your expertise. Letting you stay on the *Shady Lady* while you do all the slog is my lazy way of doing a bit for charity. Also, there's no way I'll get to the boat until the autumn, so you're providing me with a boat-sitting service. Don't let her be boarded by pirates! ☺

You've familiarised yourself with the *Shady Lady* on paper and someone will be at the boat who knows how everything works. There's nothing that's hard to operate but it's a bit like a floating caravan and things tend to be tucked away in odd corners.

As Davie and Loz aren't expecting you to start work until Wednesday, you'll have a couple of days to provision the boat and get used to things like filling up the water. Chill. All you're doing is living on board – not sailing her across the ocean single-handed!

Simon xxx

PS Is this a good time to ask if you've changed your mind about Lucas?

To: Simon.Rose
From: Elle.Jamieson
Subject: Troubled waters

Pirates??? Should I expect any?

E xxx
PS No, re Lucas. I don't want to hear about the fabulous life he's probably living with you in the US ... so long as he's OK.

To: Elle.Jamieson
From: Simon.Rose
Subject: Safe harbour

No pirates in the Ta' Xbiex yacht marina. (Remember it's pronounced 'Tashbeesh' not, as someone once told me, 'Tax-bee-ex'.)

S xxx
PS He's OK.

Chapter One

Elle stared out through the taxi window, heart soaring as high as the blue sky over the sea.

She'd left sensible, dutiful, walking-work-ethic Elle behind in England and she was really here, being driven along the waterfront between the moorings and gardens fringed with waving palm trees. She was going to live on a boat and be carefree and adventurous. Rolling down her window, she breathed the warm briny air.

'You know where is the boat?' asked her Maltese driver.

'She's called the *Shady Lady*. She's all white and quite far along towards Manoel Island bridge, but not as far as the kiosk.' Elle knew Simon's directions by heart.

'OK, the other end.' The driver nodded.

The boats were moored stern-to, in sailing terminology – tied by their blunt ends. The first they passed were huge, two or three decks with gleaming chrome railings projecting out into the creek.

After a couple of minutes Elle could see a kiosk cafe and glimpses of a long low stone bridge that connected their quayside to another. There, shifting gently on her mooring ropes as if impatient for Elle to arrive, was a boat with *Shady Lady* in flowing navy script on her sleek white hull.

'There she is,' Elle breathed. Definitely one of the junior members of the marina at forty-two feet long, the *Shady Lady* gleamed in the sun, her sliding glass doors open. Fantastic. The person Simon had said would be at the boat must have arrived already.

The driver brought the car to a halt. 'I get your bags.' He jumped out, legs bare and tanned below khaki shorts.

Elle climbed out more slowly, almost in sensory overload as a hot breeze tossed her hair over her face, the sun on the water dazzling. Behind her, traffic grumbled along a road on the other side of the gardens.

'You like hot weather?' The driver opened the car boot and tugged out a suitcase, swinging it onto the quayside.

'I love it.' Elle gazed around, identifying what she'd learned from Simon and the 'boating for beginners' website she'd been haunting for the past few weeks. The metal box rising out of the quayside was where the boat connected to the electricity and water supplies. The *Shady Lady* didn't have an integral gangplank, as the bigger vessels did, but a wooden plank lay between the shore and the big shelf on the back of the boat, the bathing platform. White fenders hung at strategic points to keep the *Shady Lady* from rubbing up against her neighbours, *Fallen Star* and *Alice*.

'Very hot, the sun in Malta.' The driver hauled out suitcase two.

'It feels great after the British drizzle.'

'You be careful.' Suitcase three slapped to the ground. 'You get—' The driver paused to open the back door to drag out suitcase four, which had travelled from Malta International Airport as a rear-seat passenger. He lined it up with the others: two black that matched, a leaving gift from her colleagues in her last job, at Waterfield Systems; a bubblegum pink one from TK Maxx and one decorated with the Union flag, purchased from a market stall by Elle Jamieson, Adventurer.

'—sunstroke!' he produced triumphantly. 'Sunstroke makes you very sick. Sweaty. Dizzy.'

And even as she held out his fare and began to thank him, Elle found herself experiencing something very much

4

as he described, complete with giddiness and sweat. It was nothing to do with the sun, though the heat was beginning to press on the crown of her head.

It was everything to do with the man who had just emerged through the door of the *Shady Lady* and frozen mid-step.

'Thank you, madam.' The friendly taxi driver slid back into his car, inched around nearby fishermen dangling their lines between the boats, turned and set off back along the marina access road.

'Lucas.' The word stuck to the sides of Elle's suddenly dry throat. Her heart, which had been floating with joy, plummeted to the dusty ground. 'Lucas,' she repeated, stupidly. His black hair was longer, blowing around his jawline in the breeze, and his dark eyes burned in a tanned face. His feet were bare and if he'd ever carried even an extra ounce, it was gone. Every part of him was hard and lean.

'Elle,' he returned, flatly, 'what the high-flying fuck are you doing here?' His disbelieving gaze swept over her luggage before returning to her face. Slowly, he stepped down onto the bathing platform and halted at the edge. Eighteen inches of water lapped between them.

Elle's chest gave a painful squeeze. She swallowed. 'S-S-' She paused to will her tongue to untie itself. 'S-Simon has lent me his boat.' She glanced down at the name on the stern, seeking reassurance that she was actually in the right place. And that Lucas wasn't.

'I don't think so. Simon has lent me the boat.'

Silence. Stupid tears prickled at the back of Elle's eyes. Lucas belonged deep in the past, not here, now, obstructing the gateway to her big adventure.

'You'd better come aboard while we sort this out,'

he snapped. And then, as Elle stooped to the Union flag suitcase, 'You can leave your baggage there.'

'Right, like I'm about to heap disaster upon catastrophe by getting my suitcases stolen.' Masking her anxiety with bravado, she hauled the first towards the edge of the quay.

With a curse, Lucas leaped the gap between boat and shore and stooped to manhandle the gangplank through a couple of iron hoops and into position.

Then he swiped the suitcase out of her hand and swung it on board, beside the cockpit seat. The other three followed rapidly and Elle was left clutching her backpack as Lucas stalked across the plank, through the sliding doors and out of sight.

Barely breathing, she followed, onto the bathing platform and through the cockpit to the saloon, registering only absently the sliding gliding movements of the craft on the sea. Already familiar with boat's interior from the photos she'd pored over, her focus was on Lucas.

He slid into one of the sofa seats, propped his forearms on the table and glowered, the air fairly crackling with his irritation. 'I'm working in Malta and Simon said I could live on the boat. I've been here a week already.'

Elle slid onto one of the vacant seats, shock beginning to recede. She straightened her spine. It was time to take charge of the meeting. 'I'm in Malta working and volunteering and Simon said I could live on the boat at least until the autumn. It was agreed months ago. I can show you the e-mails—'

'I believe you,' he cut in, obviously having taken charge of a few meetings himself. His fingertips tapped on the plastic tabletop. 'It's bloody Simon.'

Miserably, she gazed at him. 'Maybe he made a mistake—'

'More likely he didn't. Now I understand the thoughtful pause when I asked if it was possible for me to use the *Shady Lady*. I just thought he needed reassurance that I didn't intend to host wild parties, and I told him that I'm relatively sane these days.' His mouth set in a grim line. 'But I suppose he was actually wondering whether to tell me that he'd already lent the boat to you, or whether to just let me make this pleasant little discovery for myself.'

Elle recoiled. 'Why on earth would he let us end up in the boat at the same time?'

Lucas snorted. 'My guess would be that he thinks it might get us back together. Like that's going to happen.'

'Yeah, right,' she agreed, stonily.

'You'll have to find a hotel.'

'Or you could.'

His eyes glittered. 'Simon's my uncle.'

'Simon's my friend. You've already admitted that he offered me the *Shady Lady* first.'

He glared. 'But I'm *in situ*.'

'I can't afford a hotel. I've arranged to work part-time on another boat for my keep but I'm going to be spending a lot of time working somewhere else. Unpaid,' she added. And, in case it made any difference, 'For charity.'

Lucas folded his arms. He wore a sleeveless T-shirt and a dusting of dark hair outlined the muscles of his arms. 'What's Miss Great Job in IT doing volunteering?'

'Becoming Miss Redundant, House Rented Out to Pay the Mortgage.'

He eyed her. 'Really?'

Elle bristled. '*Really*.' She fought hard to keep the blood from rushing to her cheeks. She knew that scepticism in his eyes, the scornful impatience whenever he suspected anything but the unvarnished truth. Seared in her memory

7

was the way he'd once talked her round in circles until she tripped up over all the things she'd kept from him and he'd said things that couldn't be unsaid and stormed off to his new life in America. She lifted her chin. 'So, how about you? If you're here on vineyard business maybe you and Simon can find the funds to move you into a hotel?'

'Maybe, if I was,' he snapped. 'But I'm not working for Simon. It seems you and me are both trying something new this summer. My budget isn't based on coughing up for accommodation, either.'

'Then I'll have to ring Simon,' she snapped back.

He leaned back, quirking one eyebrow. 'Good idea. Give Uncle Simon my love.'

Lucas watched as Elle marched out through the cockpit and ashore. After a few moments she paced out of his view along the concrete quayside, phone clamped to her ear. Then she paced back, her frown a blonde slash across her brows. Both blue-tinted sliding doors were pushed to one side, making it look as if she were changing colour as she moved behind them. Then she became animated and began to speak. Stopped. Paced. Listened. Threw up her hands. Glared at the boat. Clocked him watching; glared more fiercely and moved out of his line of sight.

He waited for her to reappear, noticing absently that his respiration rate had returned to normal and the pressure he'd felt like a band on his forehead was easing. It had been some moment when he'd seen her standing there behind her wall of suitcases, like a beautiful apparition from a disobedient imagination that should have barred heavy doors against Elle Jamieson a long time ago. But hadn't.

Had he reacted well to her appearance? He reran what

he could remember of the conversation. No, he didn't think he'd been cool, though he usually considered that the past four years had calmed him some, especially since he'd taken up scuba diving. Underwater, everything had to be measured, at least if you wanted to breathe while down there and come up healthy. Dive tables and formulas couldn't be impetuously ditched.

Lucas had learned too from being around Simon, who usually saw the best in people. Grown. Mellowed.

Until he'd seen Elle again.

Until she'd tried to work her voodoo with her big ice-blue eyes turning to pools of confusion and outrage. Like he hadn't seen that look before. Like he hadn't been driven to fury by her innocent act.

While he waited, he went to the galley and got himself a cold beer. Cisk, the produce of the Maltese brewery, was usually one of his pleasures, but today he could scarcely taste it. It was as if his senses had shut down to anything but Elle, her spicy perfume, the storm of blonde hair piled high on her head, her soft voice shocked and defiant by turns. He'd once found that voice so sexy.

OK, he still did.

He found everything about Elle sexy. Her walk, the liquid grace of her body, the noises she made when—

He clattered the beer bottle down on the table as if to shock his mind onto a safer track, just as she swept back into the cabin.

For an instant, anxiety flashed across her face. Then the spark returned to her eyes. 'I get that you're angry. I'm angry, too. But remember that your tantrums don't work on me.'

He swallowed a sudden bubble of laughter. She still knew how to push his buttons, knew that he'd consider anything as petty as a tantrum beneath him. Righteous anger, that was another matter. He could do righteous anger. Right was his constant companion.

He made his voice sweetly reasonable. 'What's the situation with Simon?'

She dropped down on the seat, sighing her exasperation. 'Faux surprise that us sharing the boat might be a problem. Enough sheepishness to make it obvious that he's bullshitting. But he says that there are two cabins, so we ought to be able to make it work.'

Lucas could envisage Simon over in California, safely out of the line of fire as he made mischief. 'Did you tell him that we recognised his half-arsed plan as inept meddling?'

'That's about when he began to say that the call was breaking up.' Folding her arms, she glared out of the window towards the cars nosing over the bridge to Manoel Island.

Lucas sipped from his bottle. 'Have a beer while you decide where you're going to go.'

The eyes she turned on him were both ice and fire. 'Nowhere! I don't have the income to find somewhere else and I don't have a house to go back to. But you can go.'

Eyes locking on hers, he managed, just, not to let her fury detonate an answering explosion in himself. 'Just out of bloody-mindedness I wouldn't, even if I did have a chance of finding somewhere for rock bottom rent now the season's started.' He waited a beat before adding, 'And I'm expecting a visitor, soon. A woman.'

Chapter Two

Elle felt as if something was slowly dragging its way through the pit of her stomach. But she managed to say, 'W-we'll have to make sure we spare her any embarrassment.' She hoped he would have forgotten that she only ever stuttered with emotion. There was no logic to her feeling so shocked by his revelation. He was hardly the kind of man to be celibate for four years. Before they'd met, Lucas had been a bit of a lad.

And Elle had been married.

There had been men for her since Lucas, of course. All right, only two, but that was 'men'.

'I have a personal code,' he said.

'You don't have to remind me.' She smiled, bitterly. 'Few people are as decent, straight and honest as Lucas Rose. Ask anyone. Certainly ask Lucas Rose. That's the way he is, the way he wants to be, and the way he no doubt has every intention of always being.'

His voice was expressionless. 'It's a good way.'

She sighed. 'How about you point out which is my room, so I can get unpacked?'

'It's called your cabin.'

'Thank you, Lucas. Yes, a room is a cabin. And the kitchen is the galley, the toilet is the head, the pointy end is the bow, the back is the stern and the upstairs is the flybridge. The gazebo thing over the flybridge is the bimini. I can read and remember the glossary of nautical terms on Wikipedia as well as the next person. Got it. Just tell me where I sleep and wash.'

He pointed with his beer bottle to the steps beside the helm. 'First door to the right—'

'Starboard,' she put in, before he could.

'It's the guest cabin. I've already occupied the master cabin. But I suppose we ought to toss a coin for it,' he added, fairly.

She wasn't in the mood to be grateful. 'I'm sure it will be fine.'

Down the steps, she opened the narrow door and stepped down into the guest cabin. It contained two single beds, a narrow wardrobe and not a whole lot of anything else.

'You can shove the beds together to make a double, if you want,' he called after her. 'The boat's water tank has to be kept topped up so it would be good if you could keep your showers to under seven minutes. Regarding the loo, usual procedure is to use the toilet block on shore as much as possible.'

'Simon explained all that. I think I'm capable of living on a safely moored boat with all modern comforts.'

She went back out to the cockpit to fetch the first suitcase, and returned carefully down the steps and through the cabin door so as not to scratch anything. The *Shady Lady* wasn't even three years old and she'd cost Simon megabucks. Or megaeuros, as he'd bought her in Malta.

Once she'd fetched all of the cases there was absolutely no floor space. Ah. She hadn't expected space to be the issue it had turned out to be. But two of her cases contained all she'd need for now, so, pretending not to be conscious of Lucas watching her from the saloon, she began back up the steps with one of the others.

Lucas was in the same place but now there were two bottles of beer before him. He gestured to one of them in invitation. She stopped, suddenly parched. With her spare hand she swooped the bottle up, gulping half of it down in one go, enjoying the chill in her throat.

Lucas's glossy black hair slid over his eyes and he raked it back. 'What are you going to do with that suitcase?'

'Put it in the lazarette.'

'My, you have been doing your homework.'

'I always was a good student.' She ignored the unsettling sensation of his eyes following her movements as she put down the beer and went through to open a hatch in the cockpit floor. The engine was down there but it was the big stowage space beside it, the lazarette, that was her target.

'Do you want a hand?' He didn't move.

'Nope.' She managed to wrangle the suitcase into the depths without toppling in after it; then fetched the other and struggled that down, too. Out in the sun she began to appreciate the air conditioning of the boat's interior. She wiped her forehead with the back of her hand and retreated to her cabin.

The narrow wardrobe held nine hangers. Working rapidly, she hung up her summer dresses and folded shorts, skirts and tops onto the shelves. Underwear remained in the smaller case, which she stowed inside the larger and, ducking, because the ceiling of the cabin sloped, the helm seat being above it, squeezed onto the floor at the far end of the space between the beds. It could be her sea chest.

She put her sponge bag in the bathroom. There was a complicated arrangement of doors and locks so that the bathroom could be shut off from the cabin or not. She chose not.

Resolutely, she refused to remember the pictures Simon had sent her of the master cabin, the double bed built into the bow under skylights. The guest cabin of this gorgeous boat would do absolutely fine.

In the saloon, Lucas still lounged, but now the beer bottle he contemplated was empty. 'Did Simon give you a key?'

'Yes. He sent it. You?' An unnecessary question as he'd been living on board for a week.

'He leaves one with Dad.' He lifted his gaze. 'Can you skipper the boat?'

She grimaced. 'No. I suppose you can?'

'In theory.'

'Are you going to move it while I'm ashore?'

Sudden amusement lit his dark eyes. 'Don't give me ideas. It would be fun to sail off around the island, just to imagine your face when you found an empty berth where the *Shady Lady* had been.'

Elle felt anger roll in her chest. 'But is it in keeping with your rigid personal code? It sounds like deceit.'

A scowl snapped the grin from his face. 'The less you say about deceit, the better.'

She snatched up her backpack, which contained the purse full of euros she'd bought in such a bubble of happiness last week, and dug out the map and notes Simon had e-mailed. 'The moral high ground is a pretty tenuous place to hang out, Lucas. It takes a lot of clinging on to. But I suppose you have just the right rigid, uncompromising, blinkered personality to carry it off.'

She flipped open the map, turning it around to orientate herself as she marched out through the doors and off the boat, pretending to herself that the rough wooden gangplank had handrails (and wishing that it did) so that she could stride across with confidence.

The sun beat at her through the already heated air but she disregarded it.

Passing the toilet building, tucked between the end of the gardens and the outdoor dining area, she strode between the kiosk and the filling station, where a few cars were parked and a boat was up on large blocks of stone as if awaiting maintenance. Approaching the rush of traffic on the busy main road, The Strand, she became aware what an effective barrier the gardens provided between it and the tranquillity of the marina. She crossed into the shade and turned right along an uneven, busy pavement that served businesses and shops.

According to Simon's notes, she was heading for Sliema, which was full of shops, cafes and bars. Its present attraction was that it was empty of Lucas Rose.

Lucas went out into the cockpit to watch Elle leave, squinting against the sun.

His hands tightened into fists of frustration. He'd thought he was over the childlike habit of blabbing his first furious thoughts. Spinning on his heel, he headed back to the cool of the boat's saloon. He shut the sliding door and snatched his phone from his pocket, selecting *Simon* from his contacts.

When the call was answered he could hardly gather enough breath to form words. 'What the *fuck*, Simon?'

Simon sighed. 'You don't have to tell me. It was a wild idea, but Elle's already made it clear that I've thrown you into a nightmare. I'm sorry. I thought you guys needed to talk. You never talked – you declared war and split up.'

Lucas clenched his eyes shut. 'Sticking us both aboard the *Shady Lady* was brutal. I feel as if someone switched the engines on while I was wrapped around one of the propellers.'

Simon carried on as if Lucas hadn't spoken. 'I've never completely known why you split up. You never told me.'

Silence. Lucas refused to let himself fill it with explanations. Some kind of residual loyalty to Elle, perhaps? Or his own massive overgrown pride that wouldn't let him admit what he'd seen.

'I'm not sure that even your parents know the whole story,' Simon added, encouragingly.

Lucas barked a laugh. 'My parents don't care why we split up. They only care that we did. They never hid their dismay over Elle's past.'

'I suppose that's their privilege. I can't say I thought their archaic attitude did them credit, and I told them that. Your father's my big brother but that doesn't stop him being a pompous butthead who needs to get his values straight. And your mother—!' Simon halted, as if suddenly remembering who was on the other end of the phone.

'Don't hold back. You obviously feel strongly.' But the fire of Lucas's anger was beginning to burn down and he sank onto the nearest sofa, suddenly realising how shaken he was by Elle climbing aboard the boat as if she had a right to – OK, she did have a right to – shock and resentment at finding Lucas there written on every plane of her beautiful face.

For several seconds, Simon was silent. Lucas could imagine him over in California, frowning as he gazed at the neat green grape vines ranked in the morning sun on the south-facing slope above the house.

Simon was only a half-brother to Lucas's father, Geoffrey Rose. Perhaps because he was a decade younger than Geoffrey, or maybe because his mother had been an exotic American rather than an ordinary Englishwoman, Simon had always been a cool uncle to Lucas and his brother, Charlie. Laid-back, feckless and fun, Simon bounced between the UK and the US, taking mad ideas into his head and acting on them. He'd fitted in well in California when he inherited a small vineyard from his mother's family and rebranded it Rose Wines.

Are you Rose white, Rose red or Rose rosé? the state-wide advertising ran. Lucas remembered vividly how he'd leaped at the chance to take up Simon's offer of a sort of junior partnership, utilising his management and promo skills at marketing affordable wines to the Californian cool kids.

He hadn't foreseen that it would spell the end for him and Elle.

At first Elle had been jazzed at the idea of a sun-filled life in the Rose Wines vineyard. Simon had always been high on her list of favourite people.

Lucas, ploughing ahead with Project California, had quickly discovered that, without a sponsoring employer, it would be impossible for Elle to get a US work permit and social security card unless she was his wife. 'So we'd better get married,' he'd concluded, with logic but little finesse. Or romance. Or love. Or thought. Or sensitivity.

Elle's excitement had gurgled away and her eyes had become places of shadows—

Simon began talking again, jerking Lucas back to the present. 'I sure regret it. Elle's upset and you're upset, and it's obvious that what I thought was a wacky way to give you a last-ditch chance to communicate was actually super-moronic meddling. Elle's remained my friend throughout the last four years and I'd hate to think I'd endangered that.'

Simon cleared his throat. 'Here's the way I'm looking at it, Lucas. I said that Elle could have the boat for the

summer, and I said it months ago. She's lost her job and—'
He paused. 'Well, there's nothing to hold her in the UK. Being able to live free on board made it possible for her to do something she wanted to do.

'Then you suddenly got this contract in Malta and asked me if you could use the *Shady Lady* as if me saying "yes" was only a formality. I'd just arrived in England for a flying visit, jet-lagged, and I thought how fantastic it would be if everything came right for Elle, for both of you. And so I did say "yes". But life isn't a chick flick and I should just have told you that I'd promised the *Shady Lady* to Elle first.'

'But I'm family,' Lucas pointed out, mulishly.

Simon's silence was its own reply.

Lucas reached for the beer bottle Elle had abandoned. Closing his eyes, he lifted it and drank, his lips where hers had been, because nobody could see him give in to the temptation.

Once the cold liquid had eased the tightness in his throat, he said, 'It would be a budget-busting pain to have to find a room or an apartment, now. The island's heaving with tourists already.' And he might as well confess. 'I've told Elle I'll be staying out of bloody-mindedness.'

Simon growled in frustration. 'Compromise and conciliation aren't exactly your strengths, hey, Lucas?'

Despite her fury at Simon – or at Lucas, she wasn't sure – it took about three minutes for Elle to fall in love with Sliema.

She found herself a table under a dark green umbrella outside a bar to watch the tourists strolling along the broad promenade beside Sliema Creek and tried to damp down her anger with a glass of the local beer, Cisk –

pronounced 'chisk', she learned from a smiling Maltese waiter, whose English seemed as natural a part of his role as his white shirt and dark trousers.

Sipping the cold golden brew, she gazed over the busy road to the sparkle of the sea, bobbing with boats and ferries in the sunshine. She soaked up the noise and colours, the novelty of being hot even in the shade, trying to lose herself in her carefully arranged new life and get past the shock of Lucas appearing like a grouchy spectre.

Presently, the smell and sight of the food around on nearby tables reminded her that it was late afternoon and breakfast at Luton Airport was a distant memory. She picked up the menu and soon the waiter appeared beside her. 'Would you like to order, madam?'

'Is the pasta good in Malta?'

He smiled. 'Madam, we taught the Italians.'

She laughed. 'Carbonara then, please.'

'And another drink?'

She hadn't finished her first, but she nodded. 'That would be great.' It wasn't as if she was in a hurry to get back to the boat.

And Lucas.

Whose fathomless dark eyes had almost sprung from his head at Elle arriving just when he was expecting his girlfriend. The girlfriend was a heavy, cloying fact that she'd need to get used to.

Her phone began to buzz. *Simon* the screen told her. For an instant, she considered dismissing the call. She couldn't believe that Simon, *Simon*, would drop her into this horrible situation, wrecking her new beginning with the reminders of a terrible end. She let it ring several times before she answered.

'I'll pay your hotel bill,' he offered, without preamble.

Her heart softened to hear the guilt and remorse in his voice. 'I couldn't let you do that.'

'I got you into this situation. I had a stupid fantasy that you and Lucas were still in love. I've just talked to him and it's obvious I didn't understand *at all*. I feel like a shit-heel.'

Elle closed her eyes. Lucas must have made reconciliation sound about as attractive to him as dead dog soup. 'Anyway, I'd never get into a hotel for months on end in high season, and if we could find an apartment it would be astronomical.'

'But you should be making me suffer. I've been a two-faced conniving asshole.'

Despite herself, she laughed. Over the last few years it had sometimes felt as if Simon were her only friend, one who cared what happened to her and whether she was sad or lonely. Co-workers came and went. Her father was taken up with Tania, his new, young, second wife. And her mother was ... as she was. Incapable of caring about anything other than her own little world.

When Lucas had stormed off to America, Elle had left Northampton, and she sure as hell hadn't headed for her hometown of Bettsbrough. No, Elle had moved to a fresh job in a fresh place where she knew nobody. She'd kept in contact with neither Bettsbrough nor Northampton friends and colleagues. In her self-imposed isolation, Simon's long-distance friendship and funny, crazy, happy e-mails had kept her sane.

She tried to joke. 'I'll be such a bitch that he'll be glad to leave the boat.'

Simon laughed. 'I don't think you could be a bitch if you tried.' Then he sobered. 'Elle. I suppose I felt justified because you always ask if Lucas is OK. And he—'

Elle wasn't certain whether to be glad or sorry that Simon didn't finish the sentence. 'You didn't tell me that he'd left the States,' she said, softly.

'No. I'd promised not to. He said that if you ever asked, he'd rather I didn't discuss his life. But you never said more than the occasional "Is he OK?".'

She had to swallow. 'Did you know he has a girlfriend?'

'No,' he said, slowly. 'I am so, so sorry. Wow. Major, major fuck-up.' He groaned. 'Elle, I could not be more sorry.'

She tried to say, 'It's all right,' but her voice broke on the words.

After Simon had rung off, still uttering apologies and self-recriminations, she took out her phrase book and distracted herself by committing a few new Maltese words to memory. *Skola*, school; *pulizija*, police; *ċentru*, centre; *triq*, street. Then the waiter brought her meal and a kind couple on the next table began suggesting places she should visit in Malta, to add to the long list of places she had never been. Till now, a school trip to France and three glorious holidays in California with Lucas had made up her travel history.

The couple left and twilight passed through in about fifteen minutes. The arrival of darkness turned the sea black and it reflected the lights of the waterfront in crazy golden squiggles.

Elle ordered another beer. Was she going to be able to live on the same boat as Lucas for the many blue days and black nights of the summer?

The thought of him loving someone else coiled around her heart like a snake.

Eventually, she paid her bill and crossed the road to walk back beside the sea, gazing across the water to Manoel Island.

She knew from her map that Manoel was vaguely fish-shaped, joined to the mainland at its tail. It lay between two arms of land, Sliema, and Malta's capital, Valletta. They gazed at each another across Marsamxett Harbour, past Fort Manoel. Sliema Creek ran from the bridge towards Sliema, and Lazaretto Creek from the other side of the bridge and around the island.

Some really expensive craft moored on the Manoel Island side, past the finger pontoons. Footballers kept their yachts there. Floating money. Some of those boats were worth more than Elle expected to earn in her entire life.

She followed the broad promenade, enjoying the faint soft sweetness of oleander as she passed bandstand-like gazebos and back-to-back benches, and men fishing in the moonlight. Hotels and apartments lined the road like stacked hutches, one light on each balcony. Joggers and power-walkers weaved between couples arm-in-arm or sauntering with their families.

Past the bridge and onto the quayside, she reached the kiosk's open-air dining area, where a game of bingo was going on in English. Beyond the kiosk children lifted their voices against the ever-present traffic as they played between gnarled pines that looked fluffy-headed in the orange lights, date palms rising spikily between. Neat hedges boxed the gardens in.

Barely moving in the slack water, the *Shady Lady* waited as Elle picked her way over mooring lines. On board, a light shone through the blinds, which probably meant that Lucas was there and she'd have to face his unwelcoming expression.

Elle's steps stopped. Her shiny summer was tarnished by having to share just forty-two feet of boat with Lucas.

But she couldn't afford to stay in Malta if she didn't live on the boat. Not unless she managed to get a proper job, and at least half the point of her new life was volunteering at the Nicholas Centre. If she let the centre down, Joseph Zammit and his wife, Maria, would have to begin all over again with another volunteer and the children she'd committed to helping would remain unhelped for several weeks during the process of interviews, questionnaires and checks.

In a world where she'd begun to feel of no real importance to anybody, the decision to volunteer had given her at least the illusion of significance. She didn't want to give it up before she'd begun. It was a commitment.

Also, Simon had got her a part-time job with some of his friends, David and Loz St John, as 'the help' on their big motor yacht. She'd hate to let them down.

She stared at the back of the *Shady Lady*, absently registering a warm velvet breeze on her skin.

She forced her mind to dwell on Lucas's girlfriend. If ever Elle had lain awake and fantasised that somehow, some day, Lucas would tell her that he was sorry he'd judged her, sorry he'd been so black-and-white about everything, or even that he wasn't one bit sorry but he'd accept her as she was. Well, now she could stop all that bloody nonsense. It couldn't be more over.

For a few moments she allowed herself to indulge in regret. In memories of how Lucas had once made her feel. Then, squaring her shoulders, she started towards the *Shady Lady*, balancing along the plank and onto the bathing platform, stepping up into the cockpit, sliding open the doors and slipping into the saloon.

Lucas was holding an e-reader, lounging in the corner of the seating. When he looked up, his eyes were no longer glittering with anger. 'I've talked to Simon. I'm sorry I was a bit of an arse when you arrived. It was a shock. It seems we both want to stay on the boat so we'd better act like grown-ups.' He even smiled. 'You've got the prior claim but at the beginning of the tourist season it really would be a mission for me to find a hotel or an apartment I could afford. And it's not as if we haven't shared before. So unless you intend to tip me overboard while I'm asleep, I plan to stay.'

A tiny amount of tension unhunched itself from Elle's shoulders. 'I can't leave either. I simply don't have the money.'

'Fine, then,' he said.

'Yes.' She made for her own cabin, suddenly overwhelmed with weariness, almost stumbling at the head of the galley steps.

'I've just been wondering, though,' he called after her, as if musing about something inconsequential, 'whether Simon's in love with you.'

Clutching the handrail, slowly, slowly, Elle turned back, fury boiling black and tarry in her heart. 'If you try and make something strange and scuzzy about my friendship with Simon – the one worthwhile relationship in my life – I'll not only tip you overboard, I'll beat you to a bloody pulp and arrange for sharks to be out for their evening swim at the time.'

He blinked. 'I'm joking.'

She turned away, down the stairs to the lower deck, and sought the sanctuary of her bed. 'I'm not.'

Chapter Three

The next morning, Elle presented herself at the St John motor yacht. Loz had e-mailed her photos of *Seadancer* and she knew she was looking for a vessel about three times the size of the *Shady Lady*. Even so, she blinked at the height of the white-and-chrome decks rising majestically above her hull.

Not being practised at boat etiquette and there not being a door to knock on, Elle stood at the bottom of the gangplank and shouted. 'Hello, Loz? Davie?' She shaded her eyes. She'd walked only a few hundred yards to *Seadancer*'s berth but already she was dazzled by the morning sun and felt it like a weight on her shoulders.

A big pair of sunglasses and a curving fringe appeared on the side deck, then Loz's smile, as big as a slice of watermelon in her shiny round face as she rattled out a stream of exclamations. 'Elle! You're early! Come aboard, come aboard, come aboard!'

Cheered by the warmth of her welcome, Elle made her way up the sloping gangplank, its guardrail already burning to the touch. 'I've just come to say hello. I know I don't start work until tomorrow afternoon.'

Loz treated her to a hot and enthusiastic hug. Her floaty top and cotton shorts were dazzling white in the sun, her flip-flops glittering with silver sequins. 'Lovely! Davie's forward, in the shade. Let's go find him.'

Feeling much higher above the water than when aboard the *Shady Lady*, Elle filed behind Loz towards the foredeck, where they found Davie slouched in a director's chair under a blue umbrella, his baseball cap pulled low and his feet propped on a red cool box.

Loz gurgled with laughter. 'Wake up and say hello to Elle, Davie.'

Davie pushed his cap back on sleek silver hair and blinked. 'I wasn't asleep: I was thinking creative thoughts.' His blue eyes smiled at Elle from a tanned face. In his sixties, now, but still a dude, Davie St John was a name that had graced sleeve notes since 1975 as a producer and session musician. Bands everyone had heard of had recorded at his production studio, Saintly John. He was even mentioned on a Pete Frame Rock Family Tree. How cool was that? Nowadays, he spent long periods on board *Seadancer* while someone else ran things back at the studio.

'Thinking creative thoughts looks relaxing,' Elle observed with a grin.

He hauled himself up to kiss her cheek, opened a small locker and pulled out two more chairs to unfold on the shady part of the deck. 'Sit down and tell Loz your plans.' He opened the cool box and produced a bottle of mineral water and three tumblers. 'She'll get it out of you so you might as well get it over with.'

Loz passed Elle a glass. 'I'm not that bad. It's going to be so great to have you here, Elle. I don't know what to call your role, though. "Steward" sounds very formal.'

Elle widened her eyes. 'It sounds like someone who has training and experience, too. I'm just domestic help.'

'You're an answer to a prayer,' Loz corrected her kindly. 'Davie and I are lazy and like being looked after. Why don't you stay for lunch? We can prepare it together; then you'll find out where everything in the galley is.'

Elle felt warmed by the spontaneous invitation. 'Love

to. Then I'll go off this afternoon and find a shop to buy supplies. I have my induction at the Nicholas Centre tomorrow morning.'

'We'll show you. Davie can help you carry your bags back to the *Shady Lady*.' Loz looked pleased with this disposition of everybody's time. Davie didn't object and so Elle didn't, either. It sounded more fun than finding her own way around.

Kicking off her flip-flops, Loz settled herself comfortably. 'Tell us about the place where you're going to volunteer.'

Elle relaxed into her seat. From *Seadancer* she was treated to the sight of hundreds of boats across the creek glistening under the sun, and her joy in spending the summer in Malta began cautiously to re-emerge. 'It's in Triq Bonnard in Gżira. Joseph, who runs the centre, says it'll take me ten or fifteen minutes to walk from the marina. Schools don't finish until nearly the end of June so my opening sessions will largely involve sixteen- to eighteen-year-olds who are out of school already. My work with younger children will mainly be supervisory or helping them with the technology, although I'll run some fun sessions in the holidays. Timewise, my sessions will be dotted around – mornings or afternoons.'

'I've always enjoyed earning money, myself,' Davie observed. 'But I admire you for what you're doing.'

'I earned money in IT. I was appalled when I received my redundancy notice because, like every other wage slave, I judged my worth by my salary slip.' Elle sank deeper into her chair. She hadn't slept well, over-aware of the gentle swimming motion of the boat. And of Lucas sleeping in a cabin only a few feet away. 'But when I began to job hunt, what excited me were the openings abroad. Dubai, Canada, Germany. The idea of applying for overseas jobs opened my mind to possibilities. I noticed on online forums that the people who were most enthusiastic about their travelling were those who were volunteering. I'm not quite adventurous enough to volunteer in Africa or India but I asked Simon what he thought about me finding a voluntary post here. He's been mad about Malta since he bought the boat.'

She paused to smile. 'He offered me the use of the *Shady Lady* and asked around for someone who might want to give me a part-time job. Which was you.'

Davie toasted her with his water glass. 'The world's your oyster if you've got no ties.'

Elle laughed. 'Then I hope my oyster is more about pearls than grit.'

Presently, Loz took Elle on a tour of the boat, keeping up a stream of chatter. Four big cabins had their own bathrooms, a smaller cabin was more modest, and the stateroom boggled Elle's mind with its run of lacquered wardrobes and drawers, two squashy sofas and a king-sized bed. The main saloon was equally as impressive, with glass doors that opened onto the foredeck just behind where they'd been sitting. Above that was a sky lounge, a gorgeous room with only glass walls between it and the breathtaking glories of the marina.

They ended the tour in the galley, so that they could wash the salad. By the time they'd eaten lunch with a civilised couple of glasses of red wine, sipped coffee and renewed their sun cream, any shops that might have shut for siesta would have opened again. They left *Seadancer* sunbathing at her mooring and wandered through the gardens to the road.

Elle was pleasantly surprised by what she found. 'I didn't realise there would be so many shops close to the marina.'

'It's a residential neighbourhood, which works out well for the yachties.' Loz paused at a rack outside a shop to pick up a straw hat with daisies dancing around the brim. She popped it on Elle's head and stood back to admire. 'You're such a pretty girl you'd probably look good with a paper bag on your head, but that really suits you.'

Elle made to put it back on the rack. 'I don't like hats.'

'Better have one,' advised Davie.

Loz nodded. 'It's not even hot, yet. Only about twenty-seven Celsius today. It could be forty in July and August and if you don't protect yourself you'll be scarlet, in agony and probably heaving over a bowl.'

'OK,' Elle sighed. The hat was cute enough, with a brim that turned up at the back, and she bought a pair of sunglasses with green mirror lenses to go with it.

When they arrived at a grocery store with a Wall's ice cream sign outside, Elle enjoyed the mix of familiar and unfamiliar products and filled her basket with salad stuff, ham, cheese, bread, eggs, butter, milk, cereals and a few tins and packets.

'Drinking water,' said Davie, puffing as he hefted a pack of six big bottles. 'Don't drink from the boat's tanks.'

'Of course,' said Elle, gratefully. 'I'll have to remember to keep my supplies up.'

Slowed by the stultifying heat, they wandered back to the marina, Elle and Loz each toting two shopping bags and Davie staggering in exaggerated exhaustion under his load of water.

Loz put in a sudden stop as they neared the *Shady Lady*. 'Oh my,' she breathed. 'I think Keanu Reeves is on Simon's boat.'

Lucas was lounging on the cockpit seat, facing the shore. He wore only a pair of black board shorts, his skin golden in the sunlight, feet bare, the ends of his glossy black hair blowing around his jawline as he concentrated on something he held in his hands.

'Oh yes.' Elle prickled with annoyance but swung her shopping bags with studied unconcern. 'Simon's nephew's living on the boat, too.' She said it loud enough for Lucas to hear.

Slowly, he looked up, and his inscrutable gaze locked on the trio as they approached.

Elle made formal introductions. 'Loz and Davie St John, meet Lucas Rose. Lucas, these are Simon's friends, Loz and Davie. Simon lined me up a job with them.'

Lucas smiled his easy, charming smile, which Elle hadn't seen much since her arrival. 'Simon's mentioned you.' He put down what looked like three gauges on a thick stick of liquorice, and with a stride and a jump arrived on the quay without having troubled the gangplank. He took the water from Davie, swinging it easily across to the platform. 'Coming aboard?'

'That would be lovely.' Loz beamed, flushing coquettishly, thrusting her shopping bags at Davie while she shuffled towards the edge of the dock as if she didn't know quite how to broach the gangplank. Obligingly, Lucas offered his hand, which made Loz's cheeks even pinker as he steadied her over the eighteen inches of dead calm water that lay between boat and shore.

When four people and the shopping had been transferred successfully to the saloon, Lucas got hospitable with fruit juice and water from the fridge as Loz sought his views on the *Shady Lady*, the marina, the island, the Malta heat and how great it would be if Loz and Davie were still on the *Seadancer* when Simon came over from the States in the autumn. 'Your uncle's as mad as a box of frogs, but such fun. Do you know many people here? We're having a little party on Friday – why don't you come? Any nephew of Simon's is a friend of ours.'

As they chatted, Elle carried the shopping bags down the galley steps. She'd been too busy and unsettled to do more than glance into the compact galley till now. It didn't take her long to locate the fridge but she found it was jam-packed with bottles of beer and water.

She glanced over at Lucas. 'Where does the food go?' She gazed around in case another fridge might be tucked away. There was a cocktail cabinet in the saloon, but she knew it wasn't chilled.

'I eat ashore.' He returned to answering Loz's stream of questions.

Elle began removing bottles from the fridge and standing them in the little sink. The boat was rolling gently and she didn't want bottles doing the same.

Lucas cut into his own discourse. 'What are you doing?'

'I'm clearing my half of the fridge.' Turning her back to him, she searched out a pack of antibacterial wipes from one of her carrier bags and set about the top shelf, half of the middle shelf and half of the door compartment, before stowing away her perishables and some of the bottles of water Davie had hauled from the shop.

Then she began opening cupboard doors and drawers. Apart from a drawer of cutlery and a cupboard containing matching plates, bowls, mugs and glasses, most were empty of anything but dust. She chose two to wipe before stowing the rest of her shopping.

Job done, she went back up to the saloon and took a seat next to Davie listening quietly as Loz continued to interrogate Lucas. He glanced at her out of the corner of his eye once or twice but Loz was demanding most of his attention.

'Are you here for a holiday?' Loz twiddled the ends of her pale brown hair as she hung on his answers.

Lucas shook his head. 'No, I'm working here for a few months.'

Loz brightened. 'You're not a skipper, are you? Because we sometimes hire a skipper to take us out. We can sail the *Seadancer* but it's a lot of hard work, so we often get someone.'

'I'm a divemaster at a scuba school,' said Lucas.

Elle found herself turning to look at him in surprise. In all the exultation, swiftly turned to panic and disappointment, of her arrival, she hadn't asked what had brought him to Malta. She'd been too taken up with the scale of the disaster of his being there and the threat to her lovely new life plans.

Apart from the facts that Lucas had left his job in events management and headed to California to learn about running a vineyard and be Simon's business guru, she hadn't really known what he'd done with his life since he'd stormed out of hers. 'A diver?' she questioned. 'Since when?'

The dark eyes swivelled her way. 'Since a couple of years ago. I took up scuba recreationally and got hooked.'

Loz jumped back in. 'There are loads of instructors on the island because the diving's popular with the tourists. The Med's not like the Red Sea but it's pretty good.'

Lucas smiled. 'I'm a divemaster, rather than an instructor. The divemasters have all the fun while the instructors take all the responsibility.'

Loz giggled. 'What did you do before diving?'

'I worked for Simon at his vineyard for a while.'

'And before that?' Loz pressed.

Lucas picked up his drink and finished it in long, slow gulps, his Adam's apple working. Then he looked into the empty glass. 'Before that doesn't matter.'

Elle felt herself recoil.

Loz paused. 'Oh. OK. Sounds mysterious.' She waited, but Lucas just smiled enigmatically, because most of his attention was focused on his own words ringing in his head. Caustic. Dismissive. Insulting, too, judging by the way Elle's smile had vanished like a popped bubble.

He tried to convey with his eyes that he hadn't meant that to sound quite as shitty as it had, but Elle's expression reminded him of a cat just before its tail began to lash. She explained to Loz, 'What Lucas is referring to is that before he went to America, we were together.'

Loz's eyes widened to saucers. 'You're joking.' She looked from Elle to Lucas and back again. 'You're not joking!'

Elle laughed. At least, her face made the right movements for laughter. But Lucas could read her better than that. The hurt in her eyes, the tightness of her fingers on the edge of the seat cushion, the rigidity of her spine. The spine he used to trace with his tongue …

She shrugged. 'It's a bit of a pain, ending up in the same boat, but it's happened so we just have to get on with it.'

'Oh my.' Loz's eyes were full of sympathy when they rested on Elle. When they moved to Lucas they became surprised, curious, but devoid of the frank approval she'd been beaming his way until that moment.

Davie was staring at him, too. 'Probably time we went,' he said, shortly. 'Thanks for the drink.' He drained his glass.

Elle jumped up to let him scoot out of his seat as Loz thanked Lucas politely for his hospitality. They both followed Elle out of the cabin, across the plank and onto the dock.

Lucas leaned forward to watch through the open door as the older couple clustered around Elle.

Loz was smiling uncertainly, touching Elle's arm sympathetically.

Davie's hands were on his hips. He frowned, talking rapidly, indicating the *Shady Lady* with his head. He looked like a protective dad.

Loz nodded along emphatically to whatever Davie was saying.

Elle, arms folded, was half-smiling, shrugging, nodding, then shaking her head. He could imagine her part in the conversation. *Yes, I'm fine. Yes, honestly. No, I can put up with him. It was all a long time ago. You don't have to worry.*

Because that was Elle. Self-contained, self-reliant. Not letting people in.

It had been one of his regular complaints, that she always treated people as if they were going to fail her. Now, for the first time, he wondered whether her reluctance had actually been a defence mechanism.

Back in the day, sure that he could cure her of this trait if he could get to the bottom of it, he'd been caustic. 'It's as if you think everyone will let you down. Even your parents.'

She'd laughed shortly. 'You have to bear in mind how my parents reacted after I made a mistake.'

'The mistake being Ricky?'

'Yes.' She was never forthcoming on the subject of Ricky, the guy, ten years older than her, who she'd married in a registry office, straight out of university, without inviting her parents. He could see how that would go down badly with any parents, let alone the controlling kind, like Elle's, and though he was aware that there was a layer of steel under Elle's soft sweet skin, her actions had seemed uncharacteristically rebellious.

When pressed, she'd expanded reluctantly. 'You know what my mum and dad are like. No understanding or compassion over my errors. I learned young never to own up because I dreaded their cutting remarks and mean silences. Marrying against their wishes was obviously going to create an absolute storm of those things so it seemed easier to at least enjoy the wedding. Without them.'

The subject of marriage hadn't come up again until, a year later, he'd made his unfortunately business-like proposal and she'd been underwhelmed.

He should have made it absolutely crystal clear that Elle was the most desirable woman on the planet and, because he loved her, he would have proposed even if his plans hadn't made it expedient. Wincing at the memory, he told himself aloud, 'You were an idiot.'

On the quay, Elle was still listening politely as Loz and Davie discussed her situation. For an instant Lucas contemplated bowling out there and warning them that they were setting themselves up for failure if they thought they could predict Elle's reactions.

Just look at how she'd reacted when he'd tried to fix things by suggesting the big wedding he'd been sure every girl lusted after. 'I'd rather get married without telling anyone. We could go to Vegas!' Elle had countered.

But he'd refused to hurt his parents by deliberately excluding them, even though they disdained the bride's first marriage. He didn't embrace their assumption that a wedding involved a marquee on a manicured lawn, but Elle's Vegas idea struck him as mean, or even a hint that it was all his offhand proposal deserved. Or all that befitted a second husband …?

His jealous curiosity about her past had spiked.

Rather than admit his fears, he'd resorted to, 'What the hell would your parents think of being sidelined a second time?'

Elle had recoiled and become almost as reluctant to talk about marriage to Lucas as she was about her marriage to Ricky. She'd looked perpetually unhappy.

She was looking unhappy again, now, while Loz and Davie exchanged uncertain glances over her bare head. Loz and Davie had put their hats back on while the flowered thing Elle had come in wearing was on the helm seat.

If she stayed out there much longer, he'd toss it out to her. She wasn't dark-haired, like him, with skin that tanned. She'd just come off the plane and her milky complexion could turn to radish before she even realised that the sun had rubbed its fiery fingers over her.

But then Elle began saying her goodbyes, stepping across onto the boat, waving to Loz and Davie.

The moment that she slipped back into the saloon, he did the right thing. 'Sorry,' he said.

Chapter Four

She stopped short, eyebrows lifting. 'Sorry that you caused me needless embarrassment?'

'I was thrown that you chose to cough your guts to people you've only just met, contrary to your usual habit of keeping things to yourself.'

She flushed. 'I've only just met them in the flesh but we've been e-mailing for months.'

With an effort, he remembered that he was supposed to be apologising. 'What I'm sorry for is sounding so melodramatic and bitter. It came out wrong. I'd realised from the way you made the introductions that you hadn't explained our history. I meant to head her off but somehow it came out all drama queen.'

The faintest of smiles tugged at a corner of her mouth. 'It was just your way of being nice?'

Reluctantly, he grinned. 'I wouldn't go as far as that. Let's just say I wasn't actively trying to piss you off.'

After a moment, she nodded. 'OK. Thanks.'

He sighed. 'Do you think it would be a plan to talk a few things out? If we're stuck with each other we might as well try and make it as easy on ourselves as possible. I haven't forgotten what you said about the sharks. I hope to swim with a few during my time here, but not when I'm sporting Elle-inflicted injuries.'

She actually looked alarmed. 'Are there really sharks in the Med?'

'Only a few, because they've been over-fished. There hasn't been a shark attack in decades.' He picked up his wallet and tucked it in the back pocket of his board shorts, trying not to read anything into the fact that she didn't seem to care for the idea of him swimming with sharks. 'Forget the sharks, let's go get a drink on neutral ground. We can discuss the rules of engagement.'

Finally, her expression relaxed. 'I could go for a glass of wine.'

They locked the boat and he led the way along to the promenade. As well as the shore moorings, boats were dotted right across the creek on swing moorings in the marine equivalent of a car park. Leisure craft in white and navy bobbed beside rowing boats. Fishing boats in traditional combinations of blue, yellow and red sported eyes on each side of their prows to ward off evil. On the other side of the creek craft nestled in cradles at Manoel Boatyard.

Elle looked content as she drank it all in. In an effort to have at least one conversation not filled with barbs, Lucas made like a tour guide. 'Further along is where the ferries leave from. They sail round the island, around the harbours, or over to the sister islands of Gozo and Comino. You'll be offered tickets every time you pass.'

'I'd love to do some cruises. On a calm day.' She tipped back her hat so that she could look at him under the brim.

His breath caught at the blueness of her eyes. 'Are you going to have time for sightseeing?' She'd mentioned something to do with a charity as well as working for the St Johns.

'If I don't, I'm going to be very upset. The whole idea of travel is to see stuff and enjoy it, so I intend to have a couple of days off every week. Simon told me to go on the open-top bus tours but that sounds really touristy.'

He stepped aside to let a family pass, her arm brushing

his, warm and distracting. 'But you do see a lot of the island in one day.'

The Ta' Xbiex waterfront became the Sliema waterfront, and the heat of the afternoon radiated up around their bare ankles as they wove between statues and pocket gardens, kiosks and bus stops. When they reached the stand for the water taxi he bought two tickets.

She hovered. 'Are we going somewhere?'

'I thought we could buzz across to Valletta. See that cafe? It's a nice place for a beer.' He pointed across the water to a huddle of bright yellow umbrellas, the fortifications of Valletta rising like stone curtains behind.

Her eyes sparkled, lighter and brighter than the sea. 'My first cruise.'

The Maltese skipper pulled the little white-hulled water taxi closer to the side, holding on to one of the struts of the yellow canopy. 'Madam. *Sinjur*. Please board carefully.'

Lucas followed Elle as she negotiated two steps down into the bobbing craft and settled herself on the cushions of a bench seat at the back. Two passengers were seated already: tourists, looking pink and hot. A small Maltese family followed; the skipper clambered into the helm seat and a man emerged from the ticket stand to cast them off, calling to the skipper in Maltese.

With a rumble, the boat edged away from the quay, and then swooped around to face Valletta. The engine note rose as they began to accelerate, bouncing over the wake of a large cabin cruiser making its way down the deep channel.

The sun was still strong, drawing patterns on the water, prompting Lucas to put on his sunglasses. From behind their black lenses he could watch Elle as she took off her hat, turned her face towards their destination and let her blonde hair dance in the wind.

Her hair had only brushed her shoulders last time he'd seen her. Now it was long down her back and she had to catch it into a tail and hold on to it so that she could gaze at the pointed shape of Fort Manoel, like a stone ship about to plough the waves, as they left behind the jumble of modern buildings that was Sliema. Before them, the citadel of Valletta rose, its aged stone buildings studded by *gallerija*, the enclosed balconies common on the island.

It was only minutes before the boat turned to present itself to a different concrete dock and Elle swayed against him with the motion, her skin feeling hotter than the sun. With an apologetic glance, she edged away.

The road into Valletta rose steeply to the right, but they crossed to the cafe only a few yards away.

'Every table with a sea view.' Elle dropped into a chair beneath a yellow umbrella, raking her hair with her fingers until it ran like gold over one shoulder as she smiled at the young waiter who appeared at their table. He looked dazzled as he took their drinks order.

Elle's gaze followed him as he crossed the road to the restaurant building. 'They must have to carry trays across all the time.'

'They do, but it's a small road. It really just comes to the two restaurants here, a few boats and the water taxis and ferries.'

'You seem to know your way around.'

'I was here last year for several weeks, with Simon. As soon as I left I wanted to come back.'

In the shade she'd discarded her hat and sunglasses and he was able to see the shadow that crossed her face. 'So we both want to be in Malta. You're right that we need to talk about how we're going to … c-coexist.' She stumbled over the final word.

Live together he supplied, silently. They used to live together. He recalled the excitement of making the decision that she'd give up her flat and move into his house on the outskirts of Northampton. Getting used to her things around, buying a new bed because she'd joked that his old one was probably high mileage. He'd known she'd been joking but he'd changed the bed even though Elle didn't seem to do jealousy. No, that was all Lucas's thing.

And, fuck, it was still eating at him that she'd never really told him everything about Ricky.

Unreasonably nettled by the realisation, instead of opening a sensible discussion about how they were going to 'coexist', he heard himself demand, 'Why were you always so weird over talking about your ex?'

Apprehension flitted into her eyes. 'What's he got to do with anything now?' She laced her fingers together.

Lucas sat back as the waiter arrived with their drinks, realising he was in danger of sounding like a pillock. 'Sorry. Nothing. It was just idle curiosity that I don't have the right to indulge. I'll shut up.' But it was interesting that she'd reacted so warily.

To defuse the situation, he caught her up on the antics of his brother, Charlie, who she'd always loved, trying to make her laugh.

When she seemed to have uncoiled, he brought the conversation back around to his ideas of how they were going to share the boat – to have his or her own space. Live and let live. Be considerate.

'And not be grouchy.' She sent him a sidelong glance.

'I'm never grouchy,' he protested.

'You were when I arrived.'

'Apart from then.' He dismissed the moment with a grin, glad to see her recovering her spirit.

'When's your— the woman you mentioned coming over?'

'Kayleigh? I'm not certain, yet.' He tried to conjure up Kayleigh in his imagination: her striking face, her straight dark red hair and her frequent smile with the tiny gap between her front teeth. 'She makes her own plans. She's not high-maintenance.'

He included the last line to see whether Elle would point out the iniquity of valuing this trait when he'd always protested Elle was low-maintenance to the point of shutting him out.

But Elle just treated him to a polite smile. 'She sounds very capable.'

'Yes, and she has a busy job to work around but she's hoping to get a late booking at a Sliema hotel.' Not that he'd actually asked Kayleigh the details of her schedule.

Elle's eyes widened. 'She's not staying on the *Shady Lady*?'

He was aware he'd made it sound that way when Elle's obvious dismay at first seeing him had made him feel as if his insides, frozen for four years, had burst into flames but was able to say, truthfully, 'She prefers a hotel.'

Picking up the menu cards, he passed one to her. 'Hungry?'

They ate as the sun disappeared, the lights of Sliema beginning to glitter across the short stretch of water.

As they pushed away their plates, he released the question that had been jumping in his throat since she'd walked back into his life. 'And how about you?'

She raised enquiring eyebrows, so blonde that they'd nearly disappeared in the cafe lights.

He took a draught of his beer. 'Boyfriend,' he said, casually. 'Partner. Significant other. Husband.'

'Oh.' She wrinkled her nose. 'Not right now. The last man I dated was a drummer in a band. We saw each other for a while.'

They lapsed into silence. To the right, past the mouth of the harbour to the open sea, Lucas could see lights from boats, pinpricks in the darkness as if a couple of the shining stars above them had slipped. He quashed an impulse to ask more about the drummer. How long was "a while"? Had she considered making a future with him? Had he made her happy?

Or had he driven her away with demands that she reveal herself, commit herself, yet signalled his own commitment with a marriage proposal that had come out more as pragmatism than love?

Had the drummer been as obsessed with Elle as Lucas had been? Had the end of the relationship cut caverns in his heart?

He stole a glance at her as she stared out across the water, her profile perfect, her body curvy and firm, her satin hair stirring in the breeze. Then he took a breath and moved the conversation back to safer ground. 'How long do you think you'll stay in Malta?'

Blinking, she turned back to him. 'Four months is my initial commitment. I'm going to be working as a volunteer at the Nicholas Centre, a drop-in youth centre. I'll be responsible for the internet cafe. Young people hang out there, of all ages and backgrounds.' Suddenly animated, she pulled herself up in her chair, placing her elbows on the table. 'I had plenty of IT skills but I had to take online courses in child protection and safeguarding. It made me realise what the Nicholas Centre is all about.'

He listened, intrigued. How different an Elle she was, now. The Elle he'd known had been very much on the fast track of a competitive post-graduate programme in an IT company, working hard, playing the game, living the corporate life. Giving to charity had been through sensibly Gift Aided money, not with time and effort.

'So what happens after the four months?'

She spread her hands in a "who knows?" gesture. 'I might find a way of staying. I might move somewhere new. I've only myself to please.'

'What about your parents?'

Elle looked down and began to toy with a fork on the yellow tablecloth. 'They split up, actually. Dad went off with a woman who's quite a lot younger than him. Tania.' She smiled, faintly. 'She has two kids, both at university, and is a bit defensive in case I take up too much of Dad's time or money. But, of course, that's not an issue.'

He stared. 'Your dad didn't strike me as the kind who'd leave. How did your mum cope?'

A shadow crossed her face. 'It was hard for her.' She changed the subject. 'So, you're diving? What made you decide on such a completely new career?'

He accepted the change with grace. It probably wasn't nice when your parents parted, no matter how good or bad your relationship with them. Elle's parents had always seemed as unchanging as the rock the island was made of. 'I started recreationally and just loved it. I worked my way through the courses to divemaster and diving was taking up more and more of my time, so I decided to make it my main job for a while. Simon's got some graduate covering my job at Rose Wines for a year and then we'll reassess.'

She listened in silence as he told her about his job at Dive Meddi in St Julian's Bay, about Vern, the owner, and the other instructors, Lars and Polly, and the fellow divemasters, Brett and Harriet. He kept the conversation light and entertaining.

He didn't say he'd had to get away from the vineyard because it turned out that there wasn't much pleasure in living a dream alone.

Elle lay in bed and let herself explore how the middle of the night felt when you were on a boat in Malta. The water lapped and few vehicles still rumbled on the main road. The darkness was warm and complete. The sea was calm and the motion slight.

Just one sheet lay between her naked skin and the soft night air.

She'd had a long day and hadn't slept well last night. Yet, here she was, staring into the darkness and thinking about Lucas asleep in the other cabin.

Why on earth had she told him about dating a drummer in a band? She hoped Lucas never found out that it had been a marching band, because she'd made Jamie sound like a rock star. It was sad that she'd actually wanted to spark Lucas's jealousy, see that possessive expression in his eyes, the one she'd once known so well.

Sighing, she wondered about the unknown Kayleigh and Lucas's smile when he spoke of her.

She brushed a tear from the corner of her eye.

Falling out of love was a lot harder than falling in it.

Chapter Five

Elle made use of the surprisingly efficient, if compact, shower, then dried herself and slid into a flowered summer dress of unexceptional length. The welcome pack from Joseph Zammit at the Nicolas Centre had requested that volunteers dress in 'everyday clothes, not too brief and not too expensive'.

There were no signs of life from Lucas's cabin. She breakfasted on cereal, yoghurt and chopped banana, sitting in the gardens, her hair spread over her shoulders to dry in the morning sun, watching people parking their cars along the marina access road and disappearing in the direction of the shops and other businesses. The occasional yachtie moved around on a boat. The gardens smelled of pine needles and, a little way off, a gardener was watering shrubs with a hose.

Despite another unsatisfactory night's sleep, Elle had woken with a feeling of serenity.

Someone had once told her that the key to dealing with grief was acceptance. Well, during the wakeful hours she'd done some accepting.

It was cruel that fate – or, rather, bloody nutcase Simon – had to bring her and Lucas back together in order for her to finally understand that there was to be no fairy-tale ending. She hadn't quite got as far as being glad that Lucas had found someone he could be happy with. Maybe that would come later. But she had accepted it.

Lucas had moved on.

Having to share the boat with him was definitely making her fantastic new life a little less fantastic.

She'd anticipated looking forward, living in a foreign land, transforming herself from wage slave to free spirit.

Not looking backwards and wondering and reliving.

'Get over it,' she told herself aloud, scraping up the last of her yoghurt. 'History's not for changing.' She'd throw herself into working at the Nicholas Centre and aboard *Seadancer*, and she'd spend her free time exploring the island, learning about its history and its treasures, or swimming in the beautiful Mediterranean. Later in the summer she'd decide what came next and hers and Lucas's lifelines would uncross for the last time.

She went back on board the *Shady Lady* to leave her dish and pick up her tiny, lightweight backpack, popping into it her purse, hat, sun cream and a bottle of water. And, because she'd been in IT rooms before, she added a pack of cable ties and a roll of sticky labels she'd brought with her from England.

It was only eight-twenty when she went ashore, after flipping off the isolator switches, locking up the *Shady Lady* and dragging the gangplank back onto the shore with an effort.

Joseph had said it would take her fifteen minutes to stroll to the Nicholas Centre. She fished out her street map, crossed the gardens and the road, then began up Triq San Gorg, her bag over one shoulder, the bottle of water cool against her through the fabric.

Once she'd left the shops behind, houses lined the road, all with flat roofs, many built of the pale honey-coloured local stone. She'd read that some thought the name Malta came from the Greek and Latin name for honey, *Melita*. Red geraniums and other plants nodded through balcony railings. Painted shutters stood open to the morning light either side of windows, some of which were protected by curving wrought ironwork.

Around her, people went about their morning routines: beautiful brown-eyed children in school uniform, golden-skinned women with babies or wearing smart lightweight business suits, dark-haired men in short sleeved shirts, carrying their jackets and briefcases.

She tried to catch the rhythms of the language she could hear over the traffic. It sounded almost like Arabic, full of rising notes and glottal stops.

As she followed her map away from the sea, the houses became smaller and the pavement more uneven. The occasional doorstep protruded into her path, an ankle-rapping trap for the unwary. Lines of parked cars narrowed the way.

After loitering to take a picture with her phone of a blaze of vermilion flowers climbing over a high wall and creeping along a telephone wire above the street, Elle eventually found herself in Triq Bonnard.

The street was short and narrow and crowded with houses, some in disrepair. One had its windows boarded up with *For Sale* painted on the wood.

Elle paced along the pavement looking for signs of life, wiping a sheen of sweat from her forehead. She'd been e-mailed a picture of the entrance to the Nicholas Centre, a tall wall with a green door set into it, but looked for it in vain. And there was no one around for her to ask. No car tried to navigate the narrow strip of road left by parked vehicles.

At the top of the street, bemused by the absence of green doors set in tall walls, she prepared to make her way down the other side.

Then a smiling man appeared from around a jink in the

road. 'Elle? I'm Joseph Zammit. I saw you through the lounge window.'

Recognising the small, thickset man immediately from the Nicholas Centre website, Elle stuck out her hand in relief. 'Joseph. I'm glad you found me, even if I couldn't find you.'

Joseph wore black-framed glasses and his hair was conventionally short. He was middle-aged, a little overweight, and socks showed at the toes of his sandals. 'You turned away too soon.' He ushered her a few steps further and she realised that what she'd assumed to be another street was actually a continuation of Triq Bonnard, and there was the green door in the wall standing ajar beside a small black plaque: '*Ic-Ċentru Nicholas*' and, underneath, *Nicholas Centre*.

It wasn't a grand entrance, but it opened into a courtyard with a bench and a limestone fountain, although it wasn't working. Tall windows and balustraded balconies made the building itself unexpectedly imposing.

He led the way across the courtyard, up the steps to the double doors and into a hall with archways opening into other rooms. After the sun outside, the coolness was a relief.

Joseph's office was to the right. A desk was shoved against the wall under the weight of a heap of paperwork and a laptop. Several mismatched chairs faced one another untidily.

From e-mails, Elle knew that Joseph's mother was English, a retired teacher, and his late father had been a Maltese hotelier. He spoke perfect English, if with a Maltese rhythm and flow, but when his telephone rang he slid it out of his shirt pocket and answered in rapid Maltese.

Elle took a seat while he located a piece of paper from the chaos of his desk, and then read something from it to the caller.

After he ended the call, he apologised. 'I spend too much time on the phone.' He took one of the other seats, a green office chair with its sponge filling escaping, and his smile flashed. 'Welcome to Malta.'

All the joy and anticipation of the past weeks swooshed through Elle's heart and she found herself beaming as volunteering began finally to transition from pipe dream to reality. 'It's fantastic to be here.'

He inclined his head. 'And welcome to Nicholas Centre. Some of our computers are old and cranky but I hope that you can get the best out of the equipment and encourage the youngsters to make the most of what we have.'

'I'm sure I can.'

'We have all kinds of young people attending the centre. Some use the gym, others play games, some keep up with Facebook. They come for company, because they're bored or because their friends do. Some participate in workshops or want help with a project. Sometimes—' He smiled. 'Sometimes, you'll find you have to step back from your expectations. People won't turn up for a workshop or they'll bring eight friends who haven't signed up. They'll leave halfway through, they'll decide to play a game instead of completing a task. You should be aware.'

'I understand. Will it be a problem that I just speak English? I've only learned a little Maltese.'

'Sometimes,' he said, honestly. 'But English is one of our official languages. Lots of companies come to Malta because English is widely spoken. Lots of tourists, too. English is part of Maltese education.

'I'll show you around and introduce you to Maria.

You don't have your first structured session until Friday but you said that you have a programme of work to get through first?'

Elle followed him across the hall. 'I want to assess the equipment and see where improvements can be made.'

The Nicolas Centre had once been quite grand. The rooms were large and lofty and wrought iron graced the outsides of the windows. Ornately moulded plasterwork on the ceilings was a recognisable remnant of splendour, though patched and pitted.

But in the lounge, the furniture was worn and the walls scuffed. DVDs and CDs in tatty cases flanked television and music systems and a bookcase was jumbled with books and magazines.

A notice board displayed photos of Joseph; his wife, Maria; and others – a sandy-haired man with freckles and a wide smile; a darker man with a thin, sensitive face; and a more mature woman. Under the sandy man's picture it said, *Oscar, from the Netherlands* and beneath the thin man, *Axel, from Germany*. It was written in Maltese, also. The woman was, *Aileen, from England (but a long time ago)*. Elle already knew that Aileen was Joseph's mother, who came in to help, often in the computer room. She was great with written English but not a techie.

Elle was touched to see her own photo: *Welcome to Elle, from England, who will be looking after our internet cafe and running our IT sessions*. After Lucas's reaction, it was nice that someone was glad to see her.

Down the passage, a games room held a pool table and two lads playing table tennis across a ragged net. It led into a gym room containing a cross trainer and a rowing machine, a mini rainbow of gym balls and a rack of weights. 'Impressive.'

'We were lucky. This equipment was donated.' Joseph patted the cross trainer.

Across the hall he showed her a small musty room filled with racks of clothes. 'People donate what they no longer need, which Maria, in her housemother role, kindly washes. Some of the children welcome the clothes.' Joseph grimaced. 'But it sometimes seems that the more in need a child is, the less likely he or she is to accept. Even Maria cannot find a way to make a gift to some of our young visitors.

'Let's find Maria. Her first language is Maltese. Me, I speak English with a Maltese accent and Maltese with an English accent.' He laughed.

The kitchen held a refectory table, cupboards, counters, and a couple of smaller tables. They found Maria unpacking a box of fizzy drinks, her thick dark hair clipped up. A door to a small street stood open, letting in the air.

'Welcome.' Maria took Elle's hands and kissed her on both cheeks. 'We are pleased you are here, someone who understands the computers, because when they do not work ...' She pulled a comical face of frustration.

Her English wasn't quite as effortless as Joseph's. Silver was beginning to shoot an occasional strand in her hair, but her eyes were dark and sultry. Like Lucas's.

Elle shoved the thought away. 'I know that feeling.' She felt an instant liking for Maria. They hadn't conversed via e-mail, as Elle and Joseph had, because Maria didn't write English well enough to enjoy doing so, but her smile was warm.

They left Maria unpacking and returned to the broad staircase, walled on either side.

On the first floor was an activity room with tables

and chairs, paintings on the walls and sewing in trays. 'You'll usually find Axel up here and Oscar down in the games room and gym, making a noise with the energetic children.'

Joseph showed Elle where to find the clean but antiquated toilets. And then, with an air of ceremony, threw open double doors at the end of the landing. 'The big salon. At first, I thought I would divide this room. But it's useful for parties or carols at Christmas. Sometimes, entertainers will come. So the big salon remains big.'

'Wow.' Elle gazed down a room lined with windows at one side and two chandeliers dangling from the high ceiling. 'The building is quite a place.'

'It belonged to my Great Uncle Nicholas. He was a kind man and used to try to find little jobs for local children so they could earn pocket money.' He smiled, reminiscently. 'He had compassion. When he made me the beneficiary of his will, I decided to use the house in a way he would have liked.'

'That's beautiful,' said Elle, softly.

They retraced their steps along the landing to a door at the top of the staircase. 'I've left the computer room till last. I don't think you'll say "wow" to it.' He thrust open a door labelled: *Internet Cafe*. And, underneath: *Ikel u xorb projbit. No food or drink.*

Inside were eight computers ranging from what Elle would have tossed away five or six years ago, with deep monitors and dingy mismatched keyboards, to one that might actually have come out of its box this year. Two printer/scanners squatted on a cupboard. The tables and desks were a motley selection, and wires were gaffer-taped to the carpet.

'Right,' Elle murmured, hit forcibly by what it would

mean to be *'responsible for the Internet Cafe'*, as she'd proudly told Lucas she was. It was a far cry from ranks of up-to-date machines gracing matching desks.

Joseph chuckled. 'The equipment isn't pretty, but it works. I have a tiny budget put aside to improve things, but I have waited for you to tell me how to spend it.' He unlocked a pair of cupboard doors to display more monitors and computer towers, keyboards and a straggle of wires. 'The equipment that doesn't work is in here.'

Weakly, Elle laughed. 'Well, OK. I have plenty to go at.'

Joseph passed her a bunch of three keys. 'Room key, big cupboard and small cupboard, where the printer paper's kept. You know where the kitchen is – get yourself a drink when you want one. I'll be in my office—' He paused, took a step towards the open door and peered around it. 'Carmelo?'

After a moment, a young Maltese boy stepped out of the shadows with a shy smile. His eyes were wide and bright, his hair unkempt. His sand-coloured shorts were too well washed and too big, and his once-white shirt was too small. His bare feet were in sandals, also too big. He looked to be about eight years old and his face was alive with intelligence.

'Hello,' said Elle encouragingly. And then, remembering her phrase book, *'Bonġu.'*

'Hello.' His smile widened. 'I am Carmelo.'

'I'm Elle.'

'I like computers.'

'So do I.'

Joseph broke in. 'Carmelo is usually at school at this time.' He cocked a quizzical eye at the young boy, who

54

instantly gazed down at his worn sandals. 'Carmelo, you know that I must not let you come here during the hours you should be at school.'

Carmelo stepped on the bare toes of one foot with the heel of the other and pressed down, as if punishing himself.

Elle's heart went out to him. 'I need somebody to help me in the computer room this morning.' Then, as Carmelo looked up, hopefully, 'But I'm not happy about children missing school.'

The boy looked down again. 'I help today. I go to school tomorrow.'

Over Carmelo's head, Joseph glanced at Elle and nodded slightly.

'Thank you,' she said, to Carmelo. 'Just this one time, OK? And after that you need to go to school when you should.'

Carmelo peeped through his hair at her with an expression that suggested he wasn't overly fond of the idea.

She decided to take it as acquiescence. She'd requested his co-operation; now she could only await the result. 'Let's go and ask Maria for cleaning things.'

Soon, they were back in the computer room armed with cloths and hot soapy water, cola for Carmelo and water for Elle.

'I will switch them on?' Carmelo gazed greedily at the computers as Elle opened the windows in an effort to let some of the heat out of the room.

'In a while. Other things to do first.' Elle began to unplug leads from the backs of monitors.

Carmelo gasped. 'We will not know how to put the wires again!'

Elle grinned. 'Don't worry. I know. I don't like leads that look like spaghetti.'

Carmelo laughed, eyes shining.

Working steadily, they soon had the monitors lined up at the side of the room as if they were queuing for something, then a row of computer towers, each with a keyboard on top, and a nest of computer mice. They wiped down the tables and rearranged them in an island, back-to-back and side-to-side.

'They don't fit,' observed Carmelo, sliding his fingers down one of the gaps created by differing heights and shapes.

'The gaps will come in useful.' Elle surveyed her collection of monitors and began lifting – heaving in the case of the older, heavy models – them into place, one on each table. She wrung out a cloth and put Carmelo in charge of wiping the monitor cases, allocating each table a keyboard and a CPU. Then they began on the wires, swiftly plugging in and screwing into place, dropping cables between tables, looping surplus and securing it with ties.

She looked at her watch. And yelped. 'I have to go.'

Carmelo looked disappointed. 'Tomorrow—'

'School.' She fixed him with a beady eye. Then, as he nodded in resignation, she asked, 'What time will you finish?'

He looked suddenly hopeful. 'Twelve o'clock.'

'I'll wait for you here and you can show me how much you can do on a computer.'

'Yes, I will like to!' His thin, big-eyed face glowed.

'After you've been to school,' she emphasised.

He sighed. 'OK. I will do it.'

'But now I've got to rush. See you tomorrow, Carmelo.'

Elle grabbed her things, ran downstairs and gabbled a quick update to Joseph as she returned the computer room keys so that he could lock up, later; then she rushed out across the courtyard and back towards the yacht marina.

Inevitably, because she was in a hurry, she missed a turn and came out too far along the waterfront, breathless and sweating, but she followed the creek back to the *Shady Lady*, taking her life in her hands when a car suddenly swerved off the seafront road to cross Manoel Bridge.

The boat was as she had left it. She wondered where Lucas was, and then reminded herself that there was no reason for her to know.

It felt almost familiar, now, to shove the gangplank into place and unlock the door to the saloon. She flicked the isolator switches and activated the air con to counteract the sweltering heat that had built up aboard before jumping down the steps and into her cabin. A knee-length summer dress might be suitable for the Nicholas Centre but she was pretty sure it would be a pain when cleaning a yacht, so she wriggled quickly out of the dress and into denim shorts and a sleeveless top. She found her oldest flip-flops, purple with cheerful blue beads, and then whisked back through the cabin, switched everything off, locked up, and hurried along the hot concrete of the quayside to where *Seadancer* was moored.

This time, Elle went straight up the gangplank, shouting her hellos. Loz appeared from the forward deck. 'Just in time for a glass of wine.'

Elle giggled. 'I'm supposed to be working.'

Loz looked struck, before her face broke into a beaming smile. 'Oh yes. We'll get lunch together, then. Why are you out of breath? You didn't rush, did you?'

'I was only just going to make it—'

'Make what? Slow down, Elle. You're in Malta. It's hot. The boat would still have been here in five minutes. Don't worry.'

Don't worry wasn't a philosophy that Elle had ever lived by, especially since Ricky. But it sounded attractive. She resolved to try to apply it.

The *Seadancer*'s galley was considerably larger than the *Shady Lady*'s. Elle got Loz to sit down at the dinette and began to wash and slice salad things, cutting cooked chicken breasts into neat fans and buttering crusty bread – '*Ħobż*,' said Loz – and arranging it on two plates.

Loz looked aghast. 'What about you?'

'I'll have a sandwich while I clear up.' Elle needed the money from Loz and Davie and didn't want them to think she was only playing at working for them. Being domestic help was new to her but that didn't mean she couldn't be the best domestic help possible.

'I'll eat here, then,' said Loz, immediately. She disappeared up on deck and Elle heard her calling to Davie. 'I'm eating in the galley so that I can chat to Elle. Do you want to join us or stay there? Oh good, bring the wine, darling.'

She reappeared in the galley and flumped herself comfortably down. 'Davie's coming.'

'Right,' said Elle, wondering how she was ever going to actually achieve anything.

When Davie ambled in he poured Elle a glass of cold white Frascati before she could ask him not to, and she found herself cleaning down the galley as she munched a chicken salad sandwich and sipped wine that she was sure was much too expensive to be treated so casually.

'Your ex was a bit of a shock.' Loz dipped chicken in a swirl of mayonnaise. 'But, ooh.' She gave a wiggle.

Elle ran hot water and found the spray cleaner for the counter tops.

Loz attacked a slab of crusty bread. 'He's a serious hunk, isn't he?'

Cleaning industriously, Elle made a non-committal noise.

'Before I knew he was your ex I really liked him. You weren't married, were you?'

Elle kept her eyes down. 'Me and Lucas? No.'

'That's something. But it must be really awkward sharing such a small space. Do you think he's likely to expect ... you know?' Loz paused delicately, eyebrows arched and fork poised.

'No.' Elle shook her head, face flaming. *You know* would involve a lot of Lucas and not many clothes and the idea made her heart skip.

'But don't you even—?' Loz began.

Davie cut across her. 'Elle, if it ever gets too uncomfortable, there's a cabin here for you.' And he went back to his coleslaw and potato salad.

'Of course there is,' Loz agreed immediately.

Elle gazed at them both in gratitude. 'Thank you! That's so lovely of you when you haven't known me long. But I doubt it will come to that. We've talked, and we're both cool with the situation.' She opened the oven. It was sparkling clean inside.

Loz allowed the subject of Lucas to drop. 'We don't use the oven. It only gets smelly and hot in here if we cook. We like salad and we like eating ashore. At sea, I do use the microwave, though.' She waved her fork at the black and shiny appliance built neatly into a slot. Everything in the galley, oven, fridge, cupboards, drawers, was a triumph of design functionality. What wasn't pale wood was shiny black, clean white or jolly yellow.

When Loz and Davie had finished eating, Elle cleared, washed up, grabbed the polish and the lightweight vacuum cleaner and whisked off to begin on the main saloon, the favoured indoor space.

Loz, a bit pink from all the wine, followed, and kept up a stream of conversation from a sofa. 'And can you change our bedclothes, sweetie? I'll show you the clean linen and the washing machine.'

'Washing machine?' Elle grinned. 'Seriously?'

'There's sort of a hatch to it. Dreadful squeeze for me but a slender little thing like you won't find it a problem.'

Loz took her to inspect the hatch in a companionway. Four steps led down to where a full-sized washer-dryer squatted below deck as if playing hide and seek.

The bed in the master stateroom was huge. Elle stripped the bedclothes and began the laundering process, making the bed up again in fresh sheets of navy and gold before starting on the unused cabins and their bathrooms.

Loz drifted past once more. 'Would you wash the foredeck windows? They get very salty and dull.'

Elle gathered up a bucket, a squeegee and a few cloths and followed Loz out into the sunshine of the foredeck. Davie was already lounging comfortably in one canvas chair and Loz took another, as voluble as Davie was quiet.

And as Loz laughed and joked, Elle splashed water around and made the windows gleam, thinking that there were worse ways to live than with the glorious blue sky above, the boat rocking gently at its moorings and musical clinking coming from the rigging of a nearby sailing yacht. Her movements began to slow, taking their tempo from the boat. Even Loz's relentless conversation assumed a more leisurely rhythm.

Elle smothered a yawn as she gave the last pane its final polish.

'Sit down and drink another glass of wine,' Loz ordered. 'It's five o'clock and you've done enough for today. Can you do Friday afternoon and evening? We've got friends coming aboard and I'm hoping you could do the barista thing, then clear afterwards.'

'That's fine.' Elle gazed at the Frascati as Davie pulled it out of the cool box, moist with condensation, and couldn't come up with a reason to resist it. She put down her cloth and took a glass, settling herself on the deck with her back propped comfortably against the guardrail. 'Thank you.'

Loz beamed. 'That's it, darling. Loosen up.'

'I'm loose.' Elle stretched out her legs and yawned.

Chapter Six

Lucas lounged on top of the boat and watched Elle stroll towards him along the curve of the quayside.

Even from a distance he was clonked over the head by the way her legs looked in her very short shorts. Legs that he had in no way forgotten.

Hatless, she reached up and loosened her hair from its ponytail to let it blow behind her as she strolled between the yachts and the gardens that teemed with families now that the sun had lost some of its afternoon savagery. She showed no sign of being aware of how many men were checking out the hot cool blonde as she sauntered by.

He wondered which Elle was heading his way. The poised one? You could take that Elle anywhere from a formal party to a rock climbing weekend and she'd be fantastic. Fun, articulate, quick-witted, alight with laughter.

It was the wary, withdrawn Elle that he found harder to deal with. A hundred times he'd watched her slide from laughing playfulness to grave watchfulness, picking her words as if one bad choice would explode in her face. Hell of a trick to know what was going to kick off the transition, though.

The subject of her ex-husband, Ricky – that he could understand, even if it irked him. People liked to put bad relationships behind them.

His parents? Elle had never dealt well with their habit of holding themselves aloof from those who fell short of their standards. His mother was straight-talking, his father a little chill, but it wasn't as if anybody had offered Elle money to leave Lucas alone or sent heavies to scare her off. He frowned. His parents hadn't remotely succeeded in influencing him against Elle but maybe he'd been too dismissive of her anxiety that they would.

And then the subject of marriage had brought out her mild freakiness—

Don't go there, down that labyrinth of unanswered questions and half-understood baggage.

She was drawing close enough for him to hear her flip-flops on the concrete. Her hair blazed in the sunlight and blew across the shoulders of her deep turquoise top.

'Hey,' he called down.

She looked up, shading her eyes. 'You're on the flybridge. I haven't been up there.'

'Come up now.' He might have known she'd use the proper name. Most landlubbers would have called it 'the roof', but that was Elle: precise.

She disappeared from his view as she approached the gangplank and a few seconds later appeared at the top of the steps. 'Fantastic,' she breathed, gazing around at this open-air lounge – if lounges had radar and GPS equipment at the back and a helm at the front.

Lucas lazed along one seat, a bottle of water open on the deck beside him. Elle dropped down on the seat at an angle to his. Her nose was slightly pink and a few freckles had appeared on her cheekbones. She looked familiar yet unfamiliar. 'How was your day?'

'Good, thanks.' He tried to ignore an echo of old conversations, when living with Elle meant something quite different to what it meant now. 'I was on a dive with my favourite instructor, Polly, and we took four tourists over to Ghar Lapsi, on the other side of the island.'

She turned on the seat and drew up her legs, so that her

side rested on the seatback and she could lay her cheek against her knee to watch him as he talked. He kept his own gaze on her face. It would be easy to let it follow the curve of her thigh down into those tiny frayed shorts, but she'd be bound to notice his eyes straying. He didn't want to make her uncomfortable. Even more, he didn't want her to point out that he'd long ago lost the right to take liberties. But his eyeballs felt weighted, straining to shift down so he could just check out—

'Is diving dangerous?'

He blinked. 'No, it's not dangerous if you know what you're doing and follow the rules. It's a fantastic experience. Most divers are great people to be around.'

He went on talking about Dive Meddi and its clientele of tourists. The *Shady Lady* rocked peaceably, the breeze whispered in his ears over the background rumble of the traffic.

As he watched, Elle's hair blew across her face. Her eyelids slid gently shut. Then he was hit by what it was that had seemed so unfamiliar – she was relaxed. No more staring into space and frowning, no more looking away when he caught her looking at him, as if worried that he'd read her thoughts and not liked what he found.

No more evasion.

His stomach curled to remember his casual enquiry about the man he'd seen her talking to outside her workplace, and her stuttering replies. It was no wonder he'd suspected the worst. Her hesitation over marrying him had assumed massive proportions until he was one writhing mass of suspicion. The Incredible Hulk had had nothing on the green monster that had burst out of him, wreaking carnage on their relationship.

She'd flinched as if his words were daggers, panic in her

eyes as her expression had flipped through shock, horror and dismay. Then the familiar shutters had come down as he'd given her the ultimatum that had sent them careering to the end of the road.

Charlie had told him he was an arse. Charlie hadn't believed Elle was seeing someone else. Charlie had offered to talk to Elle to try and discover the truth.

Lucas had bellowed, 'What would be the fucking point of that? She's made the truth obvious!' But his fury hadn't really been at Charlie. It had been at Elle, and at himself for allowing jealousy to turn his suspicions into disaster.

His parents had been pleased, as if he'd come to see things their way at last. Pride had prevented him from telling them the bleak truth.

Now that he could study Elle unobserved, he found that his major desire was just to watch her sleep, her lips softly parted, her lashes against her cheeks. She had chosen a seat in the shade, under the bimini. But as the sun sank it grasped her in one of its beams. A sheen began to form on her face.

He reached forward and gently pressed her shoulder. 'Elle? You should probably get out of the sun.'

Her eyes opened, widening as she uncurled, testing her neck as if she'd put a crick in it. Then she gave him a beautiful, brilliant, languorous smile, just as she used to when she was delighted to wake and find herself beside him.

The smile flew like a missile to his chest and burst inside his heart. He couldn't look away. Couldn't unlock his eyes from her mouth, which kept on smiling just for him.

For an instant he thought he was going to be physically unable to resist leaning forward and—

The smile faded. Elle's expression flicked to one of

confusion and she scrambled upright. 'I've got stuff to do. Thanks for waking me.' She yawned as she dropped her feet to the floor, face flushing as she lost a flip-flop and fumbled over retrieving it.

'No problem,' he said gruffly, watching her take three attempts to slide her high-arched foot between the straps and beads. With another smile – a small, wary one this time – she disappeared down the steps in the direction of the cockpit.

Lucas sat where he was until normal rhythm returned to his heart.

When Elle set off for the Nicolas Centre in the morning her step was light. After spending ten minutes learning some more Maltese phrases, she'd spent much of the previous evening on the cockpit seat with pad and pen, insects buzzing companionably around the light as she drew up plans for maximising the efficiency of the computer room at Nicolas Centre. It might not be everybody's cup of tea because, well, not everyone found IT fun, but to her it didn't even feel like a job. There might be no huge corporation's work practices hinging on her actions, and she was used to controlling a budget of considerably more than a few euros, but she was beginning to find making something out of so little a challenge. Bringing order out of chaos was satisfying.

Arriving at the centre, she breezed across the courtyard and past the dry fountain. The door stood open and she was through it and into Joseph's office in a few steps. 'Can I talk to you—?' she began. 'Oh. Sorry.'

Two men were seated in Joseph's office. Both rose, and she recognised them as her fellow volunteers from their pictures on the noticeboard in the lounge.

Oscar, the one with sandy hair, was possibly the tallest man Elle had ever met. He seemed entirely made up of gangle. Arms and legs straight, back long, he towered over her.

Dark-eyed Axel, probably of above-average height, looked short next to Oscar. His hair was brushed straight back, accentuating a tall forehead.

'Well, hi.' Oscar stuck out a large hand. 'And you are our new lady, from England.' He spoke English fluently, though with a breathy Dutch accent. 'Please won't you sit?' He pulled up a chair.

Axel's German accent was harder and more deliberate, as if he needed to check every word. 'Welcome to Nicholas Centre.'

Oscar seemed a lot more interested in Elle than in continuing the meeting that had been in progress and led the conversation into a swapping of information about roles and nationalities. She felt uneasily conspicuous under his intent gaze.

In contrast, Axel was quiet. He frowned at Oscar from time to time, as if pained by the Dutchman's heavy humour and blasts of laughter.

Joseph brought Oscar to a halt. 'We are discussing the under-11s' five-a-side football match on Saturday, Elle, but I could meet with you when we've finished?'

Elle jumped up. 'Fine. I'll go up and start.'

'But you leave us too soon,' protested Oscar, patting her chair as if to tempt her to take her seat again.

Ignoring this clumsy playfulness, Joseph fished the computer room keys from his desk. 'I'll follow you up in a few minutes.'

Elle ran up the stairs and it wasn't long before she was engrossed in assessing the router, the speed of the broadband and the various operating systems on each machine, checking out the sizes of the hard drives and how full they were, shaking her head that the machines were automatically logged in and all users had administrative rights. Then, as Joseph hadn't made an appearance, she signed into her e-mail and found a message from Simon.

From: Simon.Rose
To: Elle.Jamieson
Subject: Forgiven me for my meddling, yet?

Elle,
As I said on the phone, I'm deeply sorry. I see now that I did a completely stupid thing. If you want me to make Lucas quit the boat, I will do. Tell me if you need me to give him shit.

Apart from awkward living arrangements, how are you liking Malta? And how are Loz and Davie? I know you'll love them.

Much love,

Simon. xxx *penitent face*

Elle replied.

To: Simon.Rose
From: Elle.Jamieson
Subject: Forgiven

Simon,
I think me and Lucas have more or less worked things out and we're getting along, even if not as best friends. I can't really feel angry any more as I have learned something from the situation – Lucas has moved on.

She paused, trying and failing to formulate some profound words about acceptance and rite of passage. Eventually, she settled on:

> So I can move on, too! ☺ Sometimes it takes the relationships that don't last to teach us the lessons that will.
> The centre is really interesting and I feel as if I'm doing something that matters a lot more than making money for a faceless corporation that dumped me when I didn't fit with some precious new structure.
> I LOVE Malta. Truly, madly, deeply love it.
>
> Love and hugs,
>
> Elle

She pressed 'Send' as Joseph arrived, puffing at the climb up the stairs.

Elle spun her chair around. 'Is there any prospect of getting better broadband? This is slow enough to embarrass snails.'

Joseph dropped into a neighbouring chair. 'I can try. Our provider gives us a discount, as a charity. It's normal practice for me to contact all benefactors from time to time to see if I can encourage them to increase their assistance.'

'Fantastic. Ask them if we can have at least double the current speed. And do you mind if I format all the machines and set up a limited-access user account for each? Then I can make downloading apps an admin-only privilege. These machines are grinding to a halt under the weight of stuff they don't need.'

Joseph nodded. 'All sounds good. Keep me in the loop and give me a note of all passwords. Can you keep some machines available while you make the changes?'

'I'll work on one at a time,' she agreed. 'Are people allowed to save data directly to the machines? The problem with that is nobody clears out outdated stuff.'

He lifted his hands, looking very Maltese. 'They shouldn't. They should bring a memory stick or burn to a disk. But ...'

'OK. There are a couple of external hard drives in the cupboard and some old towers, too. I could use their hard drives and add a server to the network. I'll move any data I find to them, and it'll provide a place for people to save their stuff if they don't have a stick or a disk. That should prevent the machines from being clogged up.'

Joseph's pocket began to ring and he nodded as he fished out his phone. 'Anything else?'

'How long will it take Carmelo to get here from his school?'

'Ten minutes if he runs. Fifteen if he walks.'

'Thanks.'

As Joseph left, speaking Maltese into his phone, Elle began on the first machine, moving data, formatting the hard drive and reinstalling the operating system.

As she worked, two boys and a girl of sixteen or seventeen came into the room. She smiled and introduced herself and they settled themselves at machines, casting their eyes around at the changes to the layout. They gave their names as Alice, Gordon and Antonio.

Once the machine she was working on was safely formatting, Elle scooted her chair closer to Alice. 'Need any help with anything?'

The girl dimpled shyly and shook her head. 'I'm just on Facebook.'

The boys were playing computer games. Elle was fine with that: computers were meant to be used and Alice,

Gordon and Antonio were all interacting with technology and the cyber world in their preferred ways.

Because she didn't want to take more than one machine out of commission at a time and neither Alice, Gordon nor Antonio seemed to have ambitions to conquer spreadsheets or lay out a CV, Elle turned to other tasks.

She cleared up the rest of her e-mail and then began poking around the machine on which she was working. It didn't take her long to discover that the hard drive had been partitioned.

And one section used for storing pornographic images.

Oh-kay.

She blinked at the first few pictures, all eye-watering but, she was relieved to see, not illegal; then, disquieted by her discovery, protected the area with the caustic password *NotCool* and shut down the machine.

She went round making the installation of new apps an admin privilege on the machines that weren't in use, giving the admin user account a new password, *FirstSteps*. She paused, wondering whether that had sprung into her mind in relation to her first steps in taking control of this chaotic computer room ... or her first steps in her new life.

Probably the latter. Even though she'd been busy all morning, a part of her mind seemed constantly occupied with Lucas. It was as if sharing the boat had thrown the past four years in the bin. Occupying the same space. Talking together. Feeling his eyes travelling over her like a shiver. Dammit, she'd even woken up beside him yesterday evening.

Her fingers moved over yet another keyboard, but her mind kept floating back to their first meeting when, part of a drunken version of free running through the night-time streets of Northampton, Lucas had literally knocked her off her feet. Elle had been wandering disconsolately through Market Square towards the taxi rank after she and a date had agreed to end the evening early and suddenly men had flooded down the street. Pounding over walls, sliding over car bonnets, hurdling chained up cycles, twenty specimens of stag night manhood. Rat-arsed.

Lucas had lost his tie and two shirt buttons as other racers tried to haul him back. Gasping for breath and choking with laughter, he hurled himself over grey guardrails at the edge of the pavement. Then a competitor crossing his line forced Lucas to alter his trajectory over the top of a bin.

Elle, passing on the other side, found herself bowled over like a skittle, head bouncing on the pavement, legs and knickers flashing.

Lucas rolled to his feet as if landing a parachute jump, abandoning the run to fall to his knees beside her. 'Are you hurt? Should I get an ambulance?'

'Don't be stupid.' Crossly, Elle yanked her skirt to its proper position with one hand and rubbed her head with the other.

His friends returned, solicitous, crowding, offering her, with equal parts enthusiasm and drunken hilarity, piggybacks, fireman's lifts or consoling cuddles.

'All I want is a taxi.' She struggled to her feet, brushing off a forest of helping hands.

Lucas despatched someone to the rank to secure a taxi and before she knew it Elle was crushed in the back seat with Lucas and a beaming bumbling red-faced reveller introduced as Lucas's brother, Charlie. Sweet Charlie, so unlike Lucas.

'We're much nicer when we're not drunk,' Charlie confided. 'What's your name?'

'Elle.'

Charlie began to laugh. 'L for what? L for leather? L on wheels?' He'd laughed so hard he couldn't catch his breath.

But Lucas hadn't laughed. '*Elle est jolie, elle est chaude, elle est parfaite.*' His eyes had been fixed on Elle as he'd described her as pretty, hot and perfect. She'd found it hard to look away. In a taxi rocking out of the late-night streets of the town centre towards Upton, where she had a flat, Lucas breathed, '*Elle, je veux.*' *She, I want.*

Lucas returned next day, sober, clutching a huge bunch of fragile pink peonies. He hadn't forgotten her building, apparently, no matter how drunk he'd been, and had located her apartment by ringing each bell in turn until she answered.

Dark hair glossy, jaw shaved, T-shirt hugging his biceps, Lucas looked a hundred degrees of hot. He stood on no ceremony. 'How about I take you to lunch?'

It wasn't in Elle's nature to be that attainable. 'I have plans.' But she gave him a small smile as she took the flowers. 'Thank you.'

'Dinner?'

'Extensive plans.'

He looked exasperated. 'Tomorrow?'

'Plans ...' She let her smile widen to a grin.

'When?'

She tilted her head, pretending to consider. And then, as his eyes narrowed, capitulated. 'Tuesday evening could work.'

It had.

Elle completed her task and fished out the key for the cupboard where computers and peripherals went to die, intending to hook up a discarded tower to see if it could

73

be salvaged. It seemed as if the computer room had been run without expertise or common sense, so it was possible that formatting a supposedly defunct hard drive might be all that was needed to make the machine once again a useful member of the IT team.

She tried to concentrate, to ignore the ache in her chest at how good it had been with Lucas before everything had begun to go horribly wrong.

Before the day when a scruffy man she'd taken to be homeless had shaken a cardboard cup in her face, its meagre handful of small change jangling.

And it had been Ricky.

At twelve-fifteen, out of breath, eyes full of anticipation, Carmelo catapulted into the computer room.

Elle had established that the tower from the cupboard was past resurrection and had moved on to stripping it of its hard drive. She smiled. 'Hi, Carmelo! Have you enjoyed school today?'

'No,' he answered, frankly. 'But I did go.' His eyes dared her to query it.

Elle made a cheering motion with clasped hands. 'I'm really pleased.'

She was rewarded with Carmelo's smile as she returned the tower to the computer graveyard, in case she ever found its carcass useful. A quick glance at the progress of the machine that was formatting, and then she settled herself at what seemed to be the most recent equipment, and Carmelo pulled up a chair at her side.

'Right. What shall we do?'

'Wikipedia,' Camelo returned, promptly.

'OK, Wikipedia.' Elle had expected him to want to play a game or chat on social media. She gave the computer mouse a little shove towards him. 'Come on then. Show me Wikipedia.'

With alacrity, Carmelo began to click. Elle gazed at the site he opened – *Wikipedija*. 'Ah. I can't read Maltese.'

'OK.' Carmelo rapidly clicked through to the English-language version. 'Now, I think of something I want to know.' He paused before asking, courteously, 'Maybe is there something you want to know?'

'This is your computer time. You choose.'

He nodded. 'I want to know about *qarnita*.' He screwed up his forehead in concentration. 'I forget how to say him in English.'

'How about we open another browser tab and go to a translation site?'

Oscar, the giant Dutchman, wandered into the room. 'We have our beautiful Englander again!'

Elle merely smiled politely and he went to use the machine that was being formatted.

'I'm working on that one,' Elle said, apologetically. 'Can you use another?'

'OK,' he boomed, jovially, as if she'd made a joke.

Then she forgot him as she showed Carmelo how to discover that the English name for *qarnita* was 'octopus' and watched as he put the word into the Wikipedia search engine with a quick cut and paste. Unsurprisingly, she found that he didn't read English as well as he spoke it and she read much of the Wikipedia article to him, stumbling herself over phrases such as 'cephalopod mollusc'.

The habits of the eight-tentacled habitué of the seas proved to be interesting, even to her. In fact, she learned, the octopus didn't have eight tentacles, but four pairs of arms. 'He has a beak,' she marvelled.

'A beak?' Carmelo frowned.

'Like a bird. If we open another tab we can look for pictures – click on images, that's right. There.'

'A beak, like a bird,' Carmelo repeated. 'I like to eat him, the octopus.'

Elle laughed. 'I might, too, because I like his cousin, squid. In the Italian restaurants they call squid *calamari*.'

'We call him *klamari*, the same.' Carmelo tapped *klamari* into the translation window to prove that the English was given as 'squid'.

She left Carmelo to his browsing while she installed the operating system on the machine she'd worked on; then password protected it before she shut it down. She didn't want anyone messing with the machine until she had it how she liked it. She designated it number 01 and wrote a sticky label for the tower.

'I'm going now,' she said to Carmelo. 'What about you?'

Carmelo's shoulders slumped. 'You go home?'

'I'll be back tomorrow morning, but I have to work somewhere else this afternoon.' She watched a thoughtful look enter his eyes, and added, 'Would you like to help me with some jobs on Saturday? You can if you go back to school tomorrow.'

'Only if I go to school?'

She pulled an apologetic face. 'Yes. Joseph needs you to go to school, so I have to know that you're going. What if he wouldn't let me work here any more?' It seemed an unlikely result of her not taking a stand against truancy, but Carmelo heaved a martyred sigh.

'OK.'

Oscar rose from his machine. 'I'll walk with you. Make sure you know your way.' He smiled a smile large enough to fit with the rest of him.

'I already know my way and I need to talk to Joseph first. But thanks anyway,' Elle answered lightly.

She left Carmelo studying Wikipedija and ran downstairs to leave the computer room keys with Joseph. 'I'll be back tomorrow morning to take the workshop. Do you know how many have signed up?'

Joseph shrugged. He looked tired. 'About eight, but the way a drop-in centre works, that means between two and twenty.'

'I'll take the session as it comes, then.' Elle paused. 'Carmelo seems a bit of a waif.'

Joseph rubbed his eyes behind his glasses. 'Yes. His family are not well-off.'

She hesitated, hoping she wasn't overstepping any marks. 'I was thinking about his clothes ...'

She didn't need to finish. Joseph was already nodding, his dark eyes full of compassion. 'He's one of the children who shies away from accepting anything from the donated clothes rack. The children with the least sometimes have the greatest amount of pride.'

Elle nodded. She'd thought it might be the case.

She paused again, even more reluctant to bring up the next subject. 'By the way, someone's been downloading, um, adult material, to at least one of the computers.'

Joseph heaved a huge sigh. 'Damn.' He paused. 'I'm afraid I have to ask you what *kind* of adult material? Not something the police would be interested in?'

'I h-hope not! At least, I don't think so. I only looked at a few pictures.' She felt her colour rising. 'And they were just ... just *adult*. Nothing criminal.'

Relief chased away anxiety on Joseph's face, swiftly succeeded by embarrassment. 'I suppose this isn't going to sound very good but I have to look at it.'

Elle laughed, not sure whose face was burning hottest. 'Yes, I, um, suppose so. I password protected it, so I'll write down the details for you.'

'Thanks for thinking of that.' He pushed a pad towards her and she wrote quickly, with a note of which machine was affected.

Elle left his office and the centre gladly. She was no prude but felt awkward discussing the presence of porn with Joseph, a man she was still getting to know, and she didn't have his foothold in Maltese culture or know its boundaries in terms of offence.

Emerging through the front door and into the sunlight was a bit like stepping too close to a fire. She stopped, scrabbling her hat out of her backpack, unable to fully open her eyes against the glare until she'd pulled it on. Then she crossed the courtyard and let herself out of the door in the wall and into the comparative comfort of the shady side of the street.

'So, we go the same way,' said a voice, as she rounded the corner where the street jinked to the right.

Elle started, and then tried to pretend she hadn't as Oscar loomed beside her. 'Really?' She hoped she sounded politely disbelieving rather than jumpy. It wasn't his fault he towered over her but Elle couldn't help shrinking away, perhaps because he wasn't the greatest respecter of personal space, always a bugbear of hers. Nor, evidently, had he respected her polite rebuff over walking her home.

She could insist on him stating his destination, she supposed, so that she could declare her route to be different, but she had the feeling that that would only lead to him dropping any pretence and declaring his interest. And his interest was already pretty obvious in the way he let his eyes roam over her – obvious verging on creepy.

'Right,' she said, discouragingly, and set off down Triq Bonnard.

He matched his long stride to her shorter one. 'So, our new volunteer, you like it here in Malta? You usually live in England, yes?'

When she returned only minimal answers, he turned to talking about himself.

'I am from the Nederlands, from Freisland. Not Holland! That's what all English people think, that the Nederlands are Holland.' He laughed heartily. 'But North and South Holland are only two of our provinces. Friesland is a province, too, right up in the north. Even some Dutch people, now, call the Nederlands "Holland" but I am proud to be a Freislander. Like you, I am a volunteer, helping some young people and enjoying some sunshine.'

Nodding politely, Elle followed her usual route towards the marina.

'And you,' Oscar continued, keeping pace up and down kerbs, falling in behind her when cars parked half on the pavement, 'you are here to make our computer room good.'

It didn't seem as if he was going to abandon the conversation just because she wasn't taking part in it, so Elle agreed, 'That's right.' She halted, spying a neighbourhood shop on a corner. 'I've just remembered that I need some shopping. I'll see you next time we're both at the centre.'

Oscar wasn't to be so easily put off. 'I am in no hurry. I will come and hold your basket.'

Hiding growing irritation, Elle looked up at him coolly. 'Some things, a woman prefers to buy alone.'

'Ah.' Oscar looked satisfactorily nonplussed.

'See you some other time.' Maybe it would have put him off more permanently if she'd let him accompany her while she stocked up on tampons, but Elle was happy just to skip into the shop and take her time over studying available brands of shampoo and conditioner.

When she emerged once more into the brightness of the afternoon the street was empty and quiet, as if the beating sun had sent everybody indoors. Elle was glad of her hat and paused in the shade of the shop's awning to search out her sunglasses, then stepped back onto the pavement and turned towards the marina.

Like an annoying stray, Oscar emerged from a shady doorway. 'I will carry that for you.' He whisked the bag out of her hand. His head was bare even in the afternoon sun, and his sandy hair lifted in the slight breeze.

'There's no need—!' But seeing the futility of attempting to reason with him Elle reluctantly turned for home, having little choice but to listen as Oscar went on about his previous voluntary posts in Morocco and Thailand. She felt like a cat that was having its fur brushed the wrong way. No matter how short her replies, Oscar seemed to have no compunction in pushing his presence upon her. Counting silently to ten, Elle reminded herself that Oscar was a fellow volunteer and they might have to work together for months. In the interests of harmony she should maintain at least neutral relations, even if he did seem too thick-skinned to realise when a girl wasn't into him.

As they came to Triq Manoel de Vilhena, the street that came out almost opposite the bridge, Elle made to retrieve her shopping with a cursory, 'Thanks.'

Oscar retained possession by the simple expedient of hoisting the bag out of her reach. 'It is a good gentleman who carries shopping for a lady. To her door.' And stood on the kerb to await a break in the swarming traffic. The heat certainly wasn't keeping car drivers at home. Maybe they all had air conditioning.

'So, you have been fiddling with the machines.' He said it as if Elle was a child who had done something wrong.

She glanced up into his red, shiny face. Perspiration was dampening his hair and running down his temples. 'Formatting them, you mean?'

He laughed. 'Why, yes!' He laughed again. 'But we all use the computers. Perhaps you should have spoken to us before making changes. We might have wanted the opportunity to change things ourselves.'

'I'm doing what I'm here to do.' But Elle pricked up her ears, interested in what lay behind his overly casual manner. The traffic thinned enough for them to cross the road, dodging the cars that whizzed on and off the forecourt of the garage near the kiosk.

'What has happened, then, to our files and folders?'

'I saved them onto the external hard drive and I password protected a folder that contained images unsuitable for children.' They were making their way along the pathways that threaded through the gardens, now, where there were patches of dappled shade. Elle could see Lucas standing on the bathing platform of the *Shady Lady*, his head turned in her direction as she approached.

Oscar made a *pshaw* noise. 'Where males are you'll find these things. It is normal.'

She halted. Her stomach contracted. If it wasn't some naughty adolescent who had downloaded the porn she'd found that morning, that put things in quite a different light. 'What if a child had opened that folder? It didn't even have a password. I'm not up on Maltese law but

I'm pretty sure that storing explicit images on machines used daily by children must contravene it. Just in case common sense and decency doesn't prevent adults from downloading stuff like that.'

Again with the *pshaw*, but louder. 'We are human.'

They were back in the full sunlight of the marina access road, almost at the *Shady Lady*, now. Lucas, unmoving, still watched.

'It's irresponsible,' she maintained. She was relieved to reach the boat, even glad to see Lucas. If Oscar had been making her uneasy before, he was positively making her skin crawl now. 'My shopping, please.'

Immediately, Oscar swung it out of her reach again, with that maddeningly wide grin. 'But I am being a gentleman. And soon, perhaps, you will be a lady and provide me with a nice cool drink to say thank you. That will be kind.'

'You OK, Elle?' asked Lucas, his voice cutting through the heavy afternoon air.

Oscar lowered the bag, glancing at Lucas as if suddenly putting two and two together. 'This is where you live?' He looked at the boat.

'Yes.' She pulled at her bag, but he kept a firm grip on it.

'Who is this man? You have a boyfriend?' His tone was accusing, as if she had no business having a boyfriend.

'We live together,' she snapped.

Lucas's eyebrows lifted a fraction.

'So.' Oscar nodded slowly. For the first time that afternoon, he didn't smile. 'So you have a boyfriend.' He let the plastic carrier bag untwist from his fingers.

Elle snatched back her shopping and when Lucas held out a hand to steady her aboard the boat she grabbed it thankfully, welcoming the show of solidarity. She didn't resist when Lucas pulled her in to his side. It felt safe.

Slowly, Oscar began to back away. 'I will see you soon, Elle. At the centre.'

'Right,' she returned, woodenly.

Together, they watched Oscar walk up the quayside then turn and disappear from view between the toilet block and the kiosk.

'Who was that charming man?' Lucas's tone was dry.

'He's one of the volunteers at the centre. I only met him for the first time today. I didn't take to him.' Elle was very aware that Lucas still held her hand. The obvious thing was to free herself, but the feel of his fingers around hers was comforting – if uncomfortably hot. For several unsettling moments she felt as if his pulse became hers.

'He looked kind of fond of you.'

She nodded, still thinking about their hands. Touching. But neither of them mentioning it.

'He seems to have taken a shine.'

'Is he a problem?'

She pulled a face. 'I hope not. I have to work with him.'

Lucas studied her for a moment and then changed the subject. 'Loz wandered past, asking for you.' He turned towards the saloon, which meant that the unlinking of their hands happened naturally, casually.

'Thanks. I'll be heading her way in a few minutes.' Then, because Elle was glad that Lucas had helped her out with Oscar, and because they were stuck with the current living arrangements for the summer, she offered impulsively, 'I'm planning to eat aboard, this evening. Want to join me?'

He took a moment to turn the idea over. Then, gruffly, 'Thanks. I'll supply the drink.'

She showered and changed, reassuring herself that she'd done the right thing, that it would show how over each other they were if they could share a meal together and be civilised. Remembering all the meals they'd eaten together in their old home, at the homes of his parents, her parents, Simon, Charlie, their friends, their colleagues, at restaurants, in bars, on picnics. And trying not to.

It was almost a relief that when she stepped back aboard much later that afternoon that Lucas was nowhere to be seen. After yet another shower and change, she began washing salad leaves and big beef tomatoes, slicing up crusty Maltese bread and spreading it with butter, rolling up pink glistening slices of ham to place appetisingly on the plates.

Then she felt the slightest dip of the boat and looked along the deck to see Lucas on board, a bag cradled in the crook of his arm.

'We could eat on the flybridge.' He raised a questioning eyebrow.

She answered lightly. 'That would be fun. A curious cross between picnicking and doing things in style.'

At least it seemed stylish to her to be perched up at the little table on top of the boat as evening cast lengthening shadows. The golden sun reaching beneath the bimini felt gorgeous on Elle's bare arms and legs now that it had lost its earlier scorching intensity, and the flybridge caught the breeze though it was only feet above the blue and glittering sea.

The usual stream of cars grumbled along the road. 'What's that way?' Elle nodded at the road leading in the other direction from Sliema as she uncapped a bottle of cold water.

Lucas held out his glass. 'Msida's just around the coast. You can either follow the Ta' Xbiex seafront road round to it or cut across the promontory. There's another marina there, and a big residential district. If you carry on, past Pieta and through Floriana, you get to Valletta. The water taxi whizzed us between the two but it takes a lot longer by road.'

They sat down to dinner together at the table. Relaxed evening meals crowded into Elle's memory: smiling, eating, talking. Kissing. In those days, Lucas might have pulled a face at the leafy salad she'd produced, but now he accepted the meal with polite thanks.

His contribution was wine from the local Marsovin vineyard and, after the main course, a lavish lemon gateau he'd stowed in the flybridge fridge, part of a unit that included a grill and a tiny sink.

Elle laughed. 'Do the Maltese produce many desserts like this?'

Lucas filled her wine glass and replaced the bottle in its cooler. 'I don't think you have to worry about calories. You look thinner than when I last saw you.'

She dropped her eyes. The last time he'd seen her she'd been clearing her stuff out of his house – he'd arrived home unexpectedly and watched her with bleak dark eyes as she'd stumbled and fumbled her way through boxes and bags, stuttering about quite understanding that he wanted out, and it being better this way.

Because it had been; better for him and better for his parents.

The memory diminished her appetite and she left more than half of her portion of gateau. Lucas, who was scraping his fork around his plate, raised his eyebrows and Elle found herself pushing her leftovers to him in an echo of old behaviour. As he industriously set about clearing her plate, she let her head tip so that she could look up past the hoop where a cluster of boxes sat beside two sleek silver horns, all related to the GPS and television and other stuff she didn't need. The sky had turned a luminous purple ready for nightfall. 'I may have a bit of a situation with that guy, Oscar. I found a porn stash on one of the computers and he said things that make me think it's his.'

Lucas paused, fork poised. 'What sort of things?'

'That it's perfectly natural and people are human. I don't know if I ought to say something to Joseph, the centre manager. I'd assumed it was the kids but Oscar's a youth leader.'

'Tricky.' Lucas sat back, checking Elle's legs weren't in the way before he stretched his out. 'Could you point out to the centre manager that it could be anyone with access to the computers, including volunteers? Let him see the danger without pointing any fingers. It's not your responsibility to prove anything.'

She watched him use his fingertip to wipe up a last smear of cream from the edge of the plate and put it to his mouth. 'You ought to have been in law, like your parents.' And then, when he didn't respond, added, 'How are they? Dad still a magistrate? Mum a lawyer?'

He smiled, guardedly. 'That's right. No significant changes.'

She looked over to the boats moored on the Manoel side of the creek, some of them huge, looking worth every one of the millions of pounds on their price tags. The wine reached her head in a slidey little rush. 'I think law would have suited you and your love of what's right.'

'From what I understand,' he said, slowly, 'the law isn't so much about right and wrong as what evidence you have and whether you can prove your case. Not always the same thing.'

He glanced down at the two empty plates as if regretful that his sugarfest was over. 'Your own parents – I was surprised when you mentioned that they're not together.'

'Dad completely reinvented himself. Left his boring job and went into business with his new wife in a B&B in west Wales, where the surfies hang out.'

'Were you shocked?'

'Yes,' she said, simply, 'Shocked. Astonished. Ambivalent. All the things adults seem to feel when their parents part. Mum took it hard. Really hard. It shook her confidence.'

He lifted his brow. 'That's hard to imagine. Is she still in sales? Or has she retired?'

Elle yawned, feeling the soporific effects of the alcohol and the day's sun creeping up on her. She'd hardly slept out of excitement on her last couple of nights in England and now with the strain of finding Lucas on the boat and starting what amounted to two part-time jobs, her body was beginning to demand sleep. 'Mum's in a home.' She yawned again, behind her hand. 'Not long after Dad left, she had a stroke. I don't know if you remember that she's eight years older than him? But, still, quite young to have a stroke. Now she can't live independently. She was alone when the stroke hit and so a lot of damage was done.' She drained the last of her wine and sighed. 'She doesn't always know who I am so I don't suppose she knows who Dad is or that he left her.'

His voice was soft, sympathetic. 'That's bad. I had no idea.'

'Why should you?' The words hung in the air like the ghost of an accusation.

'You're right, why should I?' His eyes began to glitter in the last of the light. Like the creek, they were black and shining, reflecting the lights in sparks of gold. 'I didn't know that much about you when we were together so why should I know anything about you since you left?'

Brushing away the encroaching fug of fatigue, she climbed to her feet and began to stack the plates and the salad bowl. 'You left.'

She started towards the head of the steps but suddenly his hand was on her arm, hot, hard, as he swung her around. The plates spun from her hands and clattered to the deck, scattering scraps of lettuce and chopped peppers.

'I left?' he barked. 'You were the one who cleared her things—'

She yanked her forearm free from the crackle of his touch. 'You left the relationship. I left the house because it was yours and once you'd ended things I could hardly stay, could I?'

As he began to speak, she lifted her hands, weariness pinching at her tear ducts until she was frightened that they'd overflow. She was suddenly desperate not to cry in front of him. 'Let's not argue, Lucas. We've both moved on. Let's not allow bad memories in. They'll rock the boat.' She forced a smile to support her feeble joke. He didn't smile at all.

Chapter Seven

As soon as she arrived at the centre the next morning, Elle made it her business to find Joseph. He was at his desk, sighing over a haphazard heap of paperwork, and looked pleased to have an excuse to turn away.

'Everything OK for your first computer room session this morning? Do you need anything? Are you nervous?'

Elle waved the nervousness idea away. She'd run large team meetings and presented in front of hundreds at seminars. Eight or so teenagers shouldn't hold too many challenges. 'Just thinking about the issue of anybody being able to download anything they pleased. I'll make it impossible to use the computers without logging in with an individual user name. I'll also make it impossible to save to the hard drive of the computer they're using, only to a common storage area I've made. Space will be limited and everyone will be able to see everyone else's files.'

Joseph frowned. 'Should the other volunteers be admins, too?'

Elle hesitated. 'It could have been anyone who misused the computer access.' She let the thought sink in.

'I see.' Joseph tapped on his desk. Rubbing his eyes behind his glasses, he sighed. 'Proceed as you suggest, please. We need everything here to be correct.'

The morning passed quickly. Twelve turned up for the workshop and Elle issued their usernames. As Joseph had indicated, the kids were liberal with the term 'drop in' and she noticed that most of those who showed were male. Curiosity about the blonde Englishwoman might have motivated their attendance.

But as she was there to aid computer literacy and she saw Microsoft Word as fundamental to that, she ignored the nudges and sly grins and plunged into her workshop on the functions of the Styles menu – a feature generally underused, in her view.

'Losing your way around a long document's frustrating, can muddle your information and wastes time. Most employers don't like wasted time.' Her fingers flew over the keyboard as she began her demonstration. Most of her workshops would be demonstration-based because English might be one of the official languages of Malta but it wasn't always the first language of the Maltese. It was a lot easier to show than to tell.

She'd prepared a mock document, ten pages of sample text interspersed with headings and subheadings. She got the kids on the machines, attempting to pair those who seemed less confident in their English with someone proficient.

It would have been useful to link her iPad to the Wi-Fi at the centre and have translation software permanently open as she worked, every computer being in use. But she'd ended her tablet contract with her UK provider and had stowed it safely in her case in the lazarette, not anticipating having a use for something that had previously been only a business tool. It wasn't as if she intended to spread her new life all over Facebook and Twitter.

That was how Ricky had found her last time.

Via enthusiastic demonstration, she got the kids to designate headings so that they appeared in the easy-to-navigate document map, changing the font and style of each type of heading to suit their own choices. Then they set about adding sub-headings, lists and tables, which kept her busy whizzing from machine to machine until the workshop ended, at one.

It was only when she started back down through the streets that she let herself think about what was likely to greet her at the boat – the evening before had ended in silence and Elle leaving Lucas to clear up the spilled food on the deck. Maybe the intimacy of eating together had been too much to ask of the fragile truce between them. They should have kept their respective distances rather than trying to pretend that ex-lovers make good friends.

This morning, she'd found that the dishes had been put away, neat and clean. There had been no sign of Lucas. His cabin door had been closed and the boat silent. The gangplank wasn't in place but as he often just jumped between boat and shore, that didn't mean he hadn't left for work. Rather than lean out to grab the cord on the gangplank and heave it into place, she'd taken a deep breath, gathered her legs beneath her and tried the jump herself. Landing safely on the quayside had brought her a sense of achievement and a stubbed toe.

By the time she returned to the *Shady Lady* she was worn down by the heat. She gazed at the cool sea longingly. It was bad marina etiquette to swim near the boats, and dangerous, but she couldn't believe that she hadn't yet swum in the Mediterranean in the five days she'd been in Malta.

It would be remedied on Sunday, she determined, braving the jump from quayside to bathing platform to prove to herself that the first time hadn't been a fluke, and stepping up into the cockpit to unlock the boat.

She made a fast change of clothes, diving into a lukewarm shower, welcoming the chance to cool her blood. She'd be overheated again by the time she reached *Seadancer* but even a brief respite was welcome.

Loz was waiting for her when she arrived at the larger

motor yacht, eyes hidden behind massive sunglasses. 'Don't bother coming on board,' she called. 'You and I are going straight off to do lots of lovely shopping and then Davie's going to come along with a taxi and haul everything home. You're still OK to hand round nibbles at the party, aren't you?'

'Of course,' Elle agreed, brightly. The party meant that she'd be away from Lucas for the evening.

A big turquoise bus picked them up from the far side of the road behind the gardens and deposited them fifteen minutes later in Sliema, leaving only a few yards to walk to a supermarket that was set back from the main road, a ground floor with a further two floors beneath.

The novelty of shopping in a foreign country still high, Elle enjoyed buying salad stuff and nibbles, two cooked chickens, various cooked meats, cheeses, and an armful of fruit.

'Get the blood oranges,' Loz urged, wandering along behind the plastic shopping trolley as Elle pushed. 'It's such fun that they're red instead of orange. And figs, but don't waste them in a fruit salad. They're gorgeous with ice cream and a drizzle of honey.'

After a hot taxi journey back to the marina, Elle was thankful for the galley air conditioning as she helped Loz chop and wash, unwrap and arrange. It was nearly seven when Elle arrived back at the *Shady Lady*.

Lucas was sitting on the cockpit seat at the back of the boat, reading. He looked up with a polite 'Hello' and returned to his e-reader.

Elle responded with an equally neutral greeting and went through to her cabin to take another shower. She dried her hair with the hairdryer set on cold, sitting on her cabin floor, then changed into a green sundress, which was only slightly crumpled from being squashed into the wardrobe. Loz had said her evening's duties were to hand round the nibbles, get drinks and clear glasses and Elle thought the neat but pretty dress suitable for what the help would wear at a party on a yacht. Not that she'd ever been to a party on a yacht, much less been 'the help'. Nobody who'd known her from her old life of suits and briefcases, office politics and sweated-for performance bonuses would have pictured her in such a role. They knew the Elle for whom a redundancy notice had felt like the end of the world, plunging her into icy fear that she'd never be able to get another job like that.

Then she'd realised that she didn't actually *want* another job like that.

Status and salary had come with a hefty price tag in terms of commitment, stress and lifestyle. When had she last passed a weekend without looking at her e-mails? Or rung her line manager on Monday morning and said carelessly that she was taking a couple of days' holiday? The line manager had barked in outrage but Elle hadn't cared. Her concern was what she'd like her future to look like. A new life.

In this new life she had to be careful with money for the first time in years but it was worth it. Even with Lucas inconveniently turning up in it.

After applying make-up and putting up her hair it was nearly eight and time to leave. She tucked her key in a small pocket in her dress and skipped back up the steps to the saloon and out into the cockpit, where Lucas still sat, one ankle across the other knee, his e-reader balanced against his calf.

'Bye.' She brushed past his seat and balanced her way neatly across the gangplank, which was back in place.

He stood up. 'Hang on.'

She paused as he stowed the e-reader inside the saloon, locked up, crossed the ever-shifting gap between boat and shore and hauled back the gangplank. 'What?' She felt too aware of him and she so didn't want to talk over what had happened last night. That can of worms was a wriggling mess best left securely shut.

'We might as well go together.'

'Go?'

'To Loz's party.' He held up a bottle of red wine.

Elle's surge of dismay, as she realised that cool black cargo shorts had replaced his usual denim cut-offs and his bare feet had been pushed into deck shoes, was like standing on one boat when the wake of another passed beneath. 'Loz invited you, but then—'

'—you outed me as your ex, Loz went all quiet and Davie began to send me suspicious looks,' he finished, calmly. 'But they didn't uninvite me.' He stuck his hand in his pocket. 'So we might as well walk along together.'

'Shit,' she said, succinctly, as she turned and headed for *Seadancer.*

Lucas lengthened his stride to keep up with Elle. She stared straight ahead, outrage in her every line.

He had to hide a smile. Elle, so full of secrets, was annoyed that he hadn't told her he'd decided to take up the invitation to the party.

Today had been his rest day and he'd been fidgety. Reluctant to hang around the boat, he'd walked into Sliema, then up Tower Road to Ghar id-Dud, where steps led down onto the rocky foreshore that was strewn with tourists like sausages on a giant barbecue.

He loved strolling across the rocks, pausing to look

into the pools where hermit crabs picked their way from nook to cranny. When the glare of the sun began to make his head ache, he threw off his T-shirt and dived into the waves, first shaking off his fidgets with a fast crawl, then floating on his back and watching the occasional clouds in the intense blue sky.

After, with no towel or change of clothes, he let the sun dry him, his mind absently circling the conundrum that was Elle.

For his sanity, he had to put her behind him – easier said than done when they were trapped together on the boat and, whether she was hot and tired or freshly groomed, she looked fantastic.

Life would be easier if he had no burning need to understand what went on in her head. It was as if he'd put down a cryptic crossword with the last few clues unsolved, the necessity to know the answers gnawing at him. He wished that satisfaction were as simple as buying the next day's paper and turning to the solution.

He was pretty sure that allowing Elle to put distance between them as she had last night wasn't the way to satisfy his curiosity. But spending more time with her? That might do it. He might gain her confidence.

Failing that, he might just irritate the answers out of her.

Just striding along beside her now seemed to be giving him a head start in the irritation stakes.

They reached the *Seadancer* and Elle marched up the gangplank ahead of Lucas and halted on the deck. 'I suppose I'd better show you through to the saloon.'

'Or I could find my own way.' Her dress blew against her, neat and plain. Pale lemon bra straps peeked out beside its green fabric. When she'd worn the corporate plumage of a plain and sober suit she'd often compensated with satin and lace underwear in wild colours. It had been one of his little treats to discover the colours of the day. He wondered whether her knickers matched her bra, which, in his experience of women, indicated plans to show the underwear off. The thought tingled through him.

She sighed. 'No. I'm here to help with the guests, and you're a guest. Come on.'

He followed. He'd normally leap at a chance to look around a yacht this size but today his attention was all on the rear view of Elle. Her hair, plaited down the back of her head, dangled between her shoulder blades and pointed down at her behind as if inviting him to check it out. Nice.

'Here's Lucas,' she announced as she preceded him into a spacious saloon with its doors to the foredeck flung open. He tore his gaze from her behind. Only a couple of guests had so far arrived and Davie was helping them to champagne in tall frosted flutes.

'Oh.' Loz bit her lip.

'Right.' Davie's hand halted in mid-air.

Lucas tried to charm them out of their obvious dismay. 'Thanks again for the invitation. I couldn't resist the temptation to see your fantastic yacht. I hope you don't mind that I'm one of the first but I thought I might as well walk along with Elle.'

Elle turned her back on him. 'Do you want me in the galley, Loz?'

'Have a glass of bubbles first. Nothing for you to do, yet.' Davie put a glass in her hand, lifting his own to clink with her. Then, making it an obvious afterthought, added, 'Champagne for you, Lucas?'

'Great.' Once the glass was in his hand he found himself

looking at three turned backs, Elle's, Loz's and Davie's. The charm wasn't working.

So maybe being irritating was more his forte. He crossed to the other guests, hovering on the steps between the saloon and the foredeck. 'I'm Lucas Rose. I live with Elle.'

'Did you think you were funny, tonight, telling people that we're living together?' Elle led the march back under the lamps along the deserted quayside to the *Shady Lady*. Behind them the party was still going, but the eating and the heaviest of the drinking had wound down. Having cleared everything she could and left the dishwasher empty in case Loz and Davie were tempted to reload, Elle had called it a night at midnight. She was working at Nicholas Centre in the morning.

Lucas dug his hands in his pockets. 'But we are living together.'

'We're sharing. That's not the same as "living together".'

'But it's what you told that Oscar dude.'

'Purely an Oscar-avoidance tactic, as you know very well.'

'So we should only be honest when it's convenient?'

She glared at his profile. 'You and the Great God Honesty.'

'There are worse gods. Especially when honesty is not a convenience but a principle.'

Elle knew that she'd never win any argument with Lucas that centred on honesty. It was bad enough to have to acknowledge to herself that, in a way, all his old suspicions of her truthfulness were justified.

For a mad second she almost gave in to the urge to confess, to explain, to blurt out the total truth. Ricky's power to hurt had surely begun to wane. He was unlikely to find her here.

Then she thought of Lucas's girlfriend and realised that confession would be pointless. He could believe every word and still say, 'Good to know. But it's so long ago and we're over. Doesn't really matter now, does it?'

Worse, what if he *didn't* believe her? He'd hate her all over again. She wasn't sure she could survive him thinking worse of her than he already did.

'It's not as if you were ever that easy to live with,' she muttered crossly and inconsequentially.

Lucas said, 'Ow!' and clutched theatrically at his heart.

Elle tried not to laugh, taking a long, deep breath and consciously slowing her steps so that she could enjoy the Maltese night. Gżira Gardens was a study of moonlight and shadows. The road, for once, was quiet, the few passing cars all but drowned out by the drone of insects from the twisted and stunted pines.

'Those buzzy things make a lot of noise.' Elle peered into the shadowy trees.

Lucas had slowed his steps to match hers. 'Cicadas. The males make that noise flexing their abs, according to Simon.'

'Impressive.' She couldn't spot any ab-flexing cidadas in the trees. Maybe they were watching the moths dancing in the halos around the street lamps. With a yawn, she resumed her course for the *Shady Lady*.

Lucas positioned the gangplank, standing back in an invitation for her to precede him. 'Loz kept looking at me tonight as if waiting for me to do something evil.'

'Make me cry,' Elle supplied, stepping aboard. For the first time since Elle had arrived, the *Shady Lady* was restless at her moorings. The other boats along the marina were the same, like huge dogs pulling on their leads. Elle paused to watch as Lucas checked the fenders and the lines. 'She cornered me in the galley and asked if it was likely.'

Lucas put his hand on her arm. 'That I'd make you *cry*?'

Shrugging his hand off, she unlocked the door, stepping in and switching on the light. 'Loz has decided that our past relationship ending must've been down to you. Not that I told her any such thing,' she added. It was stuffy in the cabin and she flicked on the air con. Airlessness and a rolling boat weren't a great combination. The motion hadn't been so noticeable on *Seadancer*, when she was busy. She hoped the sea would calm soon.

'I told her you're not a villain but—' The boat's motion made her sit down on one of the cabin sofas more suddenly than she'd meant to.

Lucas dropped down beside her. 'When did I ever—?' he began.

Elle so didn't want to answer *When did I ever make you cry?* Because she'd cried endlessly, helplessly, when she'd left Northampton, having taken the first job offered to her by a new company in a place where she knew nobody. That it had turned out to be a great post had been largely luck. She'd taken it because it was in Coventry, a medium-sized city in the middle of England, where she could sink into anonymity and hope that Ricky wouldn't bother to find her once she and Lucas were finished and Ricky's hold over her was gone.

'Loz was indignant that you'd turned up for the party and annoying or upsetting me was the only reason she came up with for you doing it. Then, you went round telling people that we lived together, so she was convinced.'

She turned on the seat, kicking off a flip-flop so that she

could prop her foot on the sofa and brace herself against the rolling of the boat. 'Why did you go to the party?'

He lifted an eyebrow. His eyes were mostly black in the light in the cabin.

'I haven't been on a great big gin palace before and I didn't have anything better to do.' His eyes crinkled suddenly. 'And I knew you'd expect me to stay away.'

She sighed. 'You can be the most awkward man I know.'

He'd been mega-awkward with bells on when she'd been trying to keep him and Ricky apart, on edge in case Ricky had made good his threats to turn up when she and Lucas were together. Lucas had been like a pitbull, poised to go for someone's throat as soon as he knew whose throat to go for.

The memory made her smile waver. 'I'd better get to bed. I'm not a seasoned sailor and I'm beginning to feel I might be better lying down.'

He cocked an eyebrow. 'How about a nightcap? I overheard Davie saying the swell's going to build. A brandy might settle your stomach.'

Elle paused. Maybe brandy did work magic, and considering what a pain in the arse Lucas had been tonight, she was strangely reluctant to quit his company. There didn't seem any harm in relaxing with him, just for a short while. 'Worth a try,' she agreed. *Just a nightcap,* she reminded herself, watching him cross to the steps to the galley, compensating easily for the roll of the boat as he went. *Don't think that this changes anything. It's just because he looks hot in black and every woman at the party checked him out that you're feeling weird about him all over again.*

He returned with two brandy balloons in the fingers of one hand and a bottle with a label that mentioned 'reserva', in the other. Uncapping the bottle, he poured, pausing as the boat gave a sudden wiggle.

Lifting his glass to her in silent toast, he sipped, and then sat back to swirl the liquid in the base of the balloon in the proscribed manner.

Elle had never been able to tell the difference between a swirled brandy and an unswirled one. She took a couple of sips, enjoying its heat at the back of her throat, then returned the glass to the table, fingertips on the base in case the *Shady Lady*'s slow waltz turned into something a little more rock 'n' roll.

'I like your hair longer,' he said, suddenly.

'Oh.' She touched her plait self-consciously. It had fallen forward over her shoulder. 'Thank you.' It hadn't been a choice to grow her hair from its shoulder-length bob, more a lack of interest in the whole enterprise of making a hair appointment. In the first few months of learning to survive without Lucas, grooming had been basic. She'd begun to wear her hair up because it was quick and easy.

Then she'd seen some programme on TV where D-list celebs had been airing their hair care 'secrets' and one had demonstrated brushing her long hair forward, twisting the tail tightly, and cutting off an inch. When she'd shaken her hair back it had fallen in place with the bottom neatly layered.

Elle had fingered her own hair and suddenly realised that it was long enough for the same treatment. Tried it, liked it, and, since then, every few months she'd given her blonde locks the same 'cut'. As 'surviving without Lucas' had become 'I'm OK now', she'd begun to wear her hair down more and enjoyed collecting second looks, nature having bestowed on her the shimmering gold that people paid a lot in salons to achieve.

'Yours is longer, too,' Elle responded, lightly, not wanting him to see that he was unsettling her with his gaze. 'You only ever wore it short in your marketing days.'

'The Californian influence. Even as a business manager I didn't have to maintain a clean-cut image.' He pushed his hair back from his eyes. 'Tell me about your voluntary work.'

For the next half-hour Elle talked about Nicholas Centre, about Joseph and Maria, the grace of the old building, the little bits of history that Joseph had imparted, the kids she'd met.

'And the porn king?' Lucas poured more brandy.

Elle giggled. 'Oscar, another volunteer. I didn't take to him, even before he hinted that I'd locked away his porn stash.'

Lucas's eyes had half-closed and he'd sunk down comfortably so that he could put his feet up on the opposite sofa. 'So you viewed his whole collection?'

'No! Only the first few. But Joseph had to look at it because the centre is his responsibility so he has to know what we're dealing with.'

'The poor guy.'

Elle laughed. 'No, really, you should have seen his face. He was mortified at having to discuss the subject with me.'

Lucas's eyes glittered. 'I should think—' Before he could say more, his phone began to ring. He hooked it out of his pocket. As he checked the screen, the laughter died from his eyes. Pulling himself to his feet he made an apologetic face. 'Better take this.'

Then he disappeared out of the doors, across the bathing platform and onto the quayside.

Before he quite passed out of earshot Elle heard him speak into the phone. 'Kayleigh?'

She watched him for a moment; then her eyes dropped to her glass. The dark amber circle of brandy in the base of her glass moved with the motion of the boat. Nausea welled.

She screwed the lid on the brandy bottle and, hitching up the skirt of her dress, took the steps cautiously down to the galley, rinsing her glass and then the sink so that the place wouldn't smell like a bar in the morning.

Into her cabin. Make-up removed, she undressed and slid naked beneath the sheets, the motion of the boat increasing all the time. She closed her eyes against another clammy wave of sickness.

It seemed a long time before she heard Lucas moving about and knew that he was back on board.

Chapter Eight

In the morning, Elle emerged from her cabin to find Lucas drinking coffee in the saloon.

'Sorry to run out on you last night.' He watched as she paused at the galley to take down a coffee mug and instant coffee.

The deck heaved beneath her feet and she put both coffee and mug back again. She would wait until she was on dry land to put something that strong in her stomach. 'No problem.' She reached down to the fridge for cold water.

'Kayleigh's coming tomorrow.'

Her stomach rolled and she put the water back again, too. 'Oh? Great.' She climbed the steps and forced a smile. 'That will be fantastic for you.'

His gaze sharpened. 'Feeling sick? Pick a point on the horizon and stare at it for a while.'

'I have to go, anyway. Dry land will do the trick.' She didn't bother denying that she felt rough. She'd seen her pallor in the shower room mirror.

He rose as she made to pass by. 'Elle—' He pushed his hands into the pockets of his cut-offs.

She waited politely. When he seemed uncertain how to continue, she said, 'If Kayleigh's coming here, will you be staying with her at a hotel as you said, so your cabin will be empty? I might as well take my turn in it, hadn't I? No point me slumming it and the master cabin standing doing nothing.'

He looked surprised. Then discomfited. 'She's booked a room at the Sea Creek up the road but the boat will still be my base. Kayleigh likes her own space. But I'll swap cabins with you, if you like.'

Contrarily, she shrugged. 'In that case, no, it's OK. I just assumed you'd be moving in with Kayleigh.' Then the boat lurched. 'Excuse me. The shore looks quite attractive this morning.'

Polly, one of the dive instructors at Dive Meddi, had just lucked into a flat share in Msida and, as a custodian of one of Vern's double-cab pick-up trucks, had offered to give Lucas a lift in whenever their work days coincided. Lucas liked Polly. She was almost as tall as him, untidy and permanently smiling. He crossed to the far side of the road and took up station outside a wedding dress shop, ready to hop in when the dark blue truck arrived.

'Good day off?' As soon as Lucas had shut the passenger door Polly nosed the pick-up back into the stream of traffic. 'You're with me, today. We've got some Open Water Divers who want a guided tour so I thought we'd take them down to the statue of Madonna at seventeen metres at Cirkewwa. The sea's a bit calmer up at the north end. Vern says it's pretty choppy at St Julian's.'

Lucas relaxed into his seat. He knew he'd need to contribute little to the conversation.

When Polly finally steered the truck under the bright blue sign to Dive Meddi and inched her way down the pitted incline to the dive school and parked, Vern appeared briefly to tell Polly which students were hers as Lucas listened in, ready to prepare equipment.

The divers all had their own wetsuits, fins and masks but would need buoyancy control devices – BCDs – tanks and instruments. Lucas began by filling the tanks at the compressor in an outbuilding to the main team room, swinging the heavy, unwieldy cylinders one in each hand over to the area where he and Polly would go over the kit with the divers. Polly took the lead. She was the instructor. For now he was happy not to advance to instructor, with all the studying that involved, but to remain well within his capabilities and simply enjoy his job.

As he went in and out from shade to beating sun, he breathed in the familiar smell of neoprene and saltwater. The choppy sea bounced the sun into his eyes as it worried restlessly at the rocks, sometimes bursting a wave or two hard enough to run over into the swimming pool, cut into the rock nearby.

Lars was taking out another dive over at Ghar Lapsi and Brett was already packing the other pick-up. Those diving with Lars had been booked to arrive before those diving with Polly to keep things nice and calm. Lars was already going through the usual routines with his dive: allotting equipment, examining dive logs, discussing weights and checking instrument consoles.

Dive Meddi was a great place to work. During one of Malta's frequent redevelopments a small hotel had been swallowed up and developed by a big concern that wanted a dive school in its grounds. Vern had been swift to rent the sloping rock area with sea access, a pool, and a building with flaking blue paint for the team room, changing room and office, and now a constant clientele came via the website, the brand new hotel and from discount deals with others nearby.

Lucas put his own kit together methodically, turning the instrument console over so the gauges faced the floor as he switched on the air. After checking the hoses he added slates that could be written on underwater and knives in case someone got tangled on fishing line. He took the safety aspect of his job seriously. He even kept an old CD in the top left pocket of his BCD. It would reflect the sun if he needed to surface and signal for help.

He checked it was there, a Nickelback album that had become damaged through frequent playing. Elle had bought it for him the last Christmas that they were together. He knew the playlist by heart.

Once his kit was together and checked he stowed it in the pick-up.

'How are you doing, Lucas?' called Polly, the signal that he should join the group for the usual friendly pre-dive chat, bringing out experience and expectations, checking over dive logs and medicals.

Then they moved onto selecting BCDs and Lucas produced his usual calm flow of 'This BCD has releases here, here and here. Want to try them? Shoulder dump, pull here. Inflate ... deflate ... Want to try that?' And all the time the words of Nickelback's 'Trying Not to Love You' were going around in his head.

Chapter Nine

In the late afternoon, as Polly wasn't planning to go straight home, Lucas returned to Ta' Xbiex on the bus, shopping briefly before crossing to the boat. Once showered and changed he took up his favourite spot on the cockpit seat, tucking a bottle of Cisk into one of the cupholders at the side now that the day's diving was safely done.

Kayleigh had arranged to text him when she'd checked in at the Sea Creek Hotel. It would be good to see her again, although when she'd said she wanted to come out here he hadn't known that he would be sharing the *Shady Lady* with his ex-girlfriend.

He balked at the idea of calling Elle his 'ex-fiancée'. He wasn't sure she even qualified, in view of her unexpectedly lukewarm attitude to marrying him. In fact, unless 'Let's get married in Vegas!' could be construed as an acceptance, she'd never actually said yes.

As if he'd conjured her up, Elle appeared on the quayside in a denim dress, faded grey. She looked her usual picture of health. This morning she'd looked as pallid as if she'd eaten a bad fish.

'I bought you something,' he greeted her as she stepped across the plank.

She cocked an eyebrow. 'Why?'

Most women would ask 'What?' not 'Why?' but Elle wasn't most women. Elle didn't expect things to be given. She expected to get them for herself.

'"Why?" is to stop you being seasick. "What" is that I bought ginger ale and put it in the galley fridge.'

She looked at him, squinting under the brim of her hat. 'Thank you. That's really thoughtful.' Then, as if wondering what else to say, 'The swell seems to have subsided.'

'I hadn't really noticed. I'm used to being underwater in a swell, which can be worse than being on the surface. You can become convinced that you're staying still and the rocks around you are moving. But if someone throws up underwater at least we get a lot of fish around.'

She wrinkled her nose. 'I hope you're joking.'

He wasn't, but he could see that there were better conversational subjects. Before he could think of one, he noticed, behind Elle, a small Maltese boy in big shorts watching from amongst people enjoying the Saturday afternoon in the sun (mainly tourists) or the shade (mainly Maltese).

When he realised that Lucas had noticed him, the boy stepped behind a tree. Then peeped out again.

'Don't look now,' Lucas murmured, 'but we seem to have attracted the attention of a little boy.'

Completely disregarding his request, Elle pivoted on her heel. 'Carmelo!'

The little boy smiled shyly.

Elle waved, but sighed under her breath. 'Carmelo's from the Nicholas Centre. He's been helping me. He's one of the kids Joseph gives little jobs to so they can earn fizzy drinks or cakes, or even stuff for school.'

Dropping her bag on the deck, Elle hopped back onto the quayside and strolled in the boy's direction as he edged further out from behind the trees, smiling tentatively.

'Hello, Carmelo,' Lucas heard her say. 'What are you doing here?'

Carmelo shrugged.

Elle halted a few feet short of him and tilted her head. 'Would you like a cold drink before you go home? I just have a few minutes before I go on to my other job.'

Carmelo nodded, but his smile faded.

'Come on, then.' Elle turned and strolled back to the *Shady Lady*, stepping lightly onto the bathing platform, letting the boy follow shyly behind. In an undertone, she said to Lucas, 'I had training videos about this kind of thing. He should stay out here, in plain view.'

'Noted,' said Lucas, drily, not remotely surprised that Elle was reacting to a situation entirely according to her training videos. He'd done his own child protection and safeguarding training but there was no need for him to say so. Elle seemed to have all the bases covered.

'Carmelo, this is my friend Lucas.' Elle stepped back to the gangplank to be within reach as Carmelo edged across.

Lucas lifted a hand in greeting.

Carmelo's smile peeped out briefly.

'Sit with Lucas while I get the drinks,' suggested Elle.

And Lucas found himself sharing the cockpit seat with a little Maltese boy with huge brown eyes, dark hair that hung in his face, and atrociously fitting clothes.

'Hey,' Lucas said, easily. In his experience, kids didn't need to be talked at all the time.

Carmelo nodded, as if Lucas had said something interesting.

Elle's voice floated out through the open door. 'Carmelo, would you like water or ginger ale?'

Doubt crossed Carmelo's face. 'Ginger ale. Please.'

Elle came out with three glasses of ginger ale, sparkling in the sun. She smelled of sun tan lotion as she passed Lucas's shoulder. 'I brought one for you, Lucas.'

'Thank you.'

'Thank you,' echoed Carmelo. He put the glass to his lips and took a cautious sip. Then his face cleared and he took a healthy swig.

Lucas hid a smile. He suspected that Carmelo wasn't familiar with ginger ale and had only chosen it in the supposition that anything had to be more fun than water.

Elle sank down to sit cross-legged on the deck. 'You must live close by, Carmelo, to be playing in the gardens.'

Carmelo looked down into his glass.

'Did you know I was living here on a boat?'

The little boy shrugged. Lucas would bet his bank account that Carmelo had simply followed Elle home. Carmelo's brown eyes, whenever they rested on Elle, spoke of adoration.

'I live on the boat, too.' Lucas took a sip of his ginger ale. Not bad. Usually he only drank it when there was a healthy slug of scotch in it.

Elle developed the theme. 'Who do you live with, Carmelo? Your parents?'

'Mama and Nonnu.'

'Your mother and grandmother?' Elle hazarded.

'Nonnu, he is the father of my mother.'

'Oh, your grandfather. Fantastic.' Elle's dress blew in the wind and she tucked it around her legs. 'I used to love my grandfather. My nonnu. Do you have brothers and sisters?'

Carmelo shook his head, and drank the rest of his ginger ale in one long draught.

Seized with a sudden ambition to see the solemn little boy smile a bit more, Lucas swigged his down, too. Then let out a giant burp.

Carmelo burst into giggles that rose like birdsong on the hot afternoon air.

Lucas belched again. 'Pardon me.'

With a grin that showed a wonky front tooth, Carmelo let out a burp of his own, then two more, laughing so much between gas emissions that he could barely manage his 'Pardon mes'.

'Amazing how well burps and men go together,' Elle observed, drily. But her eyes laughed.

Lucas winked at Carmelo and the little boy burst into giggles again, trying, unsuccessfully, to squeeze out a new burp. Instead, he was seized by a hiccup so loud that it made him give an 'Oh!' of surprise. Which made him giggle harder than ever. Giggles and hiccups began to alternate, his shoulders shaking.

Lucas found himself wondering when the little boy had last laughed like a little boy ought to. He'd looked so solemn, spying on Elle from behind the twisted brown-grey trunk of the pine tree.

It was Elle who was watching Carmelo, now. Although she was smiling, her expression struck Lucas as odd, as if she were fighting a hidden pain.

'Looks like somebody's having fun.' The voice came from the quayside, the speaker a woman with thick auburn hair and a wide grin.

Lucas jumped up, feeling somehow caught out. 'Kayleigh! I thought you were going to text me when you arrived.'

Kayleigh stepped easily across the gangplank. 'Why bother the satellite when I only had a few hundred yards to walk?' She looked at Lucas and flung her arms wide expectantly.

Lucas pulled her into a huge hug, glad to see her, but acutely aware of Elle, and that they were all trapped together in a small space.

As if picking up on his reticence, Kayleigh released him and turned to Elle and Carmelo. 'Good to meet you. I'm Kayleigh Dunn.'

Scrambling up, Elle flushed. 'I'm E-Elle and this is Carmelo.' Then she glanced at her watch. 'Sorry to run off the moment you turn up, Kayleigh. I need to go to work.'

'I understand,' Kayleigh replied easily.

Elle began collecting the empty glasses. 'Maybe I'll see you on Monday, Carmelo?'

The little boy got to his feet with an air of resignation.

Lucas held up his palm for a high five. 'Great to meet you, Carmelo. Good burps.'

He at least got a smile as Carmelo high fived him back.

'Do you need me to see you across the road?' Elle asked him.

Carmelo shook his head and, evidently accepting the inevitable, crossed the gangplank without a wobble and wandered along in the direction of the bridge, glancing back a couple of times.

With a bright smile, Elle turned away. 'Excuse me, I have to go, too.' She whisked through the doors and out of sight.

'Sorry I broke up the party – but hello.' Kayleigh gave Lucas another hard hug.

Lucas was apologetic. 'Carmelo was a bit of an uninvited guest but Elle obviously wanted to give him a few minutes of her time.'

'Cool lady,' nodded Kayleigh, approvingly.

Trying to push Elle from his mind, Lucas brought his attention to the woman by his side. 'Give me a moment to grab my wallet and then we can get a beer or something.'

But Kayleigh just pulled him down beside her on the

seat. 'We don't need to go rushing off. I bet you've got a cold beer here for a hot visitor?'

'You know me so well.' He fetched a couple of cold bottles from the fridge.

When he sat back down, Kayleigh hooked an arm companionably through his, asking about the quality of Maltese beer, chatting about her trip, her work. He understood her well enough to know that she'd parked herself on board the *Shady Lady* for a reason.

As if on cue, Elle reappeared, making to brush past with cheery goodbyes.

Kayleigh pulled her up short. 'I think your little friend's doubled back to hide out in the park.'

Elle braked to a stop. This time, she didn't swing around and gaze into the shadows. Instead, she sighed. 'Really? I was hoping he'd go home. He attends the centre where I'm volunteering and I think he's taken a shine to me.'

Kayleigh nodded. 'I work in a children's hospice and I recognise the signs. He's becoming attached to you. It's hard when that happens because your heart goes out to him but you can't play favourites. And you have to be careful not to do anything that can be construed as inappropriate.'

Elle looked agonised. 'Exactly. And I'm a real novice – I've only been volunteering a week.'

'Be friendly but aware of the pitfalls, is my advice. Maybe mention the situation to someone at the centre.' Kayleigh took a swig from her bottle. 'If it was me, I'd pretend I didn't know he was back in the gardens and go about my business.'

'Good plan, thanks.' With a wave, Elle left the boat and hurried up the quayside.

'Very cool lady,' repeated Kayleigh. 'Got a good heart

and doing her bit by volunteering. So tell me how it feels to be sharing the boat with her.'

Lucas groaned. 'Give me a break, Kay.'

'Nope.' She shook her head. 'You can't phone me to casually mention that you're sharing a boat with the girl who mashed your heart and expect me just to say, "Oh, that's nice," and talk about the weather. I know how you used to feel about her.'

'OK.' Lucas sighed. 'It was a hell of a shock when she turned up here. For both of us. We flared up at each other and then we both flared up at Simon for coming up with the masterful plan of arranging for us to be here at the same time.'

Kayleigh watched him. 'It seems wayward, even for Simon.'

He took a reflective pull of his beer. 'Yes, considering that there are a lot of hurt feelings still stabbing at us both.'

'Unresolved issues?'

He laughed, humourlessly. 'Not kidding.' Suddenly the beer bottle was empty in his hand and he realised that he'd hardly been aware of tipping the contents down his throat. He gazed at the froth running down inside the glass as if it held answers.

'It sounds as if your shared history's eating at you. You need to sort it out.'

Lucas shifted restlessly. 'Do we have to do this, Kay? It's great you're here but can't we just enjoy that, without analysing things that are best ignored?'

She sighed, gazing along the quay in the direction Elle had gone. 'What's ignoring it going to resolve, Lucas?' Then she squeezed his arm. 'Love you, hon, but you're not the easiest, you know.'

* * *

On the *Seadancer* Elle found Loz and Davie nursing hangovers in the shade on the foredeck.

Loz's hand seemed permanently stuck to her forehead. 'As the sea got up, last night, Davie remembered hurricanes, the cocktails we used to drink in New Orleans. So he got out the rum, fruit juice and grenadine.'

'Lovely red colour, grenadine,' Davie put in. 'But lies a bit heavy on the stomach.' He rubbed his paunch.

Loz looked at him severely over her sunglasses, her round cheeks quite pasty. 'After champagne, red wine and port it does. And you made those cocktails much too strong, because I didn't drink many and I feel atrocious.'

'So I'll just finish clearing up from the party, shall I?' Elle wasn't in the mood to referee a discussion on where the blame lay for their hangovers. Also, the sea was still lively enough to make her wish not to hear any unfortunate hangover symptoms involving bright red cocktails.

'If you don't mind,' said Loz weakly. 'And can you put the coffee on?'

In neither saloon nor galley did Elle find signs of any clearing up having taken place since her departure last night. Glasses and coffee cups clung stickily to surfaces, crumbs speckled the carpet, plates and balled up napkins lay in wait behind curtains or on the floor.

She threw open the windows to clear the stink of booze and put on the filter coffee, double strength. While it dripped, she ferried crockery and glassware from the saloon to the galley, loading the dishwasher and standing the rest on a worktop.

When the coffee was ready she poured herself a cup, placed the jug with mugs, cream and sugar onto a tray and took it out to the foredeck. 'Caffeine!' she announced, brightly.

Davie looked asleep but Loz managed a smile. 'Is it very awful in there? I feel mean leaving it all to you, sweetie, but, honestly, Davie did make those cocktails awfully strong. Are you horribly hungover, too? Get another mug and join us.'

Elle deposited the tray on top of the ever-present cool box. 'I don't have a hangover and I'd rather get on. That's what you're paying me for.'

Loz looked stricken. 'I was supposed to pay you yesterday and I forgot, didn't I? I'll settle up with you when you leave today.'

'Thanks, that's fine,' said Elle, gratefully, and went back to her clearing up, which she didn't actually mind. Restoring order suited her mood, as she moved quickly around the saloon with hot soapy water to wipe down all the horizontal surfaces – and a few vertical ones that were no longer pristine. She wanted to grit her teeth and scrub at red wine speckling white walls, to vacuum the carpet so energetically that the party debris rattled up the hose.

If only she could clean up her own life with hard work and efficiency. Hard work and efficiency she was good at. But whenever she thought she'd got her life as clean and tidy as the saloon had been pre-party, it was as if a troop of monkeys tumbled in and hurled their shit around.

Her conscience twanged. She shouldn't include pretty, smiling Kayleigh Dunn in her vision. Kayleigh's only crime was travelling to Malta to visit her boyfriend. She'd been pleasant towards Elle when a lot of girls in the current situation would definitely have turned into shit-hurling monkeys.

Why was Elle reeling that Kayleigh had turned up, though? Lucas had *told* Elle Kayleigh would be arriving any time. He'd *told* her.

Elle kept the doors between the saloon and the foredeck firmly closed and reached new heights of scrubbing and banging, shaking and vacuuming.

At the end of three hours, the interior of *Seadancer* once again shone like something from a yacht brochure. Elle was in the galley, stowing away the final load from the dishwasher, when Loz crept in, clutching the empty coffee jug.

She eyed Elle as if waiting for her to erupt with Acute Housework Disorder again. 'Gosh, aren't you scary, today?'

Elle found a reluctant grin. 'I'm not scary. I was just in the mood for it.'

Loz hugged Elle with the arm not clutching the coffee jug. 'Don't be in a bad mood! I'm sorry I left it all for you and sat outside feeling sick. Sorry I forgot to pay you.'

Elle returned the hug. 'I'm not in a mood with you,' she protested. 'Just with—' She halted. 'Haven't you ever had a good housework session to make you feel better?'

'No.' Loz looked astounded. 'I was thinking more about a nice wine spritzer.'

'Great. You go sit down and I'll bring out the wine and fizzy water.' Elle didn't want Loz dripping and dropping all over the nice clean galley.

Loz dimpled. 'I was thinking cheese and biccies, too.'

'Right.' Elle opened the cupboard for the cracker box.

'And we want you to come out and chill with us,' finished Loz, persuasively. 'You've earned it and it must be wine o'clock by now.'

Elle paused. 'That does sound good.' And a reason not to return to the *Shady Lady*.

Once she was seated in the shade with a much-restored Loz and newly awoken Davie, Elle realised that she'd eaten no lunch and drunk only one mug of coffee all afternoon so was able to bring joy to Loz's heart by helping herself to a big hunk of cheese and a handful of crackers.

Davie pulled his tatty baseball cap down to shade his eyes. 'Sorry we didn't think to rescind the party invitation to your old flame,' he said, gruffly, making her a spritzer that was almost entirely wine.

Elle accepted the glass with thanks. 'That would have been tricky. Let's not worry about it.'

Settling back in her chair and propping her feet on the cool box, Elle gave herself up to admiring the blue Mediterranean twinkling busily, the white yachts jostling at their moorings in front of the honey-coloured stone of Manoel Island.

Again, she reminded herself that this was what she'd come to Malta for, to live her new and exciting life. She was here for her.

Not to stress about the corporate competition, not to do what her parents wanted, not to live her relationship with the feeling that it was always teetering on the brink of some dread discovery. She was here to draw a line under all that.

'Lucas's girlfriend has arrived,' she announced, as if she'd just remembered. 'That should keep him occupied, shouldn't it?'

Loz leaned forward to put her soft hand on Elle's arm, her voice a whisper. 'Don't you mind, sweetie?'

Elle drank four big gulps of her drink. 'Lucas and Elle were over long before Kayleigh turned up.'

By the time Elle prepared to leave the *Seadancer* she was feeling pleasantly fuzzy and relaxed. Loz and Davie would have swept her along with them as they went ashore to dine with other yachtie friends, but she had been firm in her refusal.

'I'm too hot and sticky and I've eaten about a pound of your cheese. What I'd really like to do,' she added, 'is swim. I can't believe I've been here almost a week and haven't been in yet.'

'You don't have to go very far.' Davie gave her directions to a suitable swimming spot and within minutes she was back at the *Shady Lady*. Relieved to find the boat empty she changed into a golden yellow one-piece. Throwing on a loose dress, she grabbed a towel and set off through the early evening sunshine to where a gathering of hotels looked across Marsamxett Harbour to Valletta and an area of sea was roped off against the intrusion of boats.

People, bright towels and beach bags were scattered on the rocks between road and sea. Balancing on the rocky ripples and serrations, Elle picked her way right to the end. The water looked incredibly inviting, lapping and twinkling in the sunshine.

She threw down her towel, kicked off her dress and flip-flops and dived in.

After the heat of the afternoon, the sea felt scalp-tingling cold. Through the water she gained a blurred impression of rocks, seaweed and her own bubbles dancing around her before she broke the surface with an exultant 'Whoo!'

The sea was still choppy and she flipped over and began a languid back crawl, the sounds of children squealing gargling in her ears, warring with the tolling of a church bell and the constant grumble of traffic.

Reaching the line of rope and buoys, she paused to tread water and gaze across the harbour to admire the Carmelite Dome and the elegant spire of St Paul's church.

She swam back more slowly. Then she climbed one of

the ladders out onto the rocks and dried herself, thinking about shopping for her evening meal. Lucas would no doubt be busy with Kayleigh.

Now she had what she had expected in the first place, the boat to herself ... it was going to feel odd.

Chapter Ten

To: Simon.Rose
From: Elle.Jamieson
Subject: Two weeks into the adventure

Hi Simon,

I'm e-mailing you while all around me industrious
16–18-year-olds are creating CVs for potential employers.
Joseph's mum, Aileen, is here, too. She's a retired English
teacher so she does the words and I do the IT skills.
Having been married to a Maltese man, she speaks quite
a bit of the language, so the kids tend to behave pretty
well when she's around.

Two weeks in Malta have flashed by. But, somehow,
I feel as if I've been here much longer, too. I get on well
with Loz and Davie. Loz is so funny, isn't she? Flinging her
arms around people, always agog about their lives. She
doesn't get *EastEnders* on the boat so real people have to
take its place. She's lovely to work for, so long as I don't
mind her wandering around with me, chattering as I work.

I've sorted out the computer room at Nicholas Centre.
Everything's reformatted and working as fast as I can
make it go. I won't bore you with the details of installing a
new router with more ports, getting the broadband speed
raised, firewalls, virus checks, clearing porn blah blah.
Let's just say I had to view it as a challenge rather than a
frustration.

I very proudly filled up the water on the *Shady Lady*,
yesterday. Lucas does it most days but he was busy
because his girlfriend, Kayleigh, is here. She's been

here for a week but I've only met her once. I expect he's showing her around the island.

Elle paused, debating whether to ask Simon why he thought it was that Lucas seemed to return alone to spend every night on the boat. Lucas had told her that he and Kayleigh liked their own space but ... the Lucas she used to know had definitely woken in the mornings ready for action. Heat flooded her at the memory of Lucas's hands and mouth on her skin, waking her for languorous early-morning love-making. Or urgent early-morning love-making. Or a shake-down in the shower, if that's all they had time for.

Separate sleeping arrangements? Not likely.

With a glance around the room to check none of the kids was wearing that I-need-help-with-this-task-but-don't-want-to-ask-for-it look, she returned to her e-mail.

I've been swimming from Tigne seafront, near that footbridge to the big shopping area, The Point. The Point's too much like any shopping mall anywhere for my taste and I'd rather mooch around Sliema or Valletta. The temperatures are in the mid-30s, which is pretty hot for June (and everyone tells me it will be even hotter in July and August) so I stop often for ice cream.

I took your advice about the open-top buses and have been on two tours. Really fascinating! The only other touristy thing I've done is a harbour cruise, which was brilliant. Doesn't Valletta look amazing from Grand Harbour? For that matter, doesn't Grand Harbour look amazing from Valletta? So fabulously blue with the white wakes of boats criss-crossing it and everything from massive ocean liners to little fishing boats.

Malta is such a fantastic place, Simon. Thank you for making it possible for me to live here. Even if Lucas is here to complicate things.

Hugs,

Elle xxx ☺

Simon's reply pinged into her inbox only forty minutes later.

To: Elle.Jamieson
From: Simon.Rose
Subject: A little bit jealous

Elle,
You make me 'homesick' for Malta! The weather is boiling here in California, too, but I suppose the difference is that I work in it whereas I'm always on vacation when I'm in Malta. Now I'm longing to be sitting up on the flybridge of the *Shady Lady* with a Cisk (or five) and a pastizzi.

So, it's Kayleigh who's turned up to be with Lucas, is it? Now that's ver-y in-ter-est-ing. I met her at Geoffrey and Fiona's place at Christmas. Nice girl.

Glad you're having a great time.

Made any new friends? Especially of the male variety?

xxx

Deciding not to react to this mention of Lucas's parents, and still underemployed as her charges worked through their tasks, Elle went straight back:

To: Simon.Rose
From: Elle.Jamieson
Subject: The male variety

Why is it interesting that Kayleigh is Lucas's gf? She
seems nice. I suppose I want to hate her but she's too
easy to like. So I'm being noble and telling myself that I'm
happy he's chosen someone good.

I have two male admirers. Carmelo and Oscar. Carmelo
is eight and one of the kids at the drop-in centre. He's
pretty much a fixture here. I don't think he can have much
of a home life. When school finishes for summer at the
end of next week I expect that he'll be here 24/7. He's
followed me to the boat once or twice. He has such sad
eyes: I feel bad for him.

Oscar, he's a fellow volunteer, an incredibly tall guy,
about six-and-a-half feet. He does a lot of the active stuff
with the kids – table tennis and weights, etc. He's made
it obvious that he's interested but he's creepy. Especially
as I think he was responsible for the porn I found on the
machines when I first got here! Even leaving that little
discovery aside, I find it hard to like him. His eyes crawl
all over me and he doesn't bother to try and hide that he's
ogling. Eww.

E xxx

To: Elle.Jamieson
From: Simon.Rose
Subject: The male variety

Watch out for the Oscar dude! Tell him that if he's a sex
pest I'll come over there and – oh, wait, you said he's big?

Set Lucas on him. ☺

x

Elle grinned as she signed out from her e-mail account. A couple of the girls, Kimberley and Giorgina, were fidgeting and whispering from behind adjacent machines.

Elle pushed away from her desk and rolled her chair over to join the girls, interrupting a fit of stifled giggles. 'So, how are we getting on?'

'Finished,' they chorused. Kimberley and Giorgina were fine examples of beautiful blossoming Maltese womanhood. Dark and glossy hair was piled up behind their heads and secured by neon-coloured clips; their sultry brown eyes were made up to look even larger and more dramatic than nature intended. Elle felt insipid beside them.

She ran her eyes over what they'd done. 'Really great! Kimberley, you might want to make all your headings consistent. Do you remember how to set up a heading style? If you made all these big headings Heading 1 and the smaller ones Heading 2, it would work well. Giorgina, I'm not sure that employers will be keen on a curly purple font.'

Giorgina giggled behind her hand.

'Can we do Facebook?' requested Kimberley, with a sigh. The session was nearly over and, despite open windows and a whirring fan in the corner, it was stultifying enough in the internet cafe to shorten attention spans.

'Of course. Just make those changes first,' Elle encouraged.

On the other side of the room, Aileen was 'encouraging' Paolo, one of the brasher kids. Paolo treated education of any kind like a joke. But Elle was fast learning that treating something as a joke was a classic defence mechanism of a kid who wasn't getting enough support.

Aileen had been a great help in showing Elle the trick of getting teens to co-operate by saying yes to their requests without letting them get away with tasks undone. Her genial but authoritative approach was easy for Elle to emulate. Already Elle was prefacing instructions with a few words of positivity, such as 'This is straightforward' or 'You'll enjoy this', because that's how Aileen seemed to get results. The computer room was more classroom-like than the rest of the centre but even when Elle wasn't running workshop sessions she was helping, encouraging, teaching. She was growing to value the sense of doing something more useful than just making money.

At the end of this workshop session most of the teens slipped away, leaving space for the younger children who came in after school. Quiet, saturnine Axel came up to check his e-mail during his break time, greeting both women politely before settling down at a machine.

Aileen swivelled on her chair, stretching her limbs and reaching for her handbag. Her handbag and sandals matched, and she reminded Elle of a forties movie star, carefully set hair waving back from a conspicuously powdered face. Elle always half-expected Aileen to tie on a headscarf and hop into an open-top sports car.

'Your Carmelo will probably be dashing in at any moment.' Aileen took out her powder compact as if reluctant to brave the world outside without a fresh coat. 'He's got a real pash on you.'

Elle laughed. 'What's a pash?'

'A passion. A crush.' Aileen put away her powder and got out her lipstick.

Sighing, Elle agreed. 'I'm afraid he has. He's a lovely boy but I'm not exactly sure whether I should be discouraging him. And if so, how.'

'Talk to Joseph. He's a whiz with little lost kids like our Carmelo.'

As Aileen left, Elle made a round of the machines, closed down open documents and signed out of a couple of Facebook pages abandoned negligently by their users. She passed a few minutes with Axel, who was shopping online for books for his e-reader, then gathered up her bag and slung it over a shoulder. With a brief goodbye, she ran down to look for Joseph.

She found him sitting on the back doorstep talking to Maria.

Elle hesitated. 'Am I interrupting?'

Joseph waved her forward. 'Nothing more important than deciding whether to buy new school stationery now or wait to see if there are any offers when the time comes to go back to school. Something on your mind?'

'It's about Carmelo Tabone.'

'Ah.' Joseph smiled and exchanged a look with Maria.

It was stupid to feel self-conscious but Elle felt herself going pink. 'I was just talking to your mum about Carmelo. She – well, I – well, both of us – we feel that he's suffering from a bit of a crush. On me.' She licked her lips. 'I don't know how to handle it. I don't want to do the wrong thing and hurt his feelings, but, obviously – I – i-it's not appropriate—' She halted, irritated that her stammer had put in an appearance.

Sombrely, Joseph nodded. 'Thank you for being careful of his little heart. I'm afraid that Carmelo is seeking affection.' He paused. Then, delicately, he added, 'His mother cannot always look after him as we'd wish her to.'

Elle's heart gave a great squeeze. 'Poor little boy. What about his Nonnu?'

A shrug. 'Unfortunately, his mind is very old.'

'Then I can see he might not be a help.' Elle sighed. 'Carmelo follows me home sometimes, Joseph; how should I handle it? The first time, I took him on board the boat for a drink, but I took care that we stayed in public view and that someone else was there. Since then, I've either pretended not to see him or taken him a drink in the gardens.'

Both Joseph and Maria sighed. 'It's hard for him.' Maria shook her head, sorrowfully.

Joseph smiled at Elle. 'Continue to be sensible in your own conduct and remember your training. But be his friend. Carmelo needs friends.'

A great lump snuck up into Elle's throat. 'Thanks,' she managed.

When Elle left the centre she had seen no sign of Carmelo, so she wasn't altogether surprised, arriving at the boat overheated and slightly headachey because she'd forgotten her hat, to find him on the quayside near the *Shady Lady*. It was new behaviour, getting one step ahead of her, but there was a schedule on the wall showing when she was due to be at Nicholas Centre. He was a fiercely bright kid, easily able to work out that if she wasn't in the internet cafe she might be at the boat.

He was perched on the kerb around the garden, his attention on the *Shady Lady*'s open door. As Elle watched, she saw Kayleigh emerge, a bottle of drink in each hand. Her thick hair shone in the sunlight and swung either side of her face.

Elle paused. Till now, it had seemed as if Lucas had been keeping Kayleigh out of Elle's path and Elle had assumed that he felt safer that way. Having lover and ex-lover together in one place wouldn't be comfortable for anyone concerned so Lucas's separatist strategy wasn't something Elle was about to dispute.

But here Kayleigh was, speaking to Carmelo, gesturing towards the gardens and handing the little boy a drink. Carmelo turned and fell into step beside her. His shorts drooped and he hitched them up before he twisted the top from the bottle, tipping back his head to drink enthusiastically. His hair looked as if it hadn't been cut for months.

Elle altered her trajectory in order to intercept them in the dappled shade of Gżira Gardens. 'Hi,' she called, brightly.

Carmelo's head swung around and a smile burst like a splash of sunshine across his face. 'Kayleigh gave me Fanta.' He held up the bottle of orange pop.

'That's great.' She exchanged a smile with Kayleigh. 'And now you're going to play in the gardens?'

'You, too?' Carmelo looked hopeful.

'I can watch you for ten minutes,' Elle temporised. 'Then I have to go to work.'

'OK.' Carmelo was never demanding.

Nothing in his life had encouraged demanding behaviour, Elle supposed. Her heart squeezed. 'There's a swing free,' she said. 'Maybe Kayleigh would hold your drink while I push you?'

'Fine by me,' put in Kayleigh.

Carmelo dashed off to secure the swing before anybody else got it and the two women followed. 'I doubt that he needs to be pushed,' Elle commented, apologetically. 'But I thought he'd enjoy it.'

'There are many interpretations of the word "need",'

observed Kayleigh. 'I'd say his need, in this case, is for your company. Whether he can work the swing alone is immaterial.'

'I think so, too.' Elle flashed a look at the other woman. 'It's obvious that kids are your thing.'

Kayleigh shrugged. 'I help meet the needs of kids who are so sick they break your heart. You're making life better for some kids whose problems might be less easy to diagnose.'

They reached the spot where Carmelo waited, glancing back eagerly over his shoulder. 'Hang on tight.' Elle grasped the black rubber swing seat and pulled it backwards, as high up its arc as she could manage. 'Ready?'

'Go!' shouted Carmelo. And whooped and giggled as Elle thrust him into the air, leaning back so that he could see her upside down as the swing swooped, forward and back. Elle caught the seat every time he returned and shoved it with all her might. The play apparatus was in the full sun and she was soon wiping sweat from her forehead.

Kayleigh grinned as the swing arced forward once more. 'I have a lot of time for anyone who helps children. And you don't even get paid.'

Elle waited for Carmelo to make the return journey and soar away again. 'He's a good kid and his home life's tough. It's good to see him laugh. Besides, it's you who gave him a drink and brought him over here.'

'Only because Lucas thought you'd be back any time. We were just filling in time waiting for you. It's you Carmelo wanted to see.' Kayleigh, too, timed her comments to coincide with the furthest part of the swing's arc, so that Carmelo couldn't overhear. She nodded between the trees. 'Here comes company.'

Elle turned and saw that Lucas was strolling up to

them, three bottles of water in his hands. He offered one bottle to Elle. 'Thanks.' She stood back to take the drink gratefully. Swinging was thirsty work, especially having already walked through the streets baking in the early-afternoon sun.

Lucas gave his own bottle into Kayleigh's keeping and moved to take over the swing. Soon Carmelo was squealing gleefully as Lucas's height and strength sent him to new heights.

Elle watched the easy athletic grace of Lucas's movements as he flung his arms up to catch the swing, the play of his muscles as he propelled Carmelo forward. He didn't contribute as Kayleigh continued the conversation about working with children, nor comment when Kayleigh asked whether she could visit Nicholas Centre, and Elle agreed to ask Joseph.

Becoming restive at his silent presence, Elle finished her drink. 'Thanks for the water, Lucas. I'd better get off to the *Seadancer*.'

Lucas nodded. 'See you later.'

Shortly after Elle departed, Carmelo asked to get off the swing. He drank the rest of his Fanta and then clambered around on the climbing frame for a while. His wide smiles and wild giggles had faded away, as if Elle had taken the fun from the afternoon with her.

Lucas and Kayleigh retired to a shady bench. Kayleigh threaded her arm through Lucas's. 'Are you cross with me for getting friendly with her?'

He shrugged.

'I'm not trying to freak you out or piss you off. I just like her and what she's doing. I'd like to see that centre. Maybe I could do something for the kids, too. Maybe we could.'

'Maybe,' he agreed, neutrally.

He glanced across at the *Shady Lady* and the flash of a yellow dress as Elle disappeared inside.

'Are you still in love with her?' Kayleigh asked softly.

'Drop it.' Then, because it wasn't Kayleigh's fault, he said, 'Please. Just give me a break, Kay.'

They sat in silence as Carmelo's climbing became gradually less purposeful, until it wasn't so much climbing as fidgeting while he watched the *Shady Lady*. His patience was rewarded when Elle emerged, her hair hidden by her hat, her gaze disguised by sunglasses, khaki shorts showing legs that were becoming tanned, her breasts moving slightly under a white T-shirt.

Carmelo bounded from the climbing frame and raced to join her. She smiled at him, saying something that made him laugh as he skipped along beside her. She glanced into the gardens and waved goodbye to Lucas and Kayleigh. Carmelo copied her, throwing them a brief salute before turning all his attention back to Elle.

Kayleigh sighed. 'Any particular reason you're keeping me away from the boat? Away from Elle?'

'You've just been with her.'

'Only because me hanging out with Elle is so obviously not what you want that you're making me curious.' After a moment she added, 'If you're not being honest with me, I hope that you're at least being honest with yourself.'

Chapter Eleven

After checking it was OK with Joseph, Elle had arranged for Kayleigh to visit the Nicholas Centre on Thursday afternoon, when she'd be there herself.

She hadn't realised that Lucas would consider himself invited along.

Although she quickly realised that she had been stupid not to have anticipated him keeping his girlfriend company if he happened to have a day off, her heart jumped to see him waiting in the hallway outside Joseph's office beside Kayleigh.

But she managed to compose herself to greet them both and make the introductions to Joseph, who provided his usual quiet welcome.

Elle wasn't sure whether to stay or go as Joseph launched into a tour of the centre, weaving in its history and aims as he began in the games room, bringing in the towering Oscar. She'd just decided to fade away to where she'd left a group of kids in the computer room gathered around Lino, who was battling minotaurs on a level rarely seen in the Nicholas Centre gaming community, when Carmelo appeared behind her.

'You are not upstairs,' he declared accusingly. Then he saw Lucas and Kayleigh and peered in at them with his shy smile. 'You are here as well.'

Lucas, who had been listening to Joseph and Oscar, turned to exchange high fives, making Carmelo's eyes dance with pleasure. 'Yup, we're here.'

Kayleigh grinned. 'Hey, Carmelo. Maybe you could help Joseph show us around?'

Joseph waved Carmelo forward. 'Would you like to show your friends where you spend some of your time?'

Soon Carmelo was leading the party from room to room, clicking his fingers when he was struggling to summon the English word for something that he knew better in Maltese. Elle fell to the back of the pack, enjoying the spectacle of Carmelo coming out of his shell.

Oscar moved back to stand beside her. 'Your boyfriend arrives today with another woman?'

Elle's stomach dropped unpleasantly. Ah. She'd all but forgotten that Oscar thought Lucas to be her boyfriend. She'd just been relieved that he'd backed off.

'Kayleigh works with children in England, so she's interested in the centre,' she said, as if that explained everything.

'And she borrows your boyfriend?' Oscar persisted.

Elle tried to look blank, as if she didn't understand what Oscar was getting at. 'She doesn't need to borrow my boyfriend.' Which had to be true, as Elle didn't have a boyfriend, Lucas wasn't Elle's to lend and Kayleigh already had him.

A sly grin began to spread over Oscar's freckly face. 'This is interesting.' He watched Kayleigh link arms with Lucas. 'Very interesting.' He smiled that irritating smile again as they climbed the stairs to the next floor.

Inwardly, Elle groaned. But as Joseph turned to her at that moment for a presentation on what took place in the computer room she was able to abandon the conversation. Nevertheless, as she poured out her enthusiasm for her role at the Nicholas Centre, she was uncomfortably aware not only of Lucas's silent contemplation but of Oscar's grin.

Once her spiel was finished, Elle could have let the tour

move on without her. But that would have meant giving Oscar the chance to lurk around in the computer room, too, so she chose to stick with the group as it drifted downstairs to settle around the largest kitchen table. Elle helped Maria hand out drinks, and then waited until Oscar was seated so that she could choose a chair that wasn't next to him.

Carmelo's face shone with pleasure from his spot between Kayleigh and Elle. Talking animatedly about school soon ending for the summer, he swung his legs and sucked Pepsi through a blue-striped straw. At the end of the table Lucas and Joseph conversed quietly. Oscar watched Elle.

After twenty minutes, Lucas rose, saying to Joseph, 'That's really generous of you. If you're certain that you don't mind?'

'We can look to see what fits you on the way out.'

The pair led the group out of the kitchen. To Elle's surprise, Joseph took Lucas into the room where the rails of donated clothing hung. Surprise turned to plain astonishment as Lucas selected a pair of jeans in a thirty-two-inch waist.

'It doesn't matter if they're a bit short because I'll cut them off, anyway.'

'What are you doing?' Carmelo demanded.

'I need a couple of new things. Joseph says that as I've offered to help the centre with something, I can take these.'

Carmelo's quick eyes darted from Lucas's face, to the jeans, and then to Joseph, who looked on, hands in pockets.

With a rush of understanding, Elle glanced at Lucas with new respect. As he had no need for donated clothing, if he was accepting something he was doing it for a reason. It seemed pretty obvious to Elle what it was.

She adopted a regretful tone. 'That doesn't really apply to official volunteers.' Then, as if struck by a sudden thought. 'But Carmelo has often helped me in the computer room. Could he choose something, Joseph?' She was rewarded by a flash of warmth in Lucas's eyes.

Joseph sucked his teeth, gazing ruminatively at Carmelo. 'I think he was a big help to you, moving machines in the computer room?' He raised his eyebrows at Carmelo. 'Perhaps four items, for the help that you gave to Elle?'

Hesitantly, Carmelo hovered closer to the clothes rack, watching as Lucas worked through the hangers. Slowly, Carmelo began to smile as he chose two brightly coloured T-shirts and a pair of black shorts. And, lastly, a pair of jeans. 'I cut them off,' he declared.

After Carmelo had slipped behind a curtain to try his new clothes and Maria had OKed their fit, Kayleigh and Lucas went up to the activity room with Carmelo to seek out Axel, who was in charge of scissors, to perform surgery on the jeans, and Elle headed back to her computer room.

With translation help from one of the minotaur crowd, Elle settled down to assist a shy nine-year-old, Natasha, with creating a new e-mail account, thinking about what Lucas had done for Carmelo. Evidently, Lucas-present was a more mature and thoughtful man than Lucas-four-years-past. Lucas four-years-past might have wondered why nobody told Carmelo that his clothes didn't fit, without realising that Carmelo had very few clothes to choose from. He certainly wouldn't have created a scenario calculated to provide Carmelo with additions to his wardrobe without hurting his pride.

Natasha had fallen into inactivity, gazing at the screen. Elle tapped it. 'Click. *Hawnhekk*.' Aileen had taught her a few new Maltese words, including the one for 'here'.

And one thing that made Elle's lack of Maltese less of a handicap in the IT stakes was that most words from the world of computers were understood in their English form. Face clearing, Natasha moved the cursor to the spot that Elle had tapped, and clicked her mouse. 'Good. *Tajba*.'

Then she glanced up as Carmelo slipped into the room, looking like a mini Lucas in denim cut-offs and a T-shirt. He smiled self-consciously as he took up station at the machine closest to the one where she sat with Natasha.

'You look great,' Elle said. Carmelo's smile stretched into a huge grin.

A couple of hours later, Elle hit the sweltering streets. Late afternoon usually offered a softening of the heat, but today sweat prickled down her back and it felt as if the soles of her feet were scorching even through her sandals.

The visit of Kayleigh and Lucas to the centre had been unsettling. Lucas had done something really useful in getting Carmelo to accept donated clothes, a feat that neither Joseph nor Maria had been able to pull off.

But, in turning up with Kayleigh, he'd aroused Oscar's curiosity.

Waiting to cross the road, she felt as if the passing traffic was coating her with dust. It would be so good to get on the *Shady Lady* and shower. Or go off somewhere and swim. She imagined the cool blue water closing over her. She was so hot she'd probably sizzle.

Finally making it through to the gardens, she was able to see two figures on the *Shady Lady*'s flybridge. Her sore feet didn't falter. Elle could only be glad that at least she liked Kayleigh. How much worse would it have been if Lucas had hooked up with someone who'd mounted a campaign to oust Elle from the boat?

She discarded her bag and her sandals at the foot of the steps to the flybridge and made her way up.

Lucas lounged comfortably, the jeans from the donated clothes rail folded on the deck. Kayleigh was at the table with her feet up, reading a magazine that fluttered in the breeze.

'Good trick with Carmelo,' Elle commented, taking off her hat and using it to fan herself.

Lucas shaded his eyes. 'He's a nice kid.' He got up with an easy rolling movement and opened the fridge, gesturing to Elle to help herself.

She knew that water was better for both hydration and thirst-quenching, but her hand went to the Cisk as if magnetised. In seconds she had removed the top and gulped down the entire contents of a bottle, finishing with a sigh of satisfaction.

Lucas laughed, reached for another bottle and whisked off the top. 'Treat this one with a little more respect.'

'Cheers.' Elle took the fresh bottle as she dropped down onto a seat in the shade of the bimini.

'Lucas seems reluctant to share the strategy that got Carmelo to accept the new stuff,' observed Kayleigh. 'My guess is that he's arranged to make a donation and just made up the story about agreeing to help at the centre to make Carmelo comfortable.'

Elle retorted without thinking. 'Made up? Lucas? You don't know him very well.'

Kayleigh turned a gaze on her that was full of curiosity. 'I suppose I'd sort of forgotten for a moment that you've known him for longer than I have.'

Lucas stepped in. 'What I suggested to Joseph is that Dive Meddi do a Bubblemaker Session for the kids, which involves a fun presentation at the centre and then a sort of mini scuba taster in the pool. I haven't asked Vern, my boss, yet. What do you think, Elle? Would some of the volunteers from the centre get involved?'

Elle turned the idea over. 'I'm sure they would. There are kids there who would love it so I'm a bit worried that you might be inundated.'

'Usually, we're not. They come to the presentation but not everyone likes the idea of the actual scuba.' He glanced at his watch and rolled quickly to his feet. 'I've got a night dive, so I have to get off.'

He patted his pockets to check his possessions, blew a kiss to Kayleigh, skimmed his way down the steps, jumped off the boat and ran into the gardens, appearing only in glimpses as he headed for the bus stop.

It was quiet in his wake. Kayleigh seemed lost in thought and Elle wasn't sure what the etiquette was when your ex left his present girlfriend with you. She sighed.

Kayleigh looked up. 'Am I in your way?'

'No,' answered Elle, quickly. 'It's just that I've been promising myself a swim. You're welcome to hang on here for Lucas.'

'He'll be gone for hours.' Kayleigh dismissed Lucas with a wave. 'A swim sounds fantastic. My hotel's only just along the Strand; I could pick up my stuff.'

'Great,' Elle lied. She didn't really want to nurture her disconcerting liking for Kayleigh by hanging out with her but she was unsure how to put that across without hurting feelings. 'I've been swimming along at Tigne, in front of the Fortina Hotel, but Joseph told me about Font Ghadir. I was going to take the bus.'

'Sounds fantastic.'

So Elle found herself waiting for Kayleigh outside the Sea Creek Hotel, having refused an invitation to go up to her room. The mere idea of seeing Kayleigh's bed, where, presumably, Lucas made love to her, sent horror boiling through her veins.

Kayleigh emerged from the hotel with a big smile and a beach bag, chatting amiably as they secured a place on the big turquoise bus.

It wasn't until they alighted that Elle was able to see that this coast, which she'd only caught a glimpse of in the early days of her stay, was quite different in character to the creek.

They had another busy road to cross but then they walked down a flight of concrete steps to a significant shelf of rock filled with sunbathers and, further along, a beach cafe on stilts. The open expanse of the Mediterranean rolled waves up to the rocks and the only boats visible were well out towards where the sea met the sky.

Elle gazed around. 'This is amazing. Like a lunar landscape by the sea.' A scampering breeze blew her hair across her face and she twisted it up, finding a clip in the pocket of her bag to secure it.

In two minutes their dresses were discarded in their bags and they were picking their way over the scorching rocks towards the sparkling waves in their swim things, glad to plunge in and exchange overwhelming heat for the tingling chill of salt water.

Clearing her eyes as she bobbed up, Elle swam clear of the rocks. She didn't fancy scratches from toothy serrations or from the spiky black sea urchin colonies.

Leaving Kayleigh to her own devices, she began a brisk breaststroke. The sea was so lively that she felt a little as if she was swimming in an 'endless' pool, where the water flow cancels out any headway the swimmer makes. Her ears filled with the hiss and splash of the waves, the flutter of the wind and children shouting to one another as her shoulders and thighs grew pleasantly heavy with the exercise.

Finally, she let the waves carry her back to the ladder and hauled herself up, heading back to where she'd abandoned her bag. Kayleigh was already drying off in one of the last pockets of sun as the buildings lining the road above were now shading much of the beach.

Shaking out her towel, Elle sat down, blotting seawater from her hair and her skin. For a time she joined Kayleigh in quiet contemplation of the waves and the few small boats that had come close to shore.

Eventually, Kayleigh stirred. 'Lucas told me about you and him planning to get married.'

Elle kept her eyes on the restless ocean. 'It was a few years ago. The wedding idea never really got underway.'

'But you were a couple.'

'Yes.' Elle turned to meet Kayleigh's eyes. 'I suppose it seems weird that Lucas and I are living in the same boat. I'm surprised that you haven't created hell over it – most girlfriends would. But there's nothing between us, now, honestly.'

Kayleigh regarded her with curiosity. After a moment, her head dropped back as she laughed. 'I'm not "most girlfriends" and I wonder at your definition of "nothing". Lucas must have felt it was right to tell me about you.' Her smile broadened. 'As you obviously know, he has a well-developed sense of what's right. Or what he thinks is right. I think life's too subjective for it to be clear what's right and what's wrong, most of the time, but he doesn't see that, of course.'

'No,' Elle agreed, with feeling.

'Do you still love him?'

Elle felt her face flood with heat. 'Y-you honestly don't have to worry about anything like that.'

Kayleigh pulled out her dress and slid it over her head. 'I don't worry. I think I'll head back to my hotel, now.'

Elle was glad: Kayleigh was unsettling. 'I'll hang on here, move into the shade for a bit.'

She sat on for a long time, glumly uncomfortable with Kayleigh's suspicions that Elle still had feelings for Lucas.

Which made her wonder, with a greasy swirl of self-doubt, whether that meant that Lucas suspected that she did.

Simon obviously had.

It was depressing to think that everyone might think the same. And be pitying her.

Chapter Twelve

Next morning, Elle got up early and in a bad mood.

Kayleigh was being so unfeasibly reasonable about Elle and Lucas living together on board the *Shady Lady* that it had made her feel guilty.

She sighed as she gazed into a fridge almost devoid of food. The galley not being over blessed with storage and her not having a car made frequent food shopping a necessity, but she'd been busy with more interesting things lately.

Going hungry wasn't going to improve her disposition so, swinging the fridge door shut, she started the little coffee machine, grabbed her purse, hopped ashore and, the kiosk not being open for breakfast, ran across to a cafe on the other side of the road. Here, she sat herself at one of the small round tables on the pavement and, succumbing to the mouth-watering smell, ordered a bacon roll.

A battered green pick-up truck racketed onto the garage forecourt nearby, pausing only long enough to disgorge a man from the passenger side before it rejoined the stream of traffic.

Elle started to realise that the man was Lucas, and that he'd spotted her and was waiting for a gap in the traffic so that he could cross towards her. His hair was tangled, he needed to shave, his T-shirt looked as if he'd slept in it, but somehow the overall effect was that he'd just stepped out of an advert for something adventurous.

'What have you ordered?' He yawned.

'Bacon roll.'

'Mind if I join you? After the night dive I stayed over at

Vern's and I need something to soak up the alcohol.' He yawned again.

'I'm taking mine back to the boat.'

'Good idea.' He poked his head into the cafe and added two rolls to the order; then he turned back to Elle. 'Shall I go put the coffee on and you bring these over?'

'The coffee's on.'

'Fantastic. I feel as if I could drink pints of it.' He smiled lazily, apparently unaffected by the terseness of her responses.

Nettled by him intruding on her bad mood, for an instant she was tempted to change her plans and eat in the gardens. Then she sighed. Under the weight of her gloomy waking thoughts she'd pretty much reached the conclusion that she needed to talk to Lucas about the Kayleigh situation. Might as well be now.

So, 'You bring the food, I'll pour the coffee,' she said.

'Wonderful.' His attention was on counting out euros from his pocket.

Elle crossed back to the *Shady Lady*, white and gorgeous in morning sun already hot enough to make her shoulders tingle. She poured the coffee and carried the mugs up to the dinette in the saloon. Two plates, two sheets of kitchen roll in lieu of napkins, one bottle of tomato ketchup, and the table dressing was done.

In five minutes, Lucas appeared, a white takeaway container in his hands. 'Breakfast is served.' He put everything down and stretched tiredly. 'What's up? Your smile fallen overboard?'

She chose a roll and squirted ketchup neatly on the side of her plate. 'Yesterday, Kayleigh hinted that she suspects there's still something between us.' Then, honestly, 'More than hinted. I don't think she's happy.'

Lucas put down the roll he'd been holding. His eyes shone black. 'Why should she be unhappy?'

Elle stared. 'Seriously?'

He shook his head. 'I mean ... I don't know what I mean. You took me by surprise.'

'*Seriously?*' Elle said again. 'She's living in the Sea Creek Hotel, and you're living here on the boat with me, and you're surprised she's not happy?'

Frowning, Lucas took a huge bite of his breakfast, gazing out of the window at *Fallen Star*, one of the vessels lying between them and the bridge.

Elle waited for him to chew and swallow. But when he took another bite without responding, she put her roll down. 'Maybe she should come and live on the boat with you.'

Lucas swallowed. 'She doesn't want to.'

'Or you go and share with her.'

'She doesn't want that, either.'

'Then,' Elle took a deep breath, 'Loz and Davie said I could live on *Seadancer*. Maybe I'd better do that. While Kayleigh's visiting, anyway.'

'So our living arrangements only matter to Kayleigh when she's around to see them? If you move to *Seadancer*, logically it should be until one or other of us leaves the island.' He raised his eyebrows. When he did that, he looked a little like his mother when she felt it necessary to be particularly direct about something, and Elle's memories of Fiona in that mode were not fond.

'Then maybe I should,' she snapped. 'I'm not comfortable with upsetting Kayleigh.'

His eyes flashed. 'Bullshit. If you don't want to share the boat with me, don't, but at least be honest about it.'

'You and your honesty!' Elle found herself suddenly

146

on her feet, banging her thigh on the table, knocking the ketchup bottle noisily on its side. '*Honestly*, I'm not comfortable with upsetting Kayleigh.'

'Kayleigh's not upset—'

'Hello,' said an amused voice from the doorway. 'Sorry to butt in on your early-morning spat.' And there was Kayleigh, silhouetted against the streaming sunlight, gazing at them both curiously. 'Why are you arguing about me?'

Slowly, Elle subsided into her seat, face flaming. 'I think you might prefer it if I move off the *Shady Lady*.'

The chords on Lucas's throat stood out but he said nothing.

Kayleigh sauntered right into the saloon, dropping her bag onto a sofa. 'Why?'

Embarrassed to the point of inarticulacy, Elle's words tripped and stumbled. 'I f-feel you've been hinting that you don't like us sh-sharing the boat.'

'I haven't been hinting that.' Kayleigh sat down beside Lucas, bumping him with her hip so that he moved up and gave her more room. He fixed her with a glower.

Kayleigh's eyes flicked from Lucas to Elle. 'You two make me laugh.'

'*Laugh*?' Elle began.

What she might have said next was lost when Lucas's phone began to ring and he scrabbled it from his pocket with a growl. 'Now's not a good time,' he snapped at his caller. Then, '*What*?' He listened for several moments, before exploding: 'What a typical, half-arsed, lunatic Charlie-type plan.'

Despite her frustration, Elle found herself grinning. Lucas was so often exasperated with his brother, Charlie. And Charlie was so good at winding him up. If Elle had ever wished for a sibling, it would have been for a brother like Charlie. He was so unlike the rest of his family, not just because of his dark red hair and freckles but because of his low-maintenance, accepting, unambitious, larky nature.

Lucas's voice rose. 'It doesn't look as if I have much choice. Does it?' With a stab of his finger, he ended the call and looked up at his audience. 'My idiot little brother is nearly here in a taxi from Malta International Airport.'

Elle's heart gave a glad squeeze. She cried, 'Charlie's here?'

At exactly the same time that Kayleigh shouted it even more loudly.

'Didn't you know he was coming?' added Elle, trying not to feel a teeny pinch of jealousy that of course Kayleigh would know Charlie, and was beaming all over her face just at the sound of his name. She'd bet that Kayleigh got on with Fiona and Geoffrey better than Elle had, too.

Not that that would be hard.

Lucas grimaced. 'Even Charlie didn't know he was coming. The restaurant where he works had an after-hours kitchen fire and has been closed down for a few weeks, so he promptly went online and booked himself a flight.'

He pushed his fingers through his hair as a taxi approached up the marina access road, nosing its way towards them. 'Here he is. Bloody nuisance.'

But then he and Kayleigh were both out of their seats and bumping shoulders in the doorway in their haste to be the first with their greeting.

Elle watched through the open doors as Charlie climbed out of the taxi and dropped a big red squashy holdall to the ground while he fished for his wallet to pay the driver. He didn't look to have changed much since Elle had last seen him, still nearly as tall as Lucas but softer and less grim.

Lucas called some exasperated remark.

Then Kayleigh was bounding into Charlie's arms and Charlie was swinging her around as if she was the person in the world he most wanted to see.

Suddenly shy of intruding, for several seconds Elle hung back. But then she realised that Charlie would come on board the *Shady Lady* and it would look strange for Elle to have been sitting in the saloon and ignoring him.

So she followed in the wake of the others, stepping down onto the bathing platform and hesitantly onto the quay.

Charlie halted in mid-hug. 'Elle?' he breathed, incredulously.

In the sudden silence, Kayleigh looked from brother to brother, amusement in her eyes.

Lucas looked uncomfortable. 'Elle's living on the boat,' he mumbled.

Charlie's eyes widened. He stared at Lucas. 'Aren't you living on the boat?'

'Yes. But it's ... We're not—' Lucas ground to a halt.

'It was Si-Simon.' Elle paused to swallow her stutter. 'He took it into his head to agree to each of us living here for the summer, but didn't tell the other one what he'd done.'

'Fuck me,' marvelled Charlie, eloquently. 'As a joke?'

'No, as a matchmaking exercise,' burst in Kayleigh. And began to laugh.

Suddenly Elle discovered her sense of the ridiculous and let out a giggle. 'I don't think he realised that Lucas had a girlfriend.'

Picking up the holdall that he'd dropped, Charlie raised

interested eyebrows at his brother. 'I didn't know he had, either.'

Elle looked from Lucas to Kayleigh to Charlie. 'Of course he has,' she said, blankly. 'It's Kayleigh.'

Charlie gave a short laugh. 'Kayleigh's not his girlfriend. She's mine.' As if to prove it, he dropped his bag and yanked Kayleigh into his arms for an enthusiastic kiss.

Chapter Thirteen

Elle could only gaze at Lucas. 'What?'

Lucas looked as if he wished he could untie the *Shady Lady* and sail her far away. 'Um—'

Kayleigh snuggled her cheek against Charlie's shoulder. 'I'm over here for a European-wide conference about children with cancer, which takes place next week at a hotel in Qawra. Charlie didn't think he'd get time off work and I had holiday to take so I thought I'd come early and let Lucas show me the sights.' She grinned. 'When I arrived, Lucas got all embarrassed and said he *might* have let you think I was his girlfriend, so would I at least not tell you that I'm not.'

'I never actually said that Kayleigh was my girlfriend.' Lucas was uncharacteristically defensive. His eyes slid from Elle's. It was the only time she'd known him not be able to meet her gaze. 'I said I was expecting a girl. You assumed we were in a relationship. I didn't tell a single lie.'

Elle gaped at him. Then her eyes began to prickle. 'But you let me think it. Why did you let me make that assumption? Why ask Kayleigh to go along with it?'

'I suppose it was convenient,' he began, slowly, 'in the same way that it was convenient for you to let Oscar believe I was your boyfriend when you wanted to fend him off.'

Humiliation rose up to roar its fury in her ears. 'But I didn't need fending off! I was off! And dishonesty from *you*, *Lucas*? The man who always said that lies of omission are as bad as lies of commission? The one who had the cheek to call *me* secretive? Why the hell did you create such an elaborate deception?'

Finally, Lucas looked at her properly, at her trembling lip, her fists clenched impotently at her sides. His gaze seared into her tear-filled eyes. 'I suppose I must have really wanted to hurt you.'

Elle spent the day somewhere. Lucas had no idea where she was, but he was all too aware that she wasn't on the boat.

When she'd turned and walked woodenly away, along the waterfront towards Sliema, he'd stared after her, his words ringing in his ears, not having the first idea how to call them back, replace them, explain them or to wipe the pain from her face.

'That was shitty,' Charlie observed candidly. 'Kayleigh, why did you go along with it?'

Kayleigh's habitual smiles had vanished. 'Lucas let me assume that he was trying to get her to show she wasn't over him so that he could do something about it. Lucas, if I'd known that you were going to use me as petty vengeance, I would have told you to stuff it. That's so not you.'

'No,' he managed, huskily. 'It was shitty.'

'You need to apologise. And not to us.' Charlie picked up his luggage. 'Where's your hotel, Kay?'

Yesterday evening's dive to put Advanced Open Water Diver candidates through their paces in dark waters lit only with head lamps and flashlights, followed by a few scant hours in a bar and a night on Vern's inadequate sofa, had made Lucas weary. But being found out in his uncharacteristic deceit was heavy on his mind. He lay on the double bed in his cabin, waiting equally fruitlessly to fall asleep or to hear Elle's footsteps, staring at puffs of white cloud through the skylights, listening to the sounds from the road and voices of people passing along the quayside.

He felt shaky and queasy. And it wasn't anything to do with not having eaten more than a bite or two of breakfast.

If this horrible, slimy feeling of self-loathing was how being dishonest felt, he wondered that anybody was ever anything but honourable.

Misleading Elle hadn't been planned. But that first day, when he'd found her standing on the quayside with her suitcases, looking just so fucking horrified and aghast to find him on the boat, he'd lost hold of his composure. *I'm expecting a visitor, soon. A girl.* The words had flowed from his lips without him considering where he was going with them. But the dismay on her face had given him so much satisfaction that *She's Charlie's girlfriend* had somehow stuck on the wrong side of his lips.

He'd told himself that he wasn't telling any actual lies. That he was just avoiding the humiliation of revealing that, since Elle, he'd operated a catch-and-throw-back policy while he nursed wounds that refused to heal.

Hadn't he just intended to give himself time to turn over in his mind what Elle's recoil from his words could have meant? Kayleigh had formed a handy barrier, a refuge from his own feelings and from the necessity of deciding on action and taking it.

Kayleigh had asked if he was being honest with himself. But now he was alone in his cabin with Elle's haunted face hanging before his eyes alongside Charlie's disillusion and Kayleigh's accusation, he knew that he hadn't been honest with anyone. Until today, when he'd told Elle he'd just wanted to hurt her. That had definitely come straight from his heart.

And did him no credit.

He moved restlessly. Lucas was used to being largely at peace with himself. He might not agree with others, they might not agree with him, but usually he was confident that he was in the right.

Usually.

Loud laughter jumped him from a sleep he couldn't remember sliding into, but, as the skies were dark above the skylight, he seemed to have slept for a good portion of the day.

The marina could be noisy, especially if the kiosk's patrons were playing bingo or watching an important football match on the TV that hung on the wall.

But the laughter that had dragged him from sleep was Elle's.

Too glad to worry about his hair being on end or that he'd slept in his clothes, he jumped up the steps to the saloon and out onto the *Shady Lady*'s bathing platform.

A few yards away, Elle, Charlie and Kayleigh were gathered with Loz and Davie, Loz being her usual one-woman conversation machine.

Elle glanced across at the boat. Her gaze caught on Lucas's for a still moment. Then she looked away.

OK. So he'd been put in his place. Lucas could take his punishment like a man. He sat down on the cockpit seat to wait.

For twenty minutes, the merry knot of people entertained one another without apparently feeling the need to include, or even acknowledge, Lucas. Gales of laughter greeted anecdote after anecdote, passers-by regarded the happy group with curiosity.

Elle took her full part in the conversation, laughing, shoving Charlie playfully. She wasn't wearing the clothes she'd stalked off in this morning. From somewhere she'd procured a black maxi dress slit up both sides and decorated with flamboyant golden flowers. In the lights that lined the quay the dress looked amazing with her hair, which tumbled loose over her shoulders.

Finally, Loz and Davie began to say their goodnights, catching hands as they prepared to stroll off in the direction of *Seadancer*. 'Seven o'clock, tomorrow!' Loz called back. 'See you then.' No invitation for Lucas.

With reluctance, it seemed, Elle turned towards the *Shady Lady*. Charlie already had one arm occupied with Kayleigh, but he threw the other around Elle's shoulders. Both Charlie and Kayleigh said things to Elle that Lucas couldn't hear. Nor her response. But the trio kept on coming up the quay until they broke apart to cross the gangplank onto the *Shady Lady*. To pass into the saloon without acknowledging Lucas would necessitate them officially blanking him.

Incredulously, for a wild instant, he thought they would.

Then Elle stopped right in front of him. Close up, he could see from the glitter in her eyes and the hint of looseness in her movements that she and alcohol were no strangers this evening.

She regarded him solemnly. 'I've decided I'm still speaking to you. I thought about going to live on *Seadancer* and pretending you didn't exist, but I'm not going to.'

Lucas glanced at his brother, who was standing behind Elle, arms loosely about Kayleigh. Kayleigh was watching Elle, not Lucas.

He returned his attention to Elle. 'Good. Any particular reason?'

Her hair blew into her face. She reached up and gathered it up into a blonde stream all over one shoulder. 'I made my plans for living here and I'm not going to change them because you've been an arse,' she explained amicably. 'I suppose you thought you owed me a bit of payback, and even if you're *wrong*, I can see that making me think that you were all loved up would be tempting. It's like doing this, isn't it?' She thumbed her nose inelegantly. 'Or saying "up yours". No reason to it, no logic, it's *wrong*, but you do it, because somehow it makes you feel better.'

Her brows arched. 'It's almost comforting to know that even Saint Lucas can fall prey to mean, small *deceits*.' Looking pleased with her speech, she took a step towards the cabin door.

Then swung back. 'But, if we're going to be civilised, I don't want to talk about this any more. You did your thing. We're both over it. Let's move on.'

'Do I get to speak?' he asked, mildly.

She tilted her head thoughtfully. 'Do you really need to?'

'Yes.'

With a sigh, she backtracked, flumping down on the seat beside him. 'What?'

He turned his head to maintain eye contact. 'I'm sorry.'

She stood up. 'Good.'

Then she sat down again. 'What's the difference between a woman and a dog?'

He went along with it. 'Don't know. What the difference between a woman and a dog?'

'It's easier to find a nice dog.' She laughed, rising slightly unsteadily.

His eyes followed her. 'I would have thought you'd tell that joke against men.'

'About a man ... it's a crocodile.' And this time she made it through the door and out of sight.

Charlie and Kayleigh hovered. 'We're still talking to you, too,' Charlie confirmed kindly.

Unwillingly, Lucas smiled. 'Good to know.' The two brothers gazed at each other.

After a moment, Kayleigh said, tactfully, 'I'll go see if Elle's all right.'

Charlie sat down next to Lucas. 'She's been OK. Kayleigh rang her to find out where she was and we stayed with her most of the day. We did some retail therapy in a glitzy shopping mall.' He pointed vaguely towards Sliema. 'Then we went for ice cream and drinks, which sort of segued into dinner and drinks, and we happened to meet Loz and Davie wandering back in this direction, so Elle introduced us, and we all stopped at a bar for more drinks.' Charlie sighed. 'Why have you been such a dick?'

Lucas tipped his head back, closed his eyes. 'I thought I'd try it. Everyone else seems to.'

'Did you like it?'

Lucas shook his head. 'Can't see the attraction.'

Charlie hesitated. 'Look, Lucas, I think Elle understands that what's past is past, without you going to stupid lengths to show her that you want there to be no chance of you getting it on again. The water has gone under the bridge; you don't have to piss in it.'

After Charlie had collected Kayleigh from Elle's cabin and they'd disappeared along the waterfront in the direction of the hotel, Lucas sat for a long time out in the night air. The traffic had begun to thin and only a few stop-outs strolled beside the slack black water of the marina that flickered with reflected gold.

Of all the explanations for his deception that he'd puzzled over in the privacy of his cabin today, Charlie's suggestion that it was to show Elle that there was no chance of them getting it on again hadn't occurred to him.

He forced himself to consider it now.

But, eventually, he shook his head. No, that wasn't it.

Chapter Fourteen

Elle wasn't enjoying Loz's dinner party.

She was grateful that Loz had invited her and knew the invitation had been issued at least partly to show Lucas that he wasn't on the guest list, but it was impossible to forget her role as 'the help' even though Loz kept saying, 'Elle, you're not on the payroll this evening, you're not to do a thing.'

Actually, with the others being depressingly coupley, drinking a lot more than Elle felt like drinking and then shrieking with laughter over coupley anecdotes, Elle would rather be clearing up the galley.

When she could find no more to do, she took her last half-glass of rosé out onto the aft deck to enjoy the quayside and the gardens.

The breeze was up and a slow swell had risen again, but it wasn't unpleasant. Elle supposed she must have found her sea legs, even though she hadn't actually been to sea, unless you counted a little potter around the harbours. She hadn't done a lot of things she'd meant to do. Tomorrow, her day off, she'd put that right. She'd take a ferry to one of the sister islands in the Maltese archipelago, Gozo or Comino.

There would be at least three benefits. She could leave the party now, yawn and say it was time she went off to bed as she needed to be up early; she would be seeing new things and having new experiences, which was her mission; there would be little chance of crossing paths with Lucas.

But as she finished the last half-inch of wine and turned

to go up to the foredeck to make her excuses, a movement beside a tree at the edge of the gardens caught her eye. She paused, pretending to look up the quayside for several seconds while she tried to decide whether she'd seen what she thought she'd seen.

Then she turned back.

The little person behind the tree was too slow to anticipate her and was in plain view for half a second before he pulled his head in.

Keeping her movements slow, twirling her wine glass between her fingers, she sauntered down the gangplank in the direction of the tree. 'Carmelo! *Bonswa*. What are you doing out so late?'

Reluctantly, Carmelo detached himself from the shadows. Shrugging, he dug his hands into his pockets.

Elle saw tear tracks on his cheeks. Her heart twisted. 'Are you OK?' she asked gently. 'Is something the matter?'

Silently, Carmelo shook his head which, as it could have been in response to either question, wasn't helpful.

'Let's sit down.' She crossed to one of the benches that, by day, would be full of tourists or parents watching their children on the playthings, but now stood empty in a cool patch of moonlight. 'What are you doing here, in the dark? Have you been looking for me?'

Again, Carmelo only shrugged.

'Are you hurt?'

He shook his head.

Elle searched for what else made a child unhappy. 'Are you frightened?'

Another shrug. But Carmelo's gaze did flicker towards Elle for an instant.

Then, taking her by surprise, he threw his arms around her and clung on, silently. Every instinct demanded that

Elle hugged him fiercely back but her child protection training kicked in and she only ruffled his hair, wondering, sadly, how often anyone hugged this child. Bloody guidelines. How the hell was she supposed to help some poor little kid who obviously needed someone on his side?

Remembering her mother's avoidance tactics whenever Elle had needed someone to talk to, Elle felt quite unable to turn a deaf ear on a child who needed a listening one. She made her voice soft. 'Well, we've got to sort this out, haven't we? Because I think Mama and Nonnu will be wondering where you are, don't you?'

Again, the shrug, his shoulders as thin-edged as card against Elle's arm. She began to rise from the bench, which obliged Carmelo to break his embrace without her having to actually reject him. 'Do they know where you are? Will they be worried about you?'

Carmelo shook his head.

'Are Mama and Nonnu at home?'

'Yes.' Carmelo's voice was small with tears.

She made her voice as understanding as she could. 'You will need to go home, won't you?'

Carmelo shook his head.

'I could go with you—' she tried.

The headshake, this time, was more violent. '*No!*'

Elle subsided. Her training had covered basic challenging situations but this one was obviously outside her skill set and experience. 'I know what we'll do,' she said, making her voice glad and enthusiastic. 'We'll ring Joseph. He'll be able to help us sort this out.'

For a long moment, Carmelo considered. Eventually he shrugged.

Elle chose to take that as agreement. 'I'll just send a text to my friends on *Seadancer*.' Her thumb flew over the screen as she tapped in hastily to Kayleigh – knowing Loz would only text a hundred questions in reply – Got to go. No prob, just something that's come up re the centre. Hug Loz and Davie goodbye and say sorry from me, pls. x

Then she glanced around the lights of the quay and the shadows of the garden. There weren't many people around, although she knew some of the bars and clubs of Sliema would be open, and in Paceville, a couple of miles away, the night was still young for those who liked to rage around the dance floor. But here in the gardens and the quayside it was almost eerily quiet.

She looked to her left and saw safety and a welcoming light.

'Let's go aboard the *Shady Lady*,' she suggested. 'We can have a drink while I try and call Joseph; then we'll see about helping you get home.'

Instantly, Carmelo slipped off the bench. He even managed the ghost of a smile, his hopeful, swollen eyes fixed on Elle's face.

Elle forgot present strained relations for an instant. 'The light's on so hopefully Lucas is on board and still up.'

'He has Fanta?'

Elle grinned, glad to hear Carmelo say something normal. 'We'll ask him.'

When they stepped across the gangplank it growled and grated on the quayside as the boat moved on the swell. Through the open door, Elle could see Lucas lounging in the saloon with a copy of *Diver* and a beer. 'Lucas?'

He looked up warily. His eyebrows quirked when he caught sight of Carmelo. 'You're up late, Carmelo.'

Carmelo looked down to the bare toes that peeped out from his sandals.

'I need to ring Joseph to see if he can help Carmelo,'

Elle said. 'I don't suppose you have a Fanta or something nice in your stash, do you?'

Lucas flashed Carmelo a grin. 'I've got Seven Up. That OK?'

Carmelo grinned back. 'It's good.'

'If you sit down here, then Lucas can bring you out the drink.' Elle ushered the little boy to the cockpit seat.

Lucas took the steps down to the galley in one long stride and opened the fridge. In moments he was out in the velvet night air, a tall glass of fizzing clear liquid for Carmelo, another beer for himself and a small bottle of water for Elle.

'Thank you,' Carmelo whispered. Then he lifted the glass in both hands and set about the liquid sweetness greedily.

'Hey.' Lucas raised his eyebrows. 'You're supposed to drink it, not dive in it.'

It took Carmelo a moment to interpret the joke, and laugh, but then he replaced guzzling with drinking.

While Lucas chatted to him in his deep, calm voice, Elle picked up her phone and, making sure to stay in Carmelo's sight, stepped off onto the quayside to call Joseph, trusting that he and Maria wouldn't mind being disturbed so late.

In her ear, the phone sounded the Maltese single ringtone several times and she was just beginning to feel a skip of dismay, when, 'Allo?' Joseph answered, sounding dazed and gruff.

Elle winced. 'Joseph, it's Elle. I'm really sorry if I woke you up. But it's Carmelo. I found him in Gżira Gardens on his own in the dark. He's not very happy about something but he doesn't seem to feel comfortable talking to me about it. He says his mum and grandfather are at home but he obviously sees some barrier to going back there himself. I offered to go with him but he was pretty positive that he didn't want that.'

'I understand.' Joseph sounded as if he was waking up fast. He cleared his throat. 'I presume Carmelo is safe? Is he still with you? Where are you? What's his emotional state? How does he seem physically?'

Elle was able to reassure him but added, 'I just don't know what to do next.'

'I'll come down to the marina. Do you think Carmelo will stay until I arrive?'

'I think so. He's drinking Seven Up and talking to Lucas. Lucas is pretty laid-back and perhaps Carmelo finds him reassuring.' She didn't add that she found Lucas pretty reassuring herself. He hadn't bombarded her with questions and objections when she'd turned up with Carmelo. He'd just handled the situation.

She explained whereabouts the *Shady Lady* was moored and ended the call, turning back to the boat. In the blueish cockpit lights she could see that Carmelo was having a burping competition with Lucas, and giggling.

She stepped back on board with an exaggerated sigh. 'Pity the water Lucas got me isn't fizzy. It puts me at a disadvantage in the burp department.'

Carmelo giggled harder.

Joseph turned up at nearly half past midnight. He strolled through the gardens and stepped on board, hands in pockets, with an easy smile. 'Good evening.'

He showed polite interest in the boat for a minute before he turned to Carmelo. 'You've had a nice drink. I think we'll talk; then I'll have to take you home, won't I?'

Carmelo's face fell, but he nodded resignedly.

'We'll go in,' said Elle, immediately, picking up her water and taking it into the saloon. Lucas followed.

Joseph sat down beside Carmelo. Elle could see them and hear snatches of Maltese. Initially, it seemed as if Joseph would bear all the conversational burden while Carmelo looked down at his fingers and shrugged.

But then he began talking, voice low, his eyes still cast down.

Joseph nodded and listened.

Carmelo explained, gesticulated.

Joseph nodded and listened.

Elle sighed. She smothered a yawn and looked at her watch, then at Lucas. 'Sorry if this has kept you up.'

'Doesn't matter.' Lucas was gazing meditatively at her. 'You're quite different to the girl I used to know. Not just that you've lost the suits and the need to be at the front of the rat race. It's that I don't think I even saw you look at a child when we were together, let alone take a particularly needy one under your wing.'

She was too tired and sad to dissemble. 'Being made redundant showed me how superficial my life was. It made me want to get involved with something more significant. I didn't expect one of the children to become attached to me.' Slowly, she twisted the cap from her bottle of water and sipped. 'And what about you? In the past you wouldn't have had the patience for Carmelo. You'd probably have given him a few euros to go away and have forgotten about him in five seconds.'

He looked surprised. 'Was I that shallow?'

She smiled at his air of injury. 'Just pointing out that you're more developed.'

He began to say something that began 'Except where—'

But then Joseph came to the door, saying over his

shoulder to Carmelo, 'Let's ask Lucas to sit outside with you for a moment while I talk to Elle.'

Obligingly, Lucas went outside and began to chat to Carmelo.

Elle looked at Joseph. 'Is it anything very bad?'

With a sigh as he took a seat on the sofa, Joseph lifted his hands. 'Tonight his mother and his grandfather were drinking and they had a huge argument, shouting and swearing. Things were thrown. Carmelo was very frightened, so he ran away. It has happened before but I think a hatred for the tension is growing in him.' Behind his glasses, his eyes were sombre.

'Poor kid.' Elle felt a weight inside her for any child who had to live with that kind of daily unhappiness. Her own home had been uncomfortable at times, but the weaponry had been silence rather than screams and missiles.

'I'm going to take him home, now. I think he wants to go. I expect the adults will be sleeping off the drink and it will soon be forgotten.' He hesitated. 'He didn't want you to take him home because he's ashamed of where he lives. He sees what other children have and he knows that what he has is not a nice home. But he's powerless to change it.'

Elle felt tears burn her eyes. 'Poor kid,' she said again. 'What can we do?'

'I don't believe I need to involve the social worker. I'll speak to his priest and I think the priest will speak to Carmelo's mother. He has done so before and she always improves for a while.' Joseph brushed back his hair and stifled a yawn. He nodded up the road. 'Maria's been waiting in the car. I've just texted her and she's on her way to fetch us.'

In two minutes Maria arrived, driving slowly up the marina access road, waving cheerfully to Elle as Joseph and Carmelo said their goodnights and crossed to meet her. Maria got out to greet tired little Carmelo with a smile.

Once they had packed themselves into the car, turned and cruised slowly away, Elle turned with a sigh to find Lucas leaning against the cabin door frame. 'I hate this,' she said, vehemently. 'I hate all adults who make kids miserable when a few kind words would make them happy.'

'It certainly makes me appreciate the safety and security of my own upbringing.' Lucas's face was sombre.

Suddenly, Elle found herself wiping fiercely at hot eyes. 'Your parents were great.'

His eyebrows shot up. 'You thought they were a nightmare.'

Elle sniffed. 'Only to me, because they didn't think I was right for you.' Words flowed out of her, uncensored. 'That's how much they love you, that they'd have the guts to tell you that you were making a mistake.'

Lucas closed the space between them, wrapping his arms around her, resting her head on his shoulder and his head on top of hers. 'All the time we were together you resented my parents and now you're praising them. You are one weird woman, Elle Jamieson.'

Elle's sniffles wavered for an instant into laughter. 'I resented being considered bad for you. Now that that's no longer an issue, I can see that everything they did was because they wanted the best for you.'

His breath was hot against her hair. 'I don't think I ever understood you.'

'No,' she agreed, sadly.

Chapter Fifteen

On Sunday, when Lucas had disappeared in the green pick-up to teach tourists how to breathe underwater, and knowing that it was something she'd put off long enough, Elle phoned The Briars, the residential care home where her mother lived.

She lay on her bed, listening as she was put through to her mother's floor and footsteps fading away as their owner went to find her mother's key carer.

While she waited, she enjoyed the motion of the boat, making her feel a bit as if she were lying on a hammock or a garden swing. The air con was off and the weather was hot. It was hard to imagine that back in England her mother was living in a room not unlike an upmarket version of student accommodation, containing a bed and a wardrobe with a small bathroom leading off.

Joanna Jamieson did have a big comfy armchair with a table and TV rather than a desk, but her living quarters were a far cry from the gleaming house she'd presided over throughout her marriage. In those days they'd had more spacious, gracious rooms than the three of them had needed, the stylish furnishings including a piano that no one knew how to play.

The house had been sold when Elle's parents split up. Joanna had rented a place while she decided whether to buy a bungalow with a garden or an apartment overlooking the park. She'd seemed in no hurry to commit. Her husband 'trading her in for a younger model' had made her reassess her life. She'd joined friends on a cruise. She'd bought new clothes.

Sadly, Joanna had still been deciding between the bungalow or the apartment when the stroke had seared through her brain. Her capital was now being briskly drained away by the costs of her care, despite Elle's contributions.

The sound of returning footsteps and the phone being scraped across a surface as it was picked up interrupted Elle's thoughts. She found herself talking to Nerys, her mother's key carer, a lovely, calm, sympathetic woman with a ready smile.

'I rang to see how my mum's getting on.'

Nerys sounded out of breath. 'She's much as before. Tires easily, you know. A little bit confused. But generally going on nicely, considering.'

Considering she hardly knew who she was and certainly not what she had been, Elle supposed. She looked around her cabin at her flip-flops and other paraphernalia of her new life and for the first time felt a long way from home. 'Could I s-speak to her?'

Nerys sounded enthusiastic. 'Actually, she's only two rooms down, in the lounge. I could get her up here but it'll take a couple of minutes.'

Elle swallowed. Her mum needed a frame on wheels and someone strong at her elbow to move along the smooth corridors. 'If it's not too much trouble,' she murmured.

She listened to a few minutes of shuffling and cheerfully raised voices from more than thirteen hundred miles away.

Finally, Nerys returned, more out of breath than ever. 'She's here now, lovie. I'll help her hold the phone.'

'Hello, Mum.' Elle waited for a moment but her mother made no reply. 'I just wanted to tell you that everything's fine with me. I'm enjoying living in Malta.'

A noise that she barely recognised as her mother's voice made what might have been an attempt at a reply.

Elle talked on, describing the boat, the island, her work at Nicholas Centre. The sound of breathing and the occasional slurred noise told her that Joanna was still on the other end of the line. 'I love you, Mum,' Elle said, impulsively. 'I understand that you weren't a demonstrative mother but I do love you. And I'm sorry that you were so upset when I sneaked off and married Ricky. I shouldn't have done that but—'

'I think we'll have to get your mum back to her room, now, lovie,' broke in Nerys's voice. 'She listened for a couple of minutes but she's pushed the handset away. I think she's a bit tired.'

'Of course.' Elle tried to smile, so that it would come through in her voice. 'Thanks for going to so much trouble for me.'

After ending the call she felt restless. She'd been looking forward to a day off all week. The Nicolas Centre was open only from midday to five on Sundays, and most of the children who used it were in relaxed mode, wanting only a game of table tennis or to chat on Facebook, making it a good day for Elle not to attend. There was still enough of a swell for her to decide to shelve her earlier plans for a boat trip. If the sea showed signs of liveliness within the marina then it would be downright choppy outside of the shelter of the creek.

So she set out on foot, strolling right up to Font Ghadir and lying on the rock on a towel to read. When that got too uncomfortable and hot, she jumped into the sea to cool off. The waves broke over the rocks, hissing and sucking, and she enjoyed the exhilaration of being tossed around until she was tired.

The rocky beach was becoming crowded and noisy, tourists and locals congregating to sun themselves like a human version of a seal colony. Elle climbed up the steps to the road and wandered back into Sliema for lunch. She hadn't brought her phone, not wanting to leave valuables in her beach bag while she swam, which meant she didn't know if Joseph had tried to contact her. She hadn't tried his number earlier because she knew that he and Maria usually spent Sunday morning in church, summoned by one of the beautiful church bells that sang out every Sunday morning and evening.

Her map was in her bag. She shook it out and assessed where she was in relation to the Nicholas Centre as she sat at a small table in the window of a cafe, drinking a glass of cold white wine and waiting for her salad to arrive. She wasn't surprised to see that she'd walked away from the centre in her search for lunch, but that didn't matter. The afternoon was hers to while away.

She turned out to have a hot and dusty forty-minute walk to Triq Bonnard but she enjoyed leaving behind the streets that were always busy with tourists whatever the day of the week and finding her way through the more residential areas where the houses dozed away the hottest part of the day.

Eventually, she crossed the courtyard, glad to step into the cool, old building.

For once, Joseph wasn't in his office. She followed the sound of laughter and cheers to the games room to find a table tennis tournament in progress, Joseph refereeing and Maria keeping score on a small board.

Oscar was there, too, coaching the participants, easy to spot as he was head and shoulders above everybody else. 'We have a new spectator,' he announced as Elle slipped through the door. 'Or perhaps Elle wishes to play?'

Elle waved the idea away. 'No, I'm happy to be part of the audience.' And soon she was clapping as points were won, laughing at the groans from those who lost.

Presently, when she was driven by thirst into the kitchen, she was glad when Joseph followed her.

'How was Carmelo when you left him?' she asked, immediately.

Joseph's brown eyes were kind behind his glasses. 'His mother was awake and looking for him when I arrived, and was reassuringly maternal – cross with him for disappearing and glad to see him home. I waited while she saw him to bed so that we could have a little chat about our concerns.' He took a bottle of Kinnie, a Maltese soft drink, from the fridge and sat down at the big table, waving Elle to another chair. 'She was sheepish. I hope the episode has brought her up short.'

Elle breathed a sigh of relief. 'I hope so. His little face was so sad, all tear-streaked.' She hesitated. 'I don't know if I exactly have to tell you this but as I'm so new to it all – Carmelo threw his arms around me. I sort of ruffled his hair rather than hugging him back, and then jollied him along to the boat. Was that right?'

Joseph began, 'It's always difficult, but, yes, that sounds—'

'Ah, our friend Carmelo,' said a voice from the doorway. And Oscar stepped into the room. He helped himself to a drink and joined in their conference as if invited. 'Always little Carmelo looks sad. It will be good if the mother gives him more affection.'

He went on discussing Carmelo with Joseph. Elle felt prickly about the intrusion but had to accept that Oscar had as much right to his concerns as she did.

When, eventually, Joseph rose to return to the table

tennis tournament, Elle made to follow him. But Oscar got up quickly and blocked her way. 'I request one word with you, Elle, if I may.' His occasional formal turns of phrase would probably have been endearing if Elle could have felt any liking for the Dutchman.

'Of course,' she replied, courteously, hanging back.

Oscar smiled widely as he gave Joseph a few seconds to move off, his eyes intent. 'I think dinner one night would be good.'

Elle blinked. 'That's really nice of you but I'm not in a position to date at the moment.'

Oscar nodded. 'Of course. There is the boyfriend who may not be a boyfriend. The boyfriend who brings his woman here, under your nose.'

'Kayleigh? She's his brother's girlfriend. She was alone, initially, but Lucas's brother, Charlie, has arrived to be with her, now.' Elle couldn't keep a hint of triumph from her voice. Now that she knew the situation between Charlie and Kayleigh she could once again utilise Lucas's presence on the boat to ward Oscar off.

'Really?' Oscar was still smiling irritatingly, knowingly. 'So. Is Lucas the boyfriend or not the boyfriend?'

Summoning a friendly but dismissive smile, Elle made to move around him. 'I don't really need to discuss this with you.'

Then she gasped as she found herself trapped suddenly between the doorjamb and a man so large that he filled all of her vision. His voice was low and his breath hot on her skin. 'You avoid me, but that doesn't mean I shall go away. I have an ambition that Elle shall look at me as she looks at little Carmelo. With soft eyes and a beautiful smile. And hugs and kisses, just like for Carmelo.'

For an instant Elle froze, bad memories sending

the blood singing in her ears. Then anger flew to her rescue. Never again would a man intimidate her, make her powerless. She took a long slow breath so that she could force her voice to ring out. 'Of course I haven't kissed Carmelo. He hugged me; I could hardly shove him away. Get away from me. I'm not comfortable with this conversation and it's unacceptable that you invade my personal space.'

'Then the conversation must instantly end.' Oscar stepped back, bowing her through the door in front of him with the air of one humouring a capricious child.

'If you behave like that again,' she said, coldly, holding her ground, 'I'll complain to Joseph. That was inappropriate and there must be no repetition.'

Oscar's grin became wider than ever. 'Englishwomen! You take everything much too serious. In the Nederlands we are more relaxed, more adult.' Then, as if an idea had just struck him: 'If Lucas is your boyfriend, it is not a problem for me. I understand a relationship that is open.'

Elle laughed her scorn right into his freckly face. 'Lucas is the last man in the world to entertain an open relationship. Believe me on that one.'

Chapter Sixteen

Lucas cornered Vern in his 'outdoor office', where Vern sometimes took his hated paperwork, a table with blistered white paintwork on a flat place on the rocks. Only one chair stood at the table. Vern didn't encourage loiterers.

Although Lucas held the day's student record files, he kept them behind his back. The only thing Vern hated more than paperwork was more paperwork.

Lucas had provided surface cover at Ghar Lapsi today while Lars and Brett led tourists down into the crystal depths to spy on octopus and swim with rainbow shoals of fish. He didn't enjoy taking his turn to provide surface cover, but at least it had given him an opportunity to think. Now he was ready to share those thoughts with Vern.

'How do you feel about helping local kids from a youth drop-in centre?'

Vern didn't look up. 'What kind of help?'

'I was wondering whether we could give them a Bubblemaker Session.'

Turning PADI forms over with distaste, Vern sighed. 'What kind of drop-in centre? Nothing to do with nasty habits?'

'No. It's just somewhere for kids to hang out. Play games, do activities, use the internet cafe.' He sketched in a few more details about the Nicholas Centre and Joseph. 'My brother's girlfriend works with children and she got talking to someone I know who volunteers there, so we went up to visit. I sort of got involved.' He pushed back his hair, damp because he'd been washing off the equipment used for today's dive and had cooled himself in the spray. 'So I was thinking we could go there and do the youth programme diving presentation and then get some of them up here in the pool. Obviously, I volunteer my services.'

Slowly, Vern sat back, squinting against the slanting sun. A big tawny man with a lot of body hair, he was a bit like a mangy bear and had a habit of growling to hide his soft heart. 'We'd need some responsible adults here from their end, safeguarding and all that stuff.'

'They have their own youth leaders. Maybe one or two of them? And, hopefully, Joseph.'

'At least that many, yeah, depending on how many kids want to make bubbles.' Vern tapped his pen against his cheek.

'Might be a nice PR exercise, being nice to local kids,' Lucas suggested, persuasively.

Vern grunted. 'It's only a good PR exercise if we get the press here and sound off about what wonderful people we are to give time and resources to provide some kids with fun. Otherwise, the only benefit for us that I see is a warm glow at having done a good deed. And there's the cost of air and the damage to kit. Kids always break things.'

Lucas glanced over at the seawater pool, dancing with sunlight. He thought about Carmelo and imagined his big eyes alight with joy and wonder. 'Some of those kids don't even have properly fitting clothes. It's unlikely that they'll get to try the expensive adventure of scuba unless someone provides the chance for them.'

Slowly, Vern nodded. 'OK, let me think about it. Maybe we could work something out at the end of a day when we've had only fairly shallow dives. By the time the instructors and divemasters get back here and sort the equipment out, some surface time will have elapsed, and you'll go no deeper than two metres so it won't add much to nitro levels.'

He turned his attention back to his paperwork. 'Now give me whatever you're hiding behind your back and sod off to see your youth centre guy.'

A couple of hours later, Lucas stepped aboard the *Shady Lady* and saw Elle's top half moving around in the galley. 'Let's clear the air,' he said, dropping his bag on the floor of the saloon and crossing to the steps so that he could see all of her. Her hair was wet and she was wearing one of those things that seemed a cross between a minidress and a pair of shorts. The outfit showed a lot of leg. He didn't let her catch him looking. He could read enough wariness and mistrust in her eyes without that.

He reached around her to grab a bottle of beer from the fridge. 'I acted like a prat: I'm genuinely sorry. I don't really know what I was thinking of and I don't suppose there's any point trying to analyse it. It was childish and stupid.

'But it's important to me that you accept my apology partly because I mean it, partly because living together on the boat is going to be a pain in the arse if there's a heavy atmosphere, and partly because I want your help with something.' Then, aware from her stare and the way that her hands paused in their task of washing up that peremptory demands probably weren't endearing him to her, added a belated 'Please. I've talked to my boss about doing a Bubblemaker Session for the Nicholas Centre and you know a lot more about the place than I do.'

Elle frowned, turning back to washing up the coffee jug. 'Go on.'

He took a seat on the galley steps and recounted his conversation with Vern, outlining how the presentation would normally go and the fun experience the kids could expect from fifty minutes in a pool wearing scuba gear.

She listened to him gravely. 'Does the event have a price tag?'

'It's a freebie. The instructors and divemasters would give their time; Dive Meddi would provide the equipment and air. The kids would just need normal swim gear. And we'd have to work out a way of transporting them up to the dive centre in St Julian's.' His seat on the steps put her bare legs at his eye level. In the days when he and Elle had been together he would have considered bare legs an invitation to play. He could almost imagine the softness of her inner thigh under his mouth—

'Would you be the one to run the session?'

He forced his gaze to remain fixed on her face. 'I'd organise everything but I'm not an instructor. A divemaster assists, not instructs. The instructors at the centre are Vern, Polly and Lars, and they'd run the session. There are children-to-adult ratios we have to observe, and the instructors will want divemasters in the water. We'll need some adults from the centre, too.'

'In the water?' Her eyes suddenly brightened.

'In the water and out. We need to work out how many kids are interested and how many we can accommodate. Joseph's obviously the guy I need to talk to but it would be great if you could get involved – talk to Joseph with me, maybe.'

'Could I be one of the adults in the water?'

She looked so intrigued by the idea that he laughed, half-sorry that he hadn't talked to her about something like this before she put him on her shit list. He could have invited her to the dive centre and showed off. 'Definitely. If Carmelo's one of the kids involved I expect he'll demand it.' Then, as a shadow crossed over her face, 'How is he today?'

'I haven't seen him.' She sighed. 'Joseph's talked to the mum and seems fairly upbeat, thinks Carmelo running away was a bit of a wake-up call for her.' She managed a hesitant smile. 'Thanks, by the way, for helping with him last night. I knew I'd be able to rely on you.'

'It wasn't much.' But he was aware of a dart of pleasure that she'd put aside the tension and come to him.

'I can imagine what— I mean, s-s-some people might have reacted differently if I'd brought home a child I'd found lurking in the dark.' She turned away from him, busying herself with fitting the jug back on the coffee maker.

It meant that he could let his gaze drop to her legs but that didn't distract him completely from that tiny telltale stutter over 'some people'. So far as he knew, she hadn't lived with many people. Her parents, her uni flatmates and—

'Ricky?' he asked, making it sound like an idle enquiry.

She went on fussing with the coffee maker, taking the jug off and on again as if unhappy with the fit. Just when he thought she was going to ignore his question, she answered. 'He didn't have much compassion.' She changed the subject brightly. 'I'm going over to Valletta on the ferry with Charlie and Kayleigh. Want to come? Joseph told me about a good pizzeria in Republic Street. We can get the last ferry there and return by bus.'

'Great.' He rose easily and turned sideways so that he could pass without brushing against her. 'I'll shower.' He felt as if he'd scored some kind of victory. She'd answered a question about Ricky, and one that gave real insight, at that. And the invitation for pizza must constitute forgiveness for his behaviour over Kayleigh.

As he showered, he wondered if she'd keep the dress/shorts thing on. That much leg on display definitely came under the heading of 'A good thing'. Especially bare leg. The great thing about hot climates was that women rarely bothered with tights or stockings.

Not that he was against stockings ...

He felt himself stirring. Maybe he *should be* against stockings – on Elle Jamieson, anyway. And bare legs. And cute hats. In fact, his life would be a lot less complicated if Elle Jamieson would wear a sack with just her head sticking out. Preferably with that blond hair cut off instead of in its current glorious mane form. He might have a lot fewer frustrating thoughts and mixed emotions.

Elle didn't make extensive preparations for the evening. After she'd let her hair dry in the warm breeze up on the flybridge, she brushed it and then made up simply with mascara, eyeliner and lip gloss.

Her heart was light. Carmelo's situation looked to have improved, she was still buzzing from drawing a line in the sand that Oscar must not creep over, and a good night out was in prospect. Maltese pizza was good, she liked Kayleigh, she'd missed Charlie, and Lucas and Charlie were fun together. Now Lucas had made the effort to clear the air, she could enjoy everybody's company.

She checked that she had enough euros for the evening and emerged from her cabin at the same moment as Lucas strolled out of his, almost colliding with him in the tiny area in front of the galley. Their arms brushed and Elle sucked in her breath at the hot liquid sensation of his skin sliding over hers.

Lucas stepped back and Elle thanked him politely as she trod lightly up the steps and through the saloon. But the heat of his touch clung to her skin like ink.

They locked up the boat and walked along the seafront. Elle kept her gaze on the twinkling water of the creek as she tried to parcel up her reaction to Lucas's touch and return it safely to that folder in her memory marked 'past'. By the time they saw Charlie and Kayleigh, waving as they dodged the traffic, she'd recovered enough for conversation.

Charlie talked enough for four, anyway, joking around on the water taxi, complaining about the slippery pavement leading into the citadel of Valletta, which glowed like rose gold in the early evening sun. Huffing and puffing, they climbed the steep roads to Republic Street, the thoroughfare of limestone buildings that ran like a spine down the length of Valletta.

Elle couldn't remember when she'd last laughed so freely as she did that evening, gathered around the table at the pizzeria. Kayleigh's humour was dry, Charlie's was impish, and Lucas slid in enough acerbic jibes to keep his younger brother in his place. Having munched her way through most of a monster crusty pizza and drunk her fair share of wine, it was nearing midnight when Elle began to think that she ought to slow down on the alcohol. And then her phone rang.

She frowned. Her phone didn't ring that often when she was in Malta. She sometimes thought she only carried it around out of habit. It took her a moment to fumble it from the tiny bag she'd slung over her chair back, hoping it wasn't Joseph with bad news about Carmelo.

She hesitated when she saw the name on the screen. Then accepted the call. 'Hello?'

'This is Yvonne, duty night manager at The Briars. Am I speaking to Elle Jamieson?'

Elle's throat went dry. 'Yes.'

'I'm calling about your mother. I'm afraid she's quite poorly. It was just after dinner—' Elle's head began to spin as phrases like 'doctor', 'ambulance' and 'hospital' flew out of the phone with no real meaning.

She tried to lift her voice over the babble in the restaurant as she pushed herself to her feet, pressing the phone hard against her ear. 'Just hang on. I'm moving outside where it's quieter.'

Then Lucas was beside her, clearing a path so that she could stumble out of the warmth and noise into the street, where she could say to Yvonne, 'Can you repeat that?' so that she could force herself to understand what had been happening in Bettsbrough, far away, in another country, another time zone, another climate.

Her alcohol haze evaporated as she discussed the severity of Joanna Jamieson's situation, running scenarios and discussing likely outcomes clinically and pragmatically. She ended by arranging to contact the day shift in the morning for her mother's health bulletin.

Elle ended the call feeling calm and in control. She turned to Lucas, who'd waited, lounging against a wall nearby. 'My mum—' she began. And burst into tears.

Somehow she found herself in Lucas's arms, face pressed against the warm fabric of his T-shirt as sobs shook through her, shocked that she was bawling in the street like a child but somehow unable to stop. Vaguely, she was aware of Charlie and Kayleigh arriving, Kayleigh shoving reams of tissues into her hands and Charlie getting them all to a taxi. The car's interior was hot though all its windows were open, and, still unable to control the sobs, Elle let herself be driven back to Ta' Xbiex.

All the time, Lucas's arms remained around her, comforting and strong.

By the time the car dropped them on the road beside the gardens, she'd more or less cried herself out, but her chest ached and her eyes felt as if someone had been at them with a laser.

'I'm so sorry,' she sniffed. 'I don't know where that came from. It's ages since I cried like that.'

'Let's get you on board,' was Lucas's only reply. Nobody asked any questions until she was seated in the saloon with a bottle of cold water and a cup of milky coffee.

Elle sucked the water down, grateful for its chill to soothe her rasping throat. 'My mum's had another stroke. She'd just eaten dinner when it hit.' She swallowed a mouthful of the coffee. 'She's in Bettsbrough General Hospital. She's not in immediate danger but,' her voice wobbled, 'the night manager said that it was too early to tell much. Mum's pretty confused anyway, so if it turns out to be a slight stroke it might not make too much difference.'

She tried to laugh but it emerged as a croak. 'Somehow, that's what seemed almost too sad to bear. S-stupid, really, to be upset because she's in such a poor way already that another stroke, more or less, doesn't make a difference.'

'So what's going to happen? What do you need to do?' asked Lucas, gently.

Elle sighed. Her head was pounding and she rubbed it with her fingertips. 'I suppose I'll have to ring Dad. When Mum had her first stroke I was only an hour and a half away so I did everything but this time Dad's closer than

I am. I don't really know what the etiquette is between divorced people when something bad happens to one of them, though.' She picked up her phone and toyed with it. 'If you guys want to get off, I don't mind. I know it's late.'

Charlie hesitated, but Kayleigh took his arm. 'Come on, Charlie, she doesn't need us eavesdropping while she talks to her dad.'

They both kissed and hugged Elle and then only Lucas remained in the quiet of the saloon, the *Shady Lady* barely moving at her mooring, the road noise rising and falling outside against the constant *whrrrrrrr* of the cicadas in the gardens.

His eyes were fixed on her. 'Do you want me to disappear?'

'Not unless you want to.' His presence was comforting. Familiar. And, at that moment, almost essential.

'I'll stay.'

He watched her pick up her phone, checking the time. 'It'll be nearly midnight at home.' She scrolled through her contacts, made her selection and held the handset to her ear.

Her eyes were pink, her skin blotchy, her nose and lips faintly swollen. Like many fair women, she didn't cry prettily. Her shoulders had convulsed as he'd cradled her against him in the night-time busyness of Republic Street. He didn't really remember seeing her cry before. Maybe a few tears at a weepy movie, laughed off in embarrassment, but not heaving, hurting, helpless sobs.

It's ages since I cried like that. He'd actually had to quell the impulse to demand, 'Did you ever cry like that over our break-up? Is it one more thing you never showed?' Then felt ashamed. Tonight was not about him.

He could hear the ringtone chirruping from her phone. Then, 'Dad, it's me, I—' Her voice caught.

Lucas handed her the coffee cup and she took a swift gulp.

'Dad, Mum's had another stroke. Someone from The Briars rang me.' Elle took a breath and began to recount as much as she knew and, apart from a couple of wobbly moments, she coped, twisting her hair, sniffing, finding a tissue to blow her nose between sentences.

It was curious to hear her and her father conduct a polite and courteous discussion. He compared their conversation to those he had with his own parents, always bursting with enquiries about how he was and what he was doing, and he silently vowed never to be irritated by them again. Those demands symbolised the love and warmth that had surrounded him as he'd grown up. Even if his parents had given Elle a bit of a rough ride, he'd never doubted that their love for him was deep and unconditional.

In contrast, judging from Elle's side of the conversation, Will Jamieson hadn't even asked his daughter how she was, though her husky voice was a pretty fucking great clue that she'd been crying.

Elle's parents had always been chilly, which she would explain away with a shrug and 'That's what comes of marrying the wrong man at the wrong time and in secret.'

As she talked into the phone, he wondered about that secret wedding all over again. Elle wasn't generally an inconsiderate person. She was self-possessed and didn't ask much of anyone, but she didn't disregard people's feelings.

So why had she ignored her parents' feelings over

marrying Ricky? Had she been that crazily in love with him that nothing else seemed to matter? His stomach clenched at how much he still hated that idea.

Finally, she put down the phone and sank her forehead on her hand. 'He's going to liaise with the hospital and The Briars tomorrow morning and try and get an idea of the situation. Then we'll talk again.'

Her hand lay on the table and he covered it lightly with his. 'How are you doing?'

She covered her eyes.

'Sorry. Stupid question. You've had a shock and you're worried about your mum.' He slid his arm around her once more, catching his breath at how right it felt to have her pressed against him. The top of her head was just below his face. He could have turned his head and laid his cheek upon it.

She let out a groan. 'It's stupid, though, isn't it? We're not even close.'

'It's not stupid.' He hesitated. 'Maybe it's grief *because* you're not close.'

She paused and swallowed. 'And the chance to be has gone? That could be insightful.' A longer pause. 'I phoned the home this morning and asked to speak to her so that I could tell her that I love her. She hardly knows her own name but I wanted to tell her anyway, just in case something of what I said got through. It's as if I knew this was coming.'

'Maybe. Some instinct.'

'It was Carmelo who set me thinking. Poor kid. I feel as if he's looking for someone to love him and his mother's the obvious one. I kind of recognised—' She stopped and started in a different place. 'I just thought: my mum's always been reserved, but I'm a grown-up. I don't have to wait all my life for her to tell me that she loves me. I can say it to her. So I did.'

Shock shimmered through Lucas. 'Hasn't your mum ever said that she loves you?'

'I don't remember that she did. She was quite friendly but I used to watch other children get swooped up into huge bear hugs and wonder what it was like.'

'"Quite friendly",' he repeated. He'd been one of the kids swooped up in bear hugs. Hugs, he was afraid, from which he'd often fought free.

Elle had never opened up to him like this before. Not in all the time they were together, not all the times they lay in bed talking, or chatting across the dinner table.

Had he actually known this woman at all? He'd loved her, made love to her, shared his life with her. He'd been aware that there was a lot going on under the top layer but not how to unwrap it. He remembered demanding information from her, as if it were his right, and being frustrated when she'd widen her eyes and look away with a shrug.

His conscience sank its fangs into him. Demands hadn't been what she needed. She'd needed the opportunity to expose herself, and then the choice as to whether to take that opportunity. She'd needed someone who would make her feel safe. Someone who wouldn't judge her.

It had never crossed his mind that he should or could provide that kind of security. He'd formed an opinion of how things should be and waited for her to fulfil his expectations.

He must be able to do better. To open his mind to ways of doing and being other than his own.

'I know your dad wasn't cuddly,' he said, experimentally. She gave a short laugh. 'Neither of my parents were cuddly. Not even with each other. They wanted a child to be proud of; that was their minimum requirement. So long as I did well, they'd smile on me. If I disappointed them, they withdrew. They could give me the silent treatment for weeks at a time.'

'Man,' he said. 'I'm not surprised that you craved affection enough to marry Ricky.'

Chapter Seventeen

For several beats, he thought she was going to ignore the comment. Then she sighed. 'He certainly made me think he approved of me, in the early days. He was ten years older and yet he apparently fell for me like a ton of bricks and I didn't question it. I just thought, "We're in love! This is what everyone gets excited about. Now I'm an adult, I'm entitled." As if it came with getting the vote or holding a driving licence.'

Careful not to push, he waited. Quiet. Giving her time. She'd only ever told him the bare facts about Ricky: that she'd met him during her masters' year and married him before returning to her hometown of Bettsbrough. It hadn't worked out. She'd sidestepped further questions by saying that she didn't really want to talk about it, it was a horrible period in her life and she wanted to forget it.

Questions had often sent Elle into sullen silence. Or maybe it had been anxious silence, he acknowledged now. Maybe her parents had prompted her reserve, made her perpetually worried about saying the wrong thing.

She stirred. 'I was young for my age. I'd got my degree at Keele and then switched to Manchester for my masters. I didn't know anyone in Manchester so I found a place via the uni, sharing with a girl called Daisy. She was a bit of a room hermit but I made friends on my course, so I had people to go out with. After Keele, which is pretty rural, it seemed as if there were thousands of clubs and pubs in Manchester. I was ready to come out of my shell and I loved it.

'The academic year had hardly started when I met

Ricky in a nightclub. He DJed. Whether he was on the stage or on the dance floor, he always had a load of girls around him. It seemed "social proof" that he was really cool. When he began to pay *me* attention I couldn't believe it. It was like being singled out by a prince, a triumph of epic proportions. We got close really quickly.' She stopped.

When she'd been quiet for a minute, he tried a gentle prompt. 'But you didn't have any reason not to.'

'But I was too naive to notice his lack of substance. That he didn't seem to have many mates to hang out with and those he had were always younger than him. The girls he went for were younger, too. Looking back, I suppose it's because people his own age saw how superficial and phoney he was. At the club, he used to say he "helped out on the promotions side" and was "an ideas man". In reality, I suppose he was a mouthy DJ with a big opinion of himself, but I took everything he said at face value. He wasn't that smart but he was crafty.'

Her sigh seemed to come up from the soles of the bare feet she'd curled beside her on the sofa. 'He boasted about things that were hard to check, like being an ace on a surfboard – we were miles from the sea. He'd been brought up in East London and I never really knew what had made him leave because he countered a lot of questions with answers like "That was a different me, babe" or "You don't expect me to tell you all my secrets, do you?"'

She covered her eyes. 'I was so stupidly trusting. A couple of guys actually took me aside to tell me I should be careful. They told me—' She paused for so long that he thought she wasn't going to start again. Then: 'They told me he owed them money. When I asked him about it he said he'd "had a word and sorted everything out". When I wanted to know what there was to sort out he got sharp. "If you're going to listen to people you don't even know, what future have we got?"' Another hot sigh. 'Then he flattered me with a lot of "You're the one person I thought understood me, babe", stuff. I fell for it, even when he didn't want to introduce me to his family and said he wasn't close to them, and put on a big sad face.'

She sniffed and reached for her bag, sorting through it to find a tissue. He was almost afraid to breathe in case she stopped filling in all the blanks that had irritated him so much and for so long.

But when she'd blown her nose, she returned to her story. 'I never knew whether his mum had really died tragically after being given the wrong dose of something in hospital and if his father had really beaten him up on a regular basis but treated his sisters like princesses. Or whether it was just fantasy.'

For a moment Lucas forgot his strategy of not asking questions. 'Why would he make stuff like that up?'

'Maybe it was to support his gripe about not having parents to help him through university. I wouldn't put anything past that bastard. I discovered – too late – that when he opened his mouth it was usually lies that rolled out. I closed my eyes to the fact that he probably hadn't been to university because he wasn't bright enough. I was too gullible, young and in love to properly question his "poor me, I never got the breaks" act. And I never asked why he hadn't made his own breaks.'

Lucas's fingers had come to rest on her neck. Absently, he moved a thumb over the delicate skin. 'I can see that he might not be the kind your parents would go for.'

She snorted a bitter laugh. 'Not much.' Then, reflectively, 'I must have acknowledged it to myself because I didn't tell Mum and Dad about Ricky. I was spending as much time as I could with him, so I wasn't going home to Bettsbrough much. My parents decided to come up and check I was working hard and it was an unfortunate first meeting with Ricky. They arrived one Sunday morning and Daisy let them in. By the time Daisy banged on my bedroom door and shouted that they'd arrived, they'd heard Ricky's voice through the door. We had to get dressed before I could introduce him.' She winced at the memory. 'Not the greatest start.'

'Oops,' said Lucas. His Green Jealousy Monster began to stir at the thought of Elle in bed with Ricky, but he resolutely chained it down. Jealousy directed at past lovers was futile at best.

'Not kidding. They asked way too many questions for Ricky's liking, and he was too charming, or "soapy" as Mum called it, to impress them.'

She groaned. 'I took his side against them. I said they were too caught up in their middle-class standards to value someone like Ricky. After a host of icy remarks they left, still spouting about how important my masters was.'

Slowly, she sat up, taking her water bottle from the table and drinking from it. The place on Lucas where she'd been pressed felt cold and empty. She stretched, easing her neck. Then she leaned back into him, tilting her head to rest once again on his arm. He was shocked by the degree of relief he felt.

'The thing is, my parents were wrong if they thought Ricky didn't think my masters was important. He actively encouraged me in my education. He was always asking if I was studying enough and creeping around quietly so as not to disturb me.'

Lucas was surprised. 'So maybe he had some good qualities.'

With an air of elaborate patience, Elle sighed. 'He wanted me to get the best possible result that would get me the best job and earn the greatest amount of money. He was preparing to climb on board the Elle Gravy Train. First stop: Ricky not having to work any more.'

After that, there was no need for further prompts. It seemed as if Elle was operating on automatic, set to 'regurgitate'. It crossed Lucas's mind that he ought to say, 'Are you certain you want to tell me all of this?' But he found himself quite unable to be so generous of spirit.

'He wasn't even subtle,' said Elle, sadly. 'But I still fell for his crap. When he said that it would help get my parents onside if we went to live in Bettsbrough, it didn't even occur to me to ask myself whether he was right, but I agreed because it seemed as if I would be pleasing both Ricky and my parents. Then he developed the theme into how horrified they'd be if we went back there and lived together – so, let's do the right thing and get married before we go. They might like him more if they could see that he had done the right thing. He even said "If they can see that I'm making it all about you."'

She flung up her hands. 'Why hatch a clever plan when Elle will fall for a simple one? I went along with it. I even felt flattered that he'd give up his life in Manchester for me. Looking back on it, I expect he'd hacked so many people off in Manchester that he wanted to leave it behind, but it didn't occur to me at the time.'

He tightened his arm, pulling her closer. 'Don't be so hard on yourself. I don't think your parents provided you with many street smarts. Condemning you and going off in a huff even when they saw what kind of guy Ricky was didn't make you see that you had choices or help you recognise a user.'

'No.' She shook her head, wearily. 'But they were still mega pissed-off when Mr and Mrs Ricky Manion turned up on their doorstep.'

She yawned mightily and Lucas finally let concern for her override his thirst for knowledge. She'd had bad news; she'd sobbed as if her heart would break; she'd bared her soul. Her eyes, now they'd lost their pinkness, were huge with exhaustion. 'I think it's time for us to go to bed,' he said.

Chapter Eighteen

Even though she felt like over-boiled spaghetti, the words shot straight to Elle's groin. *Wow, that would be …!* 'O-OK,' she managed.

Lucas was as still as a rock, probably wanting to yank those words back out of the air. She tried to think of a light remark to skip them over the awkwardness, but her mind was blank.

Suddenly, everywhere they were touching felt supercharged: his arm strong around her, their sides pressed together.

No wonder the child protection training had taught her that contact could be misunderstood. She was feeling twice as hot as the Mediterranean evening and completely unequal to giving him a quick grateful smile and extricating herself gracefully. Every inch of her screamed to be in Lucas's arms for more than a comforting hug.

'I didn't mean it to sound quite like that.' His voice was strained.

She snorted a mildly hysterical laugh. 'And I didn't mean that to sound as if going to bed would be OK. I m-mean …'

The awkward moment stretched out. Elle's breathing played hopscotch.

'Elle.' His voice was a caress. He lifted a hand and stroked her hair back from her face. 'Going to bed with you was all kinds of things, all of them a lot more than OK.'

Shyly, she lifted her gaze.

His eyes were glittering like black glass. His smile began slowly. 'A *lot* more than OK.'

Unable to lubricate her voice enough to speak, she just nodded. A smile took over her lips.

He shifted so that they were facing one another, as much as they could within the confines of the dinette. He studied her face. 'If I thought—' His Adam's apple moved.

Elle found herself nodding.

And then his head was moving closer. Until their lips touched with the lightest of kisses. Again. Again. Sweet, soft, barely there kisses.

Then he slid his hands up into her hair and his mouth took hers, his tongue hot as it traced her lips, and she was pulsing against him.

And it felt like coming home.

In a blur, Elle was vaguely aware of them struggling out from the dinette, scooting along the sofas while trying not to lose contact, banging knees and elbows, almost falling onto the floor.

She heard him begin, 'Are you sure—?' A question she answered by rubbing herself against him, smiling against his mouth when he groaned.

Steering her backwards, he lifted her off her feet for the four steps from saloon to galley, putting her feet back to the floor so that he could fumble behind her for the door handle to his cabin. The door crashed open.

'Be careful with Simon's boat,' she murmured.

'All I care about Simon's boat right now is that it has a bed and you on it.' He paused to glance ruefully at his tumbled sheets. 'I didn't realise that I'd be entertaining.'

She laughed. Then Lucas's strong hands were searching until his fingers found her zip and unfastened it with a long, slow swoosh that raised goosebumps on her neck.

'I've been fantasising about getting you out of this ... *thing*,' he breathed, sliding the fabric down her arms soooooo slooooowly that every hair on her body seemed to stand up and crackle.

'Playsuit,' she supplied.

His laughter was soft and low. 'Stupid name for it. I've worked out a route to getting you out of just about every outfit I've seen you in since you came on board this boat. Dresses that tie at the neck, shorts that zip at the side, buttons, hooks – I formulated strategies for them all.' He dropped his head and nibbled her neck, his stubble brushing her skin.

She tried to take half a step back to read his eyes. 'You've been planning this?'

He pulled her up against him again. 'More dreaming than planning. If I'd known this was going to happen I would have been a lot more cheerful. I wouldn't have acted like a moron about Kayleigh.' He backed her up until the edge of his mattress caught her behind her knees. As she began to topple, he slipped his hands into her waistband and tugged, following her down so that, somehow, as she bounced onto the unmade bed, fabric was already skimming down her legs and off over her bare feet.

'Impressive,' she gasped.

He grinned as he let himself down gently on top of her. 'What else have you got to challenge my ingenuity? A front-loading bra?'

'No. Just the usual variety.'

He rolled so that she was on top of him, tasting the skin of her collarbone, her neck, exploring the strap across her back until he found the hooks and pinged them open. 'So no particular ingenuity required.' Then the laughter left his voice as the heat of his mouth found her bare breast. He groaned. 'You are so amazing. I want you—' He paused, his teeth grazing one nipple, making her jump. 'I want you—' He closed his lips around her and sucked, making her arch her back so that she could press herself against his mouth.

He sighed and his breath passing over moisture made her breast feel both hot and shivery. 'I want you.'

Lucas woke slowly.

Eyes still closed, he felt the lift-and-slide movement that told him the boat was riding a swell. The day was going to be another hot one: his naked skin was bathed in sweat, though not even a sheet covered him.

Someone was breathing beside him.

Elle.

His eyes flew open and there she was, rumpled blonde hair streaming across her face. Last night had been neither memory, nor dream, nor guilty fantasy. She had been real beneath him. And then on top. Fresh desire rippled through him, pleasure and satisfaction in hot pursuit.

He'd made love to Elle again.

She lay on her front, her head turned on the pillow, one arm tucked beneath. Her shoulders showed tan lines. Her spine sloped down then curved deliciously to the mounds of her behind. He lay still, just watching her breathe.

Almost as amazing as the sex was the fact she'd finally talked to him about Ricky.

He wasn't certain that anybody would understand how secrets made something inside of him turn to prickles and what it meant to him that not only had Elle finally shared what had happened to her, but, as a bonus, her 'secrets' had been surprisingly palatable.

What it amounted to was that she'd made a series of bad decisions out of naivety and gullibility and married the wrong guy, in secret, a snub from which her relationship with her parents had never recovered. The memories had made her visibly cringe but, if he hadn't thought it would hurt her feelings, he would have laughed and reassured her that worse things happened. *Far* worse.

For many, the post-puberty decade was crammed with crap decisions and misadventure. They experimented, risked, smoked, overindulged, sniffed, overspent, injected, rushed, loved badly, chose stupidly, suffered, lamented and repented. Show him someone who had no regrets from their young-and-stupid period, and he'd show you someone with memory loss.

Her parents' bad reaction, echoed, unfortunately, by the sniffiness of his parents, had made her frightened to talk about her mistake. His insensitive dismissal of those feelings had made her clam up still more. But now that Elle's barriers were down, there was no reason for her to be anything but open with him in the future.

His stomach twisted.

He and Elle could have a future.

Picking up his watch from the niche beside the bed, he glanced at the time and then turned to stroke the side of Elle's breast with one fingertip, savouring the softness of her skin. 'Hey, sleepy. I have to be at work by nine-thirty so Polly will be picking me up soon. What time do you have to be doing your thing at Nicolas Centre?'

Elle's eyelids flickered; then she reared up onto her elbows, eyes wide.

He grinned. 'Yeah, it's me.'

'Whoa.' She blinked.

'Bit freaky?'

'Lot freaky.' But then she smiled, slowly stretching like a cat, which made him reach for parts of her he hadn't touched yet this morning. Then she rose up on all fours, looking suddenly wary. 'Are we OK? Is this—?' She made a gesture to include their two bodies.

'This is the OKest I've been in years.' By shifting only slightly he could brush a row of kisses across her breasts. Her hair hung down and trickled over the side of his face. 'It would be even better if we didn't have places we have to be. Because I'd much rather be inside you than under the sea.'

She breathed a laugh. 'I have to shower.' But she dipped so that she could lick the side of his neck, under his ear, where some of his best nerve endings got ready to party. Then she sighed and slid away.

Reluctantly, he let her slip through his hands, and watched her walk out of the door, scooping up her clothes on the way.

Stretching, yawning, he stepped into his shower enclosure, making the visit brief, as he'd soon be jumping into the sea. Towelling off, he could hear her shower still running. If she got a move on, they could have coffee together before they had to leave for the day. He hoped she had nothing planned for this evening. Then he could spend all day looking forward to coming home to Elle, as he used to.

He imagined strolling to one of the pavement cafes, hand-in-hand, or soaking up the evening sun on the flybridge, lingering over a meal they'd prepared together.

Before they went to bed. Together.

His phone chimed, announcing the arrival of a text message. He was surprised to find it was from Charlie: How's Elle this morning? Lucas's night with Elle had almost wiped his memory on the subject of his brother's presence on the island.

He pulled on the shorts, stuck some euros in his pocket,

grabbed a T-shirt and went out to fill the kettle. No time this morning to wait for the coffee machine. He spooned instant granules and sugar into two mugs, just as Elle emerged, her hair freshly brushed and pulled up high in a ponytail.

He grabbed her quickly, before she could turn all shy on him, and showed her Charlie's message. 'Bro wants to know how you are. What shall I say?'

She blushed and giggled. '"Better than might have been expected"?'

He grinned. 'How about "Fucking amazing!"?'

'Don't you dare.' But her magnificent eyes blazed with laughter.

Pocketing his phone so that he had both hands free to curve around her buttocks, he pulled her close and kissed her. 'It was amazing.'

'It was,' she whispered, sinking against him.

He decided to be pre-emptive in discouraging any elephants to materialise in the room. He felt certain that an elephant could do a lot of damage. 'And I feel great knowing that you finally found a way to tell me all your bad stuff. Not that it was very bad. You know I'm weird about secrets.'

The sigh she gave might have been imperceptible to anyone who wasn't holding her so firmly against himself. 'Yes,' she agreed, sadly. 'I know.'

A heartbeat, then she pulled away, her smile in place and her voice bright again. 'Right, well, I have to run. I want to get to the centre because I have to take time out during the day to talk to Dad and probably The Briars and the hospital. Then I'm working on *Seadancer* this afternoon. And I'll talk to Joseph about the Bubblemaker.'

'Right,' he said, slowly. 'Prioritise your mother's

situation. I could visit Joseph tomorrow, as I've got the day off, but don't worry if you've got other stuff on your mind.'

'OK.' She pressed a quick kiss on his lips. 'See you later.' Holding her bag in front of her, she backed away, turned and jumped up the steps, across the saloon and away.

Lucas stared after her. Despite the smile, her expression had been closed.

He didn't make the coffee. Instead, he locked up the *Shady Lady*, hauled in the gangplank, called at the cafe across the road for takeaway espresso and a couple of *pastizzi*, delicious little pastries filled with ricotta cheese. His appetite seemed to have disappeared but he knew better than to dive on an empty stomach.

While he waited for the green pick-up, he took out his phone and reread Charlie's message. How's Elle this morning?

He answered: Over the initial shock. But who knows what's going on in Elle's mind?

Chapter Nineteen

Elle made her way to the Nicholas Centre. Morning was her favourite time in Malta. The streets were abuzz with people beginning their day and the air felt fresh, as if the dust hadn't yet begun to rise, making the light more lemon yellow than the heavy gold of sweltering afternoon.

But, more than her journey through the streets, her thoughts this morning were fixed on her pulsing night with Lucas Rose.

She couldn't wish it hadn't happened. How could she wish away the dream-come-true of Lucas wanting her again? The fierce joy of reunion sex? The utter untold back-where-she-belonged relief?

For four years her skin had hurt for the want of his touch.

Without even closing her eyes she could summon the hunger in him as he'd driven into her, the lips that had scalded her. The smile that had glistened in his eyes and softened the harsher lines from his mouth.

Just as clear was the memory of the satisfaction and pleasure on his face when she'd spilled so much about Ricky. Her chest tightened. Had she done the right thing? It was more than she'd ever told him. More than she'd ever told anyone.

By unburdening herself to a suddenly empathetic Lucas she'd breached the walls that she'd lived behind. The irony was that she'd let the words bubble out on the premise that it no longer mattered what Lucas thought of her.

Then he'd kissed her and, suddenly, they weren't as over as she'd thought, and it all began to matter again. Probably more than ever.

Now he'd expect more. Ask more. She'd have this exposed feeling all the time.

You know I'm weird about secrets. The words shivered through her despite the heat from the climbing sun.

Glad at the prospect of a busy morning to occupy her thoughts, she turned into the courtyard at the Nicolas Centre, in shade at this time of day. Her heart sank as she saw Oscar seated on the rim of the dry fountain.

He rose casually enough, but she had little doubt that he'd been waiting for her. 'Good morning. It is always a good morning for me when I see a beautiful woman like Elle Jamieson.' He let his eyes travel down her body and up again. 'Yes. She is beautiful.'

She could have brushed him off by saying, truthfully, that her mother was very ill and she wanted to tell Joseph then fill her time with work until the time difference would allow her to reasonably phone the UK. But that tactic would provide only temporary relief and give him an excuse to pester her with solicitous enquiries about her mother's progress.

So, instead, she bestowed on him a smile so wide that he blinked. 'It's a good morning for *me* because it followed a very, very, very good night.' She rounded off her words with a big bawdy wink and had the satisfaction of seeing his jaw drop as she swept by.

Once she was settled in the computer room, time passed slowly. Elle's attempts at calling her father's phone resulted only in hearing his decisive voice say, 'This is Will Jamieson. I can't take your call but do leave a message.' It probably meant that he was busy with the hospital and

The Briars. She knew the frustrations of being just one of many relatives trying to get information out of busy nurses and waiting for doctors' rounds to prompt the medical updates.

Despite their tepid relationship, Elle didn't like to imagine her mother small and defenceless between the crisp white sheets of a metal bed with cot sides. Elle had accepted the role of dutiful daughter until the big Ricky mistake and that habit hadn't been entirely broken by Joanna setting her affection dial to zero to express her disappointment in Elle's fallibility.

When the first big stroke had crushed Joanna under its savage heel Elle had rushed to her bedside. Over the next weeks she'd sacrificed her time in order to supervise Joanna's nursing in recovery, consult with doctors and, ultimately, research and negotiate good residential care. She'd acquired Power of Attorney, chosen the possessions and clothes she thought Joanna would like to have with her in her altered life and deposited her jewellery into the bank's safe custody. Everything else had been sold to add to Joanna's bank balance.

Her mother had never recovered sufficiently to understand what was being done for her as her ability to recognise and recall had almost gone, along with speech and mobility. But at least Elle's conscience re daughterly responsibilities had been clear before leaving England. Though the situation had now changed and she felt an urge to react to that, there was no point flying to her mother's bedside until she knew that any action she took would be worthwhile.

None of that intellectual reasoning prevented Elle from visiting the websites of Air Malta and Ryanair to check out the ticket situation, discovering availability for the next day, which was Tuesday, and also Friday and Saturday. That only a single seat remained on the Tuesday flight made her twitchy.

Then two lads in their late teens came clattering into the computer room and she was glad to turn her thoughts away from what might be happening in a hospital many miles away to a woman who probably didn't comprehend that it was happening.

'*Kif inti?*' she greeted them, varying her limited Maltese greetings from *bonġu*. In reply, she received a scowl from the big kid and a smirk from his smaller friend. OK. Not every youth that visited Nicholas Centre was easy to like. Aggression, cockiness or suspicion were all common.

After waiting ten minutes to let the boys settle, she wandered around their side of the island of computers. 'Is there anything you'd like help with?'

She received another darkling look and a torrent of Maltese from the bigger lad. The smaller one burst into delighted laughter.

Elle didn't react except to say, 'Tell me if you do.' She returned to her machine and picked up her phone to text her father. Let me know when you know anything about Mum, pls. x

She checked her e-mail, in case her father or someone at The Briars had sent a message. They hadn't, but there was something from Simon, sent Friday, giving her the news from Rose Wines, how incredibly busy he was and that he'd had hardly any time for drinking in bars and chasing women! So how are you surviving with your shipmate? he went on. I hope that by now you've buried old hatchets (not in each other's heads) and found a way to get along. Update me! She began to type.

Simon,

Charlie has just flown out here and now I know why you were surprised that I said Kayleigh was Lucas's girlfriend! I suppose you felt some male solidarity not to rat Lucas out.

Adding a couple of rapid paragraphs, she caught him up with events regarding her mother, the boat, the island and Nicholas Centre, the sort of chatty news she usually exchanged with him a couple of times a week. She signed off: No hatchets in heads. Elle xxx

Last night was too surprising, too fragile, to share. What if it turned out not to be something new, but something doomed? Last night, they'd expressed nothing deeper than desire.

In the cold light of day – or the hot light of day, as they were in Malta – Elle's heart was too wary to easily shuck off its stab jacket. She was too mindful of how long her scars had taken to heal, too aware of all that was unresolved. *You know I'm weird about secrets.* So the obvious answer lay in telling him the rest of the story. Now. Before they got in deeper. Before she had more to lose. She found herself staring into space while her head and heart debated the situation. *You know it's the only sensible way forward,* declared her head. *But you know how he can hurt me!* quavered her heart.

She snapped out of her reverie as two girls tumbled, giggling, into the computer room, one of them Giorgina, the avid Facebooker. Instantly, the boys increased the volume of their voices. The largest – and noisiest – kept calling things in Maltese to the girls, which, judging from their outraged expressions, were not welcome and, in view of the apprehensive looks they cast Elle's way, probably not clean.

'Shall we keep it down a bit?' Elle suggested pleasantly. She picked up her phone to text Joseph and ask if he had a few minutes to come up and spread a little calm in Maltese, then she rolled her chair over to Giorgina's and Alice's machines to offer support in ignoring the big mouths. She joked and chatted calmly and showed them a Pinterest account she'd created for the Nicholas Centre, where she'd pinned photos of the computer room, the games room and the gym.

It was only a few minutes before Joseph wandered in, hands in pockets. He paused to chat to Elle, Giorgina and Alice; then strolled over to the boys, who were now stifling laughter behind their computer monitor.

Joseph addressed them in Maltese. The boys' replies seemed truculent, although it was hard for Elle to judge as Maltese frequently sounded staccato to her ears. Joseph stayed as cool and easy as always, but the large lad suddenly jumped up and barged out of the room. The smaller one followed at a trot, still sniggering.

Proving that they could speak some English, a stream of it floated up into the computer room in company with the sound of running feet on the stairs.

'Shit!'

'Fuck!'

'Piss!'

Their laughter faded into the distance.

Joseph lifted a querying eyebrow in Elle's direction.

She smiled an *I'm OK*. She had to get used to the occasional outbreak of the verbals and also that, at Nicholas Centre, there were no recriminations over bad behaviour. Joseph did sometimes send kids away, inviting them to return the next day, when, he said, he was sure their behaviour would be more acceptable, but Elle hadn't yet seen any youngster made to feel that she or he would never be able to drop in to the centre again.

Her phone rang, instantly diverting her thoughts. The screen told her who was calling and she picked the phone up with a hand that wasn't quite steady. 'Dad?'

Joseph waved to indicate that she was free to leave the room and seated himself at a vacant machine. It wasn't that the computer room had to be constantly supervised but disenchanted youths taking out their frustrations on the equipment had to be allowed for. The behaviour of the two who had just left would definitely raise such concerns.

She made her way quickly across the landing to the big salon at the front of the building, sure of privacy there, as it was generally used only for planned events. 'How's Mum?'

Will was reassuringly businesslike. 'The hospital say that your mother passed a comfortable night, which I think meant that nothing much changed and she wasn't in pain, and she's being kept in for observation. It wasn't such a big stroke, this time, but you know how these things are.'

'Anything could happen.' She sighed. 'Have you talked to The Briars? She might need additional care when she comes out.' She let herself down on one of the blue chairs set around the edge of the big room, staring up at the high ceiling and the twin old-fashioned fans hanging motionless.

'All they say is that they'll have to wait and see how she progresses.'

Elle let her head tip back against the wall. Her eyelids were heavy. She supposed she hadn't got a lot of sleep last night. 'If that's all they can say, and she doesn't seem in any immediate need of me, I'll hang on here for now. I can probably be of more use when she's ready to come out.' She swallowed, the vision of her mother in the hospital bed flashing once again across her consciousness. 'H-have you seen her?'

Her father cleared his throat. 'That's a trifle awkward, what with Tania and the fact that I'm several hours' drive away. And since your mother doesn't seem to be in any danger—'

'You're right.' Elle felt the responsibility for her mother coming to roost squarely on her shoulders. 'She probably wouldn't know you, anyway.'

They talked for a few more minutes, agreeing that Elle would ring the hospital herself the next day. Will sounded relieved. She ended the call feeling uncomfortably conflicted, her remnants of love for her mother bound up in duty and tainted by unresolved issues.

Love, for Elle, always did seem confused and complicated, instead of the certain, shiny, clean thing she wanted it to be.

She sighed, and returned to the computer room to complete the morning session.

Giorgina and Alice had been joined by three fresh boyish faces and conversation was loud, but this time good-natured and punctuated with laughter.

Briefly, she updated Joseph on her mother's circumstances.

His brown eyes darkened with concern. 'Do you need some personal time? My mum's due to come in this afternoon, anyway. I can ask her to come early.' He tapped his top shirt pocket, from which his phone could be seen peeping.

Elle summoned a smile, even though, for once, she would be glad to be out of the centre and alone with her thoughts. 'There's only an hour to go. Don't disturb her. It's not as if I have a workshop session to run.'

He nodded. 'If you're sure. The schools break up in two days so we'll be busier, then. I have two of Mum's friends, both retired teachers like her, who I can call on for help with general supervision of the beginning-of-holiday excitement.' He smiled. 'It's one of my favourite times to be here. It can be chaotic but I like the smiling faces.'

Trying to share his enthusiasm and, mindful of her promise to Lucas, Elle took the opportunity to sound Joseph out about the Bubblemaker session.

His eyes brightened. 'That sounds like it could be a wonderful opportunity. Please make Lucas welcome to visit for coffee tomorrow afternoon. I'm always interested in discussing what somebody is prepared to do for our children.'

The rest of the session passed without incident and Elle returned to the marina. When she reached *Seadancer* it was to find Loz and Davie happily ensconced with drinks in their hands on the improbably named *le Chateau*, a yacht moored three berths down. Loz waved and yoohooed and Davie came off the boat to wind down *Seadancer*'s gangplank so that Elle could board.

'You'll have the place to yourself today.' Wine fumes rolled off him into the hot afternoon air. 'Our friends Patrice and Birgit have just arrived and I expect it will take Loz the next twelve hours to catch up on their news.'

'I don't mind,' Elle said, truthfully. 'The centre's gearing up for the summer holidays so I'm glad of the peace.' Loz was a sweetheart but her constant conversation took up a lot of headspace. And if she were to ask how things were going with Lucas, Elle was sure she would blush, exciting Loz's ever-present curiosity.

Once Davie had ambled back to continue pickling his liver, Elle whisked through the galley, the saloon, and then Loz and Davie's stateroom and bathroom, leaving behind her the smells of bleach and polish.

Seadancer rocked peaceably on her lines and, as she worked, Elle wondered when to ring the hospital again, and The Briars. When it would be best for her to return to England and check out her mother's situation for herself. And whether the need for that was on her side or her mum's.

She sighed, wishing for love unburdened by old baggage. It was too late to achieve that with her mother. Her father was focusing on his new wife/new life scenario.

But with Lucas …?

Her hands slowed as she wiped the glass of the foredeck doors. Their past love had been tainted by Ricky. Her attempts to keep the new relationship separate from the old had only resulted in completely alienating Lucas.

The answer to the earlier debate between her head and her heart was suddenly as clear as the glass beneath her industrious hands.

She'd tell him. Tonight. Before things went any further.

Chapter Twenty

Lucas liked to feel the sun slanting onto his back while he hosed seawater from wetsuits and hung them on plastic hangers to drain.

He'd been in the water today with Polly while Lars provided surface cover. Polly was possibly his favourite instructor, just because she looked as if she was a bumbly, shy, awkward woman and he liked to see the clients' faces when she actually proved to be confident and incisive.

Today, two buffoons, Bryan and Jim, had decided to break a golden rule and drink alcohol between dives.

Polly had tried to indicate how bad an idea it was with a friendly, low-key request. 'Come on, guys, don't buy beer if you're diving this afternoon. Alcohol accelerates your no decompression limits and makes it difficult for your body tissue to reabsorb oxygen. Decompression sickness is easier to contract.'

Lucas grinned to remember Bryan and Jim rolling their eyes as they went ahead with their order at the beach bar.

Knowing that entertainment was about to follow, Lars and Lucas had just waited.

Polly watched Bryan and Jim hand over their euros. 'How's the beer, guys?' she called.

'Good!' Jim called back, lifting his foaming pint in a mocking toast to her.

'Glad you're enjoying it.' Polly turned to Lucas. 'Put Jim and Bryan's tanks back on the pick-up: they're spending the afternoon waterside unless they toss the beer right now.'

The grins fell from Jim and Bryan's faces. They tossed the beer.

Lucas wasn't sure whether they realised what idiots they'd made of themselves by indulging in a thinly disguised sulk for most of the afternoon but the other four guys in the party, pleasant Irish lads, all experienced Open Water Advanced Divers, didn't let Bryan and Jim spoil their date with the sea. They loved everything underwater from orange fireworms to the encrusted remains of a gun from a World War II ship and happily signed up for the next day's dives.

Bryan and Jim had not signed up for more and were probably already in some bar, downing their long-awaited beer and bitching about Polly.

As Lucas worked, moving the wetsuits up the rail once rinsed, he paused to put on his T-shirt. He'd learned to respect the sun in California.

Vern popped his head around the corner of the team building. 'Can you clean up the stuff from my dive, too, so Harriet can go? Hot date.'

'No problem.' Lucas grinned as small, dark Harriet instantly appeared with three more clients to hang up their wetsuits and BCDs. Harriet would repay the favour some time and, today, nothing was a problem.

Elle had spent last night in his bed.

Thinking about it made his heart flip like a coin. Preparing equipment, supervising and assessing the divers, participating in the briefs and debriefs, checking logs, Lucas had had to keep his mind on the job because safety was everything. But now that he needed only two per cent of his mind for this end-of-day chore he could let Elle occupy the rest.

Last night had been *hot*. This morning ... His hands

slowed. This morning, the old pattern had shown signs of emerging. He'd told Elle that her sharing her past with him had made him happy, and her own happiness had drained from her face.

He moved the last wetsuit over on the rail and began on the BCDs, letting the chill fresh water splash over his bare feet as he washed the sea from each of the padded waistcoat-like devices in turn.

Vern's head reappeared around the corner. 'We thought we'd go over to Fat Harry's. Polly and Lars are coming.'

'I'll give it a miss this time.' Lucas hung up the last dripping BCD and ran the water over the row of fins standing up against the wall before turning off the tap. He was hoping that Elle would be waiting for him at the boat.

To his disappointment, when Lucas jumped off the bus and sauntered through the gardens, he found the *Shady Lady* locked up. Hoping Elle would soon show, he put on the air con and showered.

As he finished towelling himself his phone began to ring from the pocket of the cut-offs on the cabin floor. He snatched it up, frowning slightly to see not Elle's name on the screen, as he'd hoped, but Simon's.

'What's up?' he asked shortly.

'Nothing.' Simon sounded wary. 'What's up with you?'

Lucas laughed. 'Sorry. Nothing.' He extended his arm back into the shower room to lodge the towel on the rail. 'Everything's good.'

They chatted for a few minutes. Lucas reported all OK on the *Shady Lady* and Simon asked him to see the harbour master and check that his last lot of mooring fees had arrived, as he hadn't received an acknowledgement.

Lucas yawned as he listened to Simon talking about the grapes swelling in California. The day's diving after a happy and energetic night with Elle began to have their effect. Yawning even more widely, he scratched those parts of man that sometimes demanded scratching.

A giggle made him swing around. Elle stood in the galley, eyes dancing, a bag of shopping in each hand.

Simon's voice continued in Lucas's ear. 'I talked to Elle on e-mail and she indicated the two of you were getting along.'

Lucas felt himself begin to harden as Elle put down the bags and came to lean on the door frame while she looked at him, her blonde hair pouring over one shoulder. 'Glad that she feels that way,' he said, truthfully.

Elle smiled and Lucas felt her gaze like a caress, making it difficult to concentrate on anything else. 'Got to go,' he said into the phone. 'Something's just come up. Bye, Simon.' Lucas ended the call.

Elle prowled closer. 'Naked man,' she breathed.

He drank her in, those cool blue eyes almost predatory beneath her fine blonde brows. The tops of her breasts rose where the fabric of her dress crossed over and narrowed into straps, blue and green and all the colours of the sea. He had to swallow before he could speak. 'Care to join me?'

'Love to.' The corners of her mouth lifted slightly but there was no laughter in her eyes. Instead there was wonder, tenderness. Hunger.

Slowly, she reached under her dress and pulled down her underwear, stepping from the white thong and dropping it to the floor. Then she stretched behind herself and tugged until he heard the soft hiss of a descending zipper. Dropping her arms, she shrugged, and her dress began to slide south. The colours seemed to shimmer as the fabric caught briefly on her breasts, or maybe it was Lucas's vision that shimmered. He did seem to have stopped breathing.

The dress slithered to the floor.

Lucas wasn't sure who reached out first but in an instant hot naked woman was jammed up against him and his only recognisable thought was that he must get inside her.

Elle knew it was unlikely that she'd die of pleasure but when there was so much of it, it was difficult not to at least cry out as if wounded. After the initial urgency, Lucas had created a breathtaking rhythm, pulling oh-so-slowly out of her, to pause, then push *urgggggh*-so-*slooooowly* back in. Another pause until she was grinding against him, then he started all over again.

The intensity, the concentration, was ferocious. Despite the air conditioning, the cabin pulsed with heat.

She gasped as he pulled out of her. 'This would be almost frightening'—he slid back inside her and she groaned—'if it didn't feel so good.'

Sweat shone on his cheeks. He screwed up his eyes. Then his control broke and the urgency flooded back and Elle couldn't make her breathing sync with her heartbeat to even say his name.

If it were possible to die of pleasure, she realised, she didn't care.

Slowly, their breathing calmed. Lucas had rolled onto his side, done the gentlemanly thing with the condom and pulled Elle against his skin, holding her as their sweat dried.

Elle's phone chirped. She'd abandoned it with her purse on the floor by the door. She managed to open her eyes. 'That might be Charlie or Kayleigh. They're off for a romantic dinner but they asked us if we'd go for a drink first.'

'Right.' Lucas's eyelids flickered but didn't completely open. 'Are we going?'

Elle stretched. 'A drink does sound good. Then we could come back to the boat for dinner. I bought the food.' She hoped she sounded normal, but her heart shivered. Over dinner. That's when she had scheduled telling him the rest of the Ricky story. She'd even put the romantic meal idea into Charlie's head to try and prevent him and Kayleigh turning up at the boat or suggesting that they all ate together.

Although she was bone-deep thankful to have at least this one time with Lucas, she repeated, 'A drink does sound good,' creating a reason to get out of bed. Once she was no longer tangled in the sheets with him, it wouldn't be so tempting to put off the conversation she was dreading. But if she put it off once she'd put it off again and again and sooner or later the indecision would come back to bite her rear end.

'Better shower, then.' He pulled her a little higher up his body so that he could kiss her.

Elle was trying not to dwell too much on the evening before them. But it was hard not to let various scenarios run through her head. 'Do you m-mind—' She took a breath. 'Do you mind if we don't tell Charlie anything, just for now?'

Lucas looked faintly surprised.

She pressed an apologetic kiss on his neck. 'I'd just rather not have to face a barrage of questions about this.'

He tipped her face up, frowning into her eyes. 'Before you understand what "this" is?'

'I suppose so. I know you don't like secrets, but—'

After a thoughtful stare, he shrugged. 'But you'd be more comfortable keeping our business as our business?'

She smiled, gratefully. 'At least for now.' And if 'this' was all over by the end of the evening, then it would be a hell of a lot less embarrassing not to have accepted Charlie and Kayleigh's congratulations and exclamations. Especially for Lucas.

Chapter Twenty-One

Lucas loved his brother. He'd loved him since he'd visited his mother on the maternity ward and she'd shown him the baby in the plastic cot. 'This is your brother.'

He'd taken the 'your' part of that sentence seriously and spent the next years alternately ordering Charlie around and looking after him. They'd grown up close.

Two days ago, if someone had told Lucas that his little brother would turn up in Malta and they'd be able to sit around a table in the last of the evening light, drinking beer and talking, he would have been delighted. If he could have held Elle's hand and fended off Charlie's jokes and hoots because Lucas and Elle had got it together again, he would still have been delighted.

As it was, Charlie and Kayleigh were the ones holding hands, while Lucas and Elle occupied individual spaces.

Any idea he might have had of protesting against Elle's request that they keep a lid on what was going on between them had died when he'd looked into her eyes and seen her uncertainty. What he'd been chewing over had crystallised forcibly.

Elle was acutely uncomfortable when she was pushed into revealing things she'd rather keep to herself, and just because he liked everything out in the open didn't give him the right to expect her to feel the same. She was a private person. So what? That was allowed.

In the past, maybe he'd been blinded by his white-hot need to possess. It had taken a while but now he was finally beginning to see that 'your brother' would always be your brother, but 'your girlfriend' was only yours for as long as she wanted to be.

A lot of past aggro had been created by allowing his suspicions to feed on Elle's natural inclination towards reserve. That didn't make him particularly proud of himself.

So he went along with Elle's wishes, keeping to his own space while she updated them on her mother's condition.

Even after Charlie and Kayleigh headed off to a romantic restaurant on the bastions of the silent city of Mdina he strolled back to the *Shady Lady* decorously at Elle's side as if nothing had changed between them.

They prepared dinner together and he nibbled her neck a couple of times, rewarded by her relaxing, laughing, rubbing her curves against him in the confined area.

But when they went up to the flybridge to eat in public view, he did no more than let his bare leg rest discreetly against hers beneath the table as they dined on cheese with Maltese bread and big dark red tomatoes, and all the leafy stuff that she seemed to like so he went along with.

As the rapid twilight descended and the lights began to cast their golden squiggles in the creek he watched her take a draught of wine. And then that tight, shut look stole across her face again. His heart dipped.

So when she put on a smile and said, 'It seems only fair to give you part two of the Ricky saga,' he found himself shaking his head.

She stopped, confusion bringing down her blonde brows.

'You've probably told me enough,' he said, gently. 'I've been thinking it over all day and come to the conclusion that we can leave most of it behind us.' Relief blazed in her eyes and he congratulated himself on making the right decision.

He knew everything he needed to know. Except for—

A vision rose in his mind: Elle standing very still in the street outside her office, a man almost as close to her as he could get, talking vehemently into her upturned face. Seconds had passed, five, ten, then Elle had spun on her heel and disappeared back through the revolving door. The man had stared after her. And smiled. Lucas had found his breathing coming so hard that it blurred his vision, making him unsure how to interpret what he'd seen.

He reached across the table for Elle's hands. 'There's only one thing I do need to know. Something that would affect the present.' He kept his gaze on her, letting her read his eyes. 'It might not be fair to ask and I probably shouldn't, but I've grown up enough to know my own frailties. If I don't ask it, the question will always fester. Is it OK to ask you?'

Her face was very still. Then she nodded, jerkily, her gaze fixed on his.

He drew in a breath. 'Were you seeing anyone else when you were with me?'

Visibly, new tension entered her body. Her voice emerged huskily but her gaze never wavered, blue and true. 'Are you asking if I cheated? Not once, not to any extent!'

A mixture of relief, joy and regret made his heart beat heavily. 'So I just fucked everything up by viewing what were obviously your wedding issues as suspicious. I saw you outside your office building talking to a guy I didn't know, and somehow turned that into you having an affair.'

Her hands gripped his as if she were clinging on to wreckage in the middle of a large and hostile ocean. '*We* fucked everything up,' she countered, fiercely. 'Neither of us dealt well with the pressures caused by needing to get married to go to America. But back up. You say you don't need to know about my past – but don't trust me enough to believe I could speak to a man you don't know without cheating? If you want me to tell you about that, now's definitely the time—'

'No!' She jumped at his vehemence, but he'd just seen sickeningly clearly that he could have spent the past four years with Elle, rather than without her, and all he wanted now was to find a way to go forward. 'You've told me the only thing I need to know. Let the rest go, Elle. And I will, too. I apologise for not trusting you. I'm sorry that I used to get in your face. I'm working on respecting your way of doing things rather than trying to manoeuvre you into my way.'

It took several moments for her to soften a degree or two. She managed a tiny smile but it looked like an effort. 'Do you mean I have to get used to you not saying exactly what you're thinking?'

He gave a twisted grin, relieved to see the relaxed Elle breaking through. 'I'm not sure I'd go as far as that.'

Her eyes glittered in the lights from the quay and she opened her mouth as if she were going to say more. Much more. As if truth was going to bubble out of her like molten lava.

Instead, she leaned over the table and kissed his mouth, long and deep. She didn't seem to care who saw her do it, either.

Welcoming the passion, the heat, he silently reaffirmed his decision not to ask for more. Definitely. As it was, he'd almost asked one question too many.

But … what the hell had she been going to say?

Chapter Twenty-Two

Elle felt as if she'd spent the last years encrusted in concrete. But last night had blasted it to smithereens. She'd made an honest attempt to explain what else had happened with Ricky and Lucas had stated that he didn't need to know. Apart from having her fidelity questioned, which she was trying hard to make allowances for, uncomfortably aware of her secrets, she could float as high as the Maltese sky.

Her euphoria wasn't even dimmed by the kind of morning at Nicholas Centre that would usually have made her doubt her suitability for volunteering.

The two 'children' in question, both bigger than Elle, were the swearing duo from the previous day. Elle understood that their behaviour probably cloaked self-esteem issues or fear and that the troubled and vulnerable used challenging behaviour to disguise their real feelings. But it still wasn't fun to be shouted at and a perfectly good keyboard slammed to the table over and over as anger blazed in the bigger lad's eyes.

The trigger was that Elle had addressed him in English.

It was only a friendly, 'So, tell me what you're doing?' designed to encourage the boys to interact with her rather than disrupt the whole room. But it was met with a hail of Maltese and only a few words intelligible to her – several swear words, which she'd picked up pretty quickly over the last weeks – and 'English!' accompanied by emphatic spitting on the floor.

Turning to three other lads who were huddled

blamelessly around another computer, she repeated her casual enquiry and was relieved to receive a more courteous response. 'We're playing a sim, *Football Manager*.'

Her 'That's great, can I watch for a while?' was almost drowned out by fists hammering on desks and heels drumming on the floor from the other end of the island layout. Not a promising situation, considering she was soon supposed to begin a workshop on designing posters and flyers.

'Can we keep the noise down a bit?' and 'Is there something I can help you with?' seemed only to increase the ferocity of the drumming. Elle felt the first stirrings of alarm. When the noise brought Joseph upstairs, she even found herself glad to see Oscar strolling up behind him.

However, in the genial way that somehow produced co-operation, Joseph simply asked the two boys to come back tomorrow. With one last bang of keyboard on desk they were gone, clattering down the stairs, shouting something that Elle didn't mind not being able to understand.

Oscar went to chat reassuringly to the boys playing on the football sim. Joseph caught Elle's eye and she joined him at the machine the boys had been using.

'Thanks,' she said. 'I'll just take a look at what they've been doing.' The screen displayed a networking site she wasn't familiar with but she didn't like what she saw. She put the site name into a search engine. 'Great,' she groaned as she signed in as an admin. 'Looks as if this site has recently been involved in cyberbullying. I'll add it to the blocked list.'

'Good catch,' said Joseph, making Elle feel better about not making headway with the rowdiness of the boys. He lowered his voice. 'No recurrence of the undesirable images being downloaded?'

She shook her head. 'Not so far. I've been keeping an eye out for it.'

She searched the browsing history and blocked another site she didn't like the look of and Joseph and Oscar drifted back to whatever they'd been doing before the ruckus.

Elle prepared to begin her intended workshop, feeling slightly shaken. Because of the disruption, she 'stepped back from her expectations', as Joseph would put it, and the session ended up being more about creating random clashing nonsense images than planning posters. At least it gave the participants plenty of practice at using the various tools, and the half-dozen kids who turned up seemed to enjoy it.

The session ended at noon but Elle had stowed a sandwich lunch in the kitchen fridge. She was due to sit in on the Bubblemaker discussion at two-thirty but, more importantly, she hadn't seen Carmelo since Saturday and hoped that he'd put in an appearance if she hung around. Yesterday, she'd only been able to hang on for ten minutes before she'd had to leave to get to *Seadancer*. It wasn't quite enough time for Carmelo to make it from school to the centre – supposing he'd been to school.

Today, her patience was rewarded. Carmelo panted into the room at twenty past twelve. His face lit up when he saw Elle and he arrived at her side with a bounce. 'Finished!' he announced, dramatically. 'School is finished. I am in holidays now.'

'Fantastic!' Elle was delighted to see him so happy. Actually, just delighted to see him. 'School's great, but we probably learn better when we've had a break from it.'

Carmelo didn't argue with her optimism, he just perched his skinny frame on the chair next to hers. 'I will look at YouTube today.'

'OK, you'd better use earphones. The room's filling up and if you all begin to watch YouTube or play games it'll be too noisy.' At peak times, the computer room could be like a teenage party on a sugar rush.

Instantly, Carmelo changed tack. 'I look at cars.' It was obvious that he didn't want the earphones to interfere with a chance to talk to Elle. He began happily to browse through the Top Gear site, lingering over the sleekest, brightest and most expensive miracles of automotive design, chattering constantly about what he saw. She felt a tug at her heartstrings as he ogled Ferraris and Lamborghinis that seemed cruelly out of his grasp.

She moved around the room, checking out activity, offering help, showing interest without interfering. Most of the kids were happy to share what they were doing on Instagram or Pinterest, or what video they were giggling at on YouTube.

At one o'clock Aileen arrived and Elle went down to the kitchen for lunch. Carmelo followed, taking the seat beside her and swinging his legs as he told her about the visiting priest who had said end-of-term mass at his school that morning. If Carmelo was dissatisfied at making a meal out of tap water, it didn't show, though several other children and Axel shared the big table with them and all ate or drank something more sustaining.

Maria was in the room, too, with fizzy drinks, fruit, crisps, cereal bars and fruit on sale.

Sandwich eaten, Elle bought a pomegranate and a large lush orange with telltale red blotches on the skin. She began to peel it, but then halted. 'What on earth is this?'

'*Laringa tad-demm*,' said Carmelo, helpfully.

'It's red.' Using a piece of kitchen towel from the middle

of the table, she pulled aside the segments distrustfully. 'Oranges are supposed to be orange.'

Carmelo looked at her in puzzlement. '*Lariṅġa taddemm* is a bit red. It's good.'

Maria glanced over. 'Blood orange,' she translated. 'They're grown here in Malta.'

Cautiously, Elle bit the end off a segment. Lovely. But she manufactured a grimace. 'Hmm.' And put the orange down on the kitchen paper.

'You don't like it?' Carmelo sat upright in indignation.

Elle shook her head apologetically. 'I'm probably being too English but it's odd for something red to taste like an orange. If you like it, will you eat it for me? I'll move on to the pomegranate.' She jumped up to borrow a small knife from Maria so that she could cut the pomegranate in half, and a teaspoon with which to ease out its jewel-like seeds. Returning to the table, she gave an inner cheer to see Carmelo tucking into the blood orange, juice pink on his chin.

Mindful not to be judgemental, she acknowledged inwardly that he could have lunch awaiting him and had chosen to come to the centre rather than go home to eat it. But if he had, then an orange was unlikely to spoil his appetite.

Nor would half a pomegranate, should she find herself unable to eat a whole one.

At two-thirty, Elle presented herself in Joseph's office.

Lucas was already seated on one of the eclectic collection of chairs: grey, with a ladder in the fabric on the arm like a run in a woolly sock. A white T-shirt made his hair and eyes look particularly dark. He greeted her casually but she found herself blushing as she took her seat, glad that Joseph was scrabbling through his paper-heaped desk for a pad and pen.

'So,' Joseph began, settling his glasses. 'Elle tells me that you would like to discuss doing something for the children?'

Lucas crossed his ankle over the other knee and ran briefly through the details of his job and where he worked. 'I've spoken to Vern, the owner of Dive Meddi, and we wonder if you'd like us to put on a Bubblemaker Session? A Bubblemaker session's for under-twelves and it gives them a taste of using scuba equipment in an enclosed, safe environment. It's all about fun and enjoyment but, of course, safety is paramount.'

He spent some time describing the facilities at Dive Meddi and what the ratios would need to be of child to instructor in the water. 'The first step would be for Vern and I to visit the centre with a fun presentation on diving, including slides showing the equipment and some of the aquatic life that inhabits the waters around Malta.'

As Lucas and Joseph discussed parental consent necessary for children to take part in the pool session, transport, on-shore supervision, equipment, insurance and Joseph visiting the dive school and meeting Vern, Elle watched Lucas's lips, enjoying his quick intelligence as he poured out information in a way that was interesting, comprehensive and comprehensible. Her eyes dropped to his hands as he borrowed Joseph's pad to augment an explanation with a sketch.

Presently, it was agreed that Joseph would check out Dive Meddi late that afternoon, when the diving groups were back, with a view to the presentation happening late Friday afternoon.

Joseph asked Elle to devise and print posters for the

noticeboard in the lounge and for the doors in the activity rooms.

'Fine,' she agreed, promptly. 'Lucas, do you have time to run up to the computer room with me to help me get the blurb right?'

'I'm happy to be in your hands,' he said easily, making Elle blush again.

They left Joseph to whichever of the million-and-one admin tasks had risen to the top of his 'to do' list and stepped out into the hall. At the foot of the stairs they had to pause to let Oscar come cantering down.

He pulled up with a broad grin and a loud and over-effusive greeting. Then he checked the corridor in both directions and lowered his voice. 'So, boyfriend-not boyfriend-boyfriend. Maybe it's with you she had the big sexual night, yes? She told me about it.'

Horror shot through Elle's chest. 'Oscar!' she hissed, her cheeks on fire. 'That is so not appropriate.'

Oscar laughed. 'Then you should not tell me.'

She turned to Lucas. 'I was trying to stop him h-hitting on me. I didn't go in to detail—'

But Lucas was grinning. 'You went public that we spent the night together?' he drawled. 'That's the best news I've had all day.'

'Oh!' Elle laughed, reluctantly. 'Yes, I suppose I can see how that would work for you.' Relieved that Oscar's poison dart had turned out to be so easily deflected, she couldn't resist sending the Dutchman a triumphant smile. It got her a glower in return.

Chapter Twenty-Three

Elle arranged her Friday so that she could whisk through *Seadancer* in the morning.

'You're very chirpy, young lady!' commented Loz.

Elle hugged her and laughed. 'A sister at Bettsbrough General Hospital says my mother's doing better and it looks as if she might be able to move back to The Briars some time.' Joanna would need a higher level of care than before but it was too early to plan. Out of her limited choices, it seemed the most desirable.

But of course it wasn't her mother's health that was making Elle dance through her day. It was Lucas. She couldn't believe how the wariness that she'd thought graven on his face had vanished and that the suspicion in his eyes had gone. Last night they'd talked for hours. Talked and laughed and teased and made love.

They'd talked about only happy things, hopeful things. Summer in Malta. Making children laugh. Travel. Charlie obviously being nuts about Kayleigh – as opposed to his usual state of simply being nuts. The pleasure of a cool shower after an overheated day; what the surface of the sea looked like from beneath; why bed was positively the only place to share Marsovin wine.

After everything that had happened, it was bliss.

But once Lucas had fallen into the sleep of the physically replete she'd remained awake, battling with the spectre of Ricky, worrying whether Lucas's parents would hate her all over again if or when they learned of the current situation. Had Lucas made the right decision? She didn't know. Should she insist on full disclosure? She shied away, too relieved and too scared of losing Lucas again to be that noble.

But now, in daylight, Elle had returned joyfully to wallowing in the bliss. Everything looked worse at night. It was a well-known fact.

In the afternoon, Elle went up to Nicholas Centre, where Vern would give the Dive Meddi presentation and Lucas, according to him, would press the buttons for the slide show and laugh in the right places.

The setting out of chairs began an hour before the presentation and many of the kids had already congregated noisily in the big salon by the time Elle heard Lucas's voice coming up the stairs. Elle instantly abandoned the computer room, where she'd been whiling away the time helping Carmelo set up a Nicholas Centre Twitter account. Carmelo was even faster.

'Lucas!' Carmelo beamed, intercepting Lucas as he reached the landing, hand raised expectantly.

'Hey, Carmelo.' With a big grin, Lucas dropped one of the black bags he carried to whip out an enthusiastic high five. If he noticed that Carmelo was dressed in cut-offs and a T-shirt just like Lucas's cut-offs and T-shirt, he didn't betray it. 'This is my boss, Vern.'

Vern high fived Carmelo, too, and then shook hands with Elle. 'Great to meet you.' His hand was like a paw around Elle's.

Elle took to Vern immediately. His thinning hair was coppery and curly and his eyebrows were set in a permanent arch, making him look like an oversized, faintly exasperated cherub.

In the big salon, leaving Lucas to set up a laptop and pop-up screen out of one of the capacious bags, Vern addressed the children with a brief and easy, 'I'm Vern and this is Lucas.' To Elle it seemed a casual opening, used as she was to the business world. But Vern seemed to have the knack of connecting instantly with everybody in the room and there was no sign in the audience of the kind of teen Aileen had warned Elle of, those who attended events solely to tut and roll their eyes.

As Vern talked, Lucas put up an underwater shot on the screen.

Vern glanced at it. 'Anyone know what that is?'

'Starfish!'

'You're too good.' The slide changed. 'And this?'

'Sea urchin! *Rizzi*.'

Another change. 'Octopus! *Qarnita*.'

Vern made an enlightened face. 'I can see that I'm going to learn the Maltese names for lots of things that live in the sea, this afternoon.' For several minutes the kids *oohed* and *aahed* over marine life with Vern and Lucas.

Then came cartoons of a bony-looking man holding a snorkel and scratching his head. 'This is Scooter the Scuba-nut,' explained Vern. 'I wonder if you can help him? He wants to swim under the water but he knows he's missing some things—'

'Fins!'

'Air!' the children called.

'You obviously know a lot already.' Vern glanced around at the kids with a congratulatory grin. 'Yes, he's not a fish so he needs air. "Scuba" stands for "self-contained underwater breathing apparatus" but you don't need to worry about that. What does Scooter need over his eyes so that he can see underwater?'

'Mask!'

Lucas put up an image of Scooter wearing a mask, his

eyes magnified to fish-like proportions behind the glass. The audience laughed.

Elle's attention was on Lucas as he took his cues from his boss, moving through what was obviously a well-organised presentation, however nonchalantly it was rolled out. As if becoming aware of her regard, he shifted his gaze straight to where she sat on the end of a row close to the back.

Swiftly, she winked.

One corner of his mouth quirked up, before he transferred his attention back to Vern.

Once Scooter the Scuba-nut had been seen through the entire process of equipping, learning technique in enclosed water and then in more open water in the company of shoals of fish, Vern began to unpack and discuss various pieces of scuba equipment from the big black bags and soon a couple of the children were trying things on and everyone was giggling at how they looked in fins and masks and BCDs.

It was right at the end of the 'show' when Vern demanded, 'OK, hands up everyone who thinks they want to try scuba in our pool at St Julian's?' About half of the children waved enthusiastically; the others shook their heads or pulled nervous faces. 'OK, those of you who think you might like a go, Joseph has some letters to go to your parents. They have to sign a form to say it's OK for you to visit Dive Meddi and take part in the Bubblemaker session. It's very important that we do that.' Vern went through what happened at a Bubblemaker, calling on Lucas for corroboration, talking about safety and following instructions, putting up slides of the instructors working with learner divers in and around a pool cut from rock.

'And'—Vern grinned around conspiratorially—'I think we need some of the adults from the centre, don't you?'

'Yes!' shouted the children.

Elle waved both hands. 'I'd love to!'

'And me also,' said Oscar, immediately.

Joseph nodded. 'I'll drive the minibus and stand on shore to watch everyone in the pool.'

'That's great,' said Vern. 'Two in the water and one on the side is exactly what we need.'

That evening, Elle and Lucas went out with Charlie and Kayleigh. Charlie was grouchy because Kayleigh was moving on to her convention on Sunday and she'd no longer have a hotel room for him to share. He'd spent three hours in a cyber cafe hunting for accommodation, but nothing he could afford was available this far into the summer season. He wasn't sure he had the cheek to try and invite himself on board *Seadancer.*

Kayleigh was equally glum at the prospect of him flying back to the UK.

Elle touched the back of Lucas's neck. The zing that shot down his spine got his attention. 'If I moved in with you, Charlie could have the guest cabin,' she mused nonchalantly.

Lucas glared at her in mock exasperation. 'I thought *I'd* get to tell Charlie.'

Charlie and Kayleigh's reciprocal grouchiness paused. Charlie looked from his brother to Elle and back again. 'Move in with …? Are you two … um?'

Elle made a contrite face at Lucas. 'Sorry. Please could you tell Charlie that yes, we are "um", but he can only have the cabin on condition that he doesn't tell anyone else. It's too—' She scrabbled for a word.

'Scary,' Lucas supplied. 'And certain people are going to demand a whole lot of explanations.'

'I'm not scared!' she protested stoutly. 'I just want to enjoy it as it is, for now.' Then she pulled a face. 'And try not to think about the explanations.'

Lucas pulled her close, hooking his hand comfortably around her waist. 'Let's go with enjoying it.' Because he sure as hell didn't want to get into the likely reaction of his parents. He'd leave a long fuse on that time bomb.

They celebrated with plentiful prosecco and were the butt of Charlie's and Kayleigh's teasing all evening. Lucas couldn't remember ever having a better time. Especially when the party broke up and he got to stroll home under a starry sky, take Elle to his – their – cabin and slowly undress her.

Finally, he fell asleep feeling as he assumed lottery winners must feel: floating a foot above the ground, hardly able to believe what had happened, wearing a grin that felt as if it might look stupid.

Equally euphoric was to wake with Elle beside him, her grin every bit as stupid as his own, the sunlight that streamed through the skylights turning her hair into molten gold. She shone like the Elle he first knew, the one whose eyes had blazed with indignation when he literally bowled her over, the one who had teased him when he'd asked for a date, as if she'd already understood that he always knew what he wanted and that it wouldn't work well for either of them if he got it too easily.

The Elle he'd fallen in love with.

On Tuesday, Joseph, Elle, Oscar and eight children who had managed to get their consent forms signed in time – including Carmelo – piled into a minibus that Joseph got cheaply from a local hire company, with Joseph driving.

Elle made certain to grab the vacant seat next to Carmelo, so that she could be sure not to have to sit with Oscar. Carmelo rewarded her with a huge grin.

With all the windows open, they made the twenty-minute drive from Gżira to St Julian's, pulling up at a gateway marked by a tall blue sign with 'Dive Meddi' dancing across it in yellow lettering, fizzing with bubbles. The noise the children made as they poured out of the minibus and down the pathway towards the pool had to be heard to be believed. Elle wasn't surprised to find a grinning Lucas already emerging from the Dive Meddi building to meet them.

'So who's for a Bubblemaker?' he demanded.

'Yes! Yes!' The volume of noise actually rose.

Vern ambled out and had to raise both his hands before they quietened enough for him to speak. 'One thing we all have to do very well on a Bubblemaker,' he said, 'is *listen*.' He pulled his ears out from the side of his head, making the children burst into giggles. 'So that means you need to be quiet when I, or any of the instructors or divemasters, ask you to be.'

He talked on, cracking jokes but getting over a lot of information, making certain that the children understood that they would be safe. Not only were Joseph and Vern to watch from the poolside but in the water would be Lucas, Brett, Polly – who Elle recognised as the driver of the green truck that sometimes came for Lucas – and Lars, a serious Swedish man. With so many observant eyes and trained bodies, Elle felt cocooned.

Then it was time to shuck off clothes to reveal swimming gear underneath. Carmelo's trunks and those of one bigger boy looked a lot like ordinary shorts, but it didn't seem to make any difference to anyone.

Elle had opted for her plain one-piece but she still didn't like the way that Oscar looked at her. And she was pretty certain it was no coincidence that her wetsuit, black with blue flashes, was the first that Lucas handed out, so that she could drag the unwilling neoprene up to cover her exposed flesh.

She'd never fought her way into a wetsuit before. It was like squashing her way into a onesie that was two sizes too small and ten times too thick. The thing seemed unwilling to have her inside it and she was out of breath by the time she managed to zip it up.

The time flew by as equipment was selected and tried on, and each person had the opportunity to see how it felt to breathe through a regulator, unfamiliar and cumbersome in the mouth. Buoyancy control devices were fitted, and Elle recognised child safeguarding at work as instructors and divemasters turned each child towards Joseph and Vern and provided a running commentary on what they were doing. 'I'm tightening the shoulder straps by pulling here. I'm fastening the BCD here, here and here.'

The first four children and Oscar were soon, under Polly and Brett's supervision, dipping their faces into the water to check that, yes, they really could still breathe through a regulator once it was submerged. Before long, all she could see of them was bubbles and heads moving under the surface as Polly got them all to kneel down and practice hand signals.

Carmelo had managed to get himself into Lars's group with Lucas and Elle. 'What will happen if I can't breathe underwater?' he demanded, as Lucas showed him how to adjust his mask so that none of his hair intruded and broke the seal.

'You will be able to. But if you couldn't, you'd just stand up and breathe normally. I won't let you go out of your depth.'

Carmelo didn't look quite convinced. 'Could I die?'

'No,' said Lucas, calmly. 'Because I'm here looking after you, and so are Lars and Elle.'

For Elle, it was a golden afternoon. She loved seeing Lucas doing his job. Calmly confident, making everything fun, yet always making sure the group he was helping felt safe and secure. The children, eyes excited behind their masks, mouths distended by their regulators, learned how to shuffle backwards in their fins, to control their buoyancy by letting air in or out of the BCD, and how to 'pop' their ears to equalise pressure – which didn't seem too big a problem in a few feet of water. They ended their fifty-minute session with a game of underwater frisbee, swishing around one another in the cool salty water like mermaids and mermen in their fins.

Elle, getting accustomed to her own Darth Vader-like underwater breathing noises, knelt on the matting at the bottom of the pool, waiting for the neon-pink frisbee to slow-motion-slice through the water in her direction. If things worked out with Lucas, she decided, as she flipped off her knees and caught the frisbee, she'd learn to dive. She pictured them together, encountering crabs and rays, and the shining fish like flitting light that she'd seen projected onto the screen at the Nicholas Centre.

Daring to even think that she might stay with Lucas temporarily deprived her muscles of all function and she let the frisbee game go on without her. Lucas put himself in her eyeline and circled his finger and thumb to signal to her, *Are you OK?*

She returned the signal to reassure him that she was

fine. In fact, she did it with both hands to show that she was bloody marvellous.

The feeling extended to when the Bubblemaker session was over, tanks turned off, equipment rinsed and hung to dry. Vern brought out ice lollies and bottles of cold water while the children wrapped themselves in towels to talk about their Bubblemaker session, to explain how they'd felt and what they'd liked or disliked. How what they'd experienced had matched up to their expectations. Every child was engaged, the outlines of masks still showing on beaming faces as their laughter rang out in the late afternoon sun.

Elle felt incredibly good to be alive, doing something worthwhile with people who would put in a couple of extra hours to give eight kids a treat. Even Oscar, who, in the presence of Lucas, wasn't hanging around Elle but was paying attention to Polly.

Polly was reacting to his heavy-handed pursuit with smiles, possibly pleased to find a man larger than herself.

Elle turned her attention to Lucas, who looked appealing in dark red swimming trunks. She was glad they'd agreed not to look ahead, for now. Just to value this amazing time, when they'd each left their old lives behind and, by luck, coincidence and the meddling of Simon, found each other again.

Chapter Twenty-Four

Back on board the *Shady Lady* when the children had been dropped safely off, Elle couldn't stop yawning as she washed salad in the galley. It was as if her first taste of scuba, albeit in five feet of water, had worn her out. Or it could be that her nights had been pretty busy, recently. Whichever, she felt relaxed and happy just to know that Lucas was somewhere on the boat.

Kayleigh was taking time out from her convention to come over from Qawra for dinner and Charlie had rushed off to wait where her bus would stop on the other side of the gardens. He'd moved onto the *Shady Lady* on Sunday, content now that he could snatch an occasional few hours with Kayleigh, and knowing they could squeeze in another four or five days in Malta after the convention wound up and before Kayleigh would have to return to the UK and work.

Charlie's job was looking dicey as insurance problems were making it unclear whether it would be possible for the restaurant to reopen. When he returned home it might be to join the unemployment queue, so he was planning to maximise opportunities for fun in the meantime.

Lucas emerged from the cabin, slotted himself behind Elle and nuzzled her neck.

'You'll make dinner late,' she complained, even while rubbing herself against him.

He gave a *hmmmmm* deep in his throat and brushed a kiss into the crook of her shoulder. 'How can salad be late?'

She shivered, trying to concentrate on rinsing glowing red tomatoes. 'Did Charlie buy the wine?'

'No idea.' He dipped a finger into her bowl of cold water and then touched it to her cleavage.

She let her head fall back as the moisture trailed between her breasts. 'You could check.' The droplet trickled down into her bra. She closed her eyes at the tiny flare of pleasure. 'You're getting me all wet.'

He laughed. 'Nice thought.' Reluctantly, he released her with a gentle bite at the spot just below her ear and she went on to washing lettuce as he investigated the drink stocks and began to ferry a selection up to the flybridge.

Charlie and Kayleigh arrived, Charlie more freckled than ever, Kayleigh's nose pink from the sun, and the four made a leisurely meal in the last of the day's sunshine, high enough up to catch the breeze. The boat rocked on the swell, a sensation that Elle had finally become inured to, as they polished off goats' cheese and ħobż along with their salad. Red wine and white stood on the table and soon a couple of empty bottles were languishing in the sink of the wet bar.

Lucas's hand rested warm and familiar on Elle's thigh as the dusk rolled swiftly into darkness.

To Kayleigh, this was still enough of a novelty to marvel over. 'Look at you two! It's kind of weird and dead right, both at the same time.' She sipped from her glass of red wine and let her cheek rest on Charlie's shoulder. 'So tell me about before, how you met and everything.'

Elle was feeling drowsy, now, not only tired but lulled by the boat and relaxed by a respectable quantity of white wine. 'These guys were having some kind of race. It was a stag do and they were racing from one bar to another.'

'The last one there had to buy the next round,' Lucas supplied.

'We were free running,' put in Charlie.

Elle laughed. 'Free running! Isn't that the thing where you race over balconies and run up walls and roofs? What I saw from Lucas was more falling over rubbish bins.'

'A big rubbish bin,' Lucas pointed out.

'Free-falling more than free running, then.' Kayleigh patted Charlie's head.

Charlie looked obstinate. 'It was free running, wasn't it Lucas?'

Lucas's fingers traced idle circles on Elle's skin. The dress she was wearing wasn't long and he'd inched the hem further up her leg so that now his fingertips were leaving delicious trails of goosebumps in their wake. 'I don't remember leaping over balconies.'

'Maybe not balconies, but we were doing rail flow on those railings beside the steps in the pedestrian centre.'

Slipping down further in his seat, Lucas laughed. 'I do remember vaguely that you got into video tutorials about that kind of stuff. I don't think I even know what rail flow is.'

'But I remember showing you how to sit and spin.' Charlie was obviously intent that Lucas should confirm his memory of events. 'You get your inside hand on the rail, swing with your inside leg, power yourself up and over so that your legs are over the other side for a second. Then you change hands and keep your legs going to complete the circle, and you end up on the side you started.'

'I think I remember you doing that.' Lucas sounded as if he was trying to humour his little brother.

'It was like this,' said Charlie, leaping up, tripping over himself, making Kayleigh laugh. Undeterred, he grabbed on to the low guardrail that encircled the flybridge, swung back a leg and looped it up and over the rail; the other leg followed on as he scissored it over the drop between the *Shady Lady* and *Fallen Star*. A quick change of hand, another scissoring of his legs and Charlie was standing back on the deck of the flybridge.

'Cool!' breathed Kayleigh.

But Lucas was definitely unimpressed. 'Charlie! Save it for a rail that isn't over a ten-foot drop into water.'

'Chill, Luke-arse, it's easy. Left hand, left leg, right leg, right hand, left leg, right leg.' Charlie demonstrated the move again, scissoring his long legs in a serious of flowing movements, over-over, twist, over-over, his boyish grin wide as Kayleigh burst into applause.

'Charlie, you've had a lot to drink,' began Elle.

'Don't be an idiot.' Lucas started to get to his feet.

Charlie swung his left leg back for impetus and began the move for a third time. The left hand, left leg, right leg sequence went to plan. But something happened. Whether he hesitated or his hand caught on the gleaming chrome rail, Elle wasn't sure. But somehow Charlie's weight shifted and instead of revolving neatly in one place in the air, he wobbled and began to tip forward. His left hand released the guardrail on schedule but the catching hand, his right, flailed uselessly, inches adrift from its target.

For an agonised instant, Charlie hung in thin air

He disappeared into the darkness with a yell. *Crash*! A splash. Then silence.

'You *fuckhead*,' bellowed Lucas. He wasted no time peering over the rail but raced to the steps, scrambling and sliding his way down, shouting over his shoulder, 'Get ready to phone the emergency services! We'll probably need an ambulance.'

Where was her phone? Their cabin. Elle had to force herself to start moving in Lucas's wake but once down the steps her legs wanted to run, to move as fast as they possibly could. She flew through the saloon, jumped down the steps, bolted into the cabin and swooped on her phone. Spinning to reverse her route, she sprinted to the gangplank and onto the quayside. 'Lucas?' She couldn't see him but could hear splashing from the black water. '*Lucas!*'

He didn't answer.

Her heart thumped into the pit of her stomach.

She began to dial 999 but then stopped. She wasn't in the UK and 999 wouldn't work. What was the emergency services number in Malta? Joseph had ensured that she knew it but the shock of seeing Charlie vanishing helplessly overboard, and now Lucas out there battling the dark water, had wiped her memory. Whirling, she darted towards a Maltese woman who was approaching the line of cars on the marina access road. 'Please, what's the phone number for the ambulance?'

The woman put her hand to her heart and took a step back, as if fearful that Elle intended to mug her.

'Please, I can't remember the number!'

The woman frowned, probably mentally translating. 'Er, one, one and two.'

'Yes, 112!' Elle stabbed at the buttons. In seconds a voice answered in Maltese. 'Ambulance!' she shouted. Instantly, the operative switched to English but Elle didn't wait to hear the rest: she shoved the phone at the woman. 'My friend has fallen off a boat. Please make them come quickly. He's in the water and I have to see if I can help.'

Without waiting to see if the woman minded her services being commandeered, Elle pelted back to the edge of the quay. The sea between the *Shady Lady* and *Fallen Star* was unlit, but, with a heart thud, she thought she could see a hand trying to get a grip on one of the boat's white fenders. Relief flooded through her when she realised that she could hear his voice, too, low and indistinct, but with calm and authority. 'Someone's getting help, Lucas,' she shouted, hoping he'd be able to hear.

Kayleigh finally caught up with Elle, trembling her way over the gangplank like an old woman. 'Oh my God. Oh my God. Oh my God, Charlie.'

From the shadowed water came a groan like that of an arthritic old dog.

'What should I do, Lucas?' Elle shouted, trying to keep panic from her voice. 'Is he hurt? I called the emergency services and a lady's giving them the details.'

But Lucas didn't waste energy on a reply. The sound of his swimming neared slightly and Elle, with a sickening roll of her stomach, realised he was hampered by lack of space between the two hulls, grabbing at fenders and saving his breath for saving his brother. What she'd considered small movements of the boats on the swell suddenly seemed like looming threats, as if the boats might jostle together and crush Lucas and Charlie at any moment.

Recovering her faculties, she swung around. The quayside was a busy area. There must be help nearby.

A family strolled towards her from the gardens, several men watched the television at the kiosk. She sucked in all the breath she could muster. 'HELP US!' she bellowed with the full force of her lungs. 'A MAN IS HURT AND IN THE WATER AND WE NEED HELP GETTING HIM OUT.'

She was vaguely aware of people beginning to run from the kiosk and from other boats. The lady with Elle's phone spoke more rapidly to the unseen operative in Maltese, no doubt reporting what she saw.

As men began to reach the scene, Lucas finally came

into sight, on his back in the traditional lifesaving position, swimming with one arm and towing Charlie along, moving slowly but steadily in the confined space.

Elle croaked, 'We've got help to get him out of the water.' Then she found herself surrounded by men, jostling for position, giving instructions, making suggestions, some in Maltese but also in English. 'Is he breathing? Shouldn't you be giving him air?'

Lucas didn't relinquish control. He trod water as he caught his breath, keeping Charlie's head above water while he assessed the crowd on the shore. 'He wasn't under long but he's unconscious and he's banged his head so I'm not taking any chances with his spine. Who's on to the emergency services? Tell them we need an ambulance. Tell them that he's weak and barely responsive. He's received a head injury. No way of telling about spine. He's breathing without help.'

'Yes, yes, I tell them,' called the woman with the phone.

'In these temperatures he's not going to get hypothermia in the next few minutes, even if he's in shock, so I want to stabilise his spine before we get him out. I need something flat and firm to put under him.'

'Inflated air bed?' suggested someone, doubtfully. 'I've got one on deck.'

'Not rigid enough.' Lucas was completely calm but he had to squeeze out words as his breathing allowed. 'What about a plastic sunbed? Anyone got one of those on board?'

'I'll get one!' a man's voice called from the back of what was rapidly becoming a crowd.

While he rushed off, Lucas looked at the boats looming above him. 'Can someone get more fenders and wedge them between these two and the side so we don't get crushed?'

'OK. Will do!'

Over the pounding of her blood in her ears, Elle was aware of other footsteps hurrying away. She kept her eyes fixed on Lucas as if she could keep him safely at the surface by sheer willpower. He was treading water mechanically and economically, totally in control of the emergency, assessing what was going on around him, pausing to look into his brother's face, observing as fenders were wedged in to keep the *Shady Lady* and *Fallen Star* from sashaying suddenly up to the quay.

In a minute, two men bustled up with a white plastic lounger. 'Do you need us to snap the legs off?'

'No time.' Lucas was beginning to sound strained. 'I'll need help in the water to get him on it. Any of you guys strong swimmers?'

There were steps down from the quay nearby and three men got themselves briskly into the water, swimming along to join Lucas. He looked up at Elle. 'If I float him closer, can you get his head? Keep it immobile.'

'Got it.' Elle lay on the concrete and stretched down, just able to lace her hands under Charlie's head, his hair brushing against her fingers, while the others arranged themselves to support his body. The sunbed was passed down carefully, Lucas making the men turn it so that the fixed part, normally under the legs, would be under Charlie's head. A man knelt beside Elle to guide the bed, angling it ready to slide it under the surface.

Lucas took over supporting Charlie's head, his fingers covering Elle's. 'Elle, can you get some sheets so we've something to cover him with when we get him out?'

'Right.' Elle gently slid her hands free before leaping up to do as directed. Reaching the guest cabin, she pulled the sheets off Charlie's bunk and bundled them up in her arms, stumbling up the steps and out to the cockpit to return to the tense scene outside.

'OK. You two'—Lucas glanced at the men on the other side of Charlie—'you stay still and support him.' He transferred his gaze to the other man on the same side of Charlie as Lucas. 'You move down to his feet.' His gaze shifted to Elle. 'Get ready to take his head again.'

'Right.' Her eyes burned with sudden tears as she looked down into Charlie's face. Even under the marina lights he was paler than she'd ever seen anybody in her life.

Lucas raised his voice to the guys still on shore. 'Can two or three of you get in and wrangle the sunbed under the water? If you can level it out, we can just float him over onto it.' He gave every word emphasis. 'We need to be steady, calm and slow, OK? Steady, calm and slow.'

The manoeuvre was accomplished with no fuss. It was as if Charlie had turned into a parcel of a million eggs and the goal was to execute the task without breaking a single one. In a pleasingly short time, Charlie, still unconscious, was lying flat on the sunbed in the water.

Lucas looked around at those who had somehow become his team. His hair was plastered to his head and hanging in his eyes. 'OK, let's get him out. We need to lift the bed level with the quay and then slide it onto the shore without letting Charlie slide off. It's going to be hard work for those in the water. Everyone OK?' He waited while the two men who had held the bed in the water got out onto the quay and Elle scrambled out of their way so that they could reach down to receive the nearest two corners.

'Slowly,' Lucas gasped, treading water hard. 'Both ends together, keep it level. OK? Ready? Three, two, one, *lift*. Steady, steady.' The four in the water lifted, their arms going above their heads as they trod water and managed to pop the end of the white plastic bed on the lip of the quay. That accomplished, there were many willing hands to ease the makeshift stretcher further along. In seconds, Charlie's bed was on solid ground and the hands turned to help Lucas and the rest of the team out of the dark water.

Lucas went straight to kneel beside his brother. Wanting to blubber with relief that Lucas was safe, Elle had to force herself not to launch herself at him in joy that he hadn't been crushed between the hulls and pride at his heroics. Instead, she kept her gaze glued to Charlie, whose eyelids had begun to flutter.

Instantly, Lucas frowned. 'Elle, can you hold his head again? I don't want him to shake it if he begins to come round.'

Cautiously, Elle crouched down at the crown of Charlie's head and placed her palms gently over the sides of his face. His skin felt colder to the touch in the air than it had in the water. Quashing her own feelings, she gave Lucas what she hoped was a reassuring smile. 'Got him.'

Lucas held her gaze for a moment, as if drawing strength. But then his focus flipped back to his brother as a siren began to wail somewhere over the ridge between them and Msida. 'We're going to get you to hospital, Charlie. The ambulance should be here in a minute.

'Great job everyone.' Lucas sounded just as if he were on a training course, reassuring his subject in case he could hear and then communicating with his team. He stooped to press his ear against his brother's chest. 'Heartbeat's faint but OK. I want to keep him warm so he doesn't go into shock. O_2 would be great but we don't carry it on the boat.'

His gaze travelled methodically along his brother's arms, shoulders and abdomen. When he moved down to

Charlie's right leg, he stopped. 'Broken, I think.' Careful not to cause unnecessary pain, he touched the foot. 'But he's got a foot pulse so the blood's getting round.'

'What about the recovery position?' someone called out.

Lucas shook his head. 'I don't want to take any chances with a broken leg and I don't know about his spine. He's breathing so I'm going to leave him on his back, but I could do with something to put under his good leg to raise it.' One of the fenders that had been wedged between *Fallen Star* and the quay appeared magically next to Lucas; he propped up Charlie's undamaged leg and covered him with the sheets Elle had fetched.

Then the ambulance was nosing its way onto the quay. Soon, green-clad paramedics were kneeling beside Charlie, speaking reassuringly, listening as Lucas gave them a situation report, nodding that they understood.

Elle made way for the professionals and edged back out of the circle of guardian angels around Charlie.

Only once the handover was complete did Lucas allow himself to sit back on his heels. The hand he passed over his face began to shake as he reverted from rescuer to brother and exhaustion etched itself on his face. Kayleigh tottered up to crouch beside him; Lucas slid a comforting arm around her and she sobbed softly into his shoulder.

As the paramedics applied a neck brace and prepared to transfer him to a backboard, Charlie began to move his hands weakly. Immediately, Lucas leaned over and spoke to him and Charlie was quiet again.

Most of the crowd was silent, now, standing back, giving the medics room to work. Elle hovered. It was hard to yearn to be of use but know that keeping out of the way was the most helpful thing she could do. She ached to go to Lucas but, as was only right, his attention was all on Charlie.

When, a few minutes later, the paramedics packed up their gear with practised economy of movement and prepared to transfer their patient to the ambulance, Lucas heaved himself to his feet and helped Kayleigh to hers. Elle realised that they intended to go in the ambulance with Charlie. It made sense, as neither of them had a car on the island.

Seeing something useful she could accomplish, she dashed back into the boat, through the saloon and into the cabin, gathering up dry clothes for Lucas and stuffing them in a bag with a towel so that once he got to the hospital he wouldn't be stuck in wet things. She snatched up his wallet from the bedside and crammed that in, too.

She arrived back on the shore on legs that were beginning to feel as if they belonged to someone else, just as Charlie was slipped smoothly into the ambulance like a precious parcel onto a shelf. Kayleigh hovered anxiously and Lucas was looking around, frowning. His expression relaxed as he saw Elle return.

She shoved the bag at him. 'Dry clothes and your wallet.'

'Fantastic.' He gathered her up against him in a hard hug, heedless of the wet, cold clothes that pressed between them. 'Thanks.' There was a break in his voice.

'You were amazing. You saved his life.' Elle wanted to ask if he thought Charlie would be all right but Lucas looked gaunt and dazed. There was no point asking him questions to which he was no doubt terrified of the answers. She wanted to stay with him and cuddle close, reassure him, reassure herself that he was safe. But there was barely room in the emergency vehicle for Lucas and

Kayleigh, so she just pressed a kiss to his mouth and released him. He almost staggered as he climbed into the ambulance. But he made it to a pull-down seat, the doors were shut and the vehicle eased away.

In the hush that followed, Elle found she was shaking. Subdued activity resumed around her. Fenders and the sunbed were retrieved by the helpful boat owners, and the lovely Maltese lady placed Elle's phone back into her hand.

'Thank you, th-thank you everybody who helped,' Elle managed, voice shaking, but her thanks were waved away as men in wet clothes prepared to move off.

'Will you be all right?' another woman asked. She seemed to be with the man with the sunbed.

'I'm fine.' She couldn't think about herself right now. All she could think about was Charlie's pallor and the apprehension in Lucas's face.

But, wow. Lucas had turned into a hero right before her eyes. Staying calm. Doing what had to be done. *Knowing* what had to be done. Keeping control of the situation. Not letting his feelings intrude until he was sure someone competent was there to take over. She was so proud of him she could burst.

Then Loz and Davie came half-running up the quay. Loz's eyes were huge. 'Elle? We came home and saw an ambulance leaving. What's happened?'

That's when Elle felt her face begin to crumple.

Loz instantly dragged her into a cushiony, comforting embrace. 'Come on, sweetie. Let's get a cup of tea or something.'

Elle didn't think she'd ever been so glad of a hug. She let herself be guided across the gangplank and into the saloon, barely conscious of the dampness of her clothes where they'd been pressed against Lucas. Gulping back tears, she poured out the story of how Charlie had taken on gravity and lost.

Davie made tea while Loz patted Elle's arm, exclaiming and clucking.

Davie had just brought the hot drinks up into the saloon when a phone began to ring.

Elle looked around. 'That's Lucas's ringtone.' She saw the handset beside a window, screen alight, and went to pick it up. Then she halted.

The name of the caller, flashing on Lucas's phone in white, portentous letters, was *Mum*.

Fiona.

Heart plummeting, Elle let the phone ring twice more. Fiona couldn't know what had happened. She was probably just calling to chat.

Elle didn't have to answer. Lucas would ring with news of Charlie as soon as he was able. Elle could text Kayleigh, who probably had her phone in her bag, and Lucas could use Kayleigh's phone to ring home.

But what if that were to take Lucas away from Charlie? Suppose that was the moment that Lucas should be signing a consent form or listening to important information?

The phone rang again.

Fiona had the right to know what had happened. Elle forced her own feelings aside and steeled herself to pick up. 'Hello,' she said, nervously. 'This is Lucas's phone. He's not here. Is that—' She swallowed. 'Is that M-Mrs Rose?'

Fiona's self-confident voice hadn't changed at all. 'Yes, hello. Will Lucas be long?' And then, curiously. 'I'm sorry, you are—?'

'Elle,' said Elle, apprehensively.

Silence.

'Mrs Rose, I only answered Lucas's phone because I have to tell you—'

'Elle *Jamieson*?' Fiona's voice had acquired several degrees of frost. Her lawyer's voice, Elle used to call it.

'Yes.' Elle closed her eyes at the revulsion in the voice of the woman who once could have been her mother-in-law. Obviously, neither Simon, Lucas nor Charlie had told Fiona that Elle was on the boat. She heard Geoffrey's raised voice in the background asking a question that sounded like: 'What about Elle Jamieson?'

Elle rushed on. 'I'm living in Malta for the summer. Look, M-Mrs Rose, I'm afraid there's been an accident.'

Fiona snapped to attention. 'Lucas?'

'No, it's Charlie. He fell off the top of the boat and into the sea. Lucas got him straight to the surface but he'd hit his head on the boat moored alongside. The *Fallen Star*,' she added, inconsequentially. With pauses for Fiona to relay information to Geoffrey, Elle recounted the facts, conscious of Loz and Davie exchanging uneasy glances as if not sure whether to stay. 'I really hope he's not too badly hurt,' Elle ended, miserably, as if the whole situation were her fault. 'I don't have more information. The ambulance only left about fifteen minutes ago.'

'What's the name of the hospital?' Fiona's voice shook slightly.

'Um, I'll try and find out.' Elle turned questioningly to Loz and Davie. 'Do you know which hospital it'll be?'

'Mater Dei, in Msida,' said Loz. 'That's where A & E is. Would you like me to give the details?'

'Please – it's Lucas's mother. Fiona Rose.' Glad to get rid of the damned phone, and Fiona, Elle sank down onto the seat, sitting on her hands to stop them shaking, not sure whether she was shivering in reaction to Charlie's accident or the slight dampness in her clothes. Or to the dislike in Fiona's voice.

Loz talked for a couple of minutes, reassuring Fiona that Mater Dei was a nice up-to-date facility and that Charlie would be well looked after. Elle had just calmed her breathing when Loz held the phone back out to her. 'Mrs Rose wants to talk to you again.'

Elle wanted to shriek, '*No!*' But, with a deep breath, she took the handset and said, 'This is Elle.'

Fiona had rediscovered her lawyer's voice, icy and authoritative. 'Would you mind enlightening me as to how you came to be on Simon's boat this evening?'

Elle's breathing picked up again. She could say, 'Yes, I do mind, actually,' and end the call. Or end the call without saying a thing. There was no law that held her answerable to Mrs Fiona Rose.

But then she thought that if by any chance, by any miracle, there was a prospect of Elle and Lucas having some kind of future together, rubbing Fiona up the wrong way was probably not politic. Lucas came with family attached.

She might as well own up to the awful crime of coming back into Lucas's orbit. She moistened her lips. 'I'm working and volunteering in Malta for the summer. Simon and I have remained friends and he said I could live on the *Shady Lady*.'

'But Simon said that Lucas could live on the *Shady Lady*.'

'Yes,' Elle acknowledged. 'I didn't know Lucas would be here when I arrived. And he didn't know I would be coming.'

Fiona drew in an audible breath. 'Bloody Simon! And

you stayed? Even though— Even after everything that happened?'

Elle felt like a defendant having her past record divulged in court. 'Yes. I couldn't do much else, financially.'

'I see.' Fiona's voice was stiff with disapproval. 'Right. Well, I need hardly tell you that Geoffrey and I will be travelling to Malta as soon as it can be arranged.'

'Right,' said Elle, numbly, fighting down the urge to exclaim, '*Oh shit!*' But of course Fiona and Geoffrey would rush out to the island to be with Charlie. They were loving parents. Their sons meant everything to them. Lucky sons.

She returned her focus to the moment. 'Kayleigh's with Lucas at the hospital. I'll text her to tell him about this call. Or do you want Kayleigh's number so that you can text her yourself?'

'I have Kayleigh's number.'

'Of course.' Because Kayleigh was Charlie's girlfriend. Dur. Kayleigh had never discussed Charlie and Lucas's parents with Elle. Maybe Kayleigh had been briefed that relations between Elle and the senior Roses had not been cordial. 'I-I'll leave you to make your arrangements, then.' She hesitated. With anyone else, Elle would have extended a friendly helping hand, so she really ought to do the same for Fiona. 'Would you like my number in case I can do anything?' she began. 'I might be able to—'

'I'm sure we'll manage.'

The old anger fired suddenly in Elle's breast. 'Goodnight, then.' She ended the call without giving Fiona any further opportunity for verbal icicles. For several long seconds she stared at the phone, half-scared Fiona might ring back to get the last word.

Instead, up on the flybridge, a new ring tone began to

shrill into the night air. Elle looked up and winced. 'That's Kayleigh's phone. She must have left it up on the flybridge. I'd better—'

Davie jumped up. 'I'll get it.' In a minute he returned and Elle was able to read 1 missed call Fiona on it.

She groaned. 'Great. I assumed Kayleigh's phone would be in her bag. Now I've fed Lucas's mother duff information, too.'

Loz cleared her throat. 'Not best friends with Lucas's folks?'

Elle tried to laugh but it stuck in her throat. 'No.' She dropped her chin on her hand. 'You know you said I could stay on *Seadancer* if I needed to? I think I probably need to.'

Chapter Twenty-Five

After seeing Kayleigh back to her hotel in Qawra and paying a pretty hefty taxi fare, Lucas arrived at the *Shady Lady* in the morning at roughly the time he should have been leaving for Dive Meddi. He would have to ring Vern, soon.

He felt as if he'd run a marathon. His legs, his everything, ached. His head buzzed with the spaced-out gritty-eyed feeling that came from lack of sleep. His hair was thick and tangled with dried salt water and his scalp itched under the morning sun.

His heart lifted to see that the *Shady Lady*'s aft door stood open, meaning Elle hadn't left to go up to the centre. He thought she'd said yesterday that this morning she was due to run some kind of workshop for the younger kids, but time seemed to have looped a bit in his memory in the stress of Charlie's accident. Was it only last night? It felt like a week ago.

Yet the memory of fishing Charlie up to the surface and towing him between boats that shifted like enormous spooked horses was fresh enough to make him feel queasy.

In a haze of fatigue, he trudged over the gangplank and into the saloon. He paused by the helmsman's chair, put down his bag of last night's wet clothes, listened, and caught the sound of a door closing. Heart lifting, he followed the sound, treading softly down the steps, past the galley, all spick and span. He paused.

Inside the cabin, Elle had a suitcase open on the bed and was folding into it her clothes, which had only recently taken up residence in the stowage areas of his cabin.

'What the fuck?' He could hear raw disbelief in his voice.

Elle swung around, dropped the dress she'd been holding and flew across the room to throw her arms around him. She smelled of shower gel and freshly washed hair. 'Are you all right? How's Charlie?'

'He got away with severe concussion and a broken leg. They're keeping him in. What's with the suitcase?' He didn't lift his arms to hug her back. Just stared at the scene over her shoulder. He'd surprised Elle packing. Again.

'No spine damage? Fantastic!' She heaved a huge, theatrical sigh of relief. 'Come and sit down.' She tried to take his hand to usher him along. 'Shall I get you coffee or something? Have you eaten? Or do you want to sleep first?'

He made himself immovable. 'First,' he returned, implacably. 'I want to know why you're packing.'

She took a deep breath and pushed back her hair. Shadows darkened the skin beneath her eyes but she smiled. 'Your parents are coming out to Malta. Loz says I can move onto *Seadancer*; then they won't have the nightmare of trying to find a hotel room in high season on top of worrying about Charlie, will they? They'll want to stay here, anyway. It's your dad's brother's boat.' She wasn't looking at him properly. He felt as if she were looking at the space between his eyes instead of into them.

He put up both his hands. 'Whoa. My parents are coming out here? How do you know?'

'Didn't they ring the hospital last night?'

He forced his muzzy brain to focus. 'Why would they? Did you phone them or something?'

Dismay fleeted across her face. 'Your mum called your phone and I thought I'd better answer. I told her about

Charlie because— because it would have been odd not to, wouldn't it? I think they tried to ring Kayleigh afterwards but she'd left her phone on the flybridge.' Her pale brows were still drawn down. 'Have I done the wrong thing? Isn't Charlie going to be all right? Do you need to prepare them for bad news?'

Relief began to trickle through him, relaxing his limbs, which, he suddenly realised, had tensed almost painfully when he'd seen that suitcase. He reached and pulled her against him, hoping he didn't smell too much of hospitals. 'Sorry. I haven't slept. My brain's not functioning. I came in here and saw you packing—' He stroked the silken fall of her hair.

She pulled back to look into his face, properly this time, comprehension in her eyes. 'Oh. Weird stuff from the past?'

He laughed. 'Sorry. Yes. How about we start this conversation again? Charlie is going to be OK. He has deep concussion and a broken leg but apart from throwing up and sleeping a lot, he's returning to his old self. I don't want to eat, I can't sleep until I've done some things, but coffee would be fantastic. Your turn.'

Her body shifted slightly as she relaxed against him, turning her head so that her cheek fitted comfortably against his collarbone. 'Your mum rang your phone. I told them what had happened; Loz and Davie had turned up just as the ambulance left and Loz gave your mum the information about the hospital. Your parents are coming straight over so I'm vacating to give them room.'

'Right.' He tried to digest the information, aware of the thrust of her breasts against him, that his hands had naturally come to rest on the curve of her buttocks. 'And you're not at Nicholas Centre because …?'

'Because I wanted to wait for you and I'm moving my stuff. I called Joseph and he's postponed my workshop.'

'I need to make calls. My parents and Vern.' He still didn't move, just holding her against him, enjoying the softness. But he couldn't hold back a question. 'How did talking to Mum go?'

Her muscles tensed. 'OK.'

'OK?'

'Yes. OK.'

If he hadn't been so damn tired he would have tried to encourage more information out of her than that. 'Don't go,' he murmured.

'I have to. You know how hard it will be for your parents to find a decent hotel at this time of the year. All the last-minute holiday companies will have booked everything up.'

'Then I'll ask Loz if I can come with you and bunk on board *Seadancer*.'

She sighed, her breath hot against him. 'Look – let's not upset your parents.'

Shit. Guilt filtered through the small part of his brain that was still doing its job. She was right. It was going to be tricky enough to manage the Elle/parents relationship without putting their backs up. He pressed his lips against her hair. 'I bet Mum was pretty surprised when you picked up the phone.'

A small silence. 'Little bit.'

He laughed at her unconvincing attempt at nonchalance. 'Don't worry about my parents this time, all right? I'll talk to them and they'll behave.'

'Great,' she said, so brightly that he knew she didn't believe he could do it. Mentally, he cursed himself for not supporting her as he should have in the past.

But this time it would be no problem. He was aware and he was in control. He yawned, hugely. 'There's nothing my parents can say to change things. I hadn't told them about us because you said you just wanted to enjoy what's happening and let the future take care of itself, and that's fine. So long as you know that I see my future with you in it.'

She didn't reply. But her embrace tightened.

Elle set the coffee machine going in the galley while Lucas retrieved his phone from the saloon. Elle had thoughtfully plugged it in to charge. Kayleigh's phone was lying next to it.

'I'll start moving my stuff over while you call your parents,' she said.

'You don't have to find an excuse to give me privacy. I'm not going to say anything I don't want you to hear.' He dropped down at the dinette.

'It's not an excuse. It has to be done. The coffee will be ready in a few minutes.' She vanished into the cabin and reappeared with two cases, one pink and one with the union flag on it.

He had a sudden vivid memory of her lining them up on the quay on the day she arrived, using them as a barrier, glaring at him from behind it. 'I'll carry them for you.'

'They have wheels. Make your phone call.' She gave him a wide smile and dragged the suitcases rapidly across the saloon and out of the door.

The boat dipped slightly as she swung each suitcase across the gap between bathing platform and quay. After a moment he heard the rumbling of the hard plastic wheels along the concrete.

He shook his head. This was not the way he would have chosen to cement Elle back into his life. Her tension every time the subject of his mother came up was palpable. He was going to have to make that stop.

He pressed the button on top of his iPhone and saw eight missed calls from his mother. There were also a couple of texts. The first, also from his mother, said: Ring me asap. Dad and I are making arrangements to fly to Malta. I spoke to the hospital and they said Charlie's in no danger but we're coming anyway. I asked the hospital to ask you to ring me but you haven't and Kayleigh's and Charlie's phones go straight to voicemail. Are you OK? Mum xxx PS Surprised to find myself speaking to Elle on your phone.

Charlie's phone had been in his pocket when he fell into the water, so its life was over, and Lucas already knew that Kayleigh had left her phone on the *Shady Lady* in the confusion after Charlie's idiocy.

The second text message said: You have two voicemail messages. When he dialled in, his mother's even tones told him that they were en route already, their flight number and an ETA of just after 1 p.m. Malta time. He pressed a button on the phone to check the time. They must already be in the air.

Pushing aside his desperation for sleep, he sent a text for his mother to pick up when she landed. I'll meet your flight. Charlie's going to be OK.

The next message was from a ruffled-sounding Vern. 'So, what's up, Lucas? Why the no-show?'

He called straight back. 'Really sorry, Vern. My brother had an accident and I've been at the hospital all night.'

Immediately, Vern's attitude changed and he demanded details. 'Good job from you,' he concluded. 'I'll work round it, mate. See you tomorrow?'

'I'll let you know, but I think so.'

Then he texted Elle: Calls made. Parents arriving early pm

and he went to throw off his clothes and get himself under the shower for a couple of minutes before crashing onto the bed. Before he could close his eyes, he set his phone alarm for noon. A moment later he heard someone coming on board and soon Elle stole into the cabin.

He held out an arm. 'Come to bed.'

Her eyes sparkled. 'You need to sleep.'

'Give me a break, Elle,' he groaned. 'I'm going to sleep. I just want to hold you for a minute.'

She arrived on the mattress beside him with a bounce, warm, soft, brushing kisses on his shoulder and his jaw. 'Lower,' he suggested.

'You're supposed to be going to sleep. By the way, Joseph says he'll take you to fetch your parents. If they want to go straight to the hospital he'll drop you all and then bring their bags here. You're to ring him half an hour before you want to leave.'

He settled her more firmly against him, stroking the roundness of her bottom through her shorts. 'That's really kind of him. It'll save me a lot of messing around with taxis.'

'So everything's taken care of and you can sleep.'

'Right.' And he let sleep have him.

Later, when his alarm went off it took him several moments to locate his phone and switch off the alert. But only an instant to realise that Elle had gone.

Picking up his parents went without a hitch. They swept into the gleaming arrivals hall towing cabin baggage suitcases, Fiona's short salt-and-pepper hair neatly styled, Geoffrey wearing an open-necked shirt. They were visibly relieved to be introduced to Joseph and find that he was to transport them to their erring younger son.

'It was Elle who arranged it,' Lucas pointed out as they shook Joseph's hand.

Joseph drove them past palm trees and the pink and white oleander that lined the busy roads as Lucas filled his parents in about the accident. 'Elle played a pivotal role. While I went to Charlie, she shot along the quay shouting for help. Sometimes, people just freeze, or they scream incoherently. But she made herself loud and accurate, told people exactly what had happened and that we needed help. Without help I wouldn't have been able to get Charlie onto a makeshift backboard and out of the water.'

'All because Charlie was showing off.' Fiona shuddered. 'Thank God you were there, darling.'

Lucas contented himself with a diplomatic 'All's well that ends well.' The huge bollocking he had saved up for Charlie could wait until his little brother was well enough to leave hospital. That's if there was anything left of Charlie after Fiona had had her say. He tried not to yawn as the sun beat down on him through the glass of the car.

Joseph dropped them at Mater Dei, a large modern building with a lot of blue-green glass. Charlie had been moved out of the emergency admissions ward, where Lucas had left him earlier that morning, and into an orthopaedic ward on the third floor. As it wasn't currently visiting hours they had to explain about Fiona and Geoffrey having only just arrived in the country; then they were allowed to visit Charlie if they promised to be quick and quiet.

Charlie woke as they arrived.

Lucas was shocked by the black eye that had doubled in magnitude since that morning and seemed to be smeared halfway across Charlie's cheek. Around this luridness, his freckles stood out against his pallor. But the big grin was reassuring and, after a few words, Lucas went to wait in the corridor to allow his parents time with their son. Fiona would need to give him a good scolding and then cry all over him.

In view of stern notices on the walls about mobile phone usage, Lucas snuck off into the Gents' and texted to Elle, All OK? xxx before taking up station again in the corridor, trying not to give in to the fuzzy arms of fatigue.

It wasn't long before Fiona and Geoffrey reappeared, leaving Charlie to sleep now they'd assured themselves that he'd got off lightly from what Geoffrey referred to as 'his bloody stupidity'. They traversed the corridors to an exit where they could call a taxi.

As they waited in the shade of the building for the car to arrive, Lucas felt his pocket vibrate. A text from Elle. All OK. I'm at the centre. He wasn't terribly surprised to learn she wouldn't be awaiting them at the *Shady Lady*. The impending arrival of his parents had taken the joy out of Elle's eyes. This uncomfortable situation occupied his woolly brain during the ten-minute drive back to Ta' Xbiex. His parents were almost silent, probably thinking about Charlie's narrow squeak.

His stomach gurgled, reminding him that he hadn't eaten since yesterday evening, which might be some of the reason he felt so spaced-out. Once he'd got his parents settled he'd arrange something about dinner. Maybe if Elle met his mum and dad again over a civilised meal in a restaurant it would be easier than staring at one another across the *Shady Lady*'s saloon.

The taxi pulled up on the quay and Lucas paid.

The boat was all shut up, as he'd expected. 'Welcome aboard,' he said, shoving the gangplank across, unlocking the door and leading his parents through.

Fiona and Geoffrey's smart little cases had been left on the floor of the master cabin, underlining Elle's determination to vacate. The bed had been changed and neatly made. He sighed. He'd had a lot of pleasure in that bed in the last week and a half. Not just awesome sex, but talking to Elle, sharing jokes, holding and being held, waking up with her golden hair tickling his face and her blue eyes sleepy. Tracing his way around the willowy body that had been haunting his dreams.

He shook his head to clear it. 'You're in here,' he told his parents. 'I'll use the guest cabin.'

But he didn't like his new situation. Shocked by Charlie's accident or not, it was time he got a few things straight with his parents. 'I need to talk to you about Elle.'

Fiona sat down on the edge of the bed with a tired sigh.

Geoffrey rocked awkwardly on his feet. 'Actually, we need to talk to you about her, too.'

Lucas frowned. 'Why?' Then an image of Elle swam before his eyes, the wary, troubled Elle who had never coped with his parents' attitude. A thump of his heart told him how much he liked the other Elle, the happy, open Elle. The Elle who had begun to slip from his grasp the moment that she knew his parents would be around.

He cut across Fiona, who had opened her mouth to speak. 'Is it something negative? Because if that's the case I'm not comfortable with discussing her behind her back.'

He watched Fiona and Geoffrey exchange looks, as if trying to communicate telepathically. 'Maybe it would be best to have her there?' suggested Geoffrey, to Fiona, not Lucas.

Fiona looked wary. 'Would it really be "behind her back"?'

Lucas watched his mother curiously. She looked the nearest to shifty that he remembered seeing her. Firmly, he said, 'I think that if you want to say something negative and we discuss it when she isn't here, then she'd definitely have a right to feel that we were talking about her behind her back.'

Into the strained silence he added, softly, 'And I don't want to have to take sides.'

Chapter Twenty-Six

The centre had quite a different vibe now the schools had shut for summer. The attendance of younger children had increased and the atmosphere became more about play.

Carmelo was hanging out in the computer room when Elle finally arrived, and his face lit up. 'You are not here this morning,' he accused.

Elle grinned. 'No, I had to do something. Nothing to worry about, though. So, what are you doing on the computer, today?'

'I make an e-mail to Mr Bernie Ecclestone.' Carmelo sat back, indicating the screen.

Startled, Elle read the e-mail over his shoulder. 'You're asking Mr Ecclestone to arrange a Formula 1 race in Malta?'

Carmelo beamed. 'I think it is a good idea. I like Formula 1. I'm for Ferrari.'

'Good choice.' She wondered quite where in Malta Carmelo envisaged a Formula 1 circuit being built. Maybe it could be added to the sports facilities at Ta' Qali or The Marsa. 'Where are you going to get Mr Ecclestone's e-mail address?'

'I don't know.' Carmelo's expression became expectant, deep brown eyes fixed on her.

She pulled up a chair. 'So we probably need to find out more about him, don't we? Where do you think you might find information? Where do you find lots and lots of information?'

'Wikipedia.'

'OK. Let's start there.'

While Carmelo found the relevant page, Elle signed into

the vacant machine beside him. Then she was drawn back into trying, without success, to find an e-mail address for Mr Bernie Ecclestone through various companies of which he was the CEO. He proved elusive.

'Not there.' Carmelo sighed despondently.

Elle didn't want to discourage Carmelo from his aims by suggesting he do something easier, even though she didn't think that Mr Ecclestone would base a decision about where to hold a race on the wishes of a small boy who would never be able to afford to go to a grand prix anyway. 'What about the Maltese government?' she suggested. 'It's probably their job to make the request.'

Carmelo brightened. 'And then I will *nikteb e-mail bil-Malti*.'

'Write the e-mail in Maltese? That would be much easier, wouldn't it?'

It didn't take long for them to find the website for SportMalta and the contact details of the offices; then Elle was able to leave Carmelo to his e-mail, writing Maltese not being within her skill set, and turn her attention to what she needed to do. E-mail Simon.

To: Simon.Rose
From: Elle.Jamieson
Subject: News about Charlie

Simon,
Just to let you know that things have changed a bit on board the *Shady Lady*. Charlie's got a concussion and a broken leg after falling off the flybridge last night.

She gave him the details of Charlie being an idiot and Lucas a hero.

He's going to be OK but Fiona and Geoffrey flew straight out here. Loz and Davie kindly offered me accommodation on *Seadancer* so I've jumped ship (ho ho) to make room for Fiona and Geoffrey.

No need to explain that Loz and Davie made the offer weeks ago and Elle only took them up on it once she knew Fiona and Geoffrey were en route. It could be viewed that she'd done a nice thing by moving out so that Fiona and Geoffrey could enjoy the comforts of the master cabin.

Or it could be viewed as cowardice. She hadn't completely made up her own mind.

She finished with an airy Just to update you as I'm in front of a computer and the others probably all have plenty to do.

How are you doing with the bars and the women? ☺ xxx.

Simon's reply came a few hours later. She was still in the computer room, making up for missing the morning session. Or knowing it was a safe hidey-hole where her path wasn't likely to cross with Fiona's. Take your pick.

To: Elle.Jamieson
From: Simon.Rose
Subject: I'll bet alcohol was involved

Elle, wtf was Charlie thinking? Just glad he's basically OK but it must've been a big scare. Good job Lucas reached him before he got into real trouble. Tell Charlie that I'm sorry to hear he's hurt and not to be such a bloody idiot. Sheesh. I'll text Lucas.

Re Fiona and Geoffrey :-/ Is that going to be a touch ticklish for you? I hope not. I never understood their stupid attitude. Anyone would think you'd done something wrong.

Re women and bars, have recently found a new bar, full of women. Win–win. ☺ xx

Elle grinned, wishing Simon weren't so far away. She could do with someone on her side.

It was past six when Elle got down to the marina and she headed straight for *Seadancer*. Lucas hadn't texted her for a while so she assumed that he was catching up on his sleep or was at the hospital with Charlie. It cost her a pang to make her way through the gardens to *Seadancer*'s mooring rather than to the familiar shape of the *Shady Lady*. She hadn't realised quite how at home she'd grown to feel on board the neat little cabin cruiser.

Seadancer suddenly seemed huge and grand. And it would be hard to keep her working and non-working hours separate. But it was incredibly kind of Loz and Davie to let her live on board for free so if it meant she was called upon to prepare the odd meal or two—

Her heart skipped. Lucas was sitting on a bench in front of her, right opposite *Seadancer*'s gangplank, hair stirring as the breeze ran through it.

She rounded the bench and dropped down beside him, pressing a quick kiss to his cheek. He needed to shave: stubble outlined his jaw. 'This is a nice surprise.' She kissed him again, just a peck, because it seemed to her that the Maltese didn't appreciate public clinches. She wouldn't want to trample on anybody's sensitivities like some unthinking tourist. 'How's Charlie?'

Lucas's eyes spoke of fatigue but he still looked glad to see her, taking her hand and stroking her palm with his thumb. 'Sorry for himself. King-sized headache, blurry vision, nausea, complaining that his leg itches in the plaster. Serves him right for acting like a twat.'

She squeezed his hand. 'I'm incredibly proud of what you did.'

He kissed the end of her nose. 'I've had the training, luckily for him. I'm just glad that the precautions we took with his spine proved unnecessary. If he'd messed that up—' He grimaced.

'Don't even think about it. Are your mum and dad at the hospital with him?' She tried not to sound as if she hoped they were safely out of her way. Walking down from the centre she'd caught herself constructing an optimistic scenario where Fiona and Geoffrey, having assured themselves of Charlie's well-being, would make this a flying visit and be off again first thing in the morning. Then Elle wouldn't need to even see them.

But Lucas immediately dashed any such hopes.

'No, they're on the *Shady Lady.*' He looked down at her hand in his for several seconds. When he looked up again she read apprehension in his face

'They wanted to talk to me about you. I said I'd feel more comfortable if you were in on the conversation.'

Around them, children called as they played in the park, the traffic rumbled on the road, sailing yachts shifted at their moorings and the clinking of their rigging sounded like cutlery being moved gently in a drawer. 'Wow,' she said, slowly. Trepidation washed through her. 'What was their response?'

'They said OK, if that's what I want.'

'OK.' She tried to work out what this could mean. It didn't give her a good feeling that the Roses felt the need to request some kind of summit, despite them being here only because their beloved younger son had been in danger, despite nothing being decided between her and Lucas. It was as if Lucas's parents were running up a huge red warning flag. Part of her wanted to whine, 'Why would I want to be in on it? Can't you talk them round for me?'

Then anger stiffened her spine. Why was she letting them make her feel threatened? All she'd ever done wrong was get married too young to the wrong man, and let Fiona and Geoffrey look down on her for her mistake, blowing it up into some massive flight of irresponsibility and stupidity. No doubt if she'd come from some upper-middle-class family it would all have been overlooked as an indiscretion of youth. But her average, ordinary family hadn't compared well to Lucas's comfortable background. She clenched her fists to remember Fiona once asking, 'Did your ex-husband have money? Divorce can sometimes be worthwhile.'

Of course, Elle had been so outraged and humiliated that her stammer had made an appearance. 'W-we kept our finances s-separate!'

Fiona had sent her a real courtroom stare.

Well, bollocks. She'd nothing to be ashamed of. Just because Fiona was a lawyer and Geoffrey a magistrate, they couldn't create some kind of dock and put her in it to be condemned as not matching up to their precious standards.

Fuck them, basically.

'Right,' she breezed. 'Give me fifteen minutes to shower and change.'

It wasn't relief that flicked across Lucas's features. It was alarm. He leaped up and grabbed her hand as she turned towards *Seadancer*, his eyes dark and troubled. 'Did I call this wrong? I'm not siding against you in some kind of half-arsed witch hunt. I just didn't want you to think I was talking about you behind your back.'

'OK,' she repeated. And tried to feel reassured.

Chapter Twenty-Seven

Elle marched along the quayside towards the *Shady Lady* with a 'let's get it over with' air. While aboard *Seadancer* she'd changed into a white dress that looked amazing with her tan, and yanked her hair up into a knot on the top of her head.

Troubled, Lucas took her hand. A few hours ago it had seemed supportive to refuse to discuss Elle without her being present. He'd felt as if he was ranking himself on her side, creating a boundary for his parents not to cross. But as he'd explained the situation to Elle, defensive wariness had frozen her expression and he could swear she'd shrunk from him. In her eyes there was something he really didn't like.

Disappointment?

As he'd waited on the quayside, trying not to attach any particular importance to her not inviting him to her cabin while she changed, he'd gazed almost unseeingly at two fishermen dangling their lines between the boats in the calm marina waters, and the expression in Elle's eyes had bothered him. A lot.

Now, striding beside her, he was beginning to feel like he was not just taking a lamb to slaughter but asking it how it would like to be cooked.

Much as he loved his parents, he was under few illusions about them. Fiona, particularly, was self-assured and direct to the extent that people in her practice affectionately called her 'Fearsome Fiona'. Or possibly not always affectionately.

He halted. 'You don't have to do this, you know.'

She made to carry on up the marina. 'It's what you want, isn't it?'

His hand tightened on hers and he tugged her back. 'Not if it's going to make you uncomfortable.'

She turned her blue eyes on him, grave and guarded. 'Your parents have always made me uncomfortable. They never made any effort to make me feel anything else. If I don't answer their summons then where do we go from here?' There was anger in her voice but also resignation.

He didn't like either one. 'Shit. I have got it wrong. Now you're uncomfortable with me.'

Her gaze switched to the *Shady Lady* and a small frown creased her brows. Slowly, she said, 'I don't think your suggesting that I be given the opportunity to hear their concerns is the issue. The issue is that your parents *have* an issue. With me. The fact that they've prioritised bringing that issue to your attention, considering the circumstances under which they're on the island, is an indicator of the level of their concern. I think ignoring that would be the wrong thing to do. Signals are there for us to learn from.'

She sounded if she was in a team meeting. Remote. Assessing. Deciding. Acting.

His heart sank and he cursed his tendency towards prompt decisions, because it was a complete bitch when those decisions turned out to be wrong. He should have heard his parents out and organised his defences – their defences, his and Elle's – once he understood the situation, instead of leaping to the stance of it being wrong to talk behind Elle's back. It had felt wrong. Wrong was wrong. So he'd said so.

Elle had always said that he saw nothing between right and wrong. She was right.

Time for damage limitation. 'Then we'd better send out a few signals of our own, hadn't we?' He lifted her hand to his mouth and kissed it.

Her gaze returned to his face and her frown lifted for just a moment. 'Let's see,' was all she said.

Fiona and Geoffrey were waiting in the saloon, long clear drinks in front of them. 'Good evening,' said Fiona, ever the spokesperson.

'Hi,' said Elle, sliding onto the sofa opposite them without waiting to be invited.

Geoffrey cleared his throat. 'Gin and tonic?'

'No thanks.' Elle hated gin and tonic. It hadn't taken the senior Roses long to provision the boat to their own tastes.

'Beer?' suggested Lucas.

With a quick smile, Elle nodded, watching him jump down into the galley and swoop up bottles from the fridge.

While showering and changing, Elle had taken a few minutes to think. Ideally, she would have liked her brain to supply her with a confidence-inspiring plan to take the fight to her opponents. She'd tried to visualise herself being more forthright than Fiona, more intimidating than Geoffrey, coolly articulate as she enquired as to the nature of their concerns, impressing them with her maturity and poise.

Unfortunately, it was a vision that refused to form. Much clearer was the spectre of Elle stammering guiltily the instant Fiona fixed her with that legal eagle glare.

So she'd decided upon the strategy of speaking only to reply, allowing Lucas's parents to state their business and expose their battle plan. She smoothed down her dress, folded her hands, and looked politely from Fiona to Geoffrey.

Fiona's brows lifted. 'It was a surprise for us to learn that you were living here with Lucas, Elle.'

'Simon's idea of helping out,' Lucas supplied. 'He felt we needed some help to get back together. And it's worked out better than we first thought it would.'

'I see.' Fiona looked at Elle.

Elle gazed back.

'Would you say that you are back together?' Fiona prompted.

Again it was Lucas who answered, his voice calm and reasonable. His thigh was warm and firm against Elle's. 'I think we're old enough to sort ourselves out, Mum. You don't need to be concerned. When we're ready to tell you something, we'll tell you.'

Fiona nodded, sadly, as if she'd feared as much. She exchanged a look with her husband and took a surprisingly enthusiastic slug of gin and tonic. For the first time, it crossed Elle's mind that Fiona wasn't enjoying herself. Everything about her spoke of a woman gearing herself up for an unpleasant task.

Being viewed as an unpleasantness gave her a jagged pain in her chest, and being so obviously disliked made her feel physically sick.

She had to resist the urge to justify herself. *Look I'm not such an awful person. I was young and stupid and I was manipulated. That's not a crime! At least give me and Lucas a chance. We can mess things up without your help.*

But begging for understanding wasn't going to win her any respect – or, for that matter, any understanding. She pressed her lips together and left the floor to Fiona.

This time, when Fiona spoke, it was to her son. Her voice was gentle. 'I would really have liked us to have this chat in private, Lucas. It would have been so much better.' She paused.

They waited.

Fiona took another slug of her gin. 'Something happened. We didn't tell you at the time because we thought it would cause unnecessary pain. You'd already left to live in America with Simon.' She licked her lips. 'A man made an appointment to see me at the office. Richard Manion.'

Elle jumped. She felt the muscles in Lucas's thigh twitch, as if some reaction was trying to burst out of him.

Geoffrey stirred, turning his gaze on Elle. 'I think you call him Ricky,' he clarified, as if she might not have noticed the name of her ex-husband on Fiona's lips.

Fiona darted a glance at Elle, but then returned her gaze to Lucas. 'I'm very sorry to tell you that Mr Manion tried to blackmail me. He also told me the truth about Elle. It seems as if the boat's not the only "shady lady" around here.'

Chapter Twenty-Eight

It was as if the air around her had turned to ice. Elle couldn't breathe. Couldn't move. She felt, more than saw, Lucas turn his head to stare at her. Fiona and Geoffrey were staring at her, too. Everybody in the world was looking at her and waiting for her to speak. 'B-blackmail?' she managed, eventually. Her voice sounded distant in her ears. 'What truth?'

Fiona turned back to Lucas. 'You know that we wouldn't do this if it weren't absolutely necessary, don't you?'

Elle felt a surge of rage at being ignored. 'WHAT TRUTH?' she yelled, not caring that everybody jumped.

Fiona visibly withdrew. 'You really want me to go through—'

'Every word.'

'I think you'd better.' Lucas's voice was without expression.

With a shrug, Fiona complied. 'This man, Richard Manion, said he was your husband.'

'Ex-husband,' Elle corrected her.

Fiona waved her hand, as if brushing the detail aside. 'He said that if I didn't give him money, he'd make sure everybody in town, including the newspapers, knew that our son's girlfriend was a crook, that she'd been involved in handling stolen goods, receiving, deception, etc. And'— she paused, impressively—'you'd let Ricky take the blame. He told me about forged cheques, the police looking for you in the past. The data you'd let him share—'

Elle gasped as if Fiona had leaned forward and driven her fist into Elle's guts. 'The shit.'

Slowly, she turned to Lucas. 'He's twisted everything,' she said, helplessly. 'I was never in on it.' Her voice shook. 'I was a victim.'

Lucas gave a single nod. 'Can you tell me how it was from your side?' Shock was in his frozen face, his expressionless eyes.

'You know the first part.' She sighed, slumping against the back of the sofa. 'You know that it didn't take me long to realise that I'd made a huge mistake but I didn't really know how to get back from it.'

Her heart beat in huge heavy thumps as she began the story she could have insisted on telling before. 'As soon as I had a decent salary, Ricky decided he was going to start his own business. He made over a spare bedroom into his office and boxes of things were always hanging around the garage. It had already become obvious that, financially, he was a nightmare. We began with a joint account but his view of that was that I put money in and he took money out.'

She swallowed. She was aware of Fiona and Geoffrey listening intently, but her focus was on Lucas. Sweat greased her palms. Her fear at finding herself cornered into regurgitating everything she'd held back for so long threatened to overwhelm logical thought. She took a deep breath, trying to steady herself, trying to order the facts.

'So I separated our finances, opening accounts in my sole name so that I could control my own money. He was really angry.' She flinched to remember the way that Ricky had roared his fury into her face. 'Ricky's manipulative. He never hit me but he was a master of emotional abuse. He'd stoked the tension between my parents and me, yet learned from them how to wield disappointment and guilt as weapons I'd respond to. So I pacified him by taking over paying the bills and rent while he kept whatever he earned for himself.'

'Why didn't you leave?' Lucas's voice was bleak.

'Because of my parents.' She went on doggedly, miserably. 'It sounds stupid and weak but they were just waiting for me to fail. The more obvious they made that, the more I couldn't face admitting that they were right, that marrying Ricky hadn't been a whirlwind fairy-tale romance but a huge mistake. That our marriage had become nothing more than mutual disappointment and separate lives. You're probably having problems understanding this because your parents brought you up to believe in yourself. My parents did nothing but fill me with doubts.

'I had my work. I put in long hours at the office; then when the last people were leaving the building and I had to go, too, I brought work home to fill the rest of the evening. Ricky was hooked on laziness, hanging out with mates I didn't like and didn't trust.' The old, ugly feeling washed over her, the shame of finding herself tied to a man who had begun to spend his life with a lager can in one hand and a TV remote in the other. 'Ricky was rude and boorish, particularly in front of these shifty new mates who began to turn up to smoke and drink with him. They picked arguments with me. They called me "Ricky's yuppie". If I was working at the kitchen table I'd try to ignore them but they'd jeer and swear until they drove me up to my room or even out of the house.' She shuddered.

'Work became all I had. I climbed the ladder. I had a position of responsibility and over the next two years my security clearance level became high. I was trusted and respected, fast-tracked, skipping up the grades. But the downside was that Ricky and his horrible mates felt more and more like a secret I had to hide.'

She risked a glance at Lucas's parents and her voice all but dried up. The condemnation on their faces was clear. She turned back to Lucas hopelessly. He was looking at her as if he'd never seen her before.

Slowly, she sank back, feeling tried and judged and declared guilty. She completed her tale listlessly. 'Long story short, one day the police turned up at the house. Ricky wasn't there and probably hadn't been for a day or two. I spent so much time avoiding him that I hadn't thought too much about his absence. The police were looking for him. Once they were happy that I didn't know what was going on or where he was'—she threw a defiant look at Fiona—'they told me that complaints had been made. Ricky had been selling stuff on the internet. Some was stolen goods, the rest didn't exist at all.'

Her voice had become small and flat. Defensive. 'I was scared to death it would affect my job. The more information the police shared, the more I began to suspect that he'd stolen data from my laptop, harvesting e-mail addresses to create mailing lists and sending out invoices for fictitious services. Some companies simply paid without checking. I think I fucked up. I must have left my laptop open when his raucous mates had driven me out of the house and one of them had been clever enough to use data held on my machine or even up in the cloud. I could imagine a nightmare inquiry and me losing my job. The only part of my life where I had respect.'

Deep breath. 'There *was* some forging of cheques,' she admitted. 'But not by me. When he left, Ricky cleared my account. I'd kept my internet banking password away from him, obviously, so he just did things the old-fashioned way, taking my cheque book and forging my signature on a succession of cheques made out to him, until the account was empty and they began to bounce. Because I wanted this horror story to go away, I took that on the chin, closed that account and opened another in a different bank to render any other cheques he wrote useless.'

Lucas was silent.

Elle forced herself further into the nightmare. 'I had no choice then but to tell my parents Ricky had left. Our relationship deteriorated further when they didn't have a word of support for me. Just all the "We told you so!" guff I'd been afraid of. So I didn't tell them about the police being after Ricky. It was just too ...' She paused. Swallowed. 'Bettsbrough's a small town. If word had got out that the police were looking for Ricky it would have made the nightmare worse. When my company moved to larger premises in Northampton, I went too.'

She tried to smile at Lucas, but her bottom lip shook. 'I settled there and I'd got a promotion along with the relocation. Ricky seemed to have disappeared from my life and I chalked the whole thing up as a horrible experience. I met you. Everything was going wonderfully.

'Too wonderfully.' She stopped to turn her gaze deliberately to the lawyer and the magistrate. 'This scruffy guy in a baseball cap and a hoodie approached me one day outside my office, begging for change. It was like my worst nightmare when I realised it was Ricky.' She looked around at each of her audience in turn. Fiona and Geoffrey wore matching sceptical expressions. Lucas was beginning to look as if he was watching a road crash.

She sighed. 'I'd done something incredibly stupid. I'd updated my Facebook profile. Northampton was listed as where I was living and as I was still working for the same company it didn't take him long to find me. He just hung around outside the building. He wanted money, of course.

He looked at my suits and my car and he saw where he could get it.'

Meeting Lucas's gaze was getting harder and harder, not because she knew herself to be guilty of anything worse than gullibility and panic, but because his eyes weren't telling her that he understood that she was innocent. 'That's why I began behaving oddly,' she whispered. 'He threatened to tell you exactly what he's told your mother. That I was the one who had practised deception and fraud and everything, and he'd been blamed. He'd been living in Spain, like some big-shot criminal, because he knew someone there with a bar. Till he fell out with the friend; then he came back to the UK.'

Fiona made a noise that might have been a tut of disbelief.

At that tiny, scornful noise, hope began to shrivel inside of Elle. 'If we'd had a big wedding, he would've turned up. He knows how to sniff out information. That's why I wanted to go to Vegas and get married,' she explained, dully. 'I thought it would halt his plans. I must admit I didn't credit him with enough tenacity to walk into a lawyer's office and try and blackmail her.'

Bitterly, Elle laughed. 'In a way, you were right to be suspicious of the man you saw me talking to outside work. That was Ricky. He'd cleaned himself up but came by regularly to threaten me with exposure, with implicating me in his crimes. I couldn't see a way out. When you went off in your jealous rage, I didn't argue when you said we were over. At least that way, I thought, Ricky would leave you and your family alone. Turns out I was wrong.'

A long silence followed her last words. Elle stared at the tabletop where the beer she hadn't touched was leaving a condensation ring.

Finally, Lucas stirred. He sounded dazed. 'I can't get my head around this. I thought it was something to do with me not proposing properly.'

Elle turned to stare at him, thrown by this change of direction. 'Not what?'

'When I suggested we get married. I thought I hadn't made it sound important enough. Just blurted out that it would be better if we got married if we were going to America.'

'Oh.' Elle tried to force her mind back. 'I suppose it was pretty ordinary. But I was probably distracted by the knowledge that the wedding would be a target, a reason for me to be threatened and coerced.'

He winced. 'Why didn't you tell me when it was happening?'

Elle smiled, though she saw his firm jaw and satin hair only through a haze of tears. 'Because I didn't think you'd believe me.'

'You didn't trust me to.' His voice was hoarse.

She had no energy left for diplomacy. She shook her head. 'Your parents hated me. They didn't try to hide that they'd expected better for their son than a silly girl who'd been married and divorced young, and no high-status contacts to counterbalance her naivety. You're very much their son. Judgemental. Sure of what's right and what's wrong. Intolerant of mistakes. So, no, I didn't trust you to believe in me. Not then.' A lone tear tracked down her cheek. 'I started to tell you once we'd—' She glanced at Fiona and Geoffrey. Fiona looked pale. 'But you told me you didn't need to know, so long as I'd never cheated on you. And I thought that I was safe, that Ricky didn't know where I was and couldn't hurt me any more.'

Lucas opened his mouth.

But Elle's phone began to ring. She slipped it from the front pocket of her dress to press 'Decline'. Then she saw *The Briars* on the screen. Her finger hovered. She pressed 'Answer' instead.

Lucas could hardly believe what he'd been hearing. Fury that Elle hadn't simply come to him with the truth four years ago warred with shame that she hadn't felt able to trust him with her fears and fragility. Threatened by that shit of an ex-husband she had borne it all alone, searching for ways out of trouble. She was that scared of disapproval.

His heart contracted that she'd been so unhappy that she'd barely noticed his proposal had been "pretty ordinary". She had deserved so much better.

He glanced at his parents. His dad's expression wasn't betraying much, as usual, but his mum looked disbelieving. He'd seen that look a million times. Fearsome Fiona had made up her mind. He wondered if that was the expression Elle sometimes saw on his face. Cold guilt curled in his stomach as he remembered Fiona referring to Elle as 'that sort of girl', and that he'd never asked her not to. He'd simply expected that his parents' misgivings would fade if he went ahead with his relationship, letting his actions speak louder than words.

He hadn't wanted to hurt them with a row.

Instead, he'd hurt Elle by not having one.

Elle's eyes were pink around the edges, now, as she listened to whoever was on the phone. He'd been so engrossed in his churning thoughts that he hadn't been paying attention to the few words she'd uttered as her part of the conversation. But he snapped back to the present as she prepared to ring off.

'Thank you for letting me know. I understand. Leave it with me. I'll be there as soon as I can.' She ended the call and posted the phone back into her pocket. Her face was white under her freckles but she seemed composed. 'That was Nerys at The Briars. They can't have Mum back under the level of care we've been paying for. I need to establish whether they can care for her with her new needs or if I have to find somewhere else.'

Lucas immediately thrust his anger and confusion aside. Or maybe he was glad of a reason to reach for her.

But she shrank from his arms. 'No, don't. Not just out of pity because you think something's going wrong for me. Mum's care's too hard to try and organise from here. I'm going back to England.'

Lucas could hardly believe his ears. 'England?' he repeated, idiotically.

Elle was already moving to extricate herself from the sofa. She went on in the same colourless voice. 'It's best. It'll give you plenty of time to think. And I need space, too. A lot of it.'

Hardly knowing what he was doing, Lucas stood up to allow her out from behind the table.

Her smile twisted and her eyes were full of tears as she gripped his hand hard between both of hers. 'Do you remember me saying I learned from my parents never to own up? I'm glad you didn't let me when I tried to. At least, this way, we've had this time.'

She turned to Fiona. 'Sorry Ricky tried it on with you. I can imagine that you must have felt vindicated, that you'd been right to be suspicious of me.' She let a pause draw out. 'I did think that you lawyers usually go on evidence and that pesky "innocent until proven guilty" thing. But don't worry, I'm not going to fight you. I wouldn't try and get Lucas to throw away parents that show their love this much.'

Neither parent seemed to have an answer. It was Lucas who found his voice, to say, 'That's pretty magnanimous of you, in the circumstances.'

Elle groaned in frustration, her blue eyes suddenly on fire. 'I'm not being magnanimous! I'm being bitter. Like most things, it's not as black and white as you make it. Your family, you live by different rules. There are a few concepts you guys need to learn about, like compromise, valuing people for what they are, there being more than one way to look at things. People being normal, imperfect human beings.'

She turned and left the saloon, slipping out through the sliding doors like a dream vanishing at dawn.

Shock giving sudden power to his legs, Lucas started after her. 'Elle—!'

He gained the cockpit in time to see her picking up pace along the quayside. Her voice floated back to him. 'Give me space, Lucas. I really need it.' Defeat was in the droop of her shoulders and the angle of her head.

Shock and lack of sleep took the power from his legs and he dropped down on the cockpit seat to watch her go until other boats obscured his line of sight. Now he knew what truths had been balanced on her lips that night he'd resolved to put the past behind them, and why she'd stayed silent. He was both ashamed and grateful.

A hand landed softly on his shoulder and his mother said, 'It might be for the best.'

He shook her off. 'Not for me.' Then, strength returning to his limbs, he jumped up and off the boat, hitting the ground running, focused only on catching up with Elle.

At the foot of *Seadancer*'s gangplank, though, he

hesitated. It wasn't that he was shy about disregarding etiquette and barging his way onto someone else's boat but that he was suddenly convinced that it was the wrong thing. Racing along the quayside, dodging mooring lines and fishermen and a motor scooter delivering pizzas, he'd formulated flash plans of helping her pack, booking her flight, calling her a taxi, seeing her to the airport. Even packing a bag and going with her back to England, though he knew Vern would take a very dim view.

Give me space. Her voice rang in his head, filled with frustration and disillusion.

He snatched out his phone and sent her a text. Can I help? What do you want me to do?

The reply came in seconds. No, thanks. I don't want you to do anything.

He glared at his phone screen. That wasn't the answer he'd wanted.

He hit 'Reply' and his thumb hovered over the keys. So, what was he going to do – insist? Disregard her wishes? Demand assurances of her return? Eventually, he texted a kiss, waited, and then turned away and trailed back to the *Shady Lady*. He jumped back on board.

In the saloon, his parents had freshened their gin and tonics. 'Kayleigh's asked us if we'd like to meet her for dinner,' said Fiona, tentatively. 'I think she's feeling the shock now the drama's over and would appreciate our support.'

Lucas drifted to a stop. 'I expect she would.'

Under his steady regard, Fiona flushed. 'That wasn't very tactful, was it? I suppose you're wondering why we never showed any support for Elle?'

'No,' he said, heavily, 'I know why you didn't. She's made mistakes. Mistakes don't sit well with you.' Then his conscience made him add, 'Or with me. She couldn't trust me to trust in her.'

He began to walk by, intending to swipe a couple of beers out of the galley and shut himself in the guest cabin to wrestle with the giant sensation of "what just happened?" But he turned back. 'Just for the record, Charlie made a pretty big mistake last night. His injuries are down only to his own reckless stupidity. But everybody always forgives Charlie just because he's Charlie. Charlie was an idiot, Kayleigh went to pieces but Elle raced around, getting help, helping me get Charlie out of a sticky situation alive and without lasting damage. And the reason that Elle's going to England tonight is that her mother needs help. Joanna's been sanctimonious and unsupportive but still Elle supports her financially and practically.'

Geoffrey cleared his throat.

Fiona said, 'I see.'

'Did either of you thank Elle for helping save Charlie's stupid fucking neck?'

His parents exchanged glances. 'No,' acknowledged Geoffrey, stiffly.

Lucas sat down, dropping his head into his hands. 'I'm not sure whether I did, either.' He rubbed at a headache that he hadn't realised he'd been nursing, thinking dully what a fantastic idea it would have been to cast off Simon's boat a few days ago and carry Elle away in it, somewhere Charlie's stupid antics couldn't bring his parents down on them, bearing their righteous judgement of Elle's past like a flaming cross. Somewhere there would be no phone calls to remind Elle of her responsibilities and burdens.

Somewhere mistakes could be forgotten.

He wished Elle had let him help.

The thought jolted him out of his pity party and got him back to his feet. 'Right, let's go and have dinner with Kayleigh.'

Instantly, his parents looked relieved, probably misreading his sudden positivity as a good thing.

He checked his phone. Elle still hadn't sent him a kiss back.

He prepared to leave the boat, flicking off the isolation switches and locking the sliding doors behind his parents. Darkness was falling and the cicadas *whirred* and *zuzzed* in the gardens as the family filed over the plank to the shore and turned right, ready to walk along the promenade towards the Sea Creek Hotel.

Then he saw, out of the corner of his eye, a small shadow hovering. 'Carmelo?'

Carmelo emerged. Apart from his shy smile, he didn't look at his best. His T-shirt was grubby and his hair unbrushed. He scampered up to Lucas with his palm upraised for their customary high five. 'Elle is here? I want to tell her about following Formula 1 drivers on Twitter.'

If Lucas hadn't been so tired and preoccupied he would have guarded his tongue. Instead, aware of his parents' gazes on Carmelo, he said, 'She's on her way back to England.'

In slow motion, Carmelo's face began to crumple. 'No! She didn't say that to me!' Two huge tears welled from his big brown eyes.

Hastily, Lucas hunkered down beside him. 'Sorry, I was a bit blunt. She's only going for a few days. She's not going forever.' He hoped. 'It's just that she has to see her mother. She got a phone call to say that her mum needs her help because she's ill.' He glanced along the quayside in the direction of *Seadancer*, wishing he could see what was happening on board, whether Elle was still packing or whether she was already in a taxi en route to Malta International Airport.

The tears made tracks down Carmelo's cheeks. Apparently unconsoled, his mouth squared off as he began to heave with sobs. 'She didn't tell me!' he wailed.

Lucas had to spend several minutes reassuring him, begging tissues from Fiona, who could be relied upon to have a supply. 'Sorry, but she didn't have time to tell you,' he said, guiltily, wishing he had Joseph's number. 'I didn't mean to upset you.' It was a good fifteen minutes before Carmelo seemed reassured enough to leave, with a few last looks behind Lucas as if willing Elle to appear from somewhere on the *Shady Lady*. He nodded glumly when Lucas asked him if he'd be OK walking home.

Finally, Lucas was free to escort his parents, crossing the gardens and the road and turning in the direction of the hotel. 'That little boy's crazy about Elle,' he observed, in case they hadn't got that. 'He's one of the kids from the youth centre where she volunteers. Nice kid. Needs a few friends.'

Fiona sounded sombre. 'He looks as if he needs someone to take care of him.'

'True. It's not always easy to know how to help, though.' And he told them about how Elle had had to call Joseph when Carmelo turned up late at night, and the Bubblemaker session that Dive Meddi had put on, which led him nicely into finding Kayleigh waiting at a table outside the Sea Creek Hotel and suggesting that she told his parents all about what had happened when Charlie fell off the boat.

By the time Kayleigh had said, 'Elle was fantastic,' for about the tenth time, leaving little option but for his parents to acknowledge Elle's part in the rescue of their irresponsible youngest son, he was sufficiently satisfied to let the conversation move on to other things while he tucked into seafood pasta and a welcome pint of golden Cisk.

He let the others decide who would visit Charlie tomorrow afternoon, so tired that the lights reflecting in the blackness of the creek were dancing in front of his eyes. He had just one thing left to do before he could crash out for the night.

Lucas waited until goodbyes had been said to Kayleigh and he and his parents were strolling back to the marina through the soft evening. 'Do you know Simon's friends, Loz and Davie?' he began, casually. 'Davie's a music producer. They have a motor yacht at the big-boat end of the marina.'

Fiona looked interested. 'Simon's mentioned them, but I don't think we've met.'

'Let's see if they're on board. I'll introduce you.' Resolutely, Lucas passed the *Shady Lady* and his yearned-for bed, leading his parents around the curve of the quayside until he could see, with a thump of gladness, the lights on *Seadancer*'s foredeck.

'Hello, *Seadancer*!' Lucas called. He couldn't quite bring himself to use the supposedly approved 'Ahoy'.

Loz appeared on the side deck in moments. 'Lucas! Did you know—'

'My parents are here,' he interrupted quickly. 'They'd like to meet you.'

'Come aboard!' Loz needed no further prompting into full hostess mode, insisting Fiona and Geoffrey join them in a nightcap on the foredeck, where the doors were open to the saloon and moths battered gently at the deck lights. As soon as her guests had been introduced to Davie and were settled on directors' chairs clutching brandy balloons and Charlie's progress enquired after, Loz fixed Lucas with a beady stare.

'Elle's gone home.'

He nodded, giving Loz plenty of opportunity to lead the conversation, pretty sure he knew where she'd take it.

Loz's eyes travelled over his parents. 'Elle was very upset tonight when she came here to pack.'

Fiona looked surprised. 'Here to pack?'

Loz's chin jutted. 'She asked if she could move in here for a bit so that you could be accommodated on the *Shady Lady*. I was pleased to make things easier for you but she's such a lovely girl I wouldn't have hesitated, anyway.' She fixed Fiona with a baleful eye. 'Poor kid needs someone on her side.'

No one could fail to notice the slight emphasis on *someone*.

'She's got us, of course,' Davie put in.

Lucas yawned, leaving Loz to do her stuff with Davie backing her up. Fiona and Geoffrey didn't look comfortable but that was OK. Food for thought wasn't always particularly palatable.

Quietly, he excused himself on the pretext of searching out a bathroom. With a silent apology to his hosts he opened doors until he found what he wanted – a cabin with its cupboard ajar and some of Elle's clothes hanging inside. He closed his eyes in relief, absorbing the fact that she hadn't cleared all her stuff.

She'd be coming back.

An hour later, picking their way between the line of gently moving boats on one side and the dark gardens on the other, Lucas found himself yawning so hugely that his jaw clicked. He was almost hallucinating about dropping into the narrow guest bed.

His parents were quiet as he pushed the plank out onto the *Shady Lady*'s bathing platform for them.

Fiona halted in the saloon. 'I'm not stupid, Lucas,' she said, drily.

Lucas cocked a brow.

'We have noted that this evening you've been on a mission to expose us to the saintliness of Elle.'

Aggravation made his voice sharp. 'Didn't you listen to what she said? Elle's no saint: she's a normal human being. But a pretty good one, one who deserves a bit of trust, maybe?' And, finally, he shut himself away in the guest cabin, dragged off his clothes and fell into bed.

He'd hardly closed his eyes when a text message came through. His heart flipped at the sight of Elle's name. Did your mother go to the police about Ricky's blackmail attempt?

He looked at his watch. She could still be at the airport, about to get on a late flight. Pulling on his boxers, he forced his tired body to the foot of the galley steps so he could see his parents seated in the saloon. He repeated Elle's question.

Fiona looked wary. 'I had to, darling. My position— It would have been odd not to report a crime. I made a statement.'

'Did they get him?'

Fiona shook her head.

Lucas retired back to the guest cabin. He deliberated over calling Elle, wanting badly to hear her voice. But she'd chosen to text so he texted the details Fiona had given him in return.

In a minute she returned OK, thx.

Despite his fatigue, he lay awake for a long time, staring into the darkness.

Chapter Twenty-Nine

Elle's first three days back in England were filled with meetings and arrangements, some awkward, some difficult and some downright unpleasant.

Healthcare workers from the hospital had to be met, staff from The Briars, staff from two different institutions that might be suitable for Joanna, other authority figures concerned with loose ends she knew had to be tied up. Explanations, consultations, instructions, assessing what would and wouldn't work.

She met her dad and Tania at the pub beside the motel where she'd booked a room. Tania, Elle was sure, had made the long haul from Wales only to make certain that Elle understood Will didn't have money to splash around contributing to the care of ex-wives.

Elle offered only brusque reassurance. 'I didn't expect anything of Dad so I'm not disappointed that it's all down to me.'

Will looked pained. 'That's not worthy of you, young lady.'

Elle picked up her wine glass, determined not to accept her father's reproof like a child. 'So who else is it down to?'

Will didn't come up with anyone, so Elle went on doggedly with her round of meetings until she thought her head would explode from information overload and hard choices. But at least it stopped her thinking about Lucas. Much.

The late afternoon of the second day, after a particularly onerous and shitty meeting, she went into McDonald's and logged on to the Wi-Fi.

Then she did something she didn't think she'd ever do.

She opened a new Facebook account and filled out the profile with her background details. *Bettsbrough Comprehensive School; Keele University; University of Manchester.*

She activated the profile and wrote a couple of status updates about being back in Northampton; then sent out a dozen friend requests to people she remembered were surgically attached to their Facebook pages so could probably be relied upon to react promptly.

Into the search window she typed: *Ricky Manion.* Three came up. *Ricky James Manion, Ricky DJ Manion* and *Ricky Manion Smith.* Ricky DJ Manion's profile picture was a musical note rather than a photo of himself, and unless the Ricky she needed had started adopting names and changing his appearance, neither of the other Rickys was the correct one.

She drank a cup of coffee and ate a chocolate brownie, slowly, and by the time she'd finished five people had friended her back, people she'd worked with who sent *Hey, where have you been – got to meet up!* messages.

She returned suitably brief and non-committal replies. Satisfied that she now had a Facebook presence, however superficial, she clicked on Ricky DJ Manion and, hoping that his settings allowed people other than Facebook friends to make contact, sent him a private message.

I need to speak to you. Call me. She added her mobile phone number.

If she had found the right Ricky Manion, he wouldn't be able to resist finding out why Elle Kirsty Jamieson would get in touch.

It was an uncomfortable feeling, doing everything she'd so carefully avoided up to now: making herself visible and discoverable. Drearily, she reminded herself that it didn't matter any more. All her dirtiest beans lay spilled in the muck.

On the morning of her fourth day back in England, she visited her mother, as she had done each day. Joanna had been moved into a geriatric ward and was in a large orange vinyl armchair, her head resting on one of the chair's wings, her fingers twisting and one corner of her mouth dragged down.

'Hello, Mum.' Elle stooped tentatively to hug her mother's shoulders; lost muscle tone had made them narrow, loose under Elle's hands. 'How are you?'

Joanna gazed back at Elle with watery blue eyes and her mouth worked as if groping for words that hovered just out of reach. Her hair was held out of her eyes with a hair slide. It was a girlish style Joanna would never have worn when she was well and Elle realised that she probably hadn't thought to book her mother haircuts while she was away. She put it on her mental 'to do' list.

To fill the silence, and because Joanna was gazing at her, Elle launched into an account of all she'd been doing since leaving the ward the day before. Encouraged by Joanna's apparent attention and by what might have been attempts to smile, she moved on to what the healthcare worker had said and what conclusions Elle had drawn from her conferences at The Briars and the alternative care homes.

'I think it'll be best for you to go back to The Briars,' she ended. 'You know the staff and they're able to give you the care you need. It means being in a new room and, hopefully, you'll keep improving.'

Elle waited while her mother tried to say something. When the attempt ended only in a sigh, she added, 'I've sorted out the money side of things.' Elle hated to think what would happen when the money from Joanna's share of the family home was gone. Elle's contribution would no longer be enough. She'd have to return to the UK and secure a proper job again. She could see her new life circling the drain.

Shoving that unwelcome thought aside, she pasted on her brightest smile. 'So there's nothing for you to worry about, Mum. It might even be as soon as tomorrow that you're back at The Briars.'

Joanna's mouth worked again, and she frowned with the effort of transferring her thoughts to her lips. Slowly, indistinctly, the words came out.

'Do I know you?'

Elle recoiled. But, as she stared at the shell that had once been her mother, her phone began to vibrate in her pocket. *Unknown number.* She dashed out of the ward and into the Ladies' to answer the call, her voice choked with tears. 'Yes?'

A pause, then, 'Why did you want me to call you?'

The sound of Ricky's voice, after four years, added a thread of panic to Elle's jangling emotions. 'I can't talk now, but it's important. Are you in Northampton?'

'What if I am?'

She wiped her eyes with the heel of her hand. 'Can you meet me?'

'Why should I?'

'I wouldn't ask if there wasn't a good reason. But I can't talk here – I don't want passers-by to hear.' And then, lowering her voice urgently, 'Ring me back if you can meet me. Up to you, but someone came to see me and gave me a whole load of information about you, and it affects us both—'

'All right. I'll meet you this afternoon, Midsummer Meadow, down by the river.'

She let out a snort. 'No thanks. I remember the kind of people you hang out with. It has to be more public than that.'

He sniggered. He hadn't changed his modus operandi of using scorn and derision to make her feel in the wrong. 'The market square public enough for you?'

'Near the entrance to The Grosvenor Centre, three o'clock,' she agreed, thickly, and ended the call. Wiping her eyes, she blew her nose and squared her shoulders.

There were still arrangements to make and bureaucracy to clear and she made time for yet another call to the authorities before feeling strong enough to return to the ward. She still needed to find out who to talk to about discharging her mother and whether she'd need an ambulance or if a taxi would be OK.

In her heart she knew that meeting Ricky was the right thing to do. She had to confront her past before she could move on. But the prospect still made her stomach lurch and she'd feel better if she kept as busy as possible.

Elle leaned on the ironstone wall beside the Market Square entrance to Northampton's flagship shopping centre, listening to the chatter of the shoppers as they passed. Jumpy, she somehow felt both cornered and exposed.

She watched what was going on around the market stalls and half-expected to catch sight of her ex-husband fencing dodgy gear to unsuspecting punters under one of the red-striped awnings.

But Ricky, when he sauntered up ten minutes late, came through the doors of the shopping centre.

'What's up then?' He took out a Marlboro packet and lit a cigarette.

Elle jammed her hands in the pockets of her jeans, determined not to let Ricky see if her hands shook. Resisting the impulse to clear her throat, she took a deep breath, not wanting to stutter over a single word. 'I hear you tried to blackmail my ex-boyfriend's mother.'

Ricky shrugged as if he had no idea what she was talking about, gazing past her at the market. Lines had settled beneath his eyes, but he looked prosperous.

She let injury resonate in her voice. 'You know that your nasty threats put paid to my relationship with Lucas. But I didn't think you'd try and get money out of his family once I'd left town.'

Ricky glanced at her. She caught a glint of something, as if he were amused or pleased at being the cause of her dismay. 'You were always too much of a cow to play fair with me,' he commented, obliquely.

'You don't know what fair is!' she snapped. 'And that kind of emotional abuse doesn't work with me now. I'm not a silly little girl you can bully any more.' Then she let it all pour out, her disgust of a man who would expect to live off her while he played at being a crook, then run away before the police turned up. How her relationship with her parents had been affected, and how, just when she thought that she'd got it together again with Lucas, her ex-mother-in-law-to-be had appeared 'and tells me that you're still sending your shit my way!'

Ricky's expression grew steadily more impatient. 'Why are you bothering to lay all this stuff on me? You don't think I give a fuck, do you?'

'Not really.' She sighed, letting her shoulders droop. 'I just thought you'd like the satisfaction of knowing.' Then she straightened her spine and forced herself to keep speaking, to say the words she knew would antagonise.

'Because that satisfaction's all you're going to get. You have nothing left to gain because I have nothing left to lose. You've pulled your masterstroke of trying to blackmail Mrs Rose and it hasn't worked. You're even a failure as a small-time crook, Ricky.'

Slowly, Ricky drew himself up, stepping into her space and right in her face, the all-too-familiar strategy to intimidate and quell. Elle was swept by sickening memories. Bellows of rage. Anger hurled like rocks. Though it was difficult not to cringe from his menacing bulk and the smoke from his cigarette, which burned her eyes and throat, she remained perfectly still by the wall, heart beating hard against her ribs.

With relief, out of the corner of her eye she spotted dark shapes rounding the nearest stalls and heading purposefully in their direction.

She forced herself to ignore Ricky taking control of her space, her air, to look up into his face. 'I'm drawing a line under you. There's some really unpleasant stuff still to come but I'm free of you and it feels pretty good.'

Ricky sneered like a goblin, the sourness of cigarette smoke on his breath. 'What are you going on about, you stupid tart? What unpleasant stuff?'

Elle didn't waver. 'Giving evidence against you. I've already made a statement.'

And as Ricky opened his mouth again, he halted, eyes swivelling to what Elle had spotted seconds before. Two uniformed police officers striding his way. 'Shit!' He tried to dart towards the glass doors to the mall but two more police officers emerged from inside, neatly blocking his escape.

Spinning on his heel, Ricky made a lunge for the narrowing gap between the uniforms but the police officers, all burly men, put on a burst of speed and were on him. 'Easy mate. Don't do anything stupid.'

Ricky, bravado and cockiness overwritten by blank shock, stared at Elle as his arms were pulled deftly behind his back. 'You fucking bitch, you ratted me out.'

Elle laughed, taking a deep breath of fresh air. 'And I enjoyed every minute. The police were glad of my help because it turned out they had quite a few reasons to want to pick you up. See you in court, Ricky. I'll be the one in the witness box.'

Her heart was still beating hard. But now it was with exhileration.

Elle had been in England for only ten days but it seemed longer. Lucas had called her and she'd been polite but in a hurry. When he'd texted her: Found hotel for Mum and Dad for a few days. Costing them! But it means they're no longer on the *Shady Lady* xxx she'd returned a polite but neutral: OK. It pained him that she didn't sound bothered. At least Charlie's out of hospital. Kayleigh's taking him home provoked a Good! ☺

A voice came from the quayside. 'Ahoy, *Shady Lady*!'

Lucas went out onto the bathing platform. He hadn't been back from work long and his shower-damp hair blew into his eyes. He had to flick it back to see Loz on the quayside. His insides hitched in case she brought him news of Elle. 'Come aboard.' He gave her his hand to cross the gangplank.

Loz beamed, settling herself on the cockpit seat in the sun. 'I've come to invite you and your parents to a drinks party this evening.'

He took the seat beside her. 'Thank you. What's the occasion?'

Loz smiled. 'Just one of our regular get-togethers. But I thought you might like to come and celebrate Elle being back.'

He bounced to his feet. 'Back? Where?'

Looking suddenly apprehensive, Loz half-pointed in the direction of *Seadancer*. 'She's—'

Lucas turned and with a run and a jump was on the shore. Too angry for good manners, he abandoned Loz alone on the *Shady Lady* and stormed along the quayside and up the gangplank onto *Seadancer*.

He found Elle in her cabin, unpacking her suitcase into the cupboard.

Fury burned so hot inside Lucas's skull that he thought flames would shoot out of his eyeballs. 'So when were you going to tell me you were back?'

Elle didn't pause in her task of sliding folded T-shirts into a wide drawer under the bed. 'I was going to come along to the *Shady Lady* soon.'

'But not to live? And that's not a detail you thought you'd share with me?' He reached out and flipped shut the lid of her suitcase, maddened beyond reason at her refusal to pay him attention.

Deliberately, Elle opened the suitcase again. Then she squared right up to him, blue eyes sparking. Her voice was dangerously soft. 'I appreciate that you're angry. Being angry is one of the things you do. But I told you to give me space. It wasn't a request. It wasn't something I expected to be ignored. I *told* you.'

Lucas halted. His anger drained away in the face of her greater fury. It was as if every slight she'd ever suffered, every frustration or injustice, was concentrated in the set of her beautiful mouth as she stared him down, refusing to accept his moment of disrespect.

'OK,' he said. And turned and walked away.

Shocked at the words that had poured from her mouth, Elle stood looking at the doorway through which Lucas had vanished. Where had her anger come from? It had been like she was possessed: her lips had opened but the voice of a furious demon came out.

Since she'd seen Joanna installed in her new room at The Briars and tied things up with the police so far as she could for the present, Elle's head had buzzed with conjecture about how matters would stand between her and Lucas when she got back to Malta. She'd hung around to pay a few afternoon visits to her mother, wanting to see if Joanna's confusion would lessen once in the familiarity of The Briars, but finally had to acknowledge that Joanna's ability to recognise her daughter was random. Elle's presence was largely irrelevant.

So she'd booked a flight with a sense of relief at removing herself from any fallout from Ricky or his mates, but also a sense of returning to face the music. Well, now she knew what tune was playing – a crashing bashing discord.

Loz came down and popped her head into the cabin. 'All right?' she squeaked tentatively.

Forcing herself to return to her unpacking, Elle nodded brightly. 'Fine.'

Loz hovered. 'Maybe you should get a nap before the party? You can be a guest, you know, you don't have to do anything.'

'I'd rather keep busy.'

'Davie's gone to do the shopping. You and me can throw a few salads into bowls.'

Elle nodded.

Loz came properly into the cabin, expression doleful. 'I'm sorry I opened my big mouth. When you agreed it was OK to invite Lucas to the party I assumed you'd told him you were back.'

'I was going to go along when I'd unpacked.' Elle blinked back the tears pricking like hot pins in the corners of her eyes. Finally, Loz seemed to get that Elle wasn't feeling chatty, and melted away. Elle stowed her case and took a shower. Then she pulled on clean shorts and a top and settled herself on the bed to text Joseph and say she was back while she reacquainted herself with the feeling of a boat moving beneath her. The breeze was up and the motion was lively. She hoped that she wouldn't have to find her sea legs all over again. She supposed she ought to go along to the galley and see if Loz had got started with the party food yet. But she felt tired and heavy – maybe she would take that nap.

She rolled down onto the bed and covered her eyes with her arm.

Probably she did doze, because suddenly she became aware of Lucas standing in the doorway of her cabin once again.

'Can I show you something?' He didn't smile, but his earlier anger seemed gone. He looked composed.

She blinked. 'Now?'

'Now would be good.'

Curiously, she slid her feet into mules and followed him up to the deck. The heat hit her as she left the air conditioning and she squinted in the brightness, wishing she'd grabbed her sunglasses. Despite Lucas's silence as he moved easily beside her along the quayside, and there being nothing to give her a clue to his mood or their destination, she felt her heart lift to once again feel the warm breeze in her hair and see the boats bobbing gently in the sunshine. This, more than the England she'd just left, felt like where she wanted to be.

When they reached the *Shady Lady* Lucas jumped across to the bathing platform without shoving the gangplank into place. Warily, Elle took the hand he extended, warm and strong, and jumped after him. Jogging lightly through the sliding doors, into the coolness of the saloon and down the galley steps, Lucas didn't pause.

He opened the door to the master cabin. Stepped inside. Turned and waited.

Cautiously, Elle stepped into the small area behind him. The bed looked freshly made in the light streaming in from the skylights and there wasn't a thing out of place.

Lucas pulled out the drawers under the bed, opened the lockers and the wardrobe. All empty.

'What am I supposed to be looking at?' Elle demanded, bewildered.

'Space.' Finally, he smiled. 'I'm giving you space. All this space is yours. I'm in the guest cabin.' Then he stepped closer to her, so close that she could smell his shampoo and feel the heat leaking from his skin. 'Until you tell me you want me in here again.'

Elle looked from empty wardrobe to empty drawers to freshly made bed. 'Got it.'

This time, it was Elle who turned and walked away.

Chapter Thirty

Lucas watched Elle as she moved between groups at the party. She looked coolly beautiful in her long black dress with golden flowers. Her hair was twisted up into a clasp, leaving the back of her neck looking soft and vulnerable as she fetched drinks and handed out canapés.

His parents were trying to engage him in conversation but he kept his focus on Elle. Beautiful Elle, fragile yet strong.

Gradually, his parents fell silent as Elle worked her way towards them, a bottle of white wine in one hand and red in the other, filling glasses, smiling, pausing to talk. Finally, she stood before them.

'Good evening,' she greeted them, formally. 'More wine?' She topped up Fiona's glass without waiting for her reply, and then shifted her gaze to Fiona's face. 'I talked to the Bettsbrough police and made a statement. I got the feeling that they wanted to chat to Ricky about all kinds of skeevy stuff he's been up to so I told them that I thought I could get him to a place where they could easily nab him for questioning. They agreed that such scenarios often work, gave me the support I required, and Ricky was arrested. The town centre CCTV caught his physically oppressive behaviour towards me, which should help.'

Fiona's jaw dropped a notch. 'I see.'

'So they'll probably be in touch with you when you get back.' Challenge was written all over Elle's face. 'And I don't think you'll gain the impression that they're investigating me. So then you'll know that I'm not guilty of fraud or deception or anything else *shady*.'

'Oh,' said Fiona, uncertainly.

Elle was being so valiant, so brave, so visibly I-will-not-take-your-shit that Lucas wanted to gather her into his arms and hug her until she gasped. But he'd sworn to wait for her to invite him into her space. So far, that invitation was conspicuous by its absence. He contented himself by saying, 'That's fantastic!'

Elle switched her grave regard to him. 'No it's not. It's a deeply embarrassing necessity, but I evidently couldn't rely on anybody simply taking my word for what happened and cutting the oxygen to Ricky's fires.'

Lucas winced.

Fiona cleared her throat. 'Thank you for telling us.'

'Yes, thank you,' mumbled Geoffrey.

Elle nodded and went to move on.

Fiona continued to speak. 'This is a wonderful motor yacht. You must enjoy living here.'

For several seconds Elle gazed at Lucas's mother. Then, clearly, she said, 'I'm the help. Loz and Davie are Simon's friends. They're lovely people and have been fantastically kind to me but I do their shopping and cleaning. I haven't suddenly gone up in the world.'

Flushing, Fiona sidestepped the issue of social status. 'I want to thank you for helping Charlie and apologise for not thanking you sooner. He's safely back in England, now.'

'Yes, Lucas told me. I like Charlie.' Elle said it in the tone of one who didn't like many people at the moment. 'Excuse me.' She moved onto the next group of people with a smile. 'More wine?'

Lucas smothered a laugh.

Fiona tried to quell him with a frown. 'Well! I suppose she thought she was putting me in my place.'

'Quite,' agreed Geoffrey. 'I suppose it gave her some satisfaction not to grasp the olive branch.'

'Dad,' said Lucas, 'if either of you think that that was an olive branch, you have a lot to learn about trees. And as far as putting you in your place is concerned, I think she succeeded.' He liked the pugnacious side to Elle he'd just seen. He let his eyes follow her. When she let her gaze slide back his way under her lashes he lifted his glass to her in a silent toast and had the pleasure of seeing her flush.

At that moment, Loz appeared in the doorway to the saloon, giggling. Beside her was a tall dark man, brushing his wavy hair out of his eyes and grinning. 'Elle,' Loz called across the saloon. 'Someone here to see you.'

Lucas felt his smile falter as Elle turned and after a stunned instant, cried out in pleasure and pelted across the saloon. 'Simon! Oh, *Simon.*'

Simon opened his arms and swept her up into a huge hug. Behind his back, Loz hastily relieved Elle of the wine bottles.

'Simon?' said Fiona, blankly. 'I didn't realise they were that friendly.'

'I had no idea that he was over here.' Geoffrey sounded as if he felt he should have been apprised.

As the rest of the guests gradually stopped craning their necks and returned to their own conversations, Lucas watched Elle and Simon hug and hug, laughing, talking over one another, laughing and hugging again, and he felt as if someone had opened up his chest and let an icy wind breathe over his heart.

Elle looked so happy to see Simon. Though Lucas had once joked about it, there was nothing lover-like about their embrace and nothing in their body language to suggest romantic love. Just open joy and huge friendly hugs.

But he could see something in Elle's face that made him want to turn away.

It was trust. In Simon's arms, Elle felt safe.

Elle disengaged herself in the end, still laughing and joking as she collected her wine bottles and prepared to resume her duties.

Simon made his way over to join his family. He shook hands with Geoffrey and Lucas and kissed Fiona briefly on her cheek. 'Can we talk?' he said. 'Loz says we can use the sky lounge.'

They followed him up to a lounge above the main saloon. From its many windows they had an impressive view of the yachts up and down the creek.

Simon seated himself in a black leather chair, took his glasses out of his top pocket and put them on to look keenly around at everybody. 'Tell me I'm not really the only one that Elle had confided the whole story to.'

A cold lump settled in the pit of Lucas's stomach. 'Have you known the truth about Ricky all along?'

'I believe so.' Simon shook his head, as if disappointed.

Fiona sat up indignantly. 'I'm not sure any of us can be held accountable for not being told the truth.'

'I can,' said Lucas, rawly. 'And I'm not proud of myself that she never felt she could confide in me. She went to lengths to conceal from me what she thought I wouldn't understand. She couldn't trust me to trust her.'

Geoffrey sighed. 'I'm afraid you were very hard on her, Fiona. I can see why she didn't feel she could confide in us.'

Fiona swung on him. 'Me hard on her?' she demanded, incredulously. 'What about you?'

Geoffrey sucked his lips and screwed up his eyes as if weighing up the rights and wrongs of a case. 'I believe I mainly reserved judgement,' he decided. 'You were the vocal one.'

Fiona jumped up in disgust. 'You're rewriting history, Geoffrey. You were plenty vocal about her behind the scenes. You just let me be the mouthpiece for us both, as always. For goodness sake, stop being so pompous. Let's go and get a stiff gin.'

'Oh dear,' said Geoffrey, taking refuge in yet more pomposity as he followed her out. 'Drink scarcely encourages you to watch what you say, darling.'

Lucas was left alone with his uncle. 'Thanks for being there for her,' he said. 'She certainly needed a friend.'

Elle was tired. Her face ached from smiling and her hands ached from being permanently clenched around the necks of wine bottles.

Her earlier ability to confront and engage felt now as if it had been a dream. Lucas and Simon had disappeared. Fiona had spent most of the party in the company of Loz and Davie and their cocktail shaker, while Geoffrey had found a retired court official and had passed the evening talking shop.

Elle yawned as she put down the wine and retired to the galley. It seemed to her that most people had already drunk their body weight in alcohol and she'd be doing them no favours by pressing more on them. She was loading the dishwasher when Loz trotted in, fingers across her mouth to hide her grin.

'Ooh er,' Loz whispered. 'Lucas's mum's not feeling very well.'

Startled, Elle straightened up. 'Is it serious?'

Loz's eyes shone with mischief. 'Nothing that wasn't caused by Davie's latest cocktails. She's been tossing down Irish Trash Cans and Pink Pantie Droppers as if they were lemonade. I'm not sure I want to tell Geoffrey. He seems in a bit of a surly mood.'

Elle wrestled briefly with her conscience, and then closed the dishwasher. 'Where is she?'

She discovered Fiona leaning miserably over the side deck rail.

'I'm not well.' Fiona sounded faintly surprised.

'You're pissed as a fart,' Elle corrected her, frankly. 'I'm sure watching the swell isn't going to make you feel any better. Come on, I'll get you some coffee.' Taking Fiona by the elbow, puffing as she took some of the weight of the staggering woman, Elle steered her towards the companionway.

Down in her cabin, Elle propped open the door to her en suite to allow rapid access; then helped Fiona down onto the bed. 'I'll see what I can rustle up to make you feel better.'

In a few minutes, she returned from the galley with iced water, black coffee and ginger ale, hoping that one of these so-called 'remedies' would help sober Fiona up.

'Thank you,' said Fiona, in a tiny voice, reaching for the coffee.

Elle deposited the water and the ginger ale on the side table. 'Thanking me twice in one evening? Be careful, you might hurt something.'

Fiona covered her eyes. 'Don't hit a woman when she's down. It's an offence under the Sisterly Solidarity Act.'

Surprised to actually find herself laughing, Elle went over to the control panel beside the door and turned the air con to its coldest.

She remained with Fiona for almost an hour, pouring water and coffee into her and helping her to the loo when she needed to purge her system, muttering, 'And you can bloody well come back and clean the head in the morning,' as she closed the door to give what privacy she could to her mother-in-law-that-never-was.

'Thank you,' whimpered Fiona, miserably.

When an insistent tapping sent Elle to her cabin door, she was unsurprised to find Geoffrey and Lucas outside. 'Is Fiona here?' Geoffrey burst in as if fully expecting to find Fiona tied to a chair and Elle sticking her with pins. He pulled up short at the sight of his wife staggering miserably between the bathroom and Elle's bed. 'You're drunk!' He wrinkled his nose.

Irked by his righteousness, Elle jammed her hands on her hips. 'It's not a crime not to be a good sailor, for goodness' sake. Haven't you noticed that there's a swell on? She feels very sick. Chill. You're not at the bench now, magistrate.'

'On the bench,' Lucas corrected softly.

Elle's fierce glare didn't waver. 'Whatever.'

'Ah.' Geoffrey looked embarrassed. 'Sorry, I assumed— Ah, sorry, Fiona. Shall we go back to the hotel, darling? I'll find our hosts and explain, and see how I get a taxi.'

'Yes, please.' Fiona clamped a hand over her eyes, piteously.

Geoffrey hurried off, and there was silence. Elle looked from Fiona to Lucas. Lucas looked at Elle and smiled, his eyes half closed.

Fiona gave an embarrassed laugh. 'I hope you understand why I didn't correct the impression you gave him. It's just that Geoffrey does rather overreact to anyone having one too many and I already have a headache.'

'I didn't tell him you weren't drunk,' Elle pointed out. 'I merely said that it was no crime not to be a good sailor. It's up to you whether you own up.'

Lucas snorted with laughter. 'You ought to have been a lawyer, Elle.'

Elle looked at him balefully. 'I don't take that as a compliment.'

'But it's an interesting point. Are you going to tell Dad the truth, Mum?' Lucas transferred his attention to his hapless mother.

Fiona clutched her head. 'I'm a lawyer. Which truth?'

Chapter Thirty-One

Elle sat on the aft deck alone with Simon. As both Elle and Simon were staying on board *Seadancer,* Loz and Davie hadn't felt they had to be the last ones standing at their party, and had tottered off to their cabin.

Elle gave Simon a hug. 'It's so fantastic to see you again.' She beamed into his crinkling eyes. His dark hair might be silvering above his ears but there was something of the free spirit about him, despite all his business success.

Simon smothered a yawn. 'It was worth it just to hear the story of you confronting your ex and enticing him into the open for the cops to handle. That must have been really hard. Confronting Ricky, confronting your past and your anxieties about him implicating you. It took guts.'

Elle answered his yawn with one of her own. She wanted to go to sleep but she wanted to talk to Simon more. 'It felt as if it was time Ricky's hold over me was broken. You're so sweet. It's hard to think of you as Geoffrey's brother.'

Simon threw back his head to laugh. 'I guess that's supposed to be a compliment so I'll take it as one.'

She giggled. 'Sorry. I'm being rude about your family.' She reached behind her head and freed her hair from its clasp, pushing her fingers through it and enjoying the sensation of the breeze whisking it around.

He gazed out across the moonlit gardens. 'I understand from Geoffrey and Fiona that you and Lucas …?' He paused, delicately.

She swallowed. 'It was looking good. But that was then.'

'I get you.' He nodded. 'It's not now. There's no way back.'

Simon putting her fears into words made Elle feel as if her options were narrowing miserably. 'Don't you think so?'

He shrugged. 'I've talked to Lucas, because he's not just my nephew, he's my friend. We used to work together and I care a lot about him. He'd never told me that he suspected you of cheating, you know. I guess his pride got in the way. He explained how you feel he let you down not just by believing you might cheat but by not supporting you with his parents. He didn't realise how that affected you. He feels real bad.'

She looked down at her hands. 'They're his parents,' she acknowledged. 'It's difficult for him if they showed their love by trying to close ranks against someone they thought was wrong for him.'

'That's true.' Simon sounded as if the thought had never struck him before. He clicked his tongue. 'But he didn't try hard enough to straighten them out about that. Then there's the thing about you not being able to trust him with the truth. His bad, again.'

She sighed.

Simon sighed, too. 'He's still kicking himself about that – although I think you could have tried.' There was only sympathy and compassion in his eyes. 'But that's history. I'm real sorry for my blundering, if well-meant, attempts to get you guys back together. I wouldn't have done it if I hadn't genuinely thought that you were eating your hearts out for each other and that past issues could be straightened out. Now that it's obvious I was wrong, it seems as if all I did was cause you both more pain.'

'Not all,' she whispered, swallowing an enormous lump

in her throat. 'We had a fantastic couple of weeks—' She stopped, unable to force out more words.

They sat in silence. *Seadancer* rocked rhythmically.

'Lucas says that he sent you texts and tried to call you while you were in England. You froze him out a little, huh?'

She nodded, lifting her eyes to stare up at the moon, which hung high in the sky, silver and luminous.

'Because he'd let you down?'

Shrugging, she listened to the cicadas whirring in the darkness to attract a mate. Eventually, she said, 'I had a lot to deal with: my mother and the police. I needed a bit of head space.'

'He told me about the space thing.' Simon picked up his wine glass from the deck beside his feet and sipped from it pensively.

Elle thought about 'the space thing', the cabin that Lucas had emptied on board the *Shady Lady* so that Elle could move in and dictate who, if anyone, came into it. Knowing it was there had given her a tiny glow of relief that she hadn't completely painted herself into a corner. A silence drew out. Elle allowed herself to think about that space. To picture herself in it, waking up with the skylights bright above her head. In the double bed.

'But, anyway,' she said, trying to sound casual, 'you'll be moving into the *Shady Lady*, won't you? She's your boat.'

'No, I lent her to you and Lucas for the summer, because summer's a busy time in a vineyard. This is just a flying visit and Loz and Davie have kindly put me up. Don't give me a thought because soon I'm going to be on my way back to California. I told Lucas the very same.'

The breeze took her hair and tickled her cheeks with it.

She turned to gaze at Simon, at the shadows that fell across his face in the deck lights. 'You're playing me, aren't you?'

He laughed, eyes crinkling with mischief. 'That phrase reeks of manipulation and cunning. I'm just a friend who cares about you very much and thinks you might need a little help to meet Lucas halfway.' Sobering, he reached out and took her hand. 'I care so much that I've abandoned my business and travelled for twenty-three hours at a cost of over two thousand dollars to "play you". The rest is up to you.'

Lucas sat up on the flybridge of the *Shady Lady*. It was dark and the kiosk was closed, the gardens and quayside deserted. The stars were pinpricks in the night sky.

A noise made him turn his head. Along the quayside came a man and a woman. The woman's blonde hair blew behind her. The man was tall and a little older. Each of them towed a suitcase, and it was the noise of the hard plastic wheels running over the concrete that had carried on the night air.

He sat motionless, hardly breathing.

They turned towards the *Shady Lady*'s gangplank and disappeared from his view. He listened to their soft voices as they manoeuvred the luggage across the gap. Then, mentally, he followed their progress through the boat.

After five minutes he heard footfall over the plank once again and the man came into view, making his way back towards *Seadancer*, alone.

Slowly, Lucas closed his eyes in relief.

Chapter Thirty-Two

Elle lived in her own space for three days.

While Lucas was on board, she remained in her cabin. Lucas didn't acknowledge her presence. She heard him in the guest cabin shower, in the galley and the saloon, and up on the flybridge. But he didn't knock on her door. He didn't text her, or telephone. She heard him leave each day and return each evening.

Between times, she attended the Nicholas Centre, Carmelo almost shouting with joy to see her back, Oscar smiling in a self-satisfied way and informing her that he was 'seeing a lot of Polly', with a lecherous wink.

Elle hoped that Polly knew what she was getting into.

On board *Seadancer*, Loz was visibly agog to hear news and Simon and Davie had to send her quelling looks.

Early in the morning of the second day, Simon came to kiss her goodbye, his bag packed.

She had to blink back the tears. 'I feel as if I've hardly seen you.'

He hugged her, hard. 'We'll have time in the future. Whatever happens, I want you to come over for some serious vacation time.'

She received an e-mail from Charlie telling her that it had been fun being whizzed past the queues at the airport in a wheelchair and now he'd been fitted with a boot instead of a cast. And thank you, Elle. I wasn't with it during the rescue but I know that you kept your head and helped my spectacular brother save my sorry arse.

Kayleigh added a rider that Charlie was being more of a pain than usual and looked like an idiot wearing the boot, from which Elle surmised they were now both over the shock.

To her surprise and bemusement she received texts from Fiona and Geoffrey, also back in the UK, each formally thanking her for helping Charlie. Fiona added and thanks also for your unexpected but very welcome observance of the Sisterly Solidarity Act, which made Elle realise that even Fiona could have a sense of humour.

Finally, on the afternoon of the third day, a text arrived from Simon. Back home. Up to my knees in grapes.

Serenity settled over Elle.

It was back to just her and Lucas and Malta. There was something very right about that.

The next day was the hottest Elle could remember since she had arrived on the island. She swam in the morning, glad to cool her blood in the waves at Font Ghadir. She changed into her dry clothes under her towel and then ate her lunch on the rocks. When the sun had dried her hair she tucked her swim things into a bag and headed for Nicholas Centre.

There she found that the computer room had reached new levels of stifling. She shoved her hat and sunglasses in her swimming bag and dumped it in a corner, closed the louvred shutters and opened the windows. But any air that made its way through the louvres had been too soaked in sunshine to offer relief. Elle felt as if she were being slowly baked.

Only a couple of kids showed up to use the computers, clicking around desultorily. Elle didn't blame them when they left. Not even Carmelo had turned up.

Thinking longingly of the air conditioning aboard the *Shady Lady*, she checked her watch. Only three o'clock.

She was down to supervise the computer room until four.

She wrote an e-mail to Simon and read a couple of articles on the history of Malta while she waited for the time to pass, too oppressed by the heat even to bother to find some IT-based housekeeping to do.

Finally, her watch dragged its way to four o'clock and she grabbed her handbag and went down to Joseph's office to give him the computer room keys. 'I'm going. There's no one upstairs but I've left the machines on.'

Joseph lifted his eyes from his laptop. 'Too hot, today.'

'I'm going to stop at the shop and buy the biggest ice lolly they have to make the walk back to the marina bearable.'

Joseph licked his lips. 'If it wouldn't leave Oscar on his own here until Axel arrives, I'd do the same.'

Elle took pity on him. 'The shop's only a couple of minutes away. I'll fetch you one.'

Joseph's eyes lit up and he took twenty euros from his pocket. 'My treat. Buy one for Oscar, too.'

The sun made Elle squint as she crossed the courtyard and she realised that her hat and glasses must still be upstairs with her swim things. She'd try to remember them when she returned.

As she stepped out into the street, she met a small whirlwind travelling in the other direction.

'Carmelo!' She laughed. 'You nearly knocked me over.'

Carmelo, panting, wiped sweat from his forehead. 'You are leaving,' he said, accusingly. 'I did shopping for Nonnu and so I am late.'

'The computers are still on.' But Elle could read disappointment in Carmelo's expression. He never hid the fact that he liked the computer room to have Elle in it.

With a little squeeze of her heart, she took a liberty with Joseph's twenty euros. 'Joseph's just sent me out to buy ice lollies. Would you like one?'

Carmelo's eyes brightened but he said, 'I do not have money today.'

'It's Joseph's treat just for people who are at Nicholas Centre this afternoon,' Elle assured him. 'I have to buy one for Oscar, too.'

'And for Lucas?' suggested Carmelo.

'Lucas isn't at the centre. By the time I see him again, the ice lolly will have melted.' She let her mind wander over the prospect of seeing Lucas again. Her heart rate increased at the thought. Nothing was settled between them, nothing was certain, but two people on one smallish boat couldn't ignore each other forever. And she was achingly aware that the next move was down to her.

It wasn't long before they were walking back across the courtyard, Carmelo sucking energetically on the tip of a big lemon ice lolly, pausing only to slurp up escaping drips from the sides. It was pleasant to step back into the comparative cool of the big hall and into Joseph's office.

'Thank you.' Joseph beamed as he stripped off the jolly yellow paper from the lolly.

Elle gave him back his change. 'I'll take Oscar's to the games room.'

Joseph turned back to his desk. 'He ran up to the computer room a couple of minutes ago, I think.'

'OK, I'll take it up. I've left a bag up there, anyway. He'll have to come away from the machines if he wants to eat it, though.' Elle opened her own lolly as she turned for the staircase, enjoying the refreshing lemon zing as she slowly made her way up. Carmelo matched her steps, absorbed in not allowing any ice melt to escape. They crossed the landing together.

Oscar was alone in the computer room, engrossed in what was on the screen.

'Joseph's bought you a lolly,' Elle announced from the doorway.

Oscar leaped to his feet, face redder than Elle had ever seen it. 'I didn't hear— Thank you, you are most kind.' He hurried to intercept her.

She stepped back. 'You'll need to eat it somewhere else.' She pointed to the *No food or drink* sign on the door.

Oscar halted, hand half extended to take the ice lolly from her. 'Of course, I—' He hesitated; then, with a sudden jerky movement, reached back to the machine he'd been using and pressed the button to switch off the monitor.

Elle tried not to show any surprise. But her heart picked up pace.

'Thank you,' he said again, as he took the now dripping ice and hovered on the landing to eat it.

Moving a step towards the stairs Elle said, experimentally, 'It might be best if we eat these in the courtyard so we don't drip all over.'

Oscar remained where he was. 'No need. I'll eat it very quickly.'

Carmelo was concentrating on his lolly so Elle shrugged and leaned against a wall. She asked after Polly, and made desultory conversation about the dive centre. When she straightened and shifted her position she noticed that, without actually blocking her way, Oscar kept himself more or less between her and the computer room.

Once all that remained of her lolly was the stick, she took out a tissue to wipe her hands, and turned away.

'Well, I'm finished for today.' Then she swung back and dodged past Oscar, not giving him a chance to react. 'I'll just get my bag. Wait on the landing, please, Carmelo.'

She was conscious of Oscar's eyes on her as she made for the far corner where her bag still stood. Then, with another sudden change of direction she swooped on the computer monitor where Oscar had been sitting. Her finger found the on button.

'What are you doing?' Oscar made a sudden lunge to switch it off again, eyes wide in panic.

But it was too late. It took only a second for the monitor to blossom back to life. The image on the screen told Elle everything she needed to know.

Oscar froze.

Shakily, Elle lifted her voice. 'Carmelo, stay out there, won't you? I'm nearly ready. Don't come into this room with your hands all sticky or Joseph will tell me off.' Then in a quite different voice she hissed at Oscar, 'What is *wrong* with you? Children use these machines. A child could have come in here at any time.'

Oscar breathed hard, eyes wide with alarm. 'Don't be stupid.' But his voice cracked. 'I was sitting so that I could see the door and nobody could see my screen. There's nobody here. I save the images to the cloud. It's safe. I am an adult.'

'You're an idiot,' she corrected, softly. 'And what makes you think you'd see anybody arrive when you didn't see me and Carmelo until I spoke to you? You were too caught up in your "private moment".' She gritted her teeth. 'It is *never* safe to view porn where children could be.'

A long pause. Carmelo came to the doorway. 'My hands aren't very sticky.'

'They might be,' said Elle, quickly. 'It would be best if you'd go into the boys' toilets and wash your hands, please. I just need to talk to Oscar.'

Carmelo heaved a sigh but turned and trailed across the landing.

Elle reached for the button and turned the monitor off once more. 'I'll have to inform Joseph.'

'No!' Oscar snarled, stepping close, towering over Elle. 'You are so prudish! I am an adult and this is nothing.'

Elle stood her ground, although the hated sensation of being crowded made her breathing flutter. 'It's not nothing,' she hissed, 'and if you don't back off I'll talk to him about harassment, too.'

With a snort of derision, Oscar crowded closer. 'I think you won't—'

Elle sucked air into her lungs and expelled it on her loudest bellow. '*JO-SEPH! Joseph, I need help!*'

Oscar leaped back as if stung. 'Stupid English—'

'Elle?' called Joseph anxiously, his hurrying footsteps crossing the hall and starting up the stairs.

As Oscar lunged for the computer tower Elle got in his way, thwarting his attempts to cut the power. 'Don't turn that off: I need Joseph to see it,' she yelled, determined that Oscar would face the music.

Then Joseph was in the doorway. 'What's going on? What do you need me to see?'

Oscar froze. Then stepped slowly back.

Elle's heart was pounding as if she'd run a thousand miles. 'It was Oscar, viewing the adult material.' Her hand shook as she switched the monitor back on.

Joseph stepped forward to look at the screen and sucked in his breath. Slowly, his accusing eyes turned on the tall man. 'What have you got to say, Oscar?'

Then Carmelo was at the door to the room, eyes wide. 'Elle, you shout—'

Elle forced a laugh as she flicked the computer monitor off again. 'It's OK. I was being silly about a bee I thought was going to sting me. Did I worry you? I'm sorry.' She slipped behind Joseph and went to Carmelo, regretful that she'd caused the apprehensive expression in his eyes but intent on getting him away from the scene as soon as possible. 'I've got to have a meeting with Joseph, now, so we have to close the centre for the rest of the day. It's way too hot to have the computers on, anyway,' she fabricated, fanning herself. 'We'll all be back as usual tomorrow. Perhaps if you're going to come in we can look at Formula 1 cars together and you can explain the race rules to me.'

Carmelo looked disappointed. 'OK.'

'Sorry we have to shut early, Carmelo,' Joseph added.

Elle gave the little boy a cheery wave, though she felt terrible at brushing him off. With a sigh, Carmelo disappeared slowly down the stairs and Elle turned back to Joseph and Oscar. The last few minutes seemed to have passed in a blur. After the adrenaline rush of catching Oscar red-handed, Elle felt almost light-headed with a mixture of apprehension and exultation.

Joseph's face was set in grim lines. 'I need to hear from you both about what happened here today.'

'I am an adult,' Oscar repeated with miserable defiance.

'Barely,' Elle snapped.

Lucas didn't get home until six. The marina had become glassily calm in the still, hot day and Elle sat on the cockpit seat and watched him walk towards her through the gardens. Saw the exact moment his gaze locked on her.

His hair swung around his face; he looked hot, in both

senses of the word. Her heart rate accelerated as he picked up his stride. Ignoring the plank, he jumped onto the bathing platform and halted in front of her.

She drank him in. The coal-dark eyes, thick fierce eyebrows, the sensitive mouth, the uncompromising jaw.

A sense of power swept through her. She'd dealt with Ricky; she'd dealt with Oscar.

And now she was going to deal with Lucas.

'Any plans, this evening?' she asked, making sure that her voice came out evenly.

He shook his head.

'Join me for dinner?'

He nodded.

'It's all prepared.'

'I'll shower and change. Flybridge?'

She tried to sound nonchalant. 'My cabin. At seven.'

For several seconds he just looked. Then he smiled, a knowing, anticipatory smile. 'I'll bring the wine.'

Exactly on seven o'clock, a knock fell on Elle's cabin door. She'd showered, put on a short strappy dress and dried her hair into a smooth fall down her back. She waited four beats before answering the door, and found Lucas with wine in one hand and two glasses in the other. She stepped back to allow him into the small space. The last of the golden light filtered in through the skylights.

There was no room for a table in the cabin so she'd set a couple of trays in the middle of the bed. It was an odd place to choose to eat dinner but it was symbolic. An invitation into her space

Her mind had been flirting with the scenario, buzzing with possibilities. She half expected him to make an early move, to kiss her or hold her, to assure himself that she was on the menu.

But Lucas just went to one side of the bed and waited politely while she climbed on and got comfortable against the headboard before settling himself, cross-legged, at right angles to her.

They ate, chatting desultorily about Dive Meddi and Nicholas Centre. Elle told him about Oscar. 'Could you give Polly a heads-up?'

He looked grim. 'I'll see her tomorrow.'

When the meal was finished, they carried the trays out to the galley.

This time when they returned to the master cabin, Lucas propped himself against the headboard and stretched his legs out alongside Elle's as he topped up their wine glasses.

'I've been thinking about the owning up thing,' he said.

'Oh?' Elle put her glass down beside the bed.

Slowly, he nodded. 'I need to own up about something.'

A curly, whirly unpleasantness took possession of Elle's stomach. 'W-what?'

'Two things, in fact.' He took a long draught from his wine glass and reached out to lodge it on the niche that stood in place of a bedside table. 'I was – am – too inclined to see things as either right or wrong.'

She licked her lips. They were as dry as if she'd been out in the wind all day. 'S-some people would see having strong convictions as a good thing.'

'Not when it means the girl I love can't tell me about things that aren't even her fault because she thinks I'll judge her. Not when we're being threatened and she protects me by letting me drive her away.'

Tears started at the back of her eyes. 'What's the other thing?'

He reached out and touched her face. 'I never fell out of love with you. Never stopped wanting you. When Simon set this whole thing up, I went through the motions of being furious but it was to hide the fact that I could have shouted with joy. He'd given me a second chance.'

Her heart gave an enormous thump. 'We could— we could thank him later.' She turned her face and kissed his palm.

His breath came out in a rush. He half-dragged her onto his lap and, when her head threatened to brush the ceiling, scooted down the bed, clasping her against him until they were lying full length, her on top, and her dress somewhere near her waist.

He groaned as his searching hands found her bare legs. 'I did own up about the wanting you bit?'

She kissed his jawline and then his neck, rubbing herself against him. 'I would have worked it out.'

He stopped. 'I have a whole load more stuff to own up to.'

She too, stilled. 'What?'

He rolled suddenly so that she was beneath him, eyes gleaming up into his. 'I want you out of that dress. I want to be inside you. I want to move back into this cabin. I want to be with you.'

'All night?' She lifted her head to taste his lips.

'All my life.'

Lucas's fingers found the zipper to her dress. Then he paused. A distant alarm bell rang.

He'd got things wrong before.

This time he was going to get things right.

He pulled back slightly so that he could look into her face.

Her eyes sprang open, wide with alarm. 'What?'

'You are the most desirable woman on the planet.'

'Oh!' She flushed. 'I—'

'I love you.' He kissed her softly. 'I want to spend my life with you. I want to sleep with you, wake up with you, live with you, love you, argue with you and laugh with you. I don't care where we live; I don't care what anybody else thinks about us. I just want you. Elle, will you marry me?'

Her eyes filled with tears. 'Yes,' she whispered.

He wiped away a tear with one fingertip. 'We'll have the wedding you want, big or small, wherever you want.'

She gave a watery smile. 'Thank you.'

He stroked back her hair. 'As long as it's soon.'

'Soon,' she agreed. Her eyes began to dance. 'Good proposal, by the way.'

He tightened his arms, loving having them full of Elle. 'I thought I must be able to do better than "pretty ordinary".'

Epilogue

To: Elle.Jamieson
From: Simon.Rose
Subject: ☺

Whenever the wedding is, wherever the wedding is, I will be there.

Much love,
Simon xxx

PS Told you. Told you. TOLD YOU! Ha! I was right. I knew it. Ha.

To: Simon.Rose
From: Elle.Jamieson
Subject: ☺

If you're going to be unbearable about it, we might uninvite you! xxx

To: Elle.Jamieson
From: Simon.Rose
Subject: ☺

I'll let you honeymoon on the *Shady Lady*.

To: Simon.Rose
From: Elle.Jamieson
Subject: ☺ ☺ ☺

In that case, your wedding invitation is in the post!!!

Elle and Lucas

About the Author

Sue Moorcroft is an accomplished writer of novels and short stories, as well as a creative writing tutor. She's also the fiction judge at Writers' Forum and a regular guest on Sue Dougan's Chat Room at BBC Radio Cambridgeshire.

The Wedding Proposal is Sue's seventh novel with Choc Lit. Her others include: *Starting Over*, *All That Mullarkey*, *Want to Know a Secret?*, *Love & Freedom*, *Dream a Little Dream* and *Is This Love?*. She also has a novella, *Darcie's Dilemma*, published on the Choc Lit Lite imprint and this is available online. *Love & Freedom* won the Festival of Romance Best Romantic Read Award 2011 and *Dream a Little Dream* was shortlisted for the 2013 Romantic Novel of the Year Award.

www.twitter.com/suemoorcroft
www.suemoorcroft.com
www.facebook.com/SueMoorcroftAuthor
www.facebook.com/sue.moorcroft.3

More Choc Lit

From Sue Moorcroft

'A delight to read. Full of laughter and tears.' Katie Fforde

Starting Over

New home, new friends, new love. Can starting over be that simple?

Tess Riddell reckons her beloved Freelander is more reliable than any man – especially her ex-fiancé, Olly Gray. She's moving on from her old life and into the perfect cottage in the country.

Miles Rattenbury's passions? Old cars and new women! Romance? He's into fun rather than commitment. When Tess crashes the Freelander into his breakdown truck, they find that they're nearly neighbours – yet worlds apart. Despite her overprotective parents and a suddenly attentive Olly, she discovers the joys of village life and even forms an unlikely friendship with Miles. Then, just as their relationship develops into something deeper, an old flame comes looking for him ...

Is their love strong enough to overcome the past? Or will it take more than either of them is prepared to give?

Visit www.choc-lit.com for more details including the first two chapters and reviews, or simply scan barcode using your mobile phone QR reader.

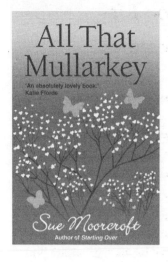

All That Mullarkey

Revenge and love:
it's a thin line …

The writing's on the wall for Cleo and Gav. The bedroom wall, to be precise. And it says 'This marriage is over.'

Wounded and furious, Cleo embarks on a night out with the girls, which turns into a glorious one-night stand with …

Justin, centrefold material and irrepressibly irresponsible. He loves a little wildness in a woman – and he's in the right place at the right time to enjoy Cleo's.

But it's Cleo who has to pick up the pieces – of a marriage based on a lie and the lasting repercussions of that night. Torn between laid-back Justin and control-freak Gav, she's a free spirit that life is trying to tie down. But the rewards are worth it!

Visit www.choc-lit.com for more details including the first two chapters and reviews, or simply scan barcode using your mobile phone QR reader.

Want to Know a Secret?

Money, love and family. Which matters most?

When Diane Jenner's husband is hurt in a helicopter crash, she discovers a secret that changes her life. And it's all about money, the kind of money the Jenners have never had.

James North has money, and he knows it doesn't buy happiness. He's been a rock for his wayward wife and troubled daughter – but that doesn't stop him wanting Diane.

James and Diane have something in common: they always put family first. Which means that what happens in the back of James's Mercedes is a really, really bad idea.

Or is it?

Visit www.choc-lit.com for more details including the first two chapters and reviews, or simply scan barcode using your mobile phone QR reader.

Love & Freedom

Winner of the Festival of Romance Best Romantic Read Award 2011

New start, new love.

That's what Honor Sontag needs after her life falls apart, leaving her reputation in tatters and her head all over the place. So she flees her native America and heads for Brighton, England.

Honor's hoping for a much-deserved break and the chance to find the mother who abandoned her as a baby. What she gets is an entanglement with a mysterious male whose family seems to have a finger in every pot in town.

Martyn Mayfair has sworn off women with strings attached, but is irresistibly drawn to Honor, the American who keeps popping up in his life. All he wants is an uncomplicated relationship built on honesty, but Honor's past threatens to undermine everything. Then secrets about her mother start to spill out ...

Honor has to make an agonising choice. Will she live up to her dutiful name and please others? Or will she choose freedom?

Visit www.choc-lit.com for more details including the first two chapters and reviews, or simply scan barcode using your mobile phone QR reader.

Dream a Little Dream

Shortlisted for the 2013 Romantic Novel of the Year Award

What would you give to make your dreams come true?

Liza Reece has a dream. Working as a reflexologist for a troubled holistic centre isn't enough. When the opportunity arises to take over the Centre she jumps at it. Problem is, she needs funds, and fast, as she's not the only one interested.

Dominic Christy has dreams of his own. Diagnosed as suffering from a rare sleep disorder, dumped by his live-in girlfriend and discharged from the job he adored as an Air Traffic Controller, he's single-minded in his aims. He has money, and plans for the Centre that don't include Liza and her team.

But dreams have a way of shifting and changing and Dominic's growing fascination with Liza threatens to reshape his. And then it's time to wake up to the truth ...

Visit www.choc-lit.com for more details including the first two chapters and reviews, or simply scan barcode using your mobile phone QR reader.

Is this Love?

How many ways can one woman love?

When Tamara Rix's sister Lyddie is involved in a hit-and-run accident that leaves her in need of constant care, Tamara resolves to remain in the village she grew up in. Tamara would do anything for her sister, even sacrifice a long-term relationship.

But when Lyddie's teenage sweetheart Jed Cassius returns to Middledip, he brings news that shakes the Rix family to their core. Jed's life is shrouded in mystery, particularly his job, but despite his strange background, Tamara can't help being intrigued by him.

Can Tamara find a balance between her love for Lyddie and growing feelings for Jed, or will she discover that some kinds of love just don't mix?

Visit www.choc-lit.com for more details including the first two chapters and reviews, or simply scan barcode using your mobile phone QR reader.

Darcie's Dilemma

How do you weigh one love against another?

Things haven't been easy for Darcie Killengrey; left with the responsibility of her troubled teenage brother Ross and a past of unhappiness and heartbreak.

And then Jake Belfast strides back into her life, as acerbic and contrary as he is exciting and handsome — he also just happens to be her best friend's brother.

Having parted on bad terms two years previously, Darcie and Jake now find themselves flung back together. Tensions reach new heights when they're forced to work in the same place and the pair struggle to put the past behind them.

And, all the while, Ross is becoming increasingly involved with a dangerous influence, which looks set to make Darcie's problems with Jake pale into insignificance …

Visit www.choc-lit.com for more details, or simply scan barcode using your mobile phone QR reader.

CLAIM YOUR FREE EBOOK

of

the Wedding Proposal

You may wish to have a choice of how you read
The Wedding Proposal. Perhaps you'd like a digital
version for when you're out and about, so that
you can read it on your ereader, iPad or even a
Smartphone. For a limited period, we're including
a **FREE** ebook version along with this paperback.

To claim, simply visit ebooks.choc-lit.com
or scan the QR Code.

You'll need to enter the following code:

Q301406

Introducing Choc Lit

We're an independent publisher creating
a delicious selection of fiction.
Where heroes are like chocolate – irresistible!
Quality stories with a romance at the heart.

Choc Lit novels are selected by genuine readers like yourself.
We only publish stories our Choc Lit Tasting Panel want to
see in print. Our reviews and awards speak for themselves.

We'd love to hear how you enjoyed *The Wedding Proposal*.
Just visit www.choc-lit.com and give your feedback.
Describe Lucas in terms of chocolate
and you could win a Choc Lit novel in our
Flavour of the Month competition.

Available in paperback and as ebooks from most stores.

Visit: www.choc-lit.com for more details.

Keep in touch:
Sign up for our monthly newsletter Choc Lit Spread for
all the latest news and offers: www.spread.choc-lit.com.
Follow us on Twitter: @ChocLituk and Facebook: Choc Lit.

Or simply scan barcode using your mobile phone QR reader:

Choc Lit   *Twitter*   *Facebook*
Spread